PLAYLIST

Paramore, "Decode" (Metal Cover by From Ashes to New ft. Caitlin De Ville)

Written By Wolves, "To Tell You the Truth"

Daughtry, "The Dam"

Erik Grönwall, "Dream On" (Aerosmith Cover)

Linkin Park ft. Evan Tunes, "Remember Me"

Coldplay, "A Sky Full of Stars"

Halestorm & I Prevail, "Can U See Me in the Dark?"

Nate Smith, Avril Lavigne, "Can You Die From a Broken Heart"

Bad Omens, "Never Know"

The Script, "No Good in Goodbye"

ABOUT THE AUTHOR

Sofia Shelley writes dark academia in a Gothic setting and haunted dead poets who adore tailored waistcoats. In her other incarnations she writes fast-paced police romances, sizzling military units, steamy cowboys with a Montana backdrop and has an annual Christmas rom-com obsession. Sofia writes kidlit for charity and has over one hundred and fifty publications across six not-so-super-secret pen names. As acquisitions editor for Evernight and Evernight Teen she loves discovering new romance and YA voices. She is a pride mum of three crazies in a returned veteran household plus two GSD fur babies who think they're teacup puppies.

Sofia lives near Brisbane, Australia, where she has her own alpaca park, Lorendel.

www.sofiaaves.com/who-is-sofia-shelley

DEAD POETS

Sorority

SOFIA SHELLEY

avon.

Published by AVON
A division of HarperCollins*Publishers* Ltd
1 London Bridge Street
London SE1 9GF

www.harpercollins.co.uk

HarperCollins*Publishers*
Macken House, 39/40 Mayor Street Upper
Dublin 1, D01 C9W8, Ireland

A Paperback Original 2025
1

A catalogue record for this book is available from the British Library.

ISBN: 978-0-00-876349-7

Set in Sabon LT Std by HarperCollins*Publishers* India

Printed and bound in the UK using 100% Renewable Electricity at CPI Group (UK) Ltd

This book contains FSC™ certified paper and other controlled sources to ensure responsible forest management.

For more information visit: www.harpercollins.co.uk/green

For every girl who wanted a midnight poet of their own.
Now you have one.

Caffeinate Me

Inerius U's college paper *The Actum*'s offices hummed with an excess of unbroken dreams and Peabody hopefuls that only an editor could smash first thing on a Monday morning.

Seven a.m. meetings were not the forte of every perky journalism student on the paper, but I'd self-caffeinated, and I was ready.

Feature writer Emma Reeves reporting for duty.

Even in my head the cliché line sounded way too upbeat, but the energy provided by my Dewar cup branded with the campus's best location for burnt beans prevailed. I refused not to ride the wave.

The yawning pair of sleep-deprived junior sports reporters who could have benefited from a shower and a dose of IV-administered mouthwash seated on either side of me, however, were not. I blamed Inerius U's football team, which made it to the National Championships Playoffs the night before, resulting in an epic frat party both had attended. In an effort to maintain my sanity, I had boycotted the event. What? A girl had to have some standards, even if they affected her social life.

Mine revolved around avoiding frat boys and spoiled sorority sisters vying for their not-so-significant other's letters on a cruddily plated necklace, ordered in bulk from the local campus frat store.

Plus, there *may* have been a little frat boy history that reminded me not to engage under any circumstances, article-fodder-worthy though they may be.

Wake up, Rhapsody." Erin Preveli, my favorite editor-in-chief, depending upon the hour, clapped her hands like we were her least favorite kindergarten attendees. "Do I need to bring in the taco?" She whipped out her favorite printed taco—something she'd made after seeing a video of a *taco slap* and deciding to make it match her entire personality—and waved it above her head. "I am not above some hand held motivation to start a Monday morning. Or maybe it could be a self-inflicted taco slap to get you moving".

I settled deeper in my plastic seat, relieved to avoid both her gaze, and her taco, for now. Janie, our sports intern who looked like her maybe two hours of scant sleep caught on someone else's sofa wasn't working out so well today, leaned forward and covered her mouth to unsuccessfully obscure a whiskey-tainted belch before she pitched her next project.

"We could take a perspective on student entertainment budgets— Oh, excuse me."

Fumes of what might have been last night's yard glass contents filled *The Actum*'s hybrid newsroom meeting area that consisted of eight chairs set out in a crooked crescent moon, each staff member armed with matching Dewar cups.

I'm too close to graduating for this shizz.

Erin raised an eyebrow as Janie stumbled from the room, her hand pressed over her mouth. Retching sounds came from the region of the fake pandanus palm in the foyer. The taco made a second appearance. "Right. One down, and it's seven-oh-five. Who's next?"

If I have to write another story about overprivileged students complaining about the lack of funding for dorm parties, I'll offer to head the obituaries column. Maybe we can print the casket sprays in color this season.

I slapped on a smile to match the grinning chibi illustrated head printed on my licensed, *Lois Lane is my Spirit Animal* tee that came complete with a perpetual coffee stain I couldn't remove and pulled a Monday-morning-worthy pitch out of my ass. "What about, 'How cancel culture has left us lonelier than ever amongst campus cliques and communities?'"

Erin faced off with me like she *knew* I planned to upstage the freshmen contingent while I rallied my best *kiss my coffee-stained belly button* stare back at her. Finally, she nodded. "Starting with a little alliteration? I like it, Emma. What else have we got? Kendall?"

She dismissed me and moved on to the next feature writer along the line—or circle—after holding my attention a fraction of a nanosecond too long that left me questioning my sanity, my life choices in studying journalism, and ever opening my mouth in a pitching meeting ever again.

Of course, that last would simply mean giving up my position on the college paper. My brain jammed at the thought. *Not on my Tiffany and Co. Diamond Ballpoint.*

That had been a gift from my grandmother when I first joined *The Actum.* Gran had the pen engraved with my name—sadly ironic, as she forgot her own when her memory faded less than a year later. Honoring her as best I could, I quickly moved through the ranks and brought my lucky pen along for the fast-tracked ride.

"I've got survey results on hacked devices during campus hours. It's not super juicy but there's some facts in there that might make the dean's remaining hairs stand on end." Griffin, our resident tech columnist and geek rep, earned himself a coveted nod from Erin and a glare from Kendall.

"There's leftover fodder from my interview with Dean Graham last month on cybersecurity. You can pick out whatever I didn't use from that," I offered.

Rhapsody sent me a side-eye that might have burned if she hadn't also turned a sickening shade of Kermit at the same moment she mumbled something about sucking up.

I smiled blandly as I sipped my coffee and managed not to wear any as the "Monday brief", for once, stuck to its name and ended on time.

"Emma, save me a few minutes afterward." Erin sent me the sort of smile executioners reserved for their next victim.

Welp, the meeting almost *ended on time.*

Mine might end permanently if I had screwed up royally in some unknown context. My coffee stuck in my throat, tried to head in both directions at once, and traveled in reverse into my nasal cavity.

Hand cupped over my mouth, eyeballs streaming, and attempting not to snort coffee across the newsroom, to Griffin's general curiosity and Rhapsody's amusement, I nodded.

"Sure," I croaked, and wore the rest of my coffee as it trickled down the front of my tee, giving my Lois chibi a lady beard.

"Not the best day so far, huh?" Griffin handed me a bunch of napkins in passing, though the germaphobe who would rather risk contracting a computer virus than touching another human avoided direct skin-to-skin contact as he did so. "Send me your notes when you have, you know, time." He waved a hand to encompass my damp, coffee-drowned ass.

Rhapsody smirked as she wandered past, swinging her empty notebook. "It's a good look for someone who won't be here much longer," she murmured not very discreetly as she sauntered toward the desk she shared with Janie.

"Go screw your desk cactus," was the first thing that popped out of my mouth—without the added bonus of lowering my voice.

I blamed the lack of caffeine that I now wore on the outside, rather than the inside, of my stomach.

Her gaze shot to the pink stress-ball cactus set off to one

side of her desk that had been her Secret Santa gifted her last Christmas—*spoilers, it was me*—that set a viral newsroom and resulting campus trend within a week. Her face flushed the same color. "Fu—"

"Play nice with others, Emma," Erin reproached me as she ushered me into her fishbowl of an office that was glassed on all sides and positioned in the middle of our workspace. She flicked her own desk cactus on the way in. "Even when they don't play well with you."

The interior of her office was visible from every angle, and soundproofed from the outside, but never had I been more conscious of the eyes of the staff members on me as she closed the door. The window glass rattled in its frame as Erin walked behind her desk.

I stood on the other side, clutching the hem of my wet tee, my blankish notebook and my empty coffee thermos vying for prime real estate in my other hand.

"Why are you standing? Sit down." She tipped her head toward the chair opposite her desk that I'd always occupied in this room.

"I do get to keep my job, then?" I joked.

Annoyingly, Rhapsody's barb hit way too close to home, considering it came from a second-rate writer, and a snarky freshman.

I wanted to write for the paper. No, I *needed* to, in order to get a job when I graduated at the end of the year. Building a successful portfolio meant everything. Without my family's backing on my chosen career, I had no contacts in the industry. It was down to me and my wits . . . and anything else I managed to make of myself in my remaining seven months.

"Of course. I need you." Erin sent me a strange glance, her Greek-Aussie accent slipping though. She pushed a manila folder toward me—my favorite editor-in-chief of the moment had an obsession with those things in the same way

I had a love affair with all things Lois Lane-related. "But I am propositioning you."

"In public?" I smiled, my energy renewed and imposter syndrome dissipating as I flipped the folder's cover open.

A quick survey of the contents showed the somewhat Gothic facade of Phi Omega Sorority House. Actual turreted towers soared above ivy-clad walls. An arched doorway with what looked like a gargoyle door knocker made a feature out of the entranceway.

As far as I knew, no pictures existed of the interior of the house. Once in, each sorority sister was sworn to the utmost secrecy. Rumor had it that the Big Sister, an initiated mentor who assisted new pledges, kept some big secrets—and a bank account to back her questionable life choices.

Even with the rumors that abounded about the sorority house, the gothicana facade made for an impressive pit stop. I half expected David Bowie to waltz out of its exclusive confines with tights, codpiece and full goblin-king wig in place. *Vale.* He was the only temptation that could draw me into a cesspit of a place like that—either dead or alive.

I'd walked past the building on campus, of course, but I'd never bothered to take much notice of the finer details.

"Cute." I closed the file and pushed it back across Erin's desk, looking at her expectantly. "But pass. What's the extra-credit project?"

That could be the only reason she pulled me in here. Or she'd found something worthy of holding back from the rest of the staff *and* cutting the Monday brief short enough to resemble its namesake. The latter seemed most likely. I leaned forward, planted my elbows on my knees, and earned myself a renewed damp belly button for my enthusiasm.

Erin watched me with a small, secret smile. I knew right then I'd hate whatever she had cooked up. "You're going undercover."

"That doesn't sound too bad." I maintained hope.

"Into the Dead Poets Sorority."

"The dead poets . . . whatsy now?" My brain caught up with the picture and the file on her desk. *Hopes thus dashed.* "Oh no. No way. I don't do sororities, sisterhoods, or frat parties. You know this. Not after the ex I shouldn't have dated in the first place. Get Janie to cover it. Or Ra— Ra—"

"Oh, please." Erin flicked her fingers imperiously like she knew she already had me knotted in her net. "You can't even say her name. You know Rhapsody isn't ready for anything beyond frivolous Friday night frat boys. Besides, this is right up your alley. She'll make a drunken mess of it at best. You won't. Plus, you're already in."

I blinked. "I am?"

"Magic, remember?" She wiggled spirit fingers at me.

The first day I walked into *The Actum*'s offices, Erin assured me that she knew everything her staff stuck their digits into, no matter what sort of secrets they thought they kept. Editor she might be, intelligence officer could be a serious second career choice. And by fingers, she meant toes and other unmentionable appendages, too.

By the time she'd walked through *The Actum*'s offices that morning, we had caught one writer focusing on a piece for a rival college paper, one staff member changing the byline on an unprinted article to their own name and two of the then lifestyle columnists making out in the copy room. Before the Monday meeting began in earnest, I believed that she did, in fact, possess a degree of editorial magic.

We bonded over Noughties-era cheerleading movies, an old Brit newspaper young adult thirst trap sitcom, and earned ourselves hangovers that neither of us ever forgot, though we couldn't quite remember the cause of any of them. I ended up as her favorite feature writer by the end of my first year at the paper, and I had remained thus.

Which made attempting to say *no* right now somehow both hellishly easy and the hardest thing I'd do all semester.

"I remember. *Magic*." I wiggled my fingers back at her, though the growing cramp in my stomach didn't ease. Erin knew my stance on sororities and frats and had never pushed me on it.

Or ambushed me.

Until now.

"You'll be tested like any of their new pledges—a little light hazing to test your mettle, nothing more. Pass, and you'll be fine."

"Pass?" I raised an eyebrow. "I'd better not end up on some dodgy video site."

"They aren't that kind of sorority. You'll survive." She flicked a dismissive hand in my direction. "Get me all the information I need to declare Kimberly Welles a fraud, and have her kicked off campus. Permanently."

Twin sweater sets, pastels and frat boyfriends, oh my. My stomach uncramped and tumbled into freefall. *This is my idea of hell.*

But more than that, something about the way Erin uttered Kimberly's name sounded . . . personal.

My palms itched. "Erin, you know my position on this. I don't do—"

"Secret societies. Emma, they're bringing back dead poets. Or at least, they're trying to in a . . . literary sense. Think *Beetlejuice* crossed with *Pride and Prejudice and Zombies*." She smiled without a skerrick of humor when my mouth dropped open.

"What, possession? Is that a real thing?" My mind started working despite my objectionable innards.

"Not live ones. At least, I don't think so. They won't pull it off in any case. It's all smoke and mirrors, parlor tricks of the *Penny Dreadful* variety. But they have an opening for a new sister or five, and I got your name on the list. That's a future favor you'll owe me. I'll add it to your tally. You'll live in Phi Omega House until you hand me an exposé on the society—"

"I'll live *where*?"

Erin ignored my butting into her sorority-fueled tirade and steamrollered along like I'd never spoken at all. "With a deadline of five weeks. I can stretch to six, but you had better turn in a sheaf of the life-changing variety for leaving me without you for that long. And your accommodation will be paid for. Write me a feature piece on the head of the Dead Poets Sorority. To recap: your target is Kimberly Welles. Be my star reporter. Get me everything I need to shut their rubbish down. She's already crazy, so it should be an easy job. Make them the laughing stock of Inerius U. You'll have a front-page feature piece, and interviews. A potential series *if* it's worthy, and a glowing recommendation not only from myself but from the dean when you graduate."

"I'll have a what from the who and why are you— Stop bribing me with all the things I want most," I muttered weakly, reaching for the folder again. "This is already set in stone?"

"Like *Psyche Revived by Cupid's Kiss*." Erin tapped her lips with her fingernails. "That favor I pulled? My best magic yet. You'll avoid the worst of the hazing. Kimberly will take you under her wing like you are her favorite duckling. Special treatment. Just. For. You."

I struggled to hold her unflinching gaze. "I thought you said she was batshit."

"So many bats have flown from that belfry." Erin smiled, though her eyes didn't.

Freaking awesome.

Erin leaned over her desk to tap the photo of the Gothic-looking building and flicked to the one beneath it. "Get me info on who is in the society. What they do, the crazy agenda they're pushing."

"That's it?"

"That, and summon yourself a dead poet."

"Summon myself a— Something's wrong with you."

"So many things. But I'm not half as mad as this woman." She tapped Kimberly Welles's photo next. "She wants to steal the voices of the past out of a sense of desperation, I think, to empower women of today for bygone transgressions. Some transcendental theory." Erin grimaced, her first show of true emotion.

I had to agree. The sentiment of literary theft to combat feminist woes sat poorly with me already. Plagiarism was plagiarism, no matter what era of stolen—ahem, *liberated*—cravat was noosed around it.

"That sounds . . . ugh. All right," I conceded with as good a dose of bad grace as I could muster while my needy fingers itched around my Dewar cup.

"Deal?" Erin sprang upright in her seat, her best business face bang in place.

I had the distinct impression I'd just been swindled.

"Deal." *Good graces be damned.*

"Excellent." She stopped shy of rubbing her hands together in a Mister Burns-esque finger pyramid and pointed to the manila folder that sat exactly where it had been when I entered her office, sorority-free, less than ten minutes earlier. "That's yours. First job: pick out what you're wearing for tonight's séance."

"What I'll be wearing to tonight's *what*?"

Erin didn't deign to reply. She shooed me out of the fishbowl as the rest of the newsroom stared, shattering my impression that my editor's office was as soundproofed as I'd previously thought.

*

Spoilers: I did *not* go and pick out my *whimsigoth* outfit like a good little reporter. Instead, I spent the afternoon loitering at the ivy-covered base of Phi Omega House, trying to remain invisible, and acquainted myself with its odd black granite foundation stones that added to its *maniera tedesca* appearance.

While a few sisters came and left via the oversized arched front doors, the gargoyle knocker that matched the great stone beasts hanging over the lintel above, to my great disappointment, went unused. I occupied myself with eavesdropping on snippets of everyday sisterhood conversation and memorized messages graffitied on the stones by long-past sweethearts who had left their initials etched on the house walls.

A bleak reminder that love turned cold and hard, which told me nothing of the history beyond two names that might no longer be joined at all, though several of the neighboring stones smelled like urine. Those were covered in a sticky stain that leached onto my hands as I discovered by an unhappy mistake when I leaned forward in an overeager moment of eavesdropping. I doubted the fluid remnants were of the animal variety.

"Classy frat boys," I muttered, peering around the vines that wound their way toward the turreted tops of the sorority house, which would soon gain at least one more resident.

My shadowed spot grew colder by the minute, as if the building's foundations were imbued with remnants of the dead poets that Kimberly Welles and her devotees were supposedly so desperate to manifest. I huffed a laugh that transformed into a shiver as the sun hid behind a cloud, deepening the pall of my dank hiding place.

Wrapping my arms around myself, I ducked behind my chosen ivy creeper as a preppy frat boy—complete with a pastel freaking sweater, as predicted, tied around his neck below his sandy brown hair grown out of its perfectly tousled broccoli cut—sauntered up the steps of the house and knocked. Without using the gargoyle, damn him.

Then he turned, giving me a glimpse of his profile, and my stomach squelched into a shape that no stomach should ever be.

It's not him, it's not him. There's no way my luck could run so bad that it could possibly be—

A muted conversation was hosted out of my line of sight while I cringed behind my ivy rosette and cluster of silent, lover-etched stones.

"It's not him."

"Fuck!" I screeched, and clamped a hand over my mouth. My fingers parted as my eyeballs drifted back to the not-ex boyfriend I couldn't see but tried to peer at anyway in a form of self-sabotage. "Are you sure?"

The conversation on the steps above us halted as I turned back and met the eyes of my best friend. Vivian Chan shrugged good-naturedly as though sneaking up on me was a regular occurrence, while I debated whether she would still *be* my best friend if I throttled her on the grounds of a sorority house. The occupants would probably do worse if they caught us on their premises, bribed membership invitation pending or not.

Which Vivian most definitely did not have, as she was not on Erin's list, likely due to her tendency to dissect people's brains and explain their worst personality traits the moment she met them.

Often before they even spoke to her.

Disconcerting for most, I found her sense of humor hilarious. We fell in together during our freshman year and shared a room for the last three years. My sanity appreciated her, as well as my deadlines, and we had a standing reciprocal clause on offer that if either of us lost our shit we would provide our own bespoke straitjacket and hand our sanity to our bestie for safekeeping.

Sort of the opposite to the celebrity clause, just handier.

"Kill me later," she whispered, grabbing my hand and correctly interpreting my only partially-faux glare. Vivian tugged me out of my crouch as footsteps clamored in our combined direction. "Come on!"

Circulation attempted to return on demand to legs that tried to emulate the consistency of the stone I crouched beside for so long. My muscles strained and screamed as I hobbled along behind her, scrabbling for my collection of notebooks that carried mainly doodles of initials and the gargoyle's side profile.

Footsteps might have followed us, but I could neither confirm nor deny our hunter's existence as we shot into a copse of brambles beyond the sorority house's shadow and ate dirt.

"This is an ignominious way to be unalived," I muttered as Vivian squashed my face into a raven's veritable treasure chest of shiny wrappers. "And not at all headline-worthy," I grumbled, keeping up my diatribe the deeper she pushed.

"Shut up." Vivian ground my face harder into the trash. I had the impression she craned out the top of our bramble while shoving me down. "No, it's definitely not him. They're looking around, leaving . . . And—we're clear. You can get up now."

"This shirt is ruined." I flapped dolefully at my favorite tee, stained and dirt-rubbed with a touch of green smear I wasn't certain I wanted to identify.

"You'll be fine." She poked my arm and slid out of the shrubbery through a Vivian-sized hole in the spiky bush that she'd pulled us into. "Come on. You can tell me why you decided to brave the Gates of Hades for an article." She paused on the other side of the bramble and stared back through the hole in the thorny bush at me. "You *were* doing it for an article, right?"

Of course she'd freaking guessed right. This was Vivian Chan, after all. Mind reading—excuse me, psychology—was her prime skill set. I hid inside the shrubbery and lamented the loss of my coffee thermos. At least I still had my notebooks. *She won't take the news well.*

"Why else would I case out a sorority?" I stalled.

Vivian tilted her head to one side. Dark razored hair hung in a cascade to her shoulders. "I mean, stalking the ex comes at the top of the list."

"That's fair."

"Come. Out. Of. The. Bramble. Right now, Emma. I don't care if you're hiding from me or the ex—who is not here, I promise—just get *out* here. Or I'll think you're as guilty as sin for something you haven't done yet anyway. And your shirt is not recoverable."

"That was mean." I glared at her through the thorns that framed her heart-shaped face.

Vivian sighed. "Come on out, and I'll help you clean the mess off."

"You mean it?" I perked up, wiggling my way through the hole she'd slipped out of that seemed half the size it had been a moment before.

"If you fess up."

I froze with my butt hanging halfway out of the prickly enclosure. "Damn psych major."

"Nosy senior journalist."

"Whatever. Give a girl a hand?"

In the end, I managed to haul my backside—with Vivian's help—from the shrubbery relatively unscathed. The traipse across campus to our dorm was of the silent variety, charged with suspicious glances I couldn't avoid. Lying to Vivian sucked, but I got the impression that my new assignment would be full of situations I'd prefer to dodge.

May as well start now.

Procrastination ever my friend, I scooted into the bathroom the moment we arrived at our second-floor dorm room. Maybe my next shirt should read *"en tempus veri-tas"*. The crappy sleight of hand bought me a few precious seconds that I wasted in not-so-spectacular style as I stared down at my scratched hands, unable to face myself in the mirror.

My life choices this morning in accepting Erin's under-cover assignment seemed both rash and necessary all at once. I hated that she'd dangled all my dreams over my head like a caffeine-coated carrot—one I was all too ready to jump for, heedless of the cost.

After stripping off my stained shirt, I soaked the filthy material in the small, scarred sink, dumping soap over Lois's name and probably doing everything wrong out of pure desperation.

Vivian's gentle knock left me jumping like a jackrabbit headed for death row.

"You can come out now, you know," she called, amuse-ment tinging her voice. "I won't eat you."

Psychoanalyze my life choices and hand me a lurid pink straitjacket.

It would be no more than I earned for myself right now. I groaned and let my head thump onto the edge of the sink. "Ow."

"I've got mulberry gin." Her voice filtered through my hair nest that I blew an air hole in as I continued to wash my shirt one-handed.

"That's a terrible idea." But I'd probably partake, anyway.

"Right? Open up." She knocked again.

"Said the doctor to the unwilling med student."

Or something like that. The G-rated version at least.

I dragged my shirt from the sink, let out the water and gave the freshly squeezed material a tentative once-over. Surprisingly, most of the stains had rinsed out. Except for that one coffee stain that refused to budge. *Stubborn thing.*

Giving it the kudos due for its latent efforts, I shrugged and hung the shirt over the shower rail, flicking crumpled grass blades out of my bra.

"Coming."

*

"It's completely unsafe."

"Yeah, but it's very me."

"It *is* very you." Vivian slid the secret society sorority file—a girl's gotta love a little alliteration before dusk—toward me and tapped the top picture. Even with that stoic proclamation, she worried at her bottom lip.

Not confidence-building.

We'd been through it all: the promise of no hazing, or reduced, at least. The requirement to live in the sorority house. Becoming Kimberly Welles's newest BFF.

And, of course, the article.

That was the truncated version, Erin-style. I had to channel someone because my vibe was destroyed half an hour after the thorny shrubbery incident, when we had unsealed the bottle of enshrined mulberry gin, which still looked as bad an idea as it had before we started. My copies of Kimberly Welles's profile and photographs were spread around the base of the bottle, where it sat in the center of our dorm-room living area. Inerius's unofficial *hot or not* retro site that was updated by Griffin glowed from my laptop to frame the collection in an eerie blue glow.

I hoped we wouldn't accidentally summon the head sister in our impromptu ritual, because it turned out that the head of the Dead Poets Sorority was a well-connected literary major with more backing—and funding—to her name than almost anyone else on campus. Her father held a partnership in an NYC legal firm and her mother owned her own luxury fragrance brand. Kimberly Welles was an heiress in her own right, and she knew it.

Plus, her obsessions were legendary. In her freshman year she started a small critique group that ended up targeting one particular member. Basically, she was a chronic literary grandstander with horrendous outcomes, socially speaking. The details were so well locked down that I struggled to locate the name of the student who had been all but stripped from Inerius U's history. Apparently, that student now resided in California and was a nursing major.

Thank you, Griffin, for your hacking skills.

The year after that, Kimberly's focus turned to botanicals. But not any regular variety of kitchen herbs. No, she wanted to recreate a 'royal poison garden' at the back of Phi Omega House. Which was how we got our coffee shop with its burnt beans and branded Dewar cups—Proserpine's Venom. Surrounded by monochromatic poppies and located within sight of the poison garden, it was named after the eternally flowering underworld garden that Persephone tended year-round.

All of that was cute in theory, as it matched the sorority's Gothic vibes, right up until two sisters who decided to follow in Kimberly's botanical footsteps ended up in the med ward treated for belladonna poisoning.

Today, it appeared Kimberly's newest fixation was dead poets. Or more to the point—raising them from the dead.

I shrugged away Vivian's concerns that ricocheted around my own mind, and pushed the perky sorority sister's photo across the file. "It's for a few weeks. Maybe a month if I can't crack this assignment open straight up. That's not too long."

It had better not be a month.

Vivian ran her fingers around the top of her empty shot glass. "Let me recap. You'll live in the house. As one of

19

them? Headbands and tea parties and bake sales? All the secrets and rumors and things you'll never tell? Except to each other, of course. Emma, you *hate* societies. *We* hate societies. You'll suffocate in their pastel all-encompassing mob mentality."

"No pain, no gain." I rallied a smile to take on the ages. Or at least, a sorority-worthy beam. *Fake it 'til you make it.* I had a dozen clichés for every occasion.

Vivian blew her cheeks out in a huff. "You've already made up your mind, haven't you? At least check in with me every few days," she pleaded.

I burst out laughing. "It's a sorority, not the army. I'll have my phone. I can message you whenever. It's not like they'll restrict my civil rights," I muttered.

"So you think now." She wagged a finger in warning as I pretended to bite it, and tapped my nose. "Head on straight, Emma Reeves. You need—"

I didn't get to find out what, exactly, I needed, because she broke off, staring over my shoulder.

"What? Did we summon her?" I joked, pretending not to react to the shiver that worked its way up my spine.

Vivian shook her head and pointed to the door, speaking in hushed, reverent tones. "I think your invitation has arrived."

I twisted in my seat, my *Care Bears Care* replacement tee riding up my stomach. I pulled the hem down as I clambered to my knees and reached for the glossy black envelope that slid toward us from its flight beneath our doorway on a breath of a gust that should never have been there in the first place.

"Do we chase?" I waved the black-on-black ribbon-tied offering.

Vivian snatched the glossy black cardstock out of my hands. "We do not."

"Hey!" I protested, lunging across our sacred circle of enshrined journalistic offerings. "I thought you weren't interested in secret societies. Or sororities." That was a tongue twister in itself.

"I wasn't."

"Until?" I leaned over her shoulder as she stroked the thick black ribbon with one finger.

"Until you received a message hand-delivered from the queen of obsession herself. Or her minions. That's worthy of a thesis chapter, at least." Vivian undid the black ribbon with her teeth while I squeezed my eyes shut.

Erin would have a seizure if she knew I'd shared the details of my assignment with my roommate and best friend. Also, this afternoon could have ended a whole lot worse than being stuck in a bramble bush had the sisters caught me loitering around the side of their building before their fancy piece of cardboard arrived.

I pried one eye open. "Read it."

Vivian cleared her throat and intoned the contents in her best funereal voice.

> Dear Miss Emma Reeves,
>
> Welcome to the Dead Poets Sorority. Please arrive at the front gate of Phi Omega Sorority House this evening at eight p.m. Bring nothing but your curiosity and willingness to explore your literary heroes in person. Your possessions will be brought to us.
>
> We look forward to raising your expectations in a literary sisterhood.
>
> Kimberly Welles

I stared at the back of the piece of paper in Vivian's hands. When she had read the entire thing over twice in silence, I grabbed it back and ran my fingers over the gold calligraphy inked on heavy cardstock.

"She's got nice handwriting."

Vivian snorted. "You think Kimberly wrote that herself?"

She flicked to a fresh browser on my laptop and drew up one of our current stalkee's assignments. A draft, by the looks of the penned piece. I raised my eyebrows, impressed at Vivian's skills and not quite prepared to ask how she knew where to look.

The handwriting was large, open and childlike at best. Neat, though almost every line involved hearts of some kind, like an overly enthused version of Cupid vomited all over the page.

"Ugh." I slapped a hand over my eyes. "You need to warn a girl about that."

Vivian laughed at me as I lowered my fingers to find her pouring our mulberry gin shots one-handed. "It's a talent. Seriously, though, the point stands. She employs lackeys for everything. Don't let her use you while you're in there."

And I'm stuck here without you.
Alone.
Hello, thesis on obsession and hive mentality.

Her unspoken words hung between us. Collective mentality had been Vivian's personal vested interest since I first met her at Inerius U's library in the psych section on a freshman research project for Erin. She helped a girl out, and we became firm friends.

Kimberly wasn't the only one to harbor obsessions, but at least Vivian hid hers better than most.

I bit my lip, keeping my chin tucked as I stared into the still-swirling depth of my mulberry gin shot that mangled my reflection back at me like a singularity confined by thick glass walls.

"Promise."

"That I'll take down a secret society from the inside?"

"That you'll be safe."

"It's done." I sent my BFF a winning smile.

"Cross your heart." She glared at me across the top of her shot glass. The viscous violet liquid reflected soulless pools in her eyes.

I crossed my heart in a childish bid to hold to my word, which I knew I'd have to break, probably within my first week in the sorority house.

Vivian muttered beneath her breath while she lit two candles placed off to one side of our impromptu shrine— away from my protected laptop—and positioned my pink and white desk cactus between them. She placed her shot glass back on the threadbare carpet and grabbed my hands, holding both tight. A chill shot between us as she stared straight into my eyes.

"Lord Byron, I call upon thee to watch over my friend when her heart is chill'd from lack of light and she cannot see the way."

"What are you doing?" I hissed, tugging on my hands for freedom and gaining nothing.

"Hush." Vivian squeezed my knuckles reprovingly, refusing to release me. "Let her not wander in the eternal darkness where poets forget their passion in dread."

"Are you paraphrasing George Byron?" My head picked out words I'd tried not to study in high school while I was too busy flirting with Justin Larcomb, who sat two rows back and possessed the best bouffant hair I'd ever laid eyes on. Even David Bowie would have approved.

"We send you this selfish prayer for light by death itself consumed."

Vivian sent me a final glare, the start of her own obsession burning in the onyx depths of her pupils. The remaining fight in me died as she pushed my shot glass forward.

I sighed and tossed my shot back, Vivian half a second behind me. Either way, the result was the same.

"Ugh." We shuddered together.

"That was feral." I shook my head, trying to banish the taste I knew would never leave me.

"Agreed. The worst. Have another?" Vivian waggled the bottle outside of my reach. "We have research on magic tricks and séance setup to do."

"Sure. Why not." There were a few hours to kill before I was due to make an appearance at Phi Omega House. I pushed my drained shot glass forward. "Top me up."

Vivian bar-wenched for us while I drank my fears away and prayed that the only thing I'd regret tomorrow was a row of bad shots, and not letting my editor bribe me with more of the things I wanted most while I gave up everything I believed in.

Or against.

I rallied a smile despite that dour thought and met Vivian's eyes across the shrine as her candles dripped wax in a pool around my desk cactus that once protected me against an ex-boyfriend.

"Bottoms up."

2

What My Heart Desires

Evening cast a shroud over Phi Omega House, the home to the Dead Poets Sorority. A near-full moon threw long shadows, providing the Gothic building with a facade that sang of excess and privilege. Like the rest of Inerius University, the structure dug into Massachusetts soil six generations deep.

There were a few newer buildings scattered about campus, but the sorority was one of the original structures. Each chipped stone, which I'd become intimate with that afternoon, from the building's lichen-kissed foundation to the spired tip of its twin belfries, promised that this society was where secrets were caged and souls could succumb to a sweet literary death.

A pair of grotesque gargoyles were seated above the masses gathered below to haze the flock of hopefuls allowed inside the sorority's coveted walls for tonight's event.

No cameras allowed, of course.

"I heard they got Byron last month," one girl whispered along the line clustered about the stone steps that led into the depths of literary insanity.

A mangled line of Vivian's prayer slipped through my mind. I stifled a laugh, even though I didn't have to hide this time.

"Not even close. My housemate said she was here when Milton appeared a few weeks ago," another mused.

"Emily Dickinson is on the list for later this year," someone else hissed.

My stomach turned over on itself. *They're talking about historical figures like they're cheap Saturday night acts at the student bar.* What in the literary hell had Erin signed me up for? These necromancer wannabes dressed in their best Victorian cosplay or French salon wear best suited to the time of Louis XIV were a far cry from the rush-week potentials covered in pastel shades of Candyland that I expected to find.

If I hadn't been dubious about the society before, that conversation would have cemented my concerns. Regardless of whether the sorority's claims were true or not, no literary behemoth deserved that level of gross disrespect.

Apologies, Byron, for mangling your prayer to Darkness earlier. It was born out of desperation.

As I eyed the gaping, wide-eyed faces mixed amongst the regular crowd I'd already cyber-stalked, I scanned for those who I knew served Kimberly Welles's intention of forming an army of belletristic wannabes for a romantic transcendence revival and who would warrant a second or third invitation.

Or so rumors had it, according to Erin and Griffin's well-collated file.

My vapid smile locked in place like a mask, eyes wide enough they'd already dried at the corners, I prayed it would be a short damn production before my fake ass fell apart at the seams and I could escape to my room.

Expose the Dead Poets Sorority. Make them the laughing stock of Inerius U.

My editor had some emotional stake in that, but an easy target meant a front-page feature bearing my name, and our goals aligned for the time being.

"Welcome, Romantics." A cloaked figure crooked a black-painted fingernail in our direction as an arched door to the side of the great entrance to Phi Omega House creaked open.

Someone at the back gasped. *Cue eye roll.* If I had enough eyeball fluid left to roll mine.

I slid my hand into my Death's-head Hawk-moth-shaped satchel and pressed the button on my voice recorder as the crowd lined up like so many sheep, chattering loud enough I knew they'd blow out my sound for the first few minutes. Not that this part mattered. I'd catch the rest of the meeting, and—

"No bags inside." The cloaked figure dropped their mystic voice as talons of death clicked in front of my nose. "Devices are to be left in the foyer for registration."

I kept my face clean of emotion as I passed everything over, my stomach clenching down. *It's not the army.* Suddenly my throwaway line to Vivian didn't seem half so pithy. "Do I get a ticket for claiming that back afterward?"

A soft gust brushed my cheek, and I swore the faceless shadow inside the hood smirked. With no answer, or cloakroom ticket, forthcoming I took the hint and followed the lemming tribe inside, taking note of the rooms we passed, each detail committed to memory. Not that I had much of a chance to study the inside of the most cloak-and-dagger sorority on campus as we were herded into a small salon set up to seat maybe twenty people in a magical, cozy environment.

My first impression was that the head of the Dead Poets Sorority had gone all out with the decorations committee. Arched, stained windows in a myriad of colors that stood the full height of the vaulted ceilings were shrouded by thick black drapes that removed all other sources of light from the room. Even the sound was dampened and our footfalls refused to echo as we tramped into the muted, designated space with all the grace of a herd of eager literary devourers.

Around the walls, an array of mismatched candles perched in ash-black alcoves, their flames flickering to create mini monsters amongst the real ones walking the halls. Ancient oil paintings set on oversized velvet backgrounds decorated the walls. Coach lanterns swung between each at intervals suspended, I suspected, on fishing line to create a ghostly ambience. I swore that if I stared long enough at any portrait in the strange, flickering light, the eyes shifted, following my path.

I needed to send myself a taco slapping gif, or maybe schedule Erin to do it for me. *Ha*. She'd love that and would probably be all in on it. *Focus, Emma*. Tonight had to be about writing my article, not turning googly-eyed about some magician's bag of tricks, no matter how much professional respect I had for the effort involved. Any more of this and my skeptic's card would be rescinded.

A throat cleared at the back of the room. The break in atmosphere prompted movement from the masses, and we filed into the proffered seats like so many trained familiars. Two cloaked sisters uncapped black salt cellars and shook them into the space in front of our chairs to create a broad circle three inches thick.

I desperately wanted to swipe my finger through their perfect line, but figured the action would be frowned upon.

A pensive air slipped between each of us and all chatter ceased. I rubber necked in true plastic-chicken style, seeking our host for the evening, but when she spoke, her voice came from high above her gathered flock.

"Begin."

The sisters seated on either side of me began to chant. Even those I'd taken as beginners muttered in haste, copying what sounded like partial phrases of old verse, though the mixed quotes fragmented my already overstimulated brain. I slid my fingers surreptitiously beneath my plush cushion, seeking a handout I'd missed in the dimmed light, but found nothing.

A talon poked me in the back. "Faith matters, sister."

Bowing my head, I muttered along to keep my cover in place, peering through my lashes to take in the scene. Most of the newbs scrunched their eyes shut, their backs hunched, clasped hands trembling.

The regulars were easiest to spot. Those sisters held their hands open on their laps, their eyes trancelike. Some rocked side to side—and their faces? Those were lit with the dangerous sort of religious fervor that burned bras and books alike.

This article would either be a brilliant, front-page-worthy feature, or I'd find myself their next unwilling sacrifice on the pyre to their literary heroes.

A chill puffed around my feet. *Secret door?* I managed to keep the grin off my face before the smoke appeared. *Called it.* Post mulberry gin shots, Vivian and I had brainstormed the possible special effects of tonight's performance. A smoke machine came out on top. My second guess was dry ice, as it didn't have the giveaway scent and came with the added benefit of dizziness as carbon dioxide permeated the closed space. Hopefully the room had ventilation and we wouldn't asphyxiate or I'd feature on the front page of the college newspaper in more than just byline come morning.

My untimely death would make a damn fine feature article, though.

I closed my eyes, listening to the chants that crossed over each other. A whisper rippled around the room, then another, each brushing my flesh, though I sensed no one nearby. My eyes sprang open as I attempted to locate the sound, but unless Kimberly had speakers planted in hidden alcoves above us, what I heard wasn't possible.

29

Ignoring the prickles rioting along my arms, I chanted along with the sisters. *Mob mentality*. Vivian would have a field day breaking this down for her collective consciousness thesis. The sisters' volume rose to a crescendo. As fast as the chants crested, the voices hushed.

Breath whooshed from me in a void. I leaned forward, gripping my seat as the floor rippled, the darkness screwing with my depth perception in momentous fashion.

"William Yeats," called a low voice at the front of the room. "We call upon thee. Show yourself!" Kimberly stepped before the multicolored stained windows, the rainbow light reflecting upon her pale hair.

"Yeats—*really*?" I muttered.

One of my neighbors elbowed me. I shut up, though the sister on my other side transformed a snort into a cough in her own personal miracle.

The pensive air returned.

A lull fell before a rumble rang out around the room. Girls whispered and clutched at each other. Kimberly turned, her mouth agape as her eyes rolled back in her head in a show of obvious possession. Slime dripped from her wrists, oozing onto the floor.

"Ectoplasm," one of the older sisters gasped, crossing herself.

Or Dollar Tree goo made up with gloopy glue before the show.

"He's here!" one wannabe pledge shrieked. A senior sister shushed her sternly.

A rumble rattled beneath us again. I frowned, tapping the floorboards with my feet. *Those didn't echo before.* I rolled my heel then banged it down. Hard.

An explosive sound ripped through the room and bounced back at me.

Rapping the boards. Another parlor trick Vivian and I

discovered mediums used to "prove" the presence of spirits in a room.

Every head turned to look at me.

"Sorry," I murmured, throwing my pithy smile back into place. "Got overexcited."

Kimberly appeared by my side, apparently recovered from her semi-sacred enthrallment. "Not every occasion warrants an appearance," she murmured as green goop dripped from her fingertips to puddle on the hollowed-out floorboards at my feet.

The same cold draft from before whispered by my cheek and a soft thunk confirmed my previous suspicion of a hidden door. *A house like this must be riddled with them.* The stuff of literal fairy tales to a journalism student. Ideas of midnight assignations and secret sisters roiled through my head. Perfect for a sisterhood who kept its secrets and true intentions hidden on campus.

And perfect for Kimberly's production. We might not have brewed a literary ghost, but the sisters were convinced of her confidence to hail one from the depths of history.

Now I needed to warrant an invitation to the next meeting without getting my metaphysical ass kicked out of Phi Omega House while I snooped around.

*

"Larissa Meyer, here." Kimberly Welles pointed to a door on our left as we—her newest recruits—followed her en masse along the corridor above the séance room and turned off to a wing I thought led along the eastern wall of the archaic building. "Sarah Jane Kinston, next door. The rest of you, please follow me."

I trotted along semi-obediently at the back of the pack. Multicolored plush carpets passed underfoot as I counted more doors than should have been reasonable for what I was certain were luxurious, oversized, well-appointed bedrooms that came equipped with their own TV, walk-in wardrobe and small, filled library. At least, according to our Big Sister's walk-through guide. No such luck on a private en suite. I'd miss what I shared with Vivian in lieu of the communal dorm one on each floor.

Phi Omega House, I swore, was bigger on the inside than the outside. Not that I felt out of my depth; at least, not yet. The excess of cheap carnival tricks at tonight's stage performance, because that's all it was—smoke and mirrors at its most Gothic—provided me with a tainted perspective on Kimberly's secret society resurrection gab. Not that I was into zombie poets, though that could have made for a decent one a.m. read.

My fingertips trailed the smooth, worn picture rail that separated Regency-patterned pearlescent wallpaper and a deep midnight-painted section above. More portraits—photographs this time—hung at regularly spaced intervals. *Someone's OCD is on show. Three guesses as to whose, and the first two didn't count.* I watched the back of Kimberly's perfectly curled head as she walked with a steady gait along the hall, pointing out door after door for her newest pledges who flitted away, reducing the flock trailing after her.

Even after the hooded episode, those Marilyn-esque pin-up spirals stayed fixed in position, as though undaring to move. I wondered if her cloak slipped, whether it would reveal her pastel twinset and spiked heels that dug into the carpets, and I swore she could have slipped straight out of the Fifties golden era, albeit with a little less sherry in the pantry.

Maybe we were here to resurrect the last spirit she consumed to keep her body eternally youthful.

Shoving the uncharitable thought deep—surely she

didn't devour souls *that* fast—I continued trailing the group as the girls drifted away to their designated rooms. Some chattered and swooned at their doorways—*that's a positive reaction, if not the sort Erin expected*—while others stood silent and still until called upon, then disappeared into their darkened rooms, their doors closing behind them.

Until I looked around to find I stood alone in the corridor, while Kimberly waited inside a doorway that stood slightly ajar.

"This one's yours."

I forced a smile on aching cheeks, even though I hadn't smiled enough for them to bear an ache in the last hour, and pressed my heel experimentally into the carpet.

No loose boards here.

I wouldn't put it past the sisterhood leader to slide a few more tricks into the first night's accommodations to scare the untried pledges, though more of her personal brand of stage-show magic was probably stowed inside the rooms. To be fair, it's what I would do, if I were the tricky sort.

Perhaps we aren't that different after all.

I glanced at the door, suddenly stalling.

You hate sororities.

Don't let her use you.

Vivian's voice of four hours prior floated back to me. My forced smile threatened to split my face as I nodded with an excess of enthusiasm I didn't feel but yanked on from the tips of my sepulcher-haze-painted toenails anyway.

"Right." I cleared my throat, half expecting my soul to evict on the obvious lie. "Yes. Thank you. And my things are . . . ?"

"Inside." Kimberly tapped the door with a single fingernail manicured into the shape of a coffin top.

The oiled door behaved like a well-trained dog, silently swaying open to expose the impenetrable void beyond.

Even the house folds to her whim.

"That's . . . great," I murmured, as we both realized I would not, in fact, be a swooner or an incessant chatterer, sucking up her twinset/cloak-covered tush. My foot hovered over the threshold.

Then I pulled it back.

"How did you—"

Kimberly's eyes flickered like the dark flame of her séance candles. I inhaled at the unnatural light, noting the same strange, cold flicker I'd experienced back in the room below. The same chill I'd felt at her grand entrance during her showtime a moment before an unseen hand that couldn't possibly belong to her pressed between my shoulder blades.

A far from gentle hand shoved me forward into the unknown abyss that would be my prison until I paid my dues in the form of an exposé that would ruin her entire world.

Or, if they discovered my true purpose, ruined mine first.

I fell into the darkness as the door closed softly behind me to the twisted jingle of her sadistic laughter.

*

The sisters chanted like Illuminati gathered beneath grave lanterns, desperate to commune with literary greatness in an effort to dispel their own mortal mediocrity.

I stopped typing. My article had started well, recounting the Dead Poets Sorority's gothicana ambience, then our entrance into the Phi Omega House. But after that . . . the words that flowed turned to ash. Being an asshole—either on or off the page—sat poorly with me. I might be skeptical of all things supernatural, but this wasn't the same. If I ripped Kimberly a new one I preferred to do it to her face, and I wasn't sure she'd earned the burn yet.

Sure, she'd put on a fun show tonight. The desperate sisters were enamored with her sideshow act. Even I bought into her ghostly bullshit for a hot minute with those whispers that seemed to come out of nowhere. Every hair on my arms stood in protest at the memory that refused to leave me. I slugged back the semi-warm beer I'd forgotten about perched on my desk beside my laptop, working on my piece.

My room was full of my things as promised, brought from the dorm room I shared—that I'd previously shared—with Vivian. Literally everything had been moved to my new sorority room and unpacked. Mostly. Some boxes of clothes were pushed into the closet. I left those exactly where they were. The rest of my room was functional, my drawers laid out like they had been in my shared room with Vivian, as though someone had photographed the original arrangement.

I could imagine how that particular event went down with Vivian. Either she spent an hour or two sassing them out, or watching in sentinel-like silence.

I missed her snarky commentary right now. Even while I was supposed to get my words down for the day, and not worry about distractions and procrastination, I missed her.

This is going to be a long three to four weeks of sorority life.

If I made it.

If they kept me and didn't oust me for breaking all the rules.

If, if, if . . .

Hence the room-temperature beer and the half-blank screen.

Write drunk, edit sober. Wasn't that the advice writers

were given? Or something like that. Even wearing my beer goggles, I knew my article lacked that front-page-worthy X-factor. It needed . . . it needed . . . empirical proof.

I needed to conjure myself a ghost.

Or at least I needed to *try* to conjure myself a ghost. It didn't actually matter if I failed; the attempt needed to be made in Phi Omega House. The summoning needed to be held right here, right now.

Uncapping a fresh beer from my small dorm-room fridge, I hunted through my drawers and pulled out every candle in my possession. Even those had been unpacked to my preferences. Most were white, though some bore flecks of color where I merged a few in my first year, broke enough to recycle anything and everything. Three were used birthday candles.

I stuck those in yesterday's blueberry muffin, which had also managed to make the location shift along with me, and cut into a bag of salt that the room's previous occupant had left behind. The crystals clung together but a few decent bangs against the counter set them free, enough to replicate the conditions of Kimberly's séance, sans her showtime paraphernalia. I did miss the goop, but hey, I could try for a bout of possession on round two, like Vivian and I had researched, though I wasn't sure I had enough goop to go around. Maybe I could ask to borrow props from Kimberly, but I suspected that might be frowned upon on my first night in the house.

Now to pick my chants. Who did I want to summon? Not Yeats. Or Byron. I'd studied T. S. Eliot in high school and probably had a copy of *Hollow Men* lying around, which had come along with the rest of my personal paraphernalia. Maybe some Edgar Allan Poe to counter the gap in centuries . . . That counted as transcendentalism, right?

"Ugh," I groaned aloud. *In over my head* didn't come

close to covering it, but I needed that reference Erin offered on a newsroom-printed platter more than she knew.

Or maybe she did, and that was the point.

My candles lit, verses secure in hand, I settled cross-legged outside my salt circle and tried not to sneeze it out of existence. With Kimberly's intoned *"begin"* in mind, I started to read, picking Poe as my first target.

"Ye who read are still among the living . . . blah. This wasn't the best pick," I informed my flickering birthday tapers, whose colored flames wobbled in agreement as I shuffled my pages and downed half the freshly cold beer I'd brought with me for the endeavor. "Here we go. Let's try a dash of Eliot. *'We are hollow men . . .'"*

The familiar verse slipped from my tongue like a lover's caress. I found my stride, swapping from Eliot to Poe and back again, my chants becoming more seamless with each stanza until my throat grew raw. Whispers that weren't mine filled my dorm room. My mind registered the extra presence, but I was too caught in my own bout of divine madness to stop.

My words didn't cease for an age. Not until the lights above me flickered, and my breath clouded before my face. Only then did that unnatural hush grip me as it had downstairs, along with the chanted frenzy of two dozen others.

Cold tendrils by a hand that didn't belong to any living creature whispered at my throat. My eyes flew wide, ready to combat whatever held me in place—

But my mortality was no longer the sole point of interest in my dorm room.

Visible through the dust motes orbiting my feeble lights, a figure wavered in the center of my salted circle. Much-needed oxygen sucked into my lungs as I stared at the man who was neither Eliot nor Poe, but some sort of Victorian-era hybrid I didn't recognize.

Spiral, shoulder-length dirty blond curls framed a narrow face and hosted cheekbones that could etch his name in diamonds, had I known it. Soul-dark eyes lit with their own spiral galaxy from within gazed at me from beneath thick lashes that would turn any supermodel a peculiar shade of Kermit. A powder blue cravat and a long frock coat that tapered at the waist and dropped to his calves completed the profile of an artist yanked straight out of the Age of Revolution.

Shock must have set in, because my sole thought was: *He will make a spectacular front-page feature.*

Priorities, Emma.

Erin's voice ran a secondary victory lap around my addled brain. That was so much more headline-worthy than my accidental death by asphyxiation at the ground floor of the Dead Poets House during séance hour.

Still, a strange man stood in my dorm room, and he wasn't the one I expected. Or probably the one that I needed.

"Who the hell are you?" I stared at the translucentish shape, who seemed as surprised to have appeared in my salt circle as I was.

"Nathaniel Harker, sonneteer and wordsmith. At your service." He swept into a deep bow, doffing a hat he didn't wear, though at least his body—no slimy ectoplasm to be seen—fluctuated into something more corporeal with every tense breath that panted from my overworked lungs.

Because there sure as hell was no air coming from *his*.

Add in my semi out-of-body experience where my feet were still attached to the floor of my new sorority room while my mind flew away with my beer-induced fantasy of the moment, and I was all in for this daydream. Or nightdream. Or whatever we called waking drunken moments where dead not-zombie boys from the past invaded dorms in costume.

"And who might you be?" he asked.

A sexy, come-hither smile curved luscious lips I swore were designed for the sole purpose of kissing virgins. His whole persona reminded me of a certain time-traveling Captain Jack mixed with a heady dose of Heath Ledger playing a period piece.

Except for those eyes that spoke of a darkness yet to be unveiled. A broody, tortured soul. Those were pure Timothée Chalamet.

He's perfect article fodder.

The perfect dead poet.

"Emma Reeves, journalist student at Inerius University."

Why did I feel inclined to add that morsel of information, which meant nothing at all to what looked like an eighteenth-century person who probably hadn't been born before the college was founded? He was my beer-and-gin-worthy dreamscape fantasy, after all. Plus, the history fit the situation. Inerius University had been established by a drunken patriarchal group, no less, who named the college after one *Irnerius*, an ancient Italian Glossator. Unfortunately, they misspelled his name on the charter that night in their soggified, over-brewed craft-beer haze. In their wisdom, the morning after, they left the college named thus, proclaiming Irnerius—known as the "lantern of the law"—, who founded the medieval school of Roman law, would appreciate their humor. Thus Inerius U was born.

I voted to resurrect ol' Irnerius to see what the Roman man had to say about this twist on his namesake now that we had the power to pull who we liked out of history.

But right now *might* not be the best time due to the ghost loitering patiently on my dorm-room floor. Kudos to the dead for understanding that patience and virtues went together. I really did need that shirt with the Latin saying about truth and time.

While I lollygagged, Nathaniel's smile never wavered, nor did his eyes break from holding mine. A shiver worked its way along my arms under his intense study. I wrapped them tighter about myself beneath his knowing gaze.

"Well, Emma Reeves of Inerius University. I am dead, and you are beautiful. What shall we do on this midsummer eve?"

Oh, swoon me sideways and hand me a Pulitzer. I'd summoned myself a freaking poet of the Romantic era.

The Dead Poets Sorority would be thrilled.

Nathaniel held out a hand that no longer looked anything other than corporeal. My heart twanging inside my chest, I shoved my skepticism card aside and let his fingers fold around mine. He drew me closer until our noses nearly touched, the warmth of my living flesh lending heat to his.

Breath left my body as he smiled, humming a song I didn't know, and whispered words I barely caught for the white noise that obliterated everything but him.

I summoned myself a poet and now he's all mine.

The sisterhood could go to hell. I wasn't one to share.

I'm Late for an Unimportant Date

Thirty minutes after I summoned my very own dead poet, I'd convinced myself that my beer goggles had lied as I attempted to sketch out notes from the night's séance before my brain dumped everything—musing my thoughts aloud and all—without a dash of peace.

My fingers didn't seem to want to work as I tapped my way through a narrative involving the smoke machine and the whispering sisters—*"Nathaniel, please don't play with the desk cactus"*—and when I reached the part about the cold shiver, I vibrated in my chair to the point I semi seized up. *"Nathaniel, leave the warm beer alone. That won't end well."*

But I might as well have been talking to myself for the comical look on his face when the beer dripped right through him to puddle on my floor, half drowning my faux bear rug.

Twice my hallucinated poet fell through my sofa, and once into the closet where he fumbled around before his hand reappeared.

I threw my metaphorical pen aside at that point, reached in and pulled him free, glaring into eyes that shimmered somewhere between flecks of gold and violet haze that matched my nail polish.

Must be a benefit of the Romantic afterlife.

I wondered what mine would look like when I died, then banished the morose thought to the back of my mind.

No more beer for you, reporter girl.

"Right." I pulled Nathaniel to the sofa that he promptly sank through despite holding my hand tightly. Warmth tinged with a strange sense of coolness melded into my fingers. *Best beer vision ever.* Pillowy lips pursed as he stared owlishly up at me, though I had the impression his show of innocence was just that. "Okay, you virgin-deflowering poet. Sit right there."

I pointed to the faux shag pile—a lurid pink bear rug, complete with faux teeth. I tested them, they were plastic. I pushed him down, pleased when he didn't sink through the floor—again. That would be a tough one to explain.

He smiled and sat, pointing at the bear's fake tail end. "Here?"

"Right. There."

Nathaniel remained seated obediently, crossing his legs, and looked up at me like *I was not a bad person.* Drunk journalist student me could definitely play that bad-girl persona up. I shook my hair back and cocked a hip. His violet-gold gaze tracked the movement with a degree of interest I wasn't sure I hated, though I ignored it for now. Or at least, I pretended to ignore his interest.

"Now. Tell me all your secrets."

Nathaniel Harker opened his mouth. "I was born in Edgartown in 1804, and died in 1827. Flu. A terrible way to die, choking on your own words, unable to write your last sonnet. Actually, not as bad as dying unknown. Never do that. A horrendous tragedy. I wrote and wrote but no one ever knew who I was in my lifetime. Perhaps, I have gained some measure of fame in my death?" He looked at me with a degree of hope.

I blinked at him, and felt like I'd kicked a puppy. *Ghost poets suck.*

"Ah. Er, no such luck of posthumous fame," I apologized, waving a hand at the book stack beyond my laptop that came pre-stocked with the sorority room. "I've got Mary Shelley—"

"Ugh, monsters and flowers."

"Descartes—"

"Some brains, at least," Nathaniel muttered.

"Coleridge, Goethe, Keats—"

"Fair enough."

"Blake, Wordsworth . . ."

"Old *Wordy*."

"And Byron."

"Bleurgh." Nathaniel blew a raspberry.

The rude noise contorted his face into a comical twist I didn't expect, and I burst out laughing.

"What's wrong with Bryon?"

"Half worth." Nathaniel snorted, staring at a fixed point above my head. "That wastrel of a man should never have been allowed to pick up a quill as a child. His sexual choices aside—those were for him alone—his poetry shouldn't be acclaimed by any who read him." His chest swelled like a grouse inflating. A dead one puffing with his own gasses.

Not my finest imagery, but my bank of witty repartee had a shelf life akin to six hours of sleeplessness when my exhausted, decaffeinated brain was still attempting to process the dead dude hanging out in my dorm room.

Erin had requested I summon a dead poet. I hadn't expected to succeed on night number one.

"Ok-*kay*, I'll stop you there." I held up a hand. "I'm sure you'll be pleased to know there was some critical controversy about his, uh, choice of penned words."

I plastered a smile on my tired face. Tired, because tonight had been all about pleasing other people and I *really* wanted to finish my article notes, though my beer buzz was fading fast, along with my energy.

"Good." Nathaniel sank into a sort of funk.

"Is there anything else you can tell me about writing? Being a poet? Poet's life?" I prodded, unsure how long I would have this poet as a grandstanding audience of one before he disappeared with the dawn and my dreams. For all I knew, he might pop out of existence at any given moment.

He refused to answer anything else, glaring balefully at the published poets' works in their neat pyramid on my desk, further showcasing the OCD of the house Big Sister because I sure as hell did not stack books—or anything— like that. Or maybe the house had a pet poltergeist. Phi Omega certainly seemed like the place to possess one.

Huh. Getting all my ghost jokes in tonight.

The breath I released was less than enthused. Nate's spate of ennui was contagious. The sulking poet who filled my shag-pile pink rug did nothing for my muse. Or lack thereof. I shook my head, but my dulled synapses refused to connect. It was like when Nate arrived, she left.

Or rather, he did.

Oh Pulitzer, Pulitzer, wherefore art thou . . .

Recognizing I'd called on a wordsmith from the wrong era, I tapped enter again and accidentally wiped the entire paragraph above my cursor from existence.

"Freaking dead poets. Are you the catnip to humanity, or just reporter kind?" I mused. My words blended together as I attempted to ease my building frustration at the blank page before me, although all I needed to do was press the *undo* button. But that small notion seemed insulting: how was I expected to cope with the extra workload after midnight.

"Thou hast eyes the color of sunset over the . . ." Nathaniel paused.

I glanced over at him and raised an eyebrow.

44

He studied my laptop. "Small printing press," he finished grandly, peeking at my screen in the most beautiful picture of utter confusion.

"It's a laptop. Where I put my words for the day before they go to my editor for the local campus paper," I said, explaining my job poorly. "Uh, magazine? It's a newspaper." I dredged my mind through older terms without Googling anything and had a less than poetic moment.

"You put your words of the day into the . . . *tappity tap*?" He frowned.

I blinked. "Yes. I write feature articles on current events." Why not add a frame of reference my pretend ghost boy couldn't possibly understand? But then this was my hallucination. And he would get what I wanted him to get. I hoped.

The frown marring his otherwise perfect features cleared. "Ah. Like a broadsheet."

I shrugged. *Never thought the language barrier of two hundred years would equate to the smallest inconveniences.*

Never thought I'd be conversing with a dead man of two hundred years ago, drunk in my bedroom, after everyone else was asleep either.

"Tell me your secrets, Nathaniel Harker," I murmured.

"When the stars fall, the sun rises over the valley of beauty." He waved a manicured hand toward me, and disappeared through my rug.

I yelped and made a grab at nothing. Nathaniel's disembodied head reappeared at floorboard level, grinning at me like he'd performed the prank of the century.

"Asshat," I muttered.

He patted his head as he slipped back to floor height, and then touched his tush. "Why would I wear my bottom on my head?"

"You scared the shit out of me, Nathaniel." I pointed toward the shadowed recliner next to the cupboard that he fell into earlier. "You are thus banished to the naughty poet's corner. Now," I added when he resumed staring at me with owlish eyes, even if they were pretty ones. *Violet set with a steam of gold flecks.* "Stop it. That's not cute."

"Ah, you are so sweet."

"Go. I have an article to write."

"Such a hard taskmaster. Mistress?" Said eyes took on a seductive gleam.

Only my hallucinations would attempt to pick me up.

"Don't you dare. I'm not doing domme kinks with you tonight."

"As she wishes." He shrugged as he loped away to the NPC. "Banished, I shall thus remain."

"Ass—"

"Hat. Yes, you said before. Be less repetitive in your insults please, mistress."

I glared at him and turned my back while he hummed some tune I didn't recognize. My screen beckoned and my muse returned, or maybe Nathaniel had. *Nate Harker.* My fingers hovered over the keyboard, then began to fly. Rather like my attention.

I didn't know what waned first—my sanity or my dream state, but I did get at least one more paragraph down on that cursed article before my eyes shut and my head crashed forward while Nathaniel sang in the naughty poet's corner.

My subconscious vaguely registered the presence of a snore that might or might not have been mine before I deleted the whole damn thing.

*

I woke in a puddle of last-night's-beverage-flavored stale saliva, and no dead poet in sight. Even without my beer goggles, my eyes gritty and sight blurry as hell, I could work out

46

that I beheld my dying laptop, and my still-made bed. Student life with a waking hangover that no pithy dorm-room séance could cure sucked as much right now as it would in six hours' time when I'd crave the comfort of that bed during class.

I shoved my hair back from my face, glad that not even a dead poet remained to witness my somewhat fragmented morning ritual. Pushing back from my desk, I shoved the power cord at my laptop charging port, missed, glared at the device, and went back for round . . . uh, three. My phone reminded me how long I'd hugged my keyboard for and how late I'd be for my first class of the day a full second before a far too jaunty knock on my door threw me into a Monday morning spiral—on a Tuesday.

"This is not fair," I muttered to my lack of morning spirit as my mind caught up with the sorority campus program.

Wait, didn't poets usually sleep past midday? I'd have to remember to ask the poet in my dreams tonight. Somewhat cowed that the whole event had been a figment of my beer-and-gin-induced haze—*beer monocle?*—and wishing I had a real dead poet to show for my night's efforts, I checked my three percent and charging laptop, groaning when I realized I'd deleted the article to date that appeared unrecoverable at a glance and yanked off last night's clothes.

"I'll be a second."

"We have Lit first up," replied Kimberly's far too cheery-as-all-feck singsong voice. "But there's a sisters' breakfast before that."

I grimaced. Erin did say I was to be Kimberly's pet duckling for the duration. At least I'd be close enough to scent the batshit firsthand. "Ah. Sisters who study together stay together, huh?"

"You got it." My door handle rattled.

I snapped my head about in alarm and a little drool slithered down my cheek.

Oh so elegant.

"I am so not morning-ready, Miss Sunshine," I snarked on automatic, then second-guessed my word choice the moment I opened my mouth.

Too late.

"Who is? Really, Emma. Let me in." Kimberly banged what sounded like her foot on the door.

"Not by the hair on my . . . uh, let's forget I tried that." I wrenched open the cupboard door that not-Nathaniel didn't fall through in my hallucination during the night and threw on the first dress I spotted.

The royal blue striped varsity dress had Inerius U's polo team's name emblazoned across the front with their mascot, and an alumni player's number on the front. Vivian had liberated it one night in our freshman year, and it ended up in my cupboard. I stuffed my feet into the first pair of sand-shoes I found, and wound my hair into a messy bun on top of my head.

"This will have to—ah. Tuesday is twinset day, huh?" I blinked at the pastel vision before me that could have put a rose garden to shame.

"Morning, Sunshine." Kimberly shook her hair out, long, loose curls bouncing like well-trained pups at her command as she shimmied for me.

Actually freaking shimmied. *That's a practiced move.* I covered a shudder as I took in the peach and violet twinset that my mother wished I would have worn, and the matching heels. Not a sign that the Gothic Big Sister from last night existed. It was like she had two distinct personalities to swap between at will. One the soulless creature who'd summoned the dead the night before; the other with sun shining out of every orifice.

Both aspects had the undeniable cult-leader addictive charisma that drew followers to her like so many pawns on

48

a chessboard. I'd been placed on a square. I just didn't know whether she needed me as a main piece . . .

Or as a necessary sacrifice.

I rubbed a hand over my face. "This place is going to send me spiraling with its double standards."

"You know it." She poked me gently, and looked over my outfit with pursed lips. "We have to be what everyone else wants to be and someone they can't touch at the same time. With me?"

"Untouchable and unattainable. I'm so good with that right now." I threw a piece of gum in my mouth that mixed with the taste of last night's stale beer horribly. "Is there caffeine on the way out?" I asked, hope burning in my empty belly. "Otherwise I need to make a stop at Proserpine's."

"That pit of burnt beans." She made a face. "I've got you covered. Coffee machine is downstairs. Burned the midnight study oil? Or a party for one?" she asked slyly.

I raised an eyebrow. "A little of both." The almost-confession fell out all too easily. "I've got deadlines encroaching, and I decided to try to replicate your ceremony from downstairs. Fueled by beer, of course." A little truth never hurt anyone. As long as it was the *right* truth to the right people. In this case at least.

Kimberly looked impressed. Some of her sunny facade dropped. "And your results?"

I smiled ruefully. "Nothing concrete. I had hope but . . . it looks like summoning with alcohol brought on bad dreams more than it did anything real. I wish I had better news to report."

Kimberly studied me for a moment longer. "All right, then. Ready to study some old Romantics? Do you have a favorite you want to pull out of the ether?"

I had the distinct impression of being one of those

crushed tiny bugs under a microscope slide before her sunny disposition returned.

This will be a fun few weeks.

The faster I got the results the paper wanted and wrote an article I didn't drunk-delete, the better. I swore the speed with which her personality shifted was designed for a nasty case of whiplash that I didn't need on a not-Monday morning that felt like one anyway.

"Ahhh, probably not Bryon. Or Wordy—uh, Wordsworth." I covered the slip, but not fast enough to prevent the dip in her too perfect brow.

That didn't deter her as she dragged me downstairs and to the promised land of the coffee machine. "I'm partial to Shelley, of course. Percy, that is. And Poe."

"Good choices. First, *we* have a new sisters' breakfast to host." Kimberly grabbed my hand and slapped a bag of bread into it as soon as we hit the kitchen, then a butter knife. "You're on toast duty."

"We?" I stared at the bread that looked nothing like coffee.

"We," she confirmed.

"Ah." That explained why we were up so early. I regretted my method of tooth brushing within seconds.

While Kimberly laid out the table with an impressive array of condiments from the largest walk-in pantry I had ever seen, I spent the next twenty minutes being kitchen bitch, depressing that toaster button on a four-slice to the rhythm of Alice Cooper's "Walk this Way" in my head, then dived into buttering my stack as the sisters—both new pledges and seasoned veterans—wandered in.

After everyone had been served their toast and an over-sized bowl of fruit salad, plus tiny mason jars of yogurt decorated with grains that Kimberly pulled from the fridge, the meeting started. As before, the Big Sister's attitude switched. I wasn't the only one who saw it in action, but clearly the original sisters were used to the change. The new pledges, from the wide eyes around the table, however, were not.

Sister Sunshine dropped off the face of the planet as Miss Batshit Psycho smiled, picking up a bread knife and stabbing it into the stack I'd spent my morning thus far meticulously buttering.

I suppressed a groan, and plastered a fake-as-hell smile on my face when her too-bright eyes fluttered my way.

"Welcome, Pledges, to Phi Omega House. Last night's event was a taste of what you'll find at the Dead Poets Sorority. One of our number spent her evening attempting to replicate the conditions of the séance. I hope you are all so thorough during your secondment within these walls or your time here will be . . . short." She sliced straight through my stack, and the toast wilted into a sad little pile.

I poked it back together with a sigh. "Dammit."

Kimberly's voice took on a business-like tone. "Before you become fully fledged members of this sorority, there will be tasks assigned to you. Please carry them out in a prompt manner. Your behavior will be assessed every waking moment . . . and sometimes while you're sleeping. Not all of you will make it to sisterhood. Please take your assigned tasks seriously."

Whispers slithered around the table at her pronouncement, but I knew better than to react.

"Basically, everything's a test." The girl opposite me took up the mantle, earning herself a Sunshine Sister glare from Kimberly. She shrugged, undeterred, and picked at her coffin-shaped manicure in grape.

"There will be regular gatherings, homework and required evening attendances," Kimberly continued as though no one had interrupted her. "We have an upcoming welcome party this weekend, and then a bake sale for charity. Please put your name down on the sign-up sheet where your appropriate talents lie." Her gaze scanned the table, and returned to fix on me.

I held her eyes, and when hers didn't waver, I looked down. A heavy black marker sat right beside my plate. *Of course.* I rolled my lips. *Here's hoping I don't poison anyone.* Because I couldn't bake for shit.

I headed straight for the sheets and ran my finger down the list of jobs.

Baker.

Cleaning.

Graphics.

Sales.

Kimberly's name was already listed against that last one. I threw my signature next to hers and turned on my heel, holding out the pen.

"Who's next?"

Kimberly smiled like I'd just aced her unspoken test. *Poets, maybe I had.*

The meeting ended fast after that, the sisters scattering to their classes as I offered to clean up, washing by hand, and I only shattered one sorority-branded mug. The house name and logo was plastered on everything from tea towels to mugs and linen. Kimberly spoke to every single pledge and sister, taking her Big Sister status seriously.

Finally, after what felt like hours, I earned my reward. The Big Sister filled a branded society thermos to the brim with dark ambrosia and added a dash of black cherry syrup at my request, because it was there. A dozen other flavors sat in a neat row that I ached to try. Our duties done for the morning, I fell into a remarkably easy conversation with Kimberly that lasted as long as our walk to the lecture hall and halfway through our first class of the day.

The entire time, Nathaniel's phantom voice snarked in the back of my mind on the state of various Romantics.

Maybe I should write a column from the point of view of a dead poet critiquing contemporary literature? I flipped the idea over in my head a few times before I turned to voice the concept to Kimberly to find the class over. She stared at me with glittering eyes that promised all the terrible things that I knew I did not want to discover.

"Did you get the notes about the assignment?"

My stomach plummeted. While I'd been sitting there daydreaming about six impossible things because I'd chosen to caffeinate and hadn't had breakfast, the girl I was supposed to effectively trash in my exposé had been studiously taking notes.

Kimberly: 1, Emma: 0

I didn't bother trying to lie to her. "Nope. Missed the whole lot. Last night really got my head going." I met her eyes head on and prayed she didn't read the omission behind them.

Besides, it wasn't all ectoplasmic trails. Last night really did blow my mind, if not quite in the way I described. The best stories had a phantom tendril of truth and all . . .

"It's not a problem. You can borrow mine. We have to write a sonnet." Her eyes glittered with that same level of obsession I thought I'd spotted last night. "Perhaps having a little assistance for inspiration might be handy, hmm?"

I pushed the corners of my mouth into a smile, despite my brain's attempt to scream, *"Plagiarism, plagiarism!"* Because that's where I knew she was going with this— summon herself a tame dead poet and liberate his or her voice and call it "inspiration". Not that different from so many across history who had stolen words from the mouths of creatives before they had a chance to publish works under their own names.

"I'm sure it would be lovely to be able to have a chat." I threw on an utterly dreadful British accent to cover my discomfort and prayed the facade worked.

Kimberly's smile never faltered. Apparently my bullshit had leveled up to match hers. "You know, I think we'd better get you ready for the initiation ceremony," she said, her voice clear enough to carry to the few rows either side of us where students were still packing up their things after the class had ended.

I froze where I sat. "I thought you didn't make those choices for a while yet?" I tried to keep my reply casual, but somehow going through with a whole initiation ceremony, knowing I would break my oath the moment I had enough article fodder on the girl seated beside me seemed . . . wrong.

After all, she wasn't that evil, right?

The corners of Kimberly's mouth crooked up in the faintest smile as she found one of my bangs and pushed it back off my face. "Oh, no, Emma. Sometimes I don't wait that long to make my choices at all. And I know the other sisters in the house agree with me. You are . . . special. And if I know that you're in, then someone else will probably leave the house tonight. No point in making them wait all the way through the week, am I right? Because that seems unnecessarily cruel. You can help me make sure they pack."

"It's not a group choice, but yours?" I fixed my vapid fake-ass smile on my face as she cleared her lap of the notebook she had filled with a child-like scrawl and left the lecture hall without another word.

Around us, the frozen eavesdropping students resumed packing up, their chatter a cover for my own hammering heart and chilled cheeks.

This is why we hate sororities. Vivian's mantra slapped both sides of my face simultaneously.

I need the job at the paper. Actually, I needed the *next* job that came after the one I had now, but the income from this one helped. Still, I had to make the article work.

I needed my dead poet to return tonight, even if he simply popped back up in my dreams. That would be enough.

The way I felt last night for some brief period with Nathaniel, my dream ghost poet boy, was . . . intoxicating. Or I was intoxicated. But he was so different from the other men that overpopulated the campus with their obvious intentions and selfish needs.

I didn't even care if he wasn't real, and I didn't care if it took me a full séance of Old Wordy, Monsters and Flowers to get me there.

Suddenly the thing that I wanted was Nathaniel and his stupid—if somewhat sweet—attempts at seducing me. He'd been seriously cute and the fantasy could have held up for at least a day. One more before it dissipated into poet dust.

I glanced down at my notebook that still lay open and froze.

His name lay scrawled across my page, doodled in different directions, and embellished with tiny quills and a stylized peacock. The image brought a smile to my face until I banished the vision with a gasp.

Kimberly had seen this. She saw that I'd written his name. The dead poet I'd named in my notebook over and over and over while I wasn't paying attention to English lit at all.

That she had offered me a place in the sorority if I bullied a girl out slammed into me headfirst. Not because of whatever deal Erin offered her or the favor she pulled. All the mean-girl bullshit aside, that seemed like the grossest betrayal.

Because in the last few hours I forgot to treat Kimberly as a study subject for my article, the prime target for an exposé, and saw her as human. For just a few hours, I even started to *like* some weird part of her crazy.

I'd trusted her. While I was struggling with that happy little backstabber of a concept, the double whammy that got me was that Kimberly now wanted me around because she thought I could raise her a dead poet of my own.

Because she couldn't do it for herself.

Vivian and I had been right all along.

My stomach rose into my throat and slid back down in a reverse luge that agreed with nothing I'd eaten or drunk all day.

All I wanted was to go back to my room and triple-check everything. *Is Nathaniel real?* Because if he was, if my beer goggles slipped—for a second—and what I'd seen . . .

No balladeer way.

But all I could do was stare at the page in my notebook as the lecture hall emptied of the remaining students who cast me their wayward looks. I sat stock-still in my seat, my eyes trained on the page and the name I'd jotted my letters over handwriting that wasn't mine. A hand that wrote in a curlicue not from this century. I traced the pretty, even letters. Mine were shaky.

His weren't.

Nathaniel Harker.

*

I could see my bedroom window outlined against Phi Omega House's gargoyles that warded away unliterary boyfriends from the angle where I crossed the commons field littered with students enjoying the sunshine between classes. Not that I could focus on anything that seemed simple as recently as yesterday.

One night of madness, and everything I thought I understood had been thrown into chaos. The drive to get back to my new room in the sorority house obliterated everything else. Even the shadow the Gothic house cast seemed to grow during the daylight hours, though the clock beneath the common's bell tower struck midday as I scurried beneath its great eye. I was so ready to get my answers and prove myself so stupidly wrong that I nearly ran face first into the last person I needed right now, the one I should have been looking out to avoid.

Vivian Chan.

Because my psych major BFF practically foamed at the mouth as she peered at me as though checking for signs of institutionalism or torture.

After last night's efforts and this morning's classes, I wasn't sure she hadn't had it right yesterday—but, I didn't have time to discuss the advent of secret societies and civil liberties.

Besides, my phone was returned after the séance yesterday, albeit with a coffin-shaped Post-It attached scrawled with a reminder not to post selfies on the local college app, called Neri, which depicted the sorority members or the internals of the house.

Everything was too *secret squirrel* for this girl. The only thing missing was a non-disclosure contract and a request for a signature in blood.

"Did she hurt you? What tricks did they use?" Viv reached for me like she might pry my mouth or eyes open to check for internal damage.

I batted her hands away awkwardly. "No. Nothing. Stop that. I'm not hurt."

"Oh." She looked crestfallen at my lack of impending doom, then perked up. "Coffee? I'll buy."

"Uh." I glanced at the window that I thought belonged to my room longingly. Vivian looked like she was in a chatty mood and I . . . wasn't. "I've got the article to write. And, you know, I have to mind what the other girls think already . . ."

The shitty lie tripped off my tongue then died a silent and thankfully quick death as Vivian stared at me like I'd sprouted a second gargoyle's head. I patted my shoulder to check I hadn't and came across the line in the green.

"You're *kidding*. Already? She's that good, huh?" Vivian circled me, poking at my arm, and grabbed my notebook straight out of my bag in a single, smooth movement.

I stared. "Give that back. And since when do you have talents hither-forth undisclosed, you little pickpocket." I swiped for my notebook but she danced away, flicking the cover open.

I knew the page she landed on the moment her eyes met mine, because they may as well have glowed.

Like Kimberly Welles's had at the end of our class together.

"Who's Nathaniel Harker?"

Well, shit.

I squeezed my eyes shut, grabbed for the notebook then held my hand out when it didn't magically appear in my palm.

"Fine. Let's go get that coffee," I grumbled.

"I knew you'd see it my way."

I cast a single covetous backward glance at my room, staring too hard at the glass pane, like it would help me edge my way closer, but Vivian's hand folded around mine.

"Oh, for heaven's sake," she muttered. "You're already acting weird. Come and do the sofa thing with Doctor Chan."

*

Viv wasn't a therapist yet, and the college café had no sofa, but that didn't stop me from divulging way too many details about the evening's séance and what had happened after. We skipped my lucid dream of a ghostly Romantic, of course. I loved Viv, but I didn't want my brain ending up in a jar of similar objects in a pickled collection.

Usually, I got it. Viv was excited about picking someone's brain apart. Most of the time I was all for watching her in cranial-dissection mode. Today, when I was her subject, I wasn't so sure of her methods.

"You know, I really do have something I want to check on." I spun my Proserpine's Venom coffee in its takeaway cup in concentric circles on the sticky plastic tabletop.

Vivian wiggled spirit fingers in my face. "Talk."

I sighed. "Fine. You were right. Trapdoor. Rapping the boards. Floating candles—I think. Definitely something dangling on a fishing line. The whole building has massive Gothic ambience. The stained windows are a bit *to die for*. You'd love those." I tried my best to look guilty and ended up sounding whimsically enthusiastic, even to my own ears.

Vivian cupped her hands around her cheeks, elbows planted on the tabletop regardless of the germaphobe brewing in both of us, and stared at me. "Smoke machine?"

"You got it." At least I hadn't asphyxiated on night number one. "False floors were used, too, or something like them. Maybe flaps in the walls, like those Roomba homes? I don't know what she had mechanized. Showwomanship, the sisterhood has aplenty. But the rest of the ritual wasn't really very organized—"

"Because there was no real ritual. Smoke and mirrors, remember?"

"But there was a moment where I thought I felt something." Every hair on my arms stood on end. I shivered, abandoning the coffee to wrap my arms around myself at the memory of the coldness that entered the room during the séance, encountered me, and then seemingly left.

"Are you doing that on command?" Viv poked at my goose bumps. They deflated at the slightest touch, and her interest waned. "Anyway. You got chills. So the ambience really worked. A place like that, it should by default." She snorted.

I frowned. "What do you mean?"

"Hello, sorority?" Vivian stared at me. "Secret society under our noses? The exposé? Not to mention a house where the stones probably talk to you in your sleep, the sisters send you subliminal messaging in your group chats, bodies are buried in the walls and the freaking gargoyles make you breakfast." She rolled her shoulders.

I knew she was just getting started, but those last two were too ridiculous.

"Breakfast? Are you kidding me? Come on." I reclaimed my coffee, took a sip—burnt beans—and put it down. "It'd be afternoon tea at the earliest that they'd serve. In loin-cloths over granite abs."

"Probably a hurtful stereotype." She considered. "Better be an eight-pack-plus with the vee." Her eyes turned dreamy.

"I forgot! There was a *possession*."

Vivian's eyes were back to glowy status. "Tell. Me."

I talked for another half hour, detailing everything I could about the remainder of the séance. Everything from the pledges and the sisters' strange chanting, the whole broken feel of the place right through to being pushed into my fully filled bedroom and the door locking behind me for the first hour.

"It's like a cult," I finished.

"The Cult de Kimberly," Vivian muttered. "It comes with a certain personality type. Narcissistic personality disorder at its finest, I suspect. Do you think she— Oh, *quackers*. Emma, quick. Lean forward, study your notebook. Look busy, for *duck's* sake." Vivian never swore if she could help it, but right now didn't seem the most opportune moment for her to shove the bound book back on the table and stuff my nose in its pages.

I stared at Nathaniel Harker's name, and registered the setting sun outside the café. *Shit.* We'd been here longer than I expected, but then Viv and I had always been able to talk. One day apart and we were already ravenous for gossip.

"Wait, why am I studying doodles I made in class when I wasn't paying attention, anyway?"

"Because Thomas freaking Carlisle is looking for you. Really obviously. Get your pen out and write something. *Now*," she hissed.

I dug a pen out of my bag, flipped over to a fresh page and started to jot notes on my article from last night—what little I could remember.

"Emma. There you are. I've been looking for you. Good to see you've come across to the other side." Thomas Carlisle's dulcet tones—those mocha-smooth notes I once was so enamored with that I missed all his other failings, like his giant ego that had no space for another person in his life—wrapped around me in an invasive sort of snuggle. I couldn't free myself from him now any more than I had then. That left me with an itch of the invasive variety, fighting a pending anxiety attack.

Even at this proximity.

I stared at the gym-toned, salon-tanned arms and knew Thomas would still resemble a plastic doll look-alike if I turned my attention to him. All bright white teeth, the square, perfectly shaved jaw girls literally swooned over from half a campus away, and the hair he spent more time styling than I did on my entire morning face of makeup—which I wasn't wearing today.

Or maybe people swooned over the state of his bank account. They certainly wouldn't be doing it over mine.

Instead of acknowledging said ex-boyfriend, I reached for my now semi-cold, bitter coffee sipped the feral mix with a forced sense of nonchalance, wondering at the best course of action in employing my favorite weapon. Vivian's silence said everything. Long ago when we were all freshmen she made a pact to stay out of Themmaville, the toxic varsity level, twelve-month not-so-honeymoon period she had to deal with of Emma + Thomas. Viv promised me our burgeoning relationship wouldn't end well, and renamed us thus. She was right, and I learned a lesson in trusting her gut that first year at Inerius U.

Thomas, of course, never got that memo. He leaned over our table to peck my cheek as I batted him away.

"Not your property, Thomas," I muttered. "Never was. Plus, I have a deadline." I didn't need an excuse but . . . I needed an excuse.

Ugh, nothing has changed.

"You know if you'd stayed with me, you wouldn't have to do that sort of . . . work," he said disdainfully.

"Some of us actually enjoy working, Thomas. It makes us feel fulfilled."

He smiled down at me. "Whatever you need to do to feel busy, Emma."

I closed my eyes, willing myself not to end my coffee's life on his overpriced blazer. After all, no coffee deserved to die that way. For all I knew it would come back and haunt me instead of him.

"I hate this fight."

"Which?"

"The one where you tell me I should shut up and put up, and be a good little wife. Then I tell you that women with brains need to occupy said gray matter so it doesn't die under the hand of a man they couldn't stand in the first damn place and who never deserved them." I finally looked up at Thomas in time to see his face shift from an expression of confusion to a mask of arrogance that bordered on anger.

Ah, there you are.

The real Thomas. Because nice little wives-to-be didn't talk back. Or berate their exes in public. Or make a scene. *Ever.*

I'd never been very good at following the rules. That was one of the reasons Thomas hurled at me on the day he tossed me aside for a Kimberly Welles doppelgänger from another sorority. Now that I looked like I would earn sorority letters of my own, he was suddenly interested again? I wondered who the next girl he took on would be, displacing his current disinterest. Men like Thomas Carlisle were never unoccupied, or alone, for long.

His snarl transformed into a sneer in a practiced movement I knew well. The moment he understood how to turn the tide of an argument, his anger transformed miraculously to disdain. Or when he thought he'd won—too often when I let him in the face of reducing conflict or walking away with my sanity intact.

"I let you have too many freedoms when we were together. Now we aren't together and you think you'll survive sorority life alone? Good luck without my influence. Kimberly Welles will eat you alive."

"Such sweet words. I hope they don't come back to bite you in your overpriced, overpromised and under-delivered ass." I blew him a kiss and continued scribbling nonsense notes, sliding my middle finger along my lucky pen.

Vivian coughed as she seemed to catch the motion and wiggled her fingers at the edge of my periphery. "Bye, Thomas," she said pointedly. "You've been dismissed."

He spluttered in our direction, watched by each curious student in Proserpine's Venom who probably had no idea who he was, and stormed out of the café. Only once he'd been gone for a solid thirty-seven seconds (I counted every single one) did I manage to inhale a full breath and let it out in an uncouth blast that he would have hated if he had stayed.

Because future housewives didn't do *that* either.

"He's so not from this century," Vivian murmured.

I nodded my agreement. "Born well outside his time. Thanks for the assist."

"Any time. Uh, Emma?"

"Yeah?"

"Who's Nathaniel Harker?"

I stared down at my scribbled notes that bore a remarkable resemblance to my class doodles. A second impatient breath blasted from between gritted teeth as I scrunched up my paper, tossed it at the nearest trash can, and downed the rest of my completely icy coffee dregs.

Kimberly Welles wasn't the only one with an obsession in the Phi Omega House, but at least she had a reason for hers.

Mine consisted of a pretend poet—a ghost boy who only ever existed inside my addled dreams in the first place.

Now, I had to prove that to myself.

Now You See Me . . . Again

The ghost of Thomas Carlisle haunted me long after our misfortunate meeting at the campus café. I finally made it back to my room unaccosted, but the whole incident left the tang of bitter, burnt beans dancing over my taste buds. Plus, I hadn't remembered to tell Vivian about Kimberly's strange offer on the initiation front. That was something I needed to research, as well as writing my article. And getting my coursework done.

Maybe find a ghost in my bed.

My to-do list grew with every chaotic, spiraling thought, but my dorm remained disappointingly empty. There was no sign of Nathaniel Harker in my bedroom when I opened my door to a brilliant display of yellows and oranges as the sun set over Inerius U.

A sense of chagrin and stained hope settled deep as I sank into my desk chair in an attempt to ignore the sorority bustling around my room—bumps against the walls as my neighbors, quiet the night before, returned, chattier than ever. Thankfully, no one knocked on my door. Kimberly's minor obsession with me seemed to have passed, or at least stagnated for the moment.

Putting my mangled thoughts to paper—or onto my keyboard—proved far more difficult than I had initially expected. Maybe I'd left it too long, but my rushed, weird morning with Kimberly, verbal diarrhea session with Vivian and run-in with Thomas left me bereft of words. I stared at the screen until long shadows crept along my desk, the light fading outside serving to highlight my failure inside the painted walls of Phi Omega House.

No professional journalist stares at a screen for an hour. Did they? The student in me screamed that I had months left to go before professionalism became a full-time requirement, while the perfectionist insisted it start here and now.

Or yesterday.

The sun's last flash of irradiated vermillion encased by periwinkle clouds died over the clock tower, leaving me in that deep haze where it was difficult to visualize anything beyond. The campus's silhouette fast melded into a penumbral wash, each building indistinct from the next. Only then did I finally succumb to the need of my aching neck, and lowered my forehead to the keyboard with a soft clack of keys.

The writer-specific version of screaming into a pillow, though maybe I could follow up with that later. Whatever came out from my forehead key-jumble press was probably more productive than the last hour's work that could have been better spent on eye yoga.

"That doesn't look healthy."

The voice didn't come from my doorway—where no voice should reasonably be audible in my otherwise unoccupied room—yet, the sound came from right behind my freaking *ear*.

My skin prickled as I recalled the cold, ethereal touch I'd experienced directly below this room during Kimberly's séance the night before as *something* trailed along my forearm, raising gooseflesh in its wake.

66

Something like a touch from a human long gone cold, albeit one I couldn't see.

An invisible human in my room who spoke to me.

Will my mystery guest please step forward?

Nathaniel Harker, it had better be you.

I shrieked in the best delayed reaction of the year—line me up for the next FailArmy Awards—and spun my desk chair on the spot.

My room stood empty.

I rose as I scanned the room wall to wall, my heart ramping up to the non-existent threat my chatty hallucination spawned, but nothing changed. Except for the puff of condensation that coalesced four feet from my face, and a little higher than where I stood.

Right at Nathaniel height.

It appeared that I had scared my ghostly visitor as much as I had scared myself. Or how much he had scared me.

Oh, sorority muse, please, please let it be Nathaniel.

After the way he'd slandered Byron, I hoped I hadn't inadvertently raised any other malevolent poets the night before. Or that Kimberly kept any pets on the upper floor, apart from us. That last thought should have irritated the most mediocre elitist out of me, but right now all I wanted was to identify my unannounced roomie.

Oh yeah, and tweak my article.

I reached behind me, scrabbling ungracefully for anything that would offer a defense, and came up with a sorority-branded pen. *Good enough.*

"Nathaniel?" I took a tentative step forward, wielding the pen. *The pen is mightier than the hauntling?* "Do you want to show yourself?"

The reporter in me offered up a printed taco for a fresh facial slap. The first rule of interviewing a potential expert subject was not to ask closed-ended questions unless you were funneling for information.

We hadn't reached that stage yet. I still had to prove he even existed.

I felt ridiculous talking to thin air. Even more ridiculous considering I'd heard my neighbors banging about before—*oh muse, don't let me hear anyone have sex in this whimsigoth hell during my enforced tenure*—and I tacked on an extra prayer that said neighbors would also not observe my conversations. Maybe there was a spell to soundproof the walls? I really was buying into Kimberly's personal brand of bullshittery today. The girl was contagious.

My fear of being overheard lasted less than half a second. The next puff that didn't belong to me came so close to crystallizing in the air in front of me that I could pick out the features of the man—person—beyond.

The soft-looking lips. The shock of school-boyish hair at least a century out of date, or two. Those soulful eyes hell-bent on annoying the utter fuck out of me the night before.

Yep. I really had raised myself an undead poet. Or a dead one. Was there a difference? Hey, I was a journalism student, not a regular haunt in the philosophy department. Actually, we probably needed representation on the paper on that front. I made a mental note to ask my editor, before an equally icy breath of a hand reached out and plucked my lucky pen right out of my fingers.

So much for the pen is mightier than the ghost boy.

The scream that had been building since Nathaniel decided to scare the literary shite out of me let rip. My voice filled my room for half of a full second before I stuffed my mouth with my fist, stumbled sideways and planted myself butt-first on my bed.

"That's an impressive skill. What else can you do?" Nathaniel asked.

Nathaniel appeared in full, perched on the end of my bed clutching my pen that no longer hovered in midair. And he looked completely not apparition-like at all. He even smiled.

Just like a real boy.

I stared at him over my hand shoved into my mouth, certain my eyes would bug out of my head at any second and land on my quilt cover. While he sat there watching me, I slowly extracted said fist from my mouth and rolled my aching jaw.

"Uh, here we call it a party trick," I said without thinking.

"Very nice," Nathaniel said politely, still smiling. "Can you do anything else?"

"I'm not a trained seal," I snapped, shoving my body backwards until my spine hit the bed board. I grabbed for my pillow, extracted it from under my butt, and cuddled it. The pen he handed tentatively back, avoiding all contact, offered little support, but the pillow created a physical shield. Not that such things seemed to matter to Nathaniel. This version of him at least. *Oh my ghost-article-worthy poet fodder.* "Where did you go? Where have you been all day?"

"I was here." He blinked at me with both eyes.

Owl time was back.

"Uh-huh." I propped my chin on the corner of my pillow. Nathaniel wore the same frock coat as he had yesterday, though his cravat appeared to be tied in a slightly different knot. No less fancy, though. His shirt remained unwrinkled, and his hair was tousled in that same gentlemanly, yet sexy come-hither-ye-virgins type way.

Apparently there wasn't much of a chance to change attire in the afterworld. Or whatever we were calling the bit that came after death. I made an additional note to ask him about that . . . but maybe later. Though if memory served, he had been forthright last night in mentioning how he died.

Last night.

Fuck my article. He was real.

My ghost boy was real. I summoned a *ghost* in my *bedroom*. My brand-new sorority bedroom. Holy freaking Pulitzer, there was a ghost boy in my bedroom. My pulse ratcheted things up times a thousand while the room took on a sparkly facade.

At least Erin will be pleased.

So would Kimberly Welles.

Shit. Kimberly.

The thought hit me in the midst of my revelation while Nathaniel, still smiling politely, began to doodle on my wall when the pen went straight through his skin without drawing blood. Well, he had no blood to be drawn, I supposed. I absently grabbed a sheet of paper.

"Thank you. Most gracious," he murmured, dipping his attention to the page and scribbling quickly.

I studied him, not wanting to break into his reverie, despite the plethora of questions brewing to overflowing point within me. I knew that headspace he was lost in as he scribbled; despite missing her terribly the night before, I hated it when Vivian decided to talk at me for no reason at all when I was in the middle of finishing a piece. When inspiration struck . . .

I waited for his hand to slow, until the pen tapped thoughtfully on the page, and then I asked my question. The one burning in my mind that seemed the most critical to ask.

"Were you watching when I changed this morning?"

He raised his face, that same damn smile still present, and nodded. "Yes."

"Why, you—"

"I turned my back." He blinked at me when I gaped at him. Our soundless conversation continued in a staccato version of Morse code where we were both sending and no one was receiving. "When I realized that there were far fewer garments than I was used to on a female, I turned my back and went into the, uh—"

He pointed to the cupboard he'd fallen into the night before that held my bags and a few hanging clothes someone else had arranged, since I hadn't had the opportunity to sort out my own things.

I had to ask Kimberly how the sorority organization worked, considering earlier today she'd suggested a hierarchical structure different to what I'd expected. For article posterity, of course. And to satisfy my own curiosity. Which, in the end, were exactly the same things.

"Oh. Thank you?" I nibbled on my lip, noting how Nathaniel's gaze tracked the motion, thick lashes sweeping across his cheeks. If he wore glasses, those lashes would hit the lens for sure. And Nathaniel, with that whimsical, slightly nostalgic, geeky look, would rock glasses. And those *curls*. "Why are the best features always given to men?"

He shrugged, his easy smile lingering rather than looking affronted. "Are you saying I'm pretty?"

I raised an eyebrow. "Was that not a hurtful stereotype in your time?"

"You are printing me painfully?" His brow dipped along with his chin.

"What?" I blinked and dredged my mind back through my more obscure historical vocabulary. Stereo . . . type. *Crap.* The old slap-it-together metal and papier mâché form of printing from his time that predated the mass-market approach. Ugh, my words meant different things to him. I closed my eyes, a tension headache already forming at my temples. "No. I meant . . ." Explaining current terms versus his limited frame of reference would constantly be a bitch. I needed a ghost's version of the Urban Dictionary.

A Ghostbook. "By describing you as a pretty man, it might offend or detract from your sense of masculinity."

I was too tired to argue over the traditional role of the sexes in his time, ours (had anything actually changed?) and all the years in between. We could table that for a different night. A Thomas Carlisle-sized headache attacked my forehead. I leaned forward with a groan, an inch shy of face-planting into my pillow, which seemed like a nice option currently.

"Not at all. I enjoy beauty in all its forms. If you think me beautiful, then I take that as a compliment, Miss Emma Reeves. You *are* a miss? Has that . . . changed?"

I got that reference. "No, it hasn't changed, and yes, I am a— I am single, if that's what you're asking." I narrowed my eyes. *Did ghost boy just hit on me?* But Nathaniel twiddled his thumbs innocently—or not *so* innocently—and studied an innocuous point over the top of my desk cactus. "Time might have passed since you were . . . alive. Two hundred years, actually," I added helpfully, counting the years between in a rush from the information he'd given me the night before.

"Good." He looked at me, a speculative glitter in those eyes that slid from sexy to soulful to sad and back again all in the space of a minute or less.

This man was born to be a poet.

Nothing better suited Nathaniel Harker. And yet he hadn't achieved the fame he desired. My heart ached for him. He knew who and what he was so early in life, when so many others fluttered at the edges of knowing, too scared to take that leap, and yet he was rewarded with a cache of unread sonnets and an early death.

"Oh, hell. The assignment. I have to write a sonnet." I did face-plant into the pillow this time and let out a small scream that burned my vocal cords.

Ghostly tendrils moved my hair. A whisper, but it was enough.

"Stop that." I batted his touch away, and looked up to find him resume his place on the end of my bed, though his legs kind of disappeared straight through it. "Neither the time nor the place, Mister Harker."

He rolled his lips inward as he tried out the term. "My time. You said that before. Time . . ."

Those curls that I wanted to run my hands through to see if they were half as silky as they looked dropped over his face as his attention waned. He scribbled again, his movements jerky and frantic.

I sighed. Apparently I wasn't getting half as much information out of my dead poet as I expected or that he claimed from me. "How come you're the one writing when I am the one with a deadline?"

"Why are we drawing lines over dead people?" He looked up at me, his brow wrinkled. "That doesn't seem very nice."

And you seem too innocent for this world.

I instantly hated the lines marring his face, but the concept was too hard for my overtired mind to untangle right now. Apparently poets weren't constrained by things like timeliness and tomorrow's copy.

"Never mind. So you've been here all day. Why didn't I see you this morning?"

He shrugged and passed back the pen. A coolness enveloped my arm, though he didn't actually make contact with my skin, at least not that I could see.

"Thank you. It's an . . . interesting instrument, though any port in a storm, I suppose." He studied the pen I took from him, careful to avoid his cold touch in case I iced over, too, though he looked as solid as any real person, seated on the end of my bed. The mattress even dipped under him like he had mass.

"How are you doing that?" I waved a hand in his direction.

He watched the movement with curious eyes. "You are very graceful. Do you dance?"

"What? No. Only when I'm drunk. Very drunk," I added. "It isn't pretty. I mean that. Sitting on the bed, then floating through it. Can you control that?"

Nathaniel looked down as he sank through the mattress and returned again. "Oh. Yes. it appears that I do have some control over my . . . floatiness."

I raised both eyebrows. "Is that a word?"

"Does it matter?" Curious Nathaniel was back.

"Of course it matters. Words have to exist to use them. Rules. Grammar."

"You've never made up a word?"

My mouth hung open. "This is a ridiculous conversation."

"Have you never made up a word to use in your tappity writing, *Miss* Emma Reeves?" Nathaniel's sly grin spread across his lips as he glided a little closer on my bed.

"Stop right there." I held the pillow out as a barrier between us, despite being under the impression that if he wanted to, he could keep on gliding right through it.

I did not want to experience what happened if he glided right through me. I'd seen enough ghost movies to know that slime like the sort Kimberly covered herself in the night before during her possession performance would be the result. I had no intention of ending my day covered in liquid ghost.

Nathaniel pulled back, stopping shy of my pillow barricade, and affected a hurt expression. "You think I would damage the mortal grace that sits before me?" Mischief lit his face.

I snorted, and threw caution—and my pillow—to the proverbial wind, tossing the latter right through him as penance.

Nathaniel clutched at his chest, or wherever ghosts stored their hearts, and toppled backward.

Right through my bed.

My pillow, blessedly ghost-goop-free, flopped to the duvet otherwise undamaged. I stared, then launched forward on my hands and knees. "Nathaniel. Where did you go?"

Did I just lose my ghost boy? Had I really hurt him? No. No way did a *pillow* do damage to an ethereal spirit crossover or whatever in all the hells we were calling him. No chance in—

A muted giggle—I swore it was a giggle—emanated from beneath me. I grabbed my pillow again and leaned over the edge, tossing the thing straight under the bed. A startled cry doused me in literal cold as my ghost reappeared on my bed, completely fine.

I stared at him and shivered, my arms wrapped around myself. Because while Nathaniel Harker, the smart-ass ghost poet, made it back fine, I was not. A light film only slightly dissimilar to the plasticky kind Kimberly dripped on the downstairs floor yesterday now covered me, only I wasn't green. Same result, though.

My ghost boy had slimed me.

*

Half an hour later, after giving strict instructions to Nathaniel to stay in my bedroom—locked away in my cupboard with a pen, his paper, and the light on—I had showered and changed into my favorite tee, still with its coffee stain, though faded. A pair of navy yoga pants, also a fave, and a wet, messy bun free of ghost slime that had thankfully dissipated beneath a thick layer of scented body wash and scalding-hot water, completed the look.

Nathaniel emerged from the cupboard on two legs,

without disappearing halfway through the floor this time. He seemed to be getting the hang of this whole body thing. A decent attempt, after a solid two hundred years without one, to my eyes.

"Where is Lois Lane?" he asked, skating ghostly fingers across the front of my spirit-animal coffee-stained tee.

"In the wash. Uh-uh. You've lost the right to touch. Or to try to touch after that little stunt." I warded his hand away, unwilling to deal with more ghost-boy goop.

"It wasn't all my fault. You threw the pillow," he said reasonably.

"In self-defense." A lie as I ignored that piece of logic. Poets were not meant to be logical. Back to his original question. "Lois Lane isn't a place, it's a who."

I could *almost* feel his ghostly touch but also I was cold and still a touch damp. Cute in theory, but I didn't want his ghost fingers all over me. A shiver not entirely related to ectoplasm rippled through me at the thought.

Nate retracted his hand. His smile dimmed a little, as though his ego might have taken a phantom hit, though his curiosity seemed as lively as ever.

"Who is Lois Lane, then?" he repeated his adjusted sentence, pronouncing it *Lewis*.

"*Lo*-is. She's a reporter. Someone I wanted to be when I was a child." I paused. "A fictional reporter for a newspaper, who dated a superhero."

"What's a superhero?"

"It's like a—" *This is impossible.* As impossible as being slimed in my own bed by the poet I brought back from the dead. Could that be the title of my sonnet, or maybe my life's memoir, if I survived this assignment? I doubted I'd get a pass for that. I huffed out a breath. "A person who can do anything. With paranormal powers. They aren't real." I held up a hand to forestall more questions. "Just, go with it?"

His brow furrowed. "Your idol is a pretend person in a scandalous relationship to someone else who also doesn't exist. Who can do anything. And you want to be this person?"

Why do I get the feeling you're stuck on the scandalous *part?*

My eyes narrowed. "Yes," I said firmly. "Since I was a little girl."

"Fascinating."

"I'm sure." I paused. "What did you want to be when you were a child?"

Nathaniel tipped his head on one side. "Once, I wanted to be a sailor."

"A sailor? Are you kidding me?"

"No, Emma Reeves. I am not." He smiled at me, and my stomach plummeted into freefall.

There are those eyes full of the soul of a man who has died and come back and never given up hope.

It was like he had an eternal well of the stuff jam-packed inside him. A rarity regardless of the year of his birth or death, or life experiences. Or perhaps because of them.

"So, tell me?" I asked, considering my desk chair, and then decided against it, settling on the hideous pink shag-pile rug in the middle of the floor, cross-legged, and avoiding the teeth part.

Nathaniel sat across from me, but he leaned on one elbow, with his legs stretched out to one side like someone might come along and paint his portrait.

The way he dressed, his hair dangling artistically over one eye, it might actually happen. I wondered if a photo of him would actually come out.

"Please," I added when he didn't talk, but watched me.

"Have you ever looked up at the stars?"

A grin teased the edges of my mouth but I tamped it

down. That was such a Nathaniel thing to say. In the short time I'd known him, he burst out with the most random, romantic ideals, yet a moment after I wanted to laugh at the thought, he made something I considered outdated very much real and something that I suddenly craved. Coveted, even.

My new obsession was understanding how the oddly beautiful man before me worked, and why this obviously brilliant mind of his hadn't been recognized in his own time . . . or later in mine.

"Yes, I know some of the stars," I acknowledged, unsure as always where he was going with the start of his conversation.

"But have you really looked at them?" Eyes swirling with hues of gold and violet stared right into me, their intensity unyielding all of a sudden. "Have you looked hard into the darkness beyond, Emma Reeves? Because if you watch the night sky in the city, the glow diminishes the beauty of the heavens. Humanity's progress—" he made a disparaging sound low in his throat that shouldn't have been as sexy as it turned out "—obliterates much of the natural allure surrounding us. But out at sea, there is no glow to dull the stars reflected on the ocean's surface. Nothing to prevent the universe from cracking open like a speckled egg before a single soul, if all they need to do is but look."

I closed my mouth and swallowed. "Why aren't you published? What happened, Nate?"

His face shuttered. "My work is my own. I choose to keep it private."

"That's not what you said last night," I objected as he turned away. How did we get here? One moment he was telling me the secrets of the universe as he saw it, me his sole student, and now he'd shut me off like a naughty child. Realization hit. "I've offended you. I'm sorry."

Nathaniel faded a little. Literally, I could see my furniture on the opposite side of the room *through* his body as he grew more transparent and less . . . real. Like he wasn't with me anymore.

By choice.

My heart sped up.

"No, please don't go!" I cried, my panic a little louder than necessary, but the words slipped out and I couldn't take them back.

The paper he'd been writing on all day fluttered across the rug as he disappeared into literal thin air, though his voice whispered in my ear.

"Read, Emma Reeves. I wrote it for you anyway."

I stared down at the lines he had scribbled over again and again, picking out the original wording that might have worked better the first time around, though the meaning was lost.

> —Breath on a windowsill on a sunless rise
> Amidst the morning golden sun's guise—

After the beauty of his speech before, I thought I understood a little more about Nathaniel Harker.

> —From ever unceasing darkness of night
> The girl who brought an unknown man to a
> place—

My dead poet. My new obsession.

Mine.

"Nate," I whispered. "Come back?"

But he refused to return, at least to my eyes. I didn't have any sense of whether Nathaniel remained in the room with me, or if he went . . . elsewhere. Wherever ghost boys went when they sulked. And I didn't know if he chose to remain away or if he was stuck, like before—

Lost.

Or did he choose to stay away, watching me as I looked for him? Add that to the list of things I didn't know or understand about my ghost boy.

The thought he might be gone forever gripped something deep inside me. A coldness seeded low in my stomach as I curled on my bed, my back pressed to wood at the bed end. My head thumped against the stone wall near my window.

Not gone, never gone, not gone—

"What?" I whipped around and nearly slapped myself with the stone wall, but no one was there.

Tentatively, and feeling like a royal fool for a ghost boy in a haunted mansion, I placed my hand to the wall.

Spoilers: the wall did not speak to me.

I settled back and watched the space in the middle of my room, but no matter how many times I whispered his name, he didn't come back to me.

Not tonight.

I prayed to my muse that Nathaniel remained nearby, at least close enough to hear my plaintive cry. I didn't know why that mattered, but it did.

My limbs and eyes warred for heaviest bodily part as I curled on the pillow that I had thrown through him on the floor, hoping he would come back. My head hung too heavy, and my eyes ached. Last night's late hours and solo drinking session post séance hit hard. I sank onto the hard floor, the shag-pile rug doing little for my exhausted body and mind now that I'd given in to it.

But the article . . .

I sank deeper, my hand crushed around the crinkled paper Nathaniel left drifting in my direction. Sometime through the night I might have moved to my bed, or maybe it was the phantom in my dream who lifted me in his arms, carried me to the mattress and tucked me in, smoothing hair back from my face with cold fingers that warmed with each soft touch.

I was too tired to know or wake. But when I did, the sun had risen, Nathaniel's not-sonnet lay tucked neatly beneath my pillow, the crumpled paper smoothed out, and I was late again.

And Nathaniel Harker was nowhere in sight.

Waking the Dead Poet

Phi Omega House was covered in green and white streamers in an attempt to welcome the incoming hordes through its doors. I hadn't been on the party's decorating committee, thankfully. Nor had Nathaniel returned to my room. Whether he had faded out of existence in totality—a horrific fate I refused to consider—or simply hid beyond where I could see or sense him, I didn't know.

As a distraction, I'd opted to hand out party favors. Literal ones. My basket overflowed with hand-twisted laurel wreaths that I placed on each partygoer's head with a welcoming smile stitched to my face, along with more foundation than I ever needed.

And I avoided touching the house stones at every opportunity in case I woke them again. I'd already resurrected one creature. I didn't need a horde of haunted brickwork following me about like puppies when I couldn't even keep a single ghost boy alive—uh, in existence.

Inanimate plastic desk cacti for the win.

Tonight's goals included not letting my required party toga expose me in a double nip-slip of epic proportions. I wore no bra beneath my sequined garb that Kimberly pinned to my only—yep, sorority-branded and event-approved—underwear. I had all the best intentions of keeping my in-theme bare feet out of everyone else's toga-streamed way for the evening, tucked away behind my basket while keeping my eyes peeled for one Thomas Carlisle, who thankfully hadn't made an appearance so far.

"How are you going?" Kimberly checked my basket, flicking at my wreaths. A frown decorated her face. "These are starting to unravel."

I tugged at the strap pinned to my underwear that redefined discomfort. "It's not the only thing," I muttered. "Please help."

She glanced up at me and shook her head. "Emma, Emma."

A moment later two of my wreaths were linked beneath my breasts in a bespoke belt that knotted at the back and kept my toga firmly in place. Her fingers trailed across my ribs, tickling me, and I giggled.

"Better?" Kimberly asked, fixing my basket and tucking my besequinned toga around me until she was satisfied.

"Much." I rolled my eyes as an influx of new guests poured in through the arched doors. "The gargoyles are busy tonight. Did you invite everyone on campus?"

She shrugged. "Almost." Her voice rose as she glared at someone tracking muddy boots across the entrance foyer. "No. *No.* Sir. Take those off and get them outside this instant. Don't you have manners at all?"

"She's wife material, all right." Thomas materialized on cue, weaving slightly on his feet and smelling strongly of hops.

"Why don't you marry her, then?" Enter Sarcastic Emma.

"She doesn't play for the right team, love."

I closed my eyes and willed him away but, when I glanced sideways, he was still there. "Don't you have someone else to bother?"

"You'll want me when I'm not around," he promised me, slobbering on my cheek in the worst a drunk ex could be.

I shuddered through his ministrations and edged sideways until he lumbered away in search of a new target. Unwilling to sully the back of my hand, I sacrificed a laurel wreath to the cause. A bumbling pledge bumped me off course. I stood on my own toga and nearly denuded myself in the middle of a doorway.

"Oh, fuckity." I held my basket over my boobs and stared at the girl, who shoved a piece of chocolate brownie into her face. My stomach chose that moment to rumble. "Where did you get that?" I struggled to pull my toga back into place, one-handed.

"The guy in the kitchens."

"The cute one." Another pledge joined her, Rosa, I thought, her toga slightly askew and with chocolate fingerprints down the front. "In the period dress. With the Heath Ledger curls."

My world zoned to just her. I threw a laurel wreath that might or might not bear Thomas's spittle onto her head as an impromptu bribe. "What guy in the period dress?"

"The sweet one." She smiled dreamily.

My stomach clenched. *He wouldn't.*

"He caught my hand and kissed it. Said some line of poetry or other. I can't quite remember—"

Oh, he would.

"Where is this wondrous man? I could do with a little . . . treat." I smiled a sugary smile that apparently had fangs from the way the two girls backed off.

"Kitchen," they uttered in unison.

I charged between them, heading straight past Kimberly and down the hall. First, Nathaniel left me alone for the last three days, wondering if I had lost him for good, and now he deigned to appear at a party, handing out chocolate treats and kissing hands? Plus, poetry?

84

My mind promised me I was in overreaction territory, but my dead poet's poetry belonged to—

Well, me.

I bit my lip and hauled my toga up, storming into the kitchen in time to witness Nathaniel standing alone in the middle of the room, trailing his fingers along the table. His eyes met mine. A breath—that was all I managed before he faded.

And was gone.

If I hadn't been looking for him and expected him to be there, I would have thought he was a figment of my imagination.

But he hadn't been.

"There you are. I wondered where you went in such a hurry." Kimberly's fingers brushed the back of the wreath belt she made up for me. "Wardrobe emergency?"

"Chocolate emergency." I grabbed for a brownie and stuffed it in my face, promising myself I'd confront him the moment the party was over.

*

Nathaniel sat on my bed and weathered my questions without answering a single one.

"Where did you go?"

"What did you do?"

"Why didn't you come back?"

"Why did you hide?"

Large, gold-flecked violet eyes watched me with the same degree of curiosity that I noted in him before, but this time they held something else. An emotion that hadn't been there previously.

"You looked pretty." It's all he said, but not in his usual voice. Tight, frowning.

He hurt. *My ghost boy was jealous*. So he showed that to me in the way he knew how. I knew exactly how that one went, but in the end, it didn't work out. Now here we were, both of us trying to figure out our *now*.

I bit my lip and stopped. Backed off. Perched on the other end of my bed.

Because, stupidly, I was jealous too.

Finally, the silence grew too big for me to manage, like a giant bubble expanding between us, pushing ever outward.

"Please say something," I whispered.

He considered, tilting his head to one side. Both eyes blinked twice. "Did you try the chocolate?"

"Yes." I ate the whole plate the moment Kimberly left the room.

"Was it nice?"

"Yes." Before I nearly threw it all up out of a panic I'd never see him again and then spent the rest of the party nauseated beyond belief.

"I wanted to come back," he whispered. "I couldn't see you."

The stones talked to me. I opened my mouth and closed it again, but the conversation was over.

I had my answer.

Nathaniel slumped against my wall and watched me like he didn't want to close his eyes.

So I didn't close mine, either.

*

Nathaniel Harker fascinated me as much as I fascinated him. At least, I thought I did. He certainly spent a fair amount of our post-class time engaged in studying me with those eyes I couldn't avoid, no matter what I did to distract him—or what I wore. Tossing technology and unusual clothing—to him—became my favorite pastime.

After the party, something changed. His flirtatious nature returned—in force—and mine matched his. Currently, my attire choice of an old bubble skirt, lavender leg warmers and black crop top I'd bought as an Eighties revival costume party in my second year drew the eye perfectly. Nathaniel never said a word, preferring to watch in silence and write lines for his newest poem. My room quickly filled with scraps of paper that he garnered from my printer ream, torn lecture handouts and the odd scribbled note on my walls that faded with the sunrise and reappeared at dusk—like Nathaniel himself.

"You are a quandary," I said over the edge of my glitter Dewar cup that matched my fluffy socks, albeit branded with the sorority's logo.

What was branded in Phi Omega House blew my mind. I managed to avoid most of the sisters for the morning and skipped my evening class so I could spend time with Nathaniel.

As far as I knew, Kimberly had avoided making good on her promise to oust one of the newer sisters. For some reason, I had the impression she waited on me.

"But of course." Nathaniel made no move to dissuade me of the premise. "I am a dead man you brought back to life." He considered his words for a moment. "And you are—"

"Beautiful. Yes, so you said on your first night."

Compliments still made me uncomfortable, especially with the notion of his ability to hand them out willy-nilly. Part of me fizzed at his solo attention, while the rest of me balked. Thomas had trained me out of the notion that anyone found me attractive. After our catastrophic dating attempt, I gave up on the entire Inerius dating scene, ignored frat parties and, sorority attempts, and focused on my career.

Until now, when Erin had dragged me back into the fray and I'd met a dead poet from a prior century who had a penchant for lounging on my hideous shag-pile rug. I flipped my phone in my hand, opened the document I'd made for Erin's assignment, and stared at the blank page before me.

That a resurrected dead poet managed to fill scraps with words and sentence fragments left my imposter syndrome dangling over a precipice I couldn't see beyond.

"The tile." He pointed at me.

I held up my phone. "This?"

"That small brick. You tap on it all the time."

He watched me do precisely that with the same intensity he absorbed everything about the new time he had landed in. I wondered at what he saw, the differences between his then and my now, and indulged his eternal curiosity, which he expected, of course.

O poet, how thou hast already trained me.

"I write on it. And there are um, games, when I'm bored or procrastinating."

His eyes lit up at that; we quickly discovered we shared a language in doing something other than what we were meant to be doing right at that moment. Somehow, I doubted this discreet bonding session was what Kimberly had in mind when she brought up resurrecting dead poets.

"Ah, the damnation of a blank page."

"Indeed." I stared pointedly at his many lines littering my room. "Somehow, I doubt you suffer the aggravation of writer's block."

"Oft times." He shrugged the concept away, though his wasn't the dismissal that Thomas would have provided in lieu of stoking his own ego in the process. "But you do more than write on it, I think?" He had cleaned his language up of the *doths* and *thous* that first day in my room after a few books went missing when I left my sorority streaming account open. Nathaniel proved the perfect chameleon to our era.

Honestly, his ability to blend impressed me, considering he had merged the language of his time with our own in just two weeks of cultural streaming immersion.

"Canny thing, aren't you?" I cast him a sideways look. Nathaniel tried to appear twice as innocent and semi succeeded. The hair helped, I swore. "It also has socials on it."

"What are—"

I sighed and launched into a diatribe on socials, pushing my phone across into the middle of the rug, and brought up Inerius's socials platform, Neri.

No, the college wasn't a unique or creative bunch when it came to names, *"Neri"* being a shortened version of *"Inerius"*.

"I want one," Nathaniel announced predictably the moment I explained what the profiles meant and how I talked to friends, showing him Vivian's profile and the chat function.

I snorted my next sip of coffee out my nose. "Over my dead body."

"Preferably not," he said in a soft tone.

Oops. I halted mid coffee-swipe. "That was insensitive, huh?"

"Perhaps, if unintentional." He made swirling patterns in the long shag pile and petted the bear head.

I might have told him not to but for the germs the faux critter probably possessed, but then I remembered that tiny things like germs didn't bother him anymore.

"I'm sorry." The apology tumbled free as my hand brushed his over the bear's glassy eyes.

A smile graced Nathaniel's curved lips even as I jerked

89

my hand back from his colder one. He didn't move away at all.

"Forgiven." He said it in the same breath, and smiled. "A lady should never feel she has to hide her feelings from those she can trust."

Is that the nineteenth-century version of "Who hurt you"?

I think I just got gently outmaneuvered.

"You're still not getting a phone," I muttered, sneaking a look at him through my lashes as I flexed my fingers. The feel of him burned into the tips that warmed, like the contact still existed.

Nathaniel's smug grin told me to put a hold on that thought, but it wasn't half as annoying as it could have been. Should have been. Joking and bantering about with him was . . . freeing.

My thoughts must have shown on my face, because he jumped right on that sonnet-shaped bandwagon with the intent of riding it through campus after dark.

"Have I proved my worth to you, o' purple siren?" Nathaniel batted his eyelids and eyed my coffee. "And can I try that?"

I raised both eyebrows. "You want to drink my bitter, burnt beans gone cold? Be my guest." I passed over my purple Dewar cup. "Better not be any ghostly backwash in there when I get it back," I warned him.

"That sounds . . . intimate." Nathaniel Harker eyed me over the edge of my cup. A smile flickered at the edges of his upturned lips as he lowered the curled lashes I adored, and sipped.

I ignored his attempt at seduction and waited.

His lips puckered on the lip of the cup and he politely spat the tepid mouthful right back in.

I waggled a finger, having given him the dregs of my

long-turned-cold coffee, and barely restrained my laughter. "I did warn you."

He passed back the coffee—I was still amazed at his ability to manipulate reality while sinking half a foot through my rug at the same time—and wiped his mouth with the back of his hand. "That is utterly disgusting. How do you stand it?"

"It's a habit."

"A feral one." A true poet, he picked up my language fast. "I shall teach you how to brew tea. And perhaps chocolate." He looked inordinately proud of himself at the concept.

My laughter bubbled over. "Oh, buddy. Do I have a surprise for you." I glanced at the door. My newfound hermit tendencies were to be short-lived, apparently. "Stay here, okay? Don't move off the rug. Got it? I'll be right back."

Nathaniel watched me with wraith-like wide eyes. "I shall stay here." He floated through the rug.

The sort of *all right* my three-year-old cousin once gave me right before he raided the candy jar in his mother's pantry and proceeded to projectile vomit all over his bed fifteen minutes later. *Taste the rainbow* took on new meaning that night.

"On this floor, ghost boy," I specified.

His brow dipped as he searched for a loophole in my logic and apparently came up empty. "All right . . ."

I stamped my foot, my leg warmers jiggling with the effort. Maybe the skirt, too. Nathaniel's gaze took on a sharpened interest, the bitter, cold coffee incident forgotten.

"Promise me, Nate."

His face closed again. "Fine."

My eyebrows hiked. They'd burrow into my hairline if I kept this up, and never return. "Did you use the F-word with me?"

He had the good sense to look affronted. Or maybe that was just him. "I would never." He tilted his head on one side. "Not with a lady."

I coughed my laugh into my hand.

On anyone else, that statement would seem affected and fake as hell. On Nathaniel Harker, it suited him.

I nodded as my slow brain chugged into gear. *He did this last night, too.* "You shut down when I call you Nate."

I could have sworn he flinched, and it wasn't because he didn't understand my modern terms.

"Nathaniel?" I prompted after a moment's held breath. Mine, not his, because he didn't breathe. My dead boy poet faded before me.

"Go, Emma," he whispered. Even his voice seemed fainter than it had a breath before. "I'll be here when you return. After all, it's not like I can leave the building, is it?"

I held his violet, gold-flecked gaze, the sadness swirling within. *Are these my rules he lives by, or ones he can't break?* House rules—had I literally tied him to the building when I tethered him to my time? Too many questions swirled unanswered in my mind. Nathaniel's lips quirked, and I half expected a smile, but only sadness emanated from my ghost poet.

My heart shattered a little on the spot.

And with that enigmatic little comment, he disappeared entirely. I half expected a *pop* to precede his absence, but the silence that pervaded my room after was worse.

So much worse.

"Fine," I muttered in a pithy echo of my invisible dead poet, and stalked for the door in a bid to escape the shroud of guilt for calling Nathaniel from his rest that cloaked me with every heavy step. "But we are having a chat about ghost-boy etiquette when I get back."

If Nathaniel wouldn't talk to me now, maybe I could

coax him back into existence with a cup of hot chocolate. Or a chai latte. I traipsed down the stairs, still debating internally with myself and not paying attention to anything but the dead poet I suspected was exactly where I left him, if hiding out of plain sight.

Which was how I ran face first into a twinset and a head of blonde curls I didn't want to see tonight.

"Emma." Kimberly's unsmiling face turned to meet mine. "I've been waiting for you."

"Oh. I was heading for—"

"This is Shyleigh. She . . . doesn't share the necessary beliefs of the Dead Poets Sorority." Kimberly placed an arm around a girl dressed in a long T-shirt dress not altogether different to the one I wore recently. Her gaze darted between me and Kimberly, a plea written in her eyes.

Oh, Pulitzer pride, no. I did not *sign up for this.*

Erin owed me after this. A permanent alumni column, and the best reference to a *New York Times* connection she could make. In person. I made a mental note to request an upgrade on her original offer.

Vivian's rant about sororities and Kimberly using me rippled about the inside of my skull, echoes of her words bouncing about in shattered fragments, obscuring most of Kimberly's speech until all I heard was—

"—and now it's time for you to leave the house. Emma will escort you out."

That was it? The girl, Shyleigh, offered me a smile tinged with relief. I didn't return it. Kimberly wasn't done yet.

"In her underwear. Your things will be returned to your dorm room the way they arrived."

Shyleigh's lip trembled. "My dorm mate already replaced me. She had to, to pay her portion of the rent—"

"Oh, too bad." Kimberly flicked her fingers in the ultimate dismissive gesture, and turned her back, effectively disowning the girl. Her gaze fixed on me. "Emma?" A warning note coated her voice.

If I wanted to stay in the sorority house and fulfill the terms that Erin had given me along with this assignment, then I had to go with the flow, no matter how much I hated it. Vivian's words rippled through my mind. I fixed my lips in a hard line and met Kimberly's gaze, making a caveat of my own.

"Once." I would do this for her exactly once, and never again.

That's all I said as I stepped around her, not waiting for an answer, and reached for the girl's clothes. Bile rose into my throat at the thought of what I was about to do, but the rock and a hard place I was put in left me with little choice.

Nope, that was a line of bullshit I fed myself on my way to sorority hell.

"Snippety snip."

A pair of scissors miraculously appeared in front of my face. I hissed out a breath, cursing Kimberly's organizational skills. Perhaps the extra reprieve hadn't been the boon I expected.

The sorority held horrors I wasn't close to prepared for, and the least of them came at the thought of raising zombie poet boys.

Actually, I was already kinda of attached to mine.

The thought of what Kimberly would do if she got her hands on Nathaniel chilled me. Keen not to give her any reason to look deeper into my actions, I grabbed the scissors, wanting to get the feral—to liberate Nathaniel's borrowed term—task done.

I met Shyleigh's watery eyes and offered her a matching smile. "At least it's me," I mouthed, my back set to Kimberly.

She gave me a fleeting smile, and held out her hand.

I stared.

When I didn't move, she took the scissors back from my unwieldy grip, sliced through the T-shirt dress with one hand, neck to hem, and handed me the swath of cut material. "In case the sorority needs a few extra rags," she murmured. "I don't need them."

"Damage the underwear, too. For . . . effect." Kimberly's voice cracked through the foyer.

Footsteps announced the entrance of the rest of the sisters and pledges, who gathered to watch their number's exit like so many hyenas desperate for Kimberly's scraps.

Ignoring the dozens of eyes surrounding us, I focused on Shyleigh, giving her a point of reference, hoping to lessen her humiliation somehow. She snipped notches in her bra straps and panty edges, as requested, that strained on their remaining threads. Her head held high, she looked at me.

"Let's go," I said quietly, my stomach filled with stones as heavy as the foundation of the building.

She nodded and together we walked toward the large, arched entranceway of Phi Omega House in utter silence. Sour notes covered my taste buds as I pulled the heavy doors open on their well-oiled hinges and walked down the steps with her, knowing this moment would forever mark me as one of *them*.

Shyleigh's shoulders remained back as she pivoted on the bottom step and looked back up at me. Her lips parted on two whispered words.

"Get out."

Then she completed her parade of tattered shame all the way back across campus to the dorms, the farthest point from the sorority house, to beg for clothing and accommodation for the night from any friends who would take pity on her plight and offer her a couch.

I doubted that Kimberly would be so kind as to return her things in a timely fashion. Swallowing back the remnants of my ruined pride and a burning sense of anger toward the girl I wanted to shred, who loitered inside her stone castle, hiding beneath her collection of gargoyles and stolen words, I watched Shyleigh until she reached the dorms and disappeared inside the plain building.

Then I walked back through Phi Omega House, headed for the kitchen, and spoke to no one. My original purpose before my fateful trip to the ground floor. Without conscious thought I made two hot chocolates, and carried them back up to my room. Kimberly's watchful eyes never left me the entire time.

And I never once looked directly at her.

By the time I opened my door with my butt, my mugs clutched to my chest, uncaring if I slopped hot chocolate all over my black feather crop, my vision had blurred beyond my ability to see if Nate had held to his promise to stay put or not.

I placed my mug collection for two beside the rug and slumped with my back to the edge of my bed. Tears coursed along my cheeks at what I'd done.

"This isn't why I chose journalism," I whispered to an empty room. I drew my knees up to my chest and wrapped my arms around them.

Cold fingers whispered along the back of my hand. Nathaniel said nothing as he reappeared at my side. A coolness preceded his appearance by half a second that I registered now as a natural part of him. He didn't say a word, but sat beside me in silence as I cried and cried and cried.

After a while, I pushed my phone into the cold bare neutral ground between us, open to my app where I'd set up a folder listed under his name, and tapped the little cross to open a new document, typing out a single sentence one-fingered as an example of what the app did and how to work it.

If I could take back all my actions within these walls,

all that I am ashamed of doing, the one thing I wouldn't rescind would be the night that I summoned you.

He stared at my phone set out between us for a long moment, then tapped once at my screen. Through my wobbly visual sheen a new letter appeared on the screen, then the next.

Snail slow, he tapped his way through the alphabet and learned the compressed keyboard with his fingertips. Nathaniel often swiped lacy cuffs back, though his excitement overrode annoyance as he gazed at the coveted device I had promised less than an hour before that I'd never let him have.

Even if it was mine, but still. After the last hour, when I engaged in activities I never thought I would be party to, some things had changed. The ideals I walked through the doors of Phi Omega House with were . . . tarnished.

Vivian was right to warn me away from this place.

But if I hadn't taken the assignment, I wouldn't have met Nathaniel. And my dead poet was worth every stain on my soul. As long as those stains didn't reach his.

He picked my phone up, cradling the device in his palm with all the care of a newborn, and glanced at me with a furrowed brow. I managed a nod and the smallest smile, glad to give joy to someone even over something as small as this, although my stomach still swooped over what I'd done downstairs.

The first row of mangled letters were erased as he discovered the backspace key, and a new line grew under his careful eye.

When she cries, all hearts shatter.

I stared at the screen as my breaths grew short, and fresh salt streamed into my mouth. Nathaniel looked at me, alarm flaring, his pretty violet and gold-flecked eyes wide. He offered the phone back. I shook my head and waved him away, pressing my fingertips to the edge of the device. I still didn't touch him, though all I wanted was to put my head on his shoulder and let my ghost poet comfort me.

Instead, he sat beside me and put my heartache into words. I wondered how much of the traumatic scene he had viewed firsthand. If he hadn't, then his understanding of the situation was remarkable as his poetry grew line by line.

If he had . . . he never judged. Nathaniel sat beside me, and he wrote.

And that was enough.

Poet, Interrupted

Nate

I am her dead poet and she is my . . .

Keeper.

Sunlight falls upon this form of breath and light where I am invisible to her eyes. Not until night falls will she be able to look upon me again, to see me as I am.

Who I am before her.

The woman who pulled me from the darkness. The place where life fears to wander and creatures like me belong.

I am not of this place. I cannot stay, yet here I wait.

Weightless, I make not even a scar upon this changed world that even now might accept me for who I am.

But I will never know.

Locked away from them, I wait behind a prison of glass until she frees me again. A creature of a forgotten hour, locked inside stones that mutter the sins of others long past.

And some not-so-long passed.

The shadows I occupy amongst her secret things.

This world is changed. She is become hard within its grasp. I see her eyes; they spark with the intelligence of her kind.

The wordsmith inside her leaches out into the ether. But she holds herself back. I don't understand that purpose.

Why not be free, and release the constraints that bind her to this place that she hates? This building and the people who exist side by side with her cripple the desire that builds within her. What she denies with every beat of her still-living heart.

Anonymity has no thrall to her. Strain to fly. Soar above.

And yet she folds, bonded to their will. Her sorrow collects, seething inside.

I watch her from my tower, through my pane of glass and whisper secrets the walls might one day impart.

Or perhaps they won't, until the day she returns me to the darkness.

An inevitable death.

And so, I wait to die.

Again.

Can't Keep a Good Ghost Down

I might have sucked at baking, but I didn't suck at selling cakes. I smiled as I cashed another handful of change in the sorority kitty tin and passed over a gift-wrapped, Gothic treat. The bleeding-heart-themed cake came complete with a tiny cake shovel that resembled a knife stuck into the white decorative icing that oozed raspberry filling.

Some of the other sisters handed out branded balloons. The sorority event was hosted in front of Phi Omega House in support of the Bleeding Hearts children's charity. Kimberly chose well for her bake sale. The sisters, both new and old, loved bonding over baking—except for me—and the entire campus came together for her charity drive.

What I didn't expect was to sell cakes bearing little pictures of Kimberly Welles's face on the tops. I passed one to Erin as she approached my side of the table, my smile fixed in place as I took her money for the tin. "It goes to a good cause."

"It'd better come with a great article," she murmured, stabbing her miniature cake knife straight through the rice paper bearing Kimberly's face. Raspberry filling oozed around the jab like so much bodily fluid.

"We're doing so well. Isn't this just great for sisterhood solidarity?" Sunshine Kimberly spewed rainbows and freaking happiness with every word she said today, I swore.

I waited for her psychotic personality switch to arise. I hadn't seen it in the last twenty-four hours, which left me wary of the Big Sister's impending crash.

"Good luck." Erin gave me a finger wave and wandered off through the crowd.

I chanced a glance over my shoulder at my room. The sun was still up but I swore something shifted behind the window pane next to my bed. Nathaniel loved the idea of the bake sale and wanted to attend but I hadn't been able to explain to him that a floaty, transparent ghost might cause panic. Plus, we hadn't worked out if he was attached to the building yet.

His frustration at being left behind, *again*, grew with each day.

I passed out another cake and tinned the cash without so much as a word.

"Smile, sister." Kimberly jabbed me in the ribs with her coffin-shaped talon.

I threw a smile on my face. "I'm not a sister yet." I spoke through clenched teeth.

"But you will be," Kimberly sang through hers.

I sold my next bleeding-heart cake with my biggest smile yet, as raspberry filling dripped its way down my wrist while my ghost boy loitered in my room, waiting for my return at sunset.

*

I faked it with the best of the sisters, but doing menial tasks for Kimberly was neither my smartest nor robust idea.

One week. One week until the new pledges were initiated into the sorority.

That's all I had to survive while I trash-talked her in my head. One week of sweeping, vacuuming, picking up laundry, not ousting housemates—thankfully—and generally being house bitch to whomever needed one. I made beds, cleaned rooms and let myself be hazed a week prior to Kimberly's supposedly scheduled main event, or so the sisters let the rumor be spread. Not that they said *what* the event was; I supposed that built a nice ambience of fear. But . . . sisters—and pledges—talked.

In return I listened, like I suspected Nathaniel did that night, hiding in the house's walls.

The one thing I learned in my week-long watch-through of *Downton Abbey* with Vivian back when we were both flu-ridden a year ago and unable to attend classes was that sometimes, they forgot the servants were present. Sure, my appearance created a novelty for the first few days, but soon I got used to the blisters and no longer flinched every time someone threw a soiled garment at my head. Then the sisters and pledges began to talk, ignoring the circles that hung and darkened beneath my eyes each day.

Because when they slept, that was when I sacrificed my downtime hours and talked to the ghost who waited in my room for me to return each night. A twisted form of therapy, with both of us all too aware that time was not our friend. And so, what no one seemed to realize was that the fixtures, of which I became one and the walls themselves, listened.

Is this how Nate spends his days?

I didn't know as he refused to divulge what he did during his sunlit hours, often swanning away to hide in the cupboard or sink beneath the floorboards. A broken part of me found that concept hilarious. While I understood that his ethereal form most likely returned to the realm of invisible ghostability, the image of his legs dangling above the séance room—I had no better term for the sacred space that

I had mopped three times now despite no one else using it at all—left me laughing on the inside. Somewhere in there, I seethed, too.

But mostly, I found a quiet headspace, and sponged all the information that might or might not be useful and every rumor I could.

"Kimberly wants the next Dead Poets meeting held outside. Not in the library like the *other one*." Bianca Chambers tipped her wine to her lips as she downed the rest of her glass. "I heard that *some* of the pledges this year aren't going to make it past her newest entrance exam. Not that she's shared the full event. Yet."

Okay, so I hadn't been entirely truthful. On occasion I was still seen, but by volunteering my meagre housekeeping skills—which nearly every other sister in the house, *especially* the more recent additions to the household, found beneath them—I was designated the most likely subject to follow Shyleigh's ultimate walk of shame. Which meant they were all reasonably loose-lipped around me. As for the *other* library—the house had several bookish nooks and crannies but there was one solitary locked room in the downstairs hallway I was desperate to gain entry to.

Kimberly's personal locked library where, rumor had it, the very first Dead Poets séance was held. Not that they'd resurrected anyone that night, despite the whispers on campus that ran with fresh names weekly at this rate. Perhaps Kimberly liked the whispers, or fueled them herself.

Either way, I wanted the key to that library.

The sisters ignored me and kept on chattering while I cleaned, lost in my head.

"Maybe it will be a strip-walk past the frat parties on a Friday night. Post-game time is meant to be quite . . . brutal." Lacy Masters played with my hair, flicking at the feathered ends of my curly cut. I gripped my cleaning cloth, swallowed the urge to shove it in her nearest orifice, and kept my face carefully blank.

"Oh! I know. It's a group trip to the ce—" Hannah Lewellyn began, to be hushed en masse.

Freed of the fingers grasping my hair as those wandering hands were slapped over Hannah's mouth, I slipped into the next room and dusted a few vases I'd already done earlier in the week.

"You're playing a good game, you know." Kimberly's voice came from directly behind me. "Most of them have no idea what you're doing."

I jumped at the unexpected voice and cursed as I mishandled the heavy porcelain piece I'd been dusting. "I hope you like this vase," I muttered, shoving my cloth under one armpit and maneuvering the thing that probably belonged to some heirloom collection back onto the mantel. "Are you always such a creeper?"

As before, I maintained the facade that she seemed to expect of me. We both knew that I hated what she made me do; what she didn't know was how much hate I had for the humiliation that Shyleigh suffered, well before my part in it.

Keeping my voice light, I twirled a magician's flourish when the vase did not immediately die an early death. "Taa-daa."

Eyes the perfect pastel blue pierced straight through me as though she could extract my secrets from reading them on my skin. "Are you ready for the ceremony this weekend?"

Kimberly's unnamed hazing event. The in-or-out door. Erin's assignment talk haunted my eardrums as I attempted to play it cool. Kimberly's knowing eyes followed me like one of her not-so-haunted paintings that lined the halls with their little peepholes for eyes.

Fail.

"That soon?" I didn't have to pretend to gulp, though I may have played it up a little because I knew her ego needed to see the fear I didn't feel. At least, not from here.

The thought of swearing a false oath I'd break a week or so later when I handed over my exposé—of which I already had plenty of material to play with—and walked away did sit oddly in my stomach. The potential trail of broken promises did little for my renewed vow of journalistic morality.

But the truth was that I wanted to see how deep and twisted Kimberly's rabbit hole went.

"This weekend," she confirmed softly, reaching out to liberate my cleaning cloth and tossing it to the table behind me. A silent protest died on my lips. "Have you completed your assignment for English lit?"

I groaned. "That would be a big no." I covered my face with my hands and peeked out, playing it up a little for a touch of showwomanship that I thought she might like after her séance antics.

Kimberly smirked. "I'd offer you a tame dead poet, but rumor has it . . ."

My spine stiffened and the floor wobbled beneath my feet. "Rumor?" I managed.

Her smile widened, and I swore those glossy white teeth beneath augmented lips had points. "Of course. Rumors are our lifeblood, sister. Or soon-to-be sister. You see, the masses . . ." She jerked her blonde head toward the doorway. "They know that not everyone will make the next cut. What they don't know, of course, is *who* won't make it. But we do, don't we?"

I stared at her, my mind lingering on the rumor she hadn't voiced as my brain slammed into overdrive. "Hannah. With the ability to disperse secrets like that. Bianca? No, she's not too bad, I suppose." I threw myself into the distasteful role.

In for a phantom penny . . . "And there were a few sisters at the ceremony who mumbled a lot. There was no power or passion in their voices," I reasoned, hoping I read the situation right before I lost Kimberly's favor.

A walk of shame was not on my to-do list, today, tonight or game night.

"Keep going." Kimberly's eyes took on that same fanatical gleam I'd come to associate with her obsession with all things dead and poet-like, and her tone whispered *impress me*.

"Lacy is tough enough to keep." No question entered my voice as I recalled my first night in the house. "There were gossips in the ranks outside. One girl whispered about Emily Dickinson." Clarity crashed over me with the lucidity of a newly freed soul from wherever souls rested during their off time. I made a mental note to ask Nate whether he remembered much of the time when he rested in the space between life and death during the centuries. "You're resurrecting *male* poets, aren't you? A . . . liberation?" My first guess.

"A transcendence." The pointed smile sharpened as she leaned in and edged the vase to the corner of the mantel.

My stomach clenched as it wobbled, precarious on the thin strip of stained wood. "I'm not familiar."

"You will be." Kimberly left one finger balanced on the vase's enameled surface and walked around me in a circle an arm's length wide. "Think of a connection with a poet over a hundred and fifty years gone. Someone who has left this world long ago, yet their printed voice remains. Imagine . . ." she paused, and leaned back until her fingertip remained on the ceramic's fragile surface ". . . connecting with that soul on a personal level. A spiritual dominance over their creative intelligence, honed to the women of today. Imagine scattering their words and sharing them between us. A poet for us, or one for all." Her lips twisted as she dropped her hand.

The vase teetered in place. The greater mass won out over gravity's pull and in slow motion, it fell. My body jerked a half second too late, the delayed reaction a silent cry for the creation's death less than a moment before it shattered on the floor at my feet.

"We will disperse the captured voices to the sisters of today. The men have had their chance. Now, we shall rise," Kimberly whispered. Her obsessive glitter fixed on me for a breath more before heeled footsteps clattered into the room that filled with a cacophony of gasps.

Cries of *Oust her!* and the like filled my ears, but all I heard was the eternal whisper of Kimberly's words that bombarded my mind on repeat, blocking out everything else.

"A mistake," she overrode the sisters' combined outrage calmly, as though nothing had happened between us. She shooed the rubbernecking pledges from the common room, and handed me the dirty cloth she had taken from me before.

A breath shuddered from me as I kneeled, collecting the shattered pieces in my rag.

A voice for all. Her twisted take on the old musketeers' quote curdled my stomach that cramped though my monthly wasn't due for another week or more.

I swallowed bile that seemed to be my constant companion in this place, as a second bout of horror slammed into me. My nausea paired with her exodus, leaving me in the room with her broken pieces.

Kimberly meant to imprison the souls of the dead poets she raised.

If she knew how close to success she had come in that last meeting . . . That couldn't happen under any circumstances. But first, I had to do the worst thing.

Nathaniel couldn't stay. Letting her imprison him to steal the voice he never got to realize and publish in the first place would be the ultimate crime.

I had to send him back.

*

"Nate? Nathaniel?" I turned in circles in the middle of my room, holding the fresh cup of hot chocolate before me like an offering. "Are you around?"

The clock tower struck midday minutes ago. I had no chance of seeing him for another four or five hours before the sun set at least. That didn't mean he wasn't around, however.

"I brought you a hot chocolate," I cooed, settling back on the bed, cradling the mug between my hands. Steam coiled in indistinct shapes beneath my chin. Half-formed beasts and monsters frolicked in my imagination before my breath whisked away their last remnants.

A whisper of steam drifted past my nose. The edges crystallized. I smiled as Nate's face slipped into view in part. His eyes bored into mine. Then he, too, dissipated in the still air.

"Come back," I breathed. My heart ached at the confession tying my tongue. "I have—something—" Hands trembling, I placed the mug carefully on my desk and knotted my fingers in my lap. "You can't stay."

"I know that."

The air at my back cooled in the closest thing we'd come to a hug. Pressure dipped on my shoulder like his chin nestled there, and a shiver of cold tendrils drifted along my forearm.

But unlike the draft that I'd experienced on the night of the séance, Nate's strange embrace was . . . comforting.

"I don't want you to go." My fingers knotted tighter; the bite of skin twisted on skin prevented the wash of tears already blurring my vision.

"I don't want that either, but I figured it would happen. Eventually," Nate whispered in his daytime ghostly voice.

I nodded. "You aren't safe."

No answer.

"I have no idea how to do it."

Nothing. At least the pressure of his presence didn't change or drift away.

"I wish it was night so I could see you."

The coldness of him fizzed around me like popping candy. I nestled deeper, letting out a long exhalation and whispering the words that could never be.

"Don't leave me, Nate. Please."

A chaotic pattern of knocks rattled my door in its frame, and the pressure at my back dissipated. The sigh that left me bordered on pure desperation, but Nate's cold fingers swiped my cheek in the barest-there caress before I lost all sense of him.

"Emma! Let us in—nnn," several voices chorused.

Groaning, I glanced sideways at the hot chocolate mug that no longer steamed. As I watched, the surface frosted at the edges, then that small touch, too, dissipated. My heart-ache resumed.

I don't want you to go.

But with no other recourse in mind, I didn't see another way out. Or rather, I didn't see another way out for Nate, apart from sending him back.

My throat closed as I forced a smile on my stiff face and pushed my legs to work. Crossing the room like a clock-work doll wound down, I was relieved that my mechanical grace dropped away; all usual feeling returned to my limbs and facial features by the time I opened the door.

"Surprise!" A vision in pastels and brights plus one emo tumbled across my threshold.

"What is this?" My momentary bemusement transformed to a show of horror as Hannah, the soon-to-be not-sister if I had read Kimberly's intention correctly, along with one other, stepped around everyone who overcrowded my doorway and placed a Ouija board I swore was three sizes too large in the middle of my fake bear rug.

My mouth opened to protest the placement, hoping she didn't squish Nate, before my brain caught up.

I have a sassy dead ghost boy who is going to love having a chance to show off.

"No. No, this is such a bad idea."

Hannah looked up at me in surprise. "Really? I mean after Kimberly ripped you a new one, we figured it would be worth a few laughs."

"We brought wine." Lacy dangled two unopened bottles under my nose.

I took the gifts without commenting on the fact that she basically abused me both physically and verbally earlier. Right now I had bigger problems.

"Uh, I haven't burned um . . . sage recently," I fibbed. The first thing that came to my mind fell out of my mouth as I grabbed for the hot chocolate turned cold.

Nate made his presence known. *Noted.* And I still hadn't solved the question of his name preference.

"Sage? You'd need to burn the whole house." Bianca waltzed in followed by two other girls. "Oh. Rosa, I think you already know, and Fae." She waved a dismissive hand over her shoulder, black matte coffin-shaped nails with their magenta spider webbed detail flashing.

I offered both girls a warm smile. "Welcome to my impromptu séance," I said politely.

"Hi," whispered Rosa, as she shuffled beneath Bianca's

112

outstretched arm and offered me a stemless wine glass covered with tiny hand-painted books that flapped their open pages around the top edge. "Are we allowed to do this?"

Fae rolled her eyes and gave the mousy sister a shove. "Who cares. Emma breaks vases. Rules can't be far behind." She winked at me and twirled what looked like a real to poetess athame.

I stared at the obsidian blade bearing a razored edge I suspected she had honed herself. The weapon—ahem, *tool*—looked sharp enough to sever a limb. I wished I could step backward, but with five sisters and pledges stuffed into my room, along with a ghost boy and a fake bear rug, I didn't have room to summon a sister for help, let alone a poet on protection detail.

"Uh, sure. Let's go with that."

Unsure if the witchy sister would become an ally I could rely on or would be more likely to plant her blade in my back, I edged around the rug and placed my cold mug on the opposite side of my desk.

"I will not make you any more if you won't drink them," I muttered to the air.

"Huh?" Hannah frowned at me. "You really are as weird as—"

"*Hannah*," four voices hushed her.

Bianca's gaze met mine. The shared knowledge that the other girl wouldn't be with us for much longer hit me square in the chest.

This isn't a fair game. But it was Kimberly's game, and thus she set the rules.

Screw the rules. Fae was right.

I planted my butt across from Hannah, the first not-fake smile stretching my lips in what felt like an eternity. Another question for Nate. I pushed the morose thought aside for later, and held out my wine glass to Rosa.

113

"Let's get started."

A small cheer went up as the girls settled around the Ouija board. The entire contraption was made of heavy wood. The words, *yes*, *no* and *goodbye* were burned into the surface in thick, dark print as though they had been branded there. Most of the versions Vivian and I had researched prior to my entering Phi Omega House were of the cardboard dime-store variety. This version resembled a family heirloom.

Hannah plopped a heavy planchette in my palm. The triangular-shaped token consisted of curved edges, and showed wear at one side where the fingers of the participants were supposed to rest.

I bit my lip and weighed my literal option. "Is this made of bone? Wait, is your grandmother a hedge witch or something?"

Hannah shrugged. "Or something. It was the singular reason Kimberly took me in. It's not like being a witch gives you wealth." She looked pointedly across at Fae who cleaned her black, short-cut nails with the tip of her athame.

The Gothic girl bared her teeth, displaying a white gold, diamond-set grill.

No lack of trust fund in evidence right there.

Hannah rolled her eyes and pressed my hand onto the board as wine glasses were passed around and topped up. "Does everyone know the rules?"

Heads bobbed around the board. I looked straight at her. "I have no problem breaking rules, but also I've got no freaking idea what we're doing. So if you raise a malevolent spirit in my bedroom, please take the fucker with you when you leave, okay?"

Fae laughed and stood up to draw my curtains. "Gotta have ambience and all."

Because doing it at night would be creepy, right?

I shrugged. "So, we say hi?"

I wanted those ground rules before I broke anything, like my tame poet. Nathaniel *needed* to know his boundaries otherwise this was going to get raucous, and fast. Because there was *no way* he wouldn't come out to play.

As bad an idea as this was, part of me was also curious to see how it would go. What questions he would answer, and what he might say that he hadn't already said to me.

Article fodder. Yep. That's all this would be.

Liar, Liar, Ouija board on fire.

Hannah wiggled her shoulders and eyed everyone past the point of awkwardness until we all extended a finger onto the planchette. Somehow I got the impression this had been a preordained excursion well before they reached my room, and I was the last to find out. Not that I cared; they were the ones in for the shock of their lives when this fiasco in the making actually worked.

Me holding back my snorts of hilarity would be the crux of it all.

O' come, let us haunt you . . .

It might be the wrong season for Christmas carols, but I still hummed it. Rosa giggled as she jammed her fingertips onto the overcrowded planchette, and we were on.

"Welcome, poetic spirits," Hannah intoned. "We beseech thee to speak with us and share your wisdom from beyond."

Bianca's nose turned pink the moment I made eye contact. *Mistake.* She gulped a healthy swallow of wine with her planchette-free hand, and I followed suit. Fae coughed into an oversized bottle of tequila she extracted from the top of her corset. Not that I knew how she fitted the thing in there. Nate would get an eyeful from that girl.

The thought of Nathaniel eyeing off anyone else left my insides simmering, and not in a positively poetic way.

I shoved that concept aside too, adding to my collection of Nate Notes to talk about later. Or not.

Maybe I should have added that thought to the *Ask Nate Never* pile.

"Is anyone there?" Hannah continued, raising her voice for round two.

"Yeah. Kimberly, if you don't keep it down," Lacy muttered. She swiped hair back from her face and fluttered pink coffin nails that matched Bianca's over the planchette. "Will this take long? I'm all for a good day-drinking session, but I have sister duties later."

"Shh." Hannah tossed her plain brown ponytail and slapped Bianca in the face. "Is there anyone there?" she called again, a hint of annoyance in her voice that fast transformed to a touch of desperation. "Any—"

I knew the exact moment that Nathaniel had it with the girl's attitude, because the planchette vibrated under our fingers and suddenly took off in a wide sweeping arc across the board to land on—

NO.

I snorted wine out my nose. "Smart-ass."

Hannah's eyes narrowed. "I didn't move it."

"Oh, not you," I apologized. "Just . . . um, whoever did." I guessed I wasn't supposed to cuss out the non-malevolent spirit in the room, despite having done just that. "Sorry, spirit," I whispered.

The planchette swept across the board again.

M

"Em?" Lacy looked at me askance. "Are you sure this isn't you?"

"Great trust circle." Fae sipped her tequila.

"Look, it's going again." Rosa watched the planchette move and raised her fingers. "It's not me."

"Me either." I grabbed my wine glass with both hands. "Look, ghostie. No hands."

"It won't *work* if you don't do it properly—" Hannah started as we all chattered, totally ignoring the Ouija board, and her.

Well, almost everyone. I kept a hard eye on that little triangular sliver of bone, keen to see what Nate would do—and ready to stop him if he handed out any state secrets too easily.

"It's moving," I said calmly, sipping my wine.

Fae was the one to watch me this time, and raised a thin, over-manicured eyebrow.

I shrugged and inclined my head toward the board where the planchette, under Nate's careful tutelage, spelled out his message.

"A," everyone chorused, as Hannah got her phone out.

I shook my head and gave her a hard glare. "You want to do it in your room, be my guest," I muttered.

"N-N-E-R-S."

"Anners?" Rosa looked confused.

Someone blew out an impatient breath.

"Manners," I said dryly. "As in *mind them*, I'm sure. Thank you, spirit, for the gentle and timely reminder."

Hannah shook her hair back and quickly primed up, despite having lost her audience to mostly day-drinking freshmen. "Do you have a message for us, spirit? Are you a poet?" She held her breath.

"Go slow," I murmured, and received a glare for my effort from Bianca.

"What? The person's probably been dead for at least a hundred years." *Or two.*

"You can't know that," Lacy objected.

"Sisters," Hannah snapped despite not being one yet,

117

breaking out of her gothicana personality as she bestowed glares around the circle. "Let the spirit speak."

"L."

The beginning of a new word began.

"O-S-T."

"Lost," Rosa mumbled, her wine glass trembling in her hands. "Oh, dear spirit. Are you lost?"

The planchette zoomed to *YES*.

My stomach clenched on nothing at all but half a glass of wine and a sonnet full of guilt.

Here I'd been worried about losing Nate, when what he'd been wanting was to return to where he came from all this time. Evening couldn't come fast enough. I needed to apologize about a zillion times over to the poet I'd pulled from both obscurity and peace, and given him nothing back for the effort.

"I'm sorry," I murmured into my wine, low enough that no one heard me, though my breath fogged the glass.

The planchette moved again.

"B-E H-E-R-E."

Lacy frowned. "Spirit, would you like us to draw you down in our next ritual?"

Nothing.

"Would you like us to invoke you and find you?" she tried again in different terms.

The planchette quivered and moved toward *YES*, then stopped.

My cramping stomach turned as cold as the hot chocolate Nate iced over before. Oh, shit. Surely there was no way I'd actually raised two spirits in my ritual that brought Nathaniel to me? I stared hard at the board, nibbling my lip, then checked my watch.

Nope, I still had three hours until sunset. I mulled over the right question to ask, but my panicked mind came up blank on cue.

"Spirit. How can we help you?" Fae asked, her voice low and filled with respect, though clear.

I sent her a grateful smile that she returned, despite the twirling athame.

The planchette scooted across the board again.

"R-E-A-D." Oh, fuckity. We were screwed. Because Nate had control, and I knew exactly what was coming.

"M-E." Bianca looked around at us, triumph lighting her dark eyes as she finished the short sentence I couldn't. "*Read me*. It is a poet. Spirit," she addressed the room with unerring command. "What is your name?"

I closed my eyes. This couldn't happen. He couldn't need this that much. Right? Oh, hell, I was a bad dead poet quixotic friend. I'd find a way for him to become famous. Maybe Erin could help me print something of his, and drag Nathaniel out of obscurity in a much safer manner than this.

The planchette glided across the board again, heading for the second row of letters. I had to do something. Maybe knock over my wine glass? Even I couldn't deal with breaking a second thing today, especially on an heirloom item like Hannah's Ouija board, but what had to be done had to be done—

The planchette stopped.

Breath halted around the circle along with it.

"Spirit," Hannah called, a frown decorating her face. "Are you there?"

Nothing.

I knew this mood. We were saved.

"Thank you," I mouthed, flicking my hair over my face and burying my attention into my wine glass.

"Are you crying?" Fae muttered into my hair. "Because if you are, I have the greatest sympathies. This was shit. Fucking magnets under the board moving the planchette about. They even broke on her."

I released a shuddering breath and raised my eyes to find Hannah glaring at us. "Uh, I think it's gone now," I said weakly.

"Yep. Done, all done." Fae clapped her hands like she'd ended an auction, scaring the wine out of everyone else in the room. "Thank you, spirit," she called in a show of literal raised hands, her athame dangling from her pinkie on a thin leather strap. "We appreciate you. Please return to wherever you came from and be no longer lost." She winked at me, downed the rest of her tequila, and rose. "Good shit show. Lemme know when we can do it again. See you in the graveyard."

Lacy and Bianca groaned as Hannah threw a victorious look in their direction. I recalled them shushing her before the vase incident. Rosa met my gaze with a raised shoulder of her own and shuffled out of the room after Fae.

"Well, now you know the secret—initiation should be fun." Lacy sent a dagger-filled look at Hannah who wisely dropped her head and hid behind her mouse-brown hair, much as I had before but for a different reason. "See you on Friday night." She and Bianca collected two still-filled wine bottles and waltzed out of my room arm in arm.

Which left Hannah sitting on the other side of the Ouija board to me, still hiding behind her hair while I sipped at my wine glass and tried not to tap my foot.

"Uh, it was a good try." I placed the planchette in her hand.

She recoiled at the contact and shoved it back at me. "Keep it. It obviously works better for you than it does for me," she spat. "My family needed a real witch to continue their line. I have the magical aptitude of a toadstool. Not even one good enough to brew a decent potion," she sobbed, dissolving into a hot sisterly mess as she dashed for my open door and slammed it shut behind her.

"Well, fuck." I sighed to the empty dorm room.

Q-U-I-T-E spelled out Nate.

My almost empty room.

"I'm so sorry I pulled you from your peace," I whispered. "It wasn't my right, and I didn't mean to. I— I'll find a way to send you back."

Nothing.

I closed my eyes and rested my forehead on my knees. Exhaustion seemed to be my new normal. Everything about today—the bitchiness and shattered hopes to be within the sorority, the sleepless nights talking with Nate that I craved while trying to balance my non-existent social and campus life, and the wine plus impromptu Ouija session crept over me with no cold tendrils for comfort.

Tears tracked my cheeks and dropped. I reached out to catch my sorrow before I splattered the board with my personal pity party and stared.

The planchette sat on *NO*.

My Crush, My Obsession

"Did you do that?" I breathed.

The planchette remained still. Then—

It moved slowly, almost tentative, across to *YES*.

"Nate, tell me it's you," I sobbed softly. "Please. I can't— Dammit, I want it to be sunset so I can see you."

M-E T-O-O.

I reached for the planchette as the door rattled under the force of its knock. Startled, I jolted where I sat, Nate's presence dissipating with the interruption. The Ouija board skewed sideways, and the planchette skittered under the bed.

The knock repeated with a ridiculous amount of force.

"Tequila is not good for you," I shouted to Fae through the door, scraping tears off my face. Only the Gothic witch would have the balls to pound half the building down postfailed-séance for laughs. She'd probably forgotten her spare blade.

I crawled to my feet, the effects of my own day-drinking habit leaving me swaying as circulation returned in a stunning array of pins and needles that rippled along my ankles, and hobbled forward.

"All right, I got it," I grumbled and pulled the door open.

And exposed Thomas Carlisle's disdainful face. "Hello, Emma," he drawled.

"Isn't there a rule about men not being in the dorm?" I said without thinking.

His smirk did distasteful things to my stomach. I immediately wished I could rescind every word.

"You look . . . less than appealing," he started, frowning and leaned forward to sniff my breath. "Have you been drinking?"

Considering the man's legendary Friday night frat party midnight gardening habit that often ended with him fertilizing the house's prized olive trees, he was in no position to speak. Of course, Thomas's double standards flowed in one direction, and never in my favor.

"Did you come here to criticize me?" I gave up wondering why he could waltz into a sorority—this was Thomas Carlisle. He could do whatever he wanted, apparently.

A deep sigh ripped through me as I ran my hand through my hair. A tuft of fluff fell out and floated to my bare feet.

His upper lip curled. "Emma, Why can't you—" He started, then closed his mouth, and took a step back.

One hand raked through his hair, messing it up. The imperfect strands triggered me. I stared at my ex-boyfriend who was once all the things that first-year Emma wanted. Here he stood, in my doorway, looking distinctly ruffled and out of sorts all over again.

Just the way he was when I first met him.

I frowned. "Are you all right?"

This is a bad idea. He's your ex for a reason.

But he was also human and, once, I cared for him.

Thomas offered me a sheepish grin. "I might have sneaked past the honor guard downstairs."

"You mean the gargoyles?" I said without thinking.

He frowned, the easy smile slipping off his face. "You say the strangest things, Emma," Thomas said softly.

Too softly.

I knew that tone. The warning in it. Not to be odd. *Different*. I met his eyes, noted the cold color in them. "What do you want, Thomas?"

He strived for the same smile as before but this time it lacked something. Warmth. Empathy.

Humanity.

"I need a date for a party," he informed me, as though this announcement should curl my toes rather than my stomach.

"Is that so," I said dryly. As always, my sarcasm was lost in Thomas's labyrinthine ego.

"Yes." He appeared pleased I had caught on to his plan so fast. He held out his hand. "You left this with me when you had your little tantrum. Not that it's important. I'm sure it's forgotten now," he lied unconvincingly. The gleam in his eye matched the glint off the gold-plated lavaliere frat necklace he extended until I reluctantly took the jewelry. It had a habit of strangling me with its excess weight.

"Thomas, I gave this back to you," I murmured, unwilling to engage in the all-out brawl he'd stage to get his way, even when he wasn't supposed to be in the building. I knew every trick Thomas possessed, and hated the lot.

"Now you can wear it again. A mark of our relationship." He beamed at me, though his confident smile wavered at the edges.

I sighed. "Why are we forcing this? There are a hundred girls who will drool after your pecs and want to climb into your pants, Thomas. We don't need to resurrect something that already died a timely death."

"You will wear what I gave you." Thomas's voice rose.

And there he is. The self-serving, pompous ass. I winced and backed up a step. "Can we discuss this some other time?" I said hopefully. *Off sorority grounds and away from my additional roomie.* Plus, I needed clarity, and maybe he needed a reminder. "Wait, are boyfriends allowed in the dorms?"

The moment the words were out of my mouth they sounded more of an invitation than a reprimand, considering we both *knew* he wasn't supposed to be there. I cursed myself for the slip in attention. Thomas's Cheshire smile could have slain dragons a mile away for the sense of conquest in it.

Dammit, Carlisle. I thought I rid myself of you already.

I squeezed the necklace I hated in my hand. The thing always felt more like a noose or a brand than jewelry. I was all in for a little kink play with the right partner, but Thomas's collar held no appeal to me whatsoever.

Behind me, something shattered. I didn't have enough energy left to jump. Things seemed to break around me on cue this week. Vases, sanity. Hearts.

Thomas ignored the inconvenience of the ghost breaking things in my room. "I need you to be present as my date on Friday night," he reiterated. "We have a match that we'll win, of course—" I concealed an ungirlfriend-worthy snort at that; Inerius's polo team hadn't claimed a win since Thomas joined them two years ago "—and you will be welcome at the after-party."

"Oh, Friday night?" I affected a pose that went straight over his coiffed head. "I can't. Sorry. Graveyard initiation. A girl's gotta get hazed. Bye, now." I slammed the door in his wide-eyed face.

I turned back to the room, flicked the lock, and slid down the door's polished surface. My heart thumped in my chest as I waited for his boot in my back with only the heavy

125

veneer between us, but it didn't come. The lock wouldn't mean much to Thomas in a mood but he'd have to trample my body if he wanted in. I held my breath as my blood pumped furiously, my vision blinking in and out of gray spots. I clenched my fingers on my knees, digging my nails into my palms against the prickles that rode my arms as my heart started to slow.

Screw you and your Friday night date, Thomas Carlisle. I'll chew grave dirt before I'll kiss a toad like you ever again.

There was no prince hiding under his plastic hair, tousled or not. My heart still ached because *something* seemed to bother him, but he could find another girl to comfort his soul—if she could locate it for him.

The planchette slid out from beneath my bed and onto the Ouija board. I watched its progress, too mentally drained to be anything but an observer to Nate's newest antics as he spelled out his next comment.

A-S-S H-A-T.

A laugh barked from my lips. Not the most pleasant sound, but Nathaniel pulled it out of me. "He was, wasn't he?" I agreed.

A tiny frisson of heat settled low in my spine as I crawled over to the bed and climbed on, ready to wait for dusk to fall. The planchette turned idle circles a few times before it stilled.

I rolled on my back and closed my eyes.

"Thank you."

For not leaving me alone.

For not wanting to leave me at all.

No matter what, I'd find a way for Nathaniel to stay. Because in the last weeks, my ethereal ghost boy who shouldn't exist had become the rock I relied upon. I didn't want that to change, no matter how unrealistic my dream might be. A panicked gasp welled in my throat as I pulled my knees to my chest.

"Stay. Please?"

He wouldn't reply. I knew that. My eyes drifted shut as I waited until I could see him again. The exhaustion I'd held at bay for the last weeks washed over me. A cool, light touch brushed by my cheek, the weight of his presence settling over me like a blanket.

"I'll see you soon," I whispered on the faintest sigh.

Nathaniel's touch flickered at my nape in reply.

A quiet comfort after a hellish day. I wished the moment with him could last forever.

*

I woke up to no poet in my room.

None. Dead or alive, Nate wasn't in residence despite the clock tower striking midnight. I'd grown so used to Inerius's prime-time chimer that I slept right through its hourly song each night. But tonight, I counted every stroke as I perched on the edge of my bed and cursed my mortal body's weakness, which my ghost boy didn't share.

Seven full hours with him I'd wasted over sleep. *Sleep*. The most useless of all the body's functions and the brain's requirements.

Huffing out a breath, I crossed my room. Careful not to step in pieces of broken lamp from earlier, I pulled open the cupboard, hoping I'd find him grinning up at me.

No such luck.

He had, in true Nate fashion, left dozens of messages all over the back of the cupboard door in his strange, flowery writing. Each letter was perfectly formed in his personal brand of calligraphy. The words wavered and faded as I touched each line or let the light fall on them as though they were both there and not at the same time. Some were nonsensical; others were filled with the heartbreak that was Nathaniel Harker and none other personified.

Here I wait, here I stay.
Promise me all that I wish to hear
O Siren, call me back. Do not let me return
Foolish woman. Oust this blight upon the
landscape of your boudoir.

Ghost poet graffiti left by your ghost boy truly. I shook my head as most of it disappeared in true Nathaniel style. It looked as though his words were just as ethereal as him. Maybe he had sulked in there while I slept, though I doubted it. I didn't remember any dreams or nightmares, and I'd begun to understand that the only time those plagued me in recent days were the hours when he didn't share my bed.

My heart panged at the thought of sharing intimacy with Nathaniel. Or not. That last seemed a fate worse than— well. We didn't use that word. Severance from this life ended any relationship we might have, and after experiencing him fading away and getting stuck between this place and the next, in a realm where the house's stones might just scream their secrets at him . . .

No, we didn't talk about such things as death or the fact that we had been sharing a bed together almost sleeplessly for several weeks.

Like I was starting to fall for a ghost boy with a secret smile and flirtatious eyes.

A laughable notion. The man had a good two hundred years on me. No, despite my resolve and our pact before over the Ouija board, he had to return to—

Wherever in the hell I'd dragged him from in the first place.

I kicked the offensive piece under the bed, knocking the lavaliere necklace onto the floor. Whatever. I hated that thing too. My anger suited the action. Right now, the jewelry could stay there.

"Nathaniel. Are you here or not?" I stamped a foot. "Please?" I tried, uncaring that I'd been reduced to begging. "Fine. If you're not around then I'll go and find Thomas."

An utter, petulant child's lie. Shit, here I was having the temper tantrum that the latter accused me of having when we broke up. *I really am that petty.* I had no intention of going anywhere near my assholic ex of epic proportions, but Nathaniel didn't know that.

I huffed a breath and grabbed my nightshirt. A quick glance around confirmed that he wasn't in the room, though the brief but naughty thought that if he did see me undressed . . . how upset would I be really? I still wasn't crystal clear on whether he had watched me change on that first day—okay, might have watched—the concept of his eyes on me with my back turned gave me butterflies. Except— No, I knew he wouldn't have watched me without asking permission. Yet, just the thought that he *could* have was . . . hot.

Did I want him to *want* to watch me . . .

No, because he wouldn't. This was *Nate*. This was my ghost boy. All I needed was to get him home. Safely. And write my article. And get my sonnet done that was due in a few days. And get my tush initiated.

Ugh. This week blew out too fast already.

I grabbed the hem of my shirt, pulled it over my head and changed in record time. If Kimberly or her minions found me wandering about the house, I could simply say I was snackish or desperate for inspirational reading material. Surely that wasn't against house rules? I flicked my phone over, but that was dead, too. I threw the device on charge, cast another glance around the room in case Nate had reappeared—he hadn't—and slipped out of the door with the belated thought that I hadn't watched Thomas leave the building.

No part of me wanted to head to the bathroom at some unholy hour and run into him in the middle of the hallway still loitering about the sorority house.

Please let him be shagging someone else. Please let it be in another sorority house.

Both of those circumstances would suit me fine, just as long as it took his creepy attention off me. I truly hoped he was happy with someone else. Anyone else, providing he left me alone, finally.

The house was settled, quiet and still now that the clock tower had finished its midnight toll. I traipsed along the middle-floor corridor, past the closed dorm-room doors, and headed downstairs. While I'd wandered around the common room and helped clean several of the girls' dorms, the one place I hadn't been able to access during daylight hours was the library.

A place Kimberly kept locked at all times. Fortunately for me, all the fully fledged sisters also held a key. Not so fortunate for them, Bianca had left hers out two days ago.

My moral compass had been screwy ever since I'd been party to Kimberly's bully session in ousting just one pledge. Besides, I intended to leave the borrowed key somewhere for her to find once I'd used it as required.

The key weighed into my palm as I stepped up to the heavy, closed door. No sound came from inside, though that didn't mean the room had no occupant. With no contingency in mind, I pushed the key into the lock and turned it. A soft *snick* announced my admittance as the door moved inward under my gentle push.

I stifled my gasp, and sealed myself inside. Kimberly was absolutely right to lock this room. The collection inside was to *die* for.

Actual illuminated manuscripts housed in glass cases were set out on lectern-like stands. Arched, stained windows—similar to the ones in the séance room—lined one side, casting a soft, multicolored glow across the heavy, lux carpeted flooring. Several velvet chaises were spread out across the round room.

Every wall was filled floor to round, domed ceiling with books. Leather-bound, hardback, some paperbacks. Sliding ladders that reached to the round picture railing with hooked ends populated the space. And in the middle sat a dark wood coffee table full of small, leather-bound books that looked like diaries.

Or spell books.

Just what I needed.

The long-term skeptic in me balked at the mere concept of magic, but since I was keeping a sweetheart of a dead man in my bedroom who happened to write me the equivalent of modern-day love letters in his spare hours . . . who was I to complain?

Plus, there might be something in them that could help me find a way to return Nathaniel to whence he came. Much more safely than any made-up chant that I could manage on my own, anyway, that could send him . . .

Anywhere.

That last thought *didn't* sit quite as well at the base of my stomach. Nathaniel, trapped in some version of hell, lost worse than before—just how many variations of purgatory could there be?—left me swaying in place. My mind didn't stop there, however. That I might be able to produce said spell books as side proof to my article for Erin, however, did.

I tripped over my own toes in my haste to get to the books, flicking through the pages one after the other. Some were exactly what I'd expect in a collection of old spell books, their pages yellowed and sometimes crackling. Each was filled with multi-use rituals, handy hints and some recipes. Other times the leather was so soft and worn with handwritten pages that the edges curled with years or generations of use.

Those seemed to warm in my hands as I held them. Two were incomplete, but one, studded with a blue gem at the spine and worn bronzed tooling along the front cover, was filled end to end. *A ritual to bind power, warding a building, drawing on a coven's combined powers to strengthen, returning that which was taken, a spell to find things that are lost, how to speak to a beloved soul, how to heal a wretched heart.*

I flicked through the pages faster and faster, desperate to find the incantation that would solve my problem—or not.

And froze on the second-to-last page on the small book that fit in the palm of my hand.

A ritual to cast out unwanted spirits from a dwelling.

A banishing spell. No matter how it was worded, as I read through the faded lines on the crinkled page, I knew that I had it. A way to send Nathaniel home. Or at least, back.

I bit my lip. I'd come this far. Now I could murmur these words, and he wouldn't be with me anymore. No more *lost*. Or, I could tear the page from the book, burn it and he'd have no recourse but to haunt my room for . . .

What, an eternity? That's beyond cruel.

Kimberly-level cruel.

Gripping the book tight in both hands, the soft leather indented with the impression of my thumbs, I made my choice. Stuffing the small volume beneath my arm, I pushed the books back into the controlled chaos as best I could make them, as they had been when I arrived, and left the sorority library, locking the door behind me.

On my way back to my room I tossed Bianca's key near her door, hoping she'd find it or that someone else would in the morning. After today, I didn't much care. Morality took a different turn. Right now, my ghost and I needed to talk.

If he hadn't run off again. Hell, I didn't even care if he'd watched me change. I needed to see him. Hell, I'd even try for that hug. Yep, right now a decent ghost hug sounded pretty perfect.

I pushed open my door and found Nathaniel lounging on my bed.

Every white-knight intention fled.

I shoved the door shut as quietly as I could, spun on my heel and hissed through my teeth. "Where the hell were you? I woke up, and you weren't here!"

"Ah, the spinster's life is revealed." His sly smile did strange things to my body, followed by his gaze that coasted from my shoulders to my toes. "Were you worried, Miss Emma?"

"I'm not a— Don't call me that," I huffed. "And yes, I was worried. Really worried. I went to get a book from the library."

He sat upright. "We have a library?"

"We do." I waved the book in his face as I approached the bed. "And I found a way to send you back."

His whole body stilled. "Why would you want that?" he asked in the softest, most unremarkable voice I'd ever heard him use.

Because there was nothing unremarkable about Nathaniel Harker. Not from the tips of his ringlet hair to the lace-embellished edges of his frock coat or the endless wells of his soul-filled eyes that I could stare into and lose myself any given night when he chose to appear.

"Because you aren't supposed to be here," I whispered. "And I'm being selfish by keeping you."

"I want you to keep me. Be my keeper, as it were. And I want a phone," he said promptly.

"You are intolerable. And you're getting neither," I pointed out.

Nathaniel didn't look deterred in the least. "I don't want to go back, Emma," he murmured, looking up at me through his lashes.

I stared. "Don't you give me ghost-boy puppy eyes." My stomach flip-flopped on demand. "That's pure manipulation."

"Is it working?"

"Nathaniel Harker. Stop that."

"Please?" He reached for me.

I froze in place as his fingertips grazed the back of my hand. When I didn't move, his gaze darkened, growing hungry. Nathaniel glided into my space, pushing all the air away with his approach.

"I can't—" I whispered, unsure what, exactly, I denied either of us.

He didn't seem to know either, but that didn't stop him.

"Can't, or won't, my keeper?" he murmured, raising his fingers to brush the same tips that touched the back of my hand a moment before across my lips.

Coldness bloomed a blazing path there that warmed a fraction of a second after the fact. I stared at him for a moment and jerked back in a far too late delayed reaction, raising my own hand to my mouth.

"Stop," I whispered breathlessly, on the meagre air that sucked back into my lungs.

Nathaniel watched me, the violet in his eyes a deeper purple than I'd ever seen before. "Why?"

I watched him back and couldn't answer.

That seemed to be enough for him.

"I'll wear you down." He slung his body around so that his head rested at the foot of my bed and his ghostly boots tapped on my pillow.

"Feet off my pillow." I pulled on every inch of energy to match his careless facade as I slapped at the offensive items and threw his own words back at him, though I tucked my hands beneath my legs afterward to hide their tremble. "Manners, remember?"

"Ah, yes. You did get sassy. The wine snort today was a classy touch, Miss Emma."

A giggle burst out of me. "Stop it, you great flirt."

"I am, aren't I?" He studied his nails, though I caught him watching me beneath those luscious eyelashes. *So not fair.* "What would I be in your time?"

"In my time? You mean, who, like . . . a job?" I planted my behind on the edge of the bed and welcomed the distraction away from the shared moment of intimacy I could process later. Much, much later. I tapped the old spell book on my knee as I thought about it, who he would be today. "Ah, you would be . . . not a starving artist, because you were the son of an aristocrat, right? You came from a wealthy family?" At his nod, I continued. "Your father was an . . . economist?" I hazarded as I began to form a fake profile for him in my mind. "Let's see. Here, you would be the son of a billionaire—a very wealthy person of either gender—and a creative who followed his heart to whatever art inspired you. You might hero certain social causes, or become a socialite."

He made a disparaging sound at that. "I like beauty, not

crowds. There is nothing beautiful about a mob mentality, Miss Emma."

"On that we agree, Nate. You should have words with my former roommate about psychology. She would enjoy picking your brain. Are you going to tell me why you hate me using the shortened form of your name?" I changed tack, seeing as he appeared to be in a chatty, flirtatious mood.

Okay, so he was always flirtatious, but I didn't want him disappearing on me again or to offend him.

"I do not hate it." He dropped into a pensive poet zone, his hands resting on my bed. "My mother called me that. Her alone, and she was the last person I saw before I died." He looked straight at me. "No one else called me Nate, or any name, until you chose to use it unbidden. The first time in two hundred years of cognizance. I do not want to go back to that place, and I do not want to leave you."

I swallowed hard on a tight throat. "Are you guilting me into not doing this?"

He grinned, and it was cute as hell.

Also, he knew it.

"Yes."

"Fine." I grumped about, pushing my laptop aside. "Dammit, I have a sonnet to write and add to my article. One was due yesterday."

"Does time work backwards here?" He sounded worried.

"It's a figure of speech." I yawned into the back of my hand. "Nate— Wait, can I call you that? Do you want me to call you something else?"

"You may use Nate." His quietness returned.

"Okay." I nibbled my bottom lip and ignored the fact he had shifted positions to sort of ghost spoon behind me.

His coolness enveloped my body, light tendrils of touch trailing my sides. If I closed my eyes I could imagine him *right* there against me. The same coolness touched my cheek, and eyes that had drifted shut sprang open. I twisted to find his mouth less than an inch from mine.

"Too close—" My eyes flared wide, lost in the gold and violet flecks of his.

"No," he said firmly, leaning in.

I expected—coldness. The touch of his mouth on mine. Warm. Some kind of contact.

In reality, I had no idea what his kiss would feel like.

What I did *not* expect was for Nate to stop mere millimeters from my mouth, his eyes closed as my stuttered breath brushed his full lips.

The only contact we shared was when his ringlet curls batted my eyes, and the moment broke.

He leaned back, his violet eyes brighter than I remembered them being, and settled behind me like he hadn't just nearly kissed me at all. Nor did he say a word as he seemed to expect me to carry on like nothing happened.

I couldn't concentrate. My hands fluttered at the page and I stabbed my lucky pen through my notes more than once. Words that formed half a dozen times in my mind and should have stayed on the inside fell out of my mouth.

"I really do think you need a contingency plan. What if something happens to me? You could be stuck here forever."

Nathaniel's coolness shimmered at my back. "Is that such a bad thing?"

"Is where you were worse?" I pivoted and found myself nose-to-lashes with my dead poet a second time. "Whoa, personal space, Nate." But I didn't mean it.

He didn't back off, and he didn't seem afraid, staring right back at me without blinking. "It was like falling forever with no one to catch me, until you pulled me out of the darkness, Emma Reeves. Until you caught me. Now I am here, with you." His voice strained, and he leaned toward me.

My breath hitched. The pressure of the last twenty-four hours, despite the fact the bell tower clock had already chimed the new day, whammed into me. I scooted backward and fell off the bed.

Blood filled my mouth as I bit my lip on impact. "Ow," I muttered, and without thinking it through, I threw the book—literally—at my dead poet's head. The leather cover slapped him on the cheek. He jerked back, affronted by the bitch slap from the spell book I delivered secondhand, and disappeared.

"Nate—" I scrambled to my feet, but it was too late.

He was gone.

Again.

"Fuckity," I gasped. "Shit. Nate. I'm sorry. I— Dammit. Please come back."

Nathaniel flickered in the moonlight. "Will you throw more things at me?" He held out the spell book that appeared next to me, hovering in midair a fraction of a second before he did.

"I'm so sorry." I shook my head frantically. "But also, you're going to get me in shit." Confusion crossed his face. "Books do not hover in rooms."

"Oh." Nathaniel shrugged, accepting the fact.

Footsteps pounded the hallway, followed by cross voices.

I widened my eyes at him, blood rushing in both directions at once through my body, leaving me dizzy. "Get under the bed."

"What?"

"Or hide in the cupboard."

"I hate the cupboard." He folded his arms, affecting a sulky tone.

"This is not the time for dramatics. Disappear. Now, Nate." I put as much urgency into my hiss as he faded on demand and I slipped under the covers of my rumpled bed.

Apparently ghost boots did muck up the pillow. Who knew. As long as he didn't leave it slimed, I was probably okay with his other habits.

The footsteps stopped outside my bedroom. A click, then another. Not footsteps—*heels*.

Kimberly.

I barely breathed as I lay on my side, already missing Nate's hugs. I wondered if I should fake snore, then decided against it, staring at my desk as my heart pounded in my chest. I didn't dare close my eyes again, having already wasted too many Nate-filled hours as it was. Finally, the footsteps moved away and I managed a full breath in an exploding chest.

"You're safe."

I nearly screamed the house down when Nate spoke in my ear. Stuffing my fist in my mouth, I allowed myself five long breaths to calm my racing heart before I extracted my hand and turned carefully in my bed beneath the quilt.

It's not me I was worried about, ghost boy.

And found Nate's face inches from mine, obscured by moon shadow and illuminated by starlight.

For the longest moment we stared at each other, studying each other's faces close up, the parts we could see. He didn't reach for me, and I didn't touch him. Only one of us breathed.

"I didn't mean to hit you, and I don't want to send you back." The confession tumbled from my lips.

"I know." Nate blinked like an owl, thick lashes sweeping over his high cheeks. "I won't leave you with that . . . What is your word for the upside-down bottom?"

"Asshat."

"Very well. I swear not to leave you with the asshat, and you will not return me to the eternal fall. Do you agree?"

I leaned into my pillow and shuffled back a little so he

could share. "Agreed, Nathaniel Harker. Now, what tips have you got for a girl who desperately needs to write a sonnet?"

His eyes lit up. "Now that, Emma Reeves, I can teach thee. Trade information for a phone?"

"In your dreams, ghost boy."

"Perhaps."

"Whatever. Don't wander around, okay? It's not safe."

"As she commands."

I fixed him with a hard glare. "Shut up, Nate, and stay in the room like a good ghost boy."

Those eyes I adored lit with the sort of mischief I knew would bite my ass at some later date but right now I was too tired to care. Still grinning, Nate talked until the false dawn faded his solid form to a waft of dead poet, and stole his voice to a mere whisper.

My eyes drifted shut, knowing he was there despite the fact my alarm would go off in less than three hours and I *still* didn't have the damn sonnet written, though my exhausted brain knew a whole lot more about them now.

"Dream of words and poets and promises," Nathaniel whispered as a coldness touched the tip of my nose.

I murmured something nonsense in reply, my lips barely moving, my mind already adrift in a sea of romantic images I swore he put there on purpose. Nate made an art form of his slow brand of seduction as he whispered words of his poems that my fatigued mind struggled to process.

That same coolness from his embraces at my back earlier brushed my lips once, the intimate touch so barely there that my mind struggled—just to acknowledge that the coolness wasn't so cool at all.

The touch was warm.

The merest contact and I was so close on the edge of sleep that I could pretend to my mind that I'd imagined it.

And then I wouldn't be breaking any of my personal rules about my ghost boy, and he could stay my fantasy, a secret inside my head.

Nathaniel Harker was the stuff of dreams. The man himself shouldn't exist and yet here he was in my bedroom, lulling me to sleep with soft words from another time. Why should his broken dawn kisses be anything more than pretend?

You Don't Own This Ghost

Nate

Shut up, Nate, and stay in the room like a good ghost boy.

Pfft. Said no real ghost keeper ever. The same sense of serenity she experiences in succumbing to her slumber douses me, her mouth soft and kissable even as her phone drops into my fingers. Funny, how things tumble off surfaces into my hands. Like the lamp, earlier.

When the asshat mouthed off at her door, I prepared to defend her honor, but Emma didn't require my assistance, only my praise afterward for her efforts.

Effort that cost her everything when she sank to the floor, her small frame trembling, all her energy reserves spent.

I am not a violent man, but I wanted to hurt him then. Remove his hairs one at a time in order to see him flinch. The ego outweighs the mind in that wastrel carcass of an oversized behemoth. One she should not spend her beautiful creativity on.

But I digress.

Her phone makes slipping through the walls harder. Doors, in her vernacular, suck.

Once I step outside her room, walking the corridors

like a regular person, freedom sings through me. I grip the phone tighter in my fading form, still able to manipulate her world, though I am barely a concerted part of it. She will rant when she wakes, as cute as a feral little kitten. Better than the tears she shed for the asshat.

My new favorite word. I must work it into my next poem. And assist her with hers.

Thankfully, she has shown me, over the hours she spends on her machine, how to work it. And to gain admittance to her toy.

My thumbprint doesn't work as hers does but the key she enters does—her birthdate, I deduced, aided with some inquiries into her satchel and cards as evidence to my point.

The house is quiet and for once as I wander the halls, its chorale of voices from the foundation stones remain silent. I am glad to be out of the walls—they cry their anguish, the remnants of souls embedded there, wedged to the places in between as I was, once. Half in this world and half out of it. They whisper the intent of the sisters to me as I traverse the tight spaces where only the dead will fit, show me who I can trust.

Who I should not. Who she should withdraw her trust from. My keeper is not wary enough of the intent within this place. Evil ferments, infusing the energy that ripples around every mortal who resides here.

She, alone, does not belong. Perhaps one other.

I pray she does not, in fact, return me to that hell-spawned place of nothingness, of the eternal fall with nothing to catch me, where everything spins in a dizzying manifest of all I fear and hate.

Alone . . . forever.

Without her.

My steps take purpose as I fade and the halls lighten. Her phone holds many apps that she's shown me. I bypass the folder with my name on it and open one with hers. Two things I'll give her tonight before the sun rises. One she can take with her, one for when she wakes.

A smile settles over my lips, the memory of the stolen kiss I shouldn't have taken, but I did, anyway.

She tasted of sweet morning innocence and strawberry jam.

No, she didn't. I can't taste anything.

And I miss strawberries. And jam.

And things I should not have or take.

The protection a woman I barely know strives to provide for me, unasked. Unrequired, but she does, regardless. Heedless of her own safety. A reversal of the roles as they should be, and I require more of myself to provide for her in my own stunted way in this strange world.

The kitchen is my destination. I head for the coffee station, having observed the sisterhood's attempt to destroy the semi-aromatic beverages that even I recall from my living years before the darkness stole all other senses and locked me away in the void. The coffee I pretended to drink and hate for her, to see her laugh.

Once the cup warms, before the sun breaks over the bell tower, which strikes the hour five times, I climb the stairs and slip into her room, avoiding the waking household.

My offering I place beside her bed, and the phone I place into her bag.

She can find my second gift later. For now, I let her sleep, lost in dreams of things that can never be.

I fade beside her, wishing I could offer warmth as my heart breaks for the mortal that a dead man has fallen in love with.

And hold her in arms that, like my heart, have no substance at all.

I, Poet

Nathaniel made me tea like he promised the day I let him drink bitter, cold coffee. I suspected even then he couldn't taste anything and put on a show just for me. I sat in my bed, clutching the steaming mug. The aromatics wafting from that simple tea bag were like nothing I'd ever inhaled before.

His tea remained unsipped, and Nathaniel Harker had converted me already.

"Damn that man," I muttered, my eyes closing. "What else did you do while I slept?"

The room didn't reply, not that I'd come to expect anything.

I placed the scalding liquid on my desk without touching it, my cold offering from the day a static mirror on the opposite side.

"When you drink yours, I'll drink mine," I whispered, unsure why it mattered to me so much. It wasn't like the liquid meant anything to him, only that it did. "I'll make you a fresh one each day until you do. Deal?"

Nathaniel didn't answer. Not that I expected him to talk to me after dawn.

I threw my quilt off and patted about for my phone. The damn thing wasn't anywhere. A niggle started in my mind that fizzed into full-blown panic within seconds. "Where is it?" Not under the bed with the Ouija board. Not on my desk, and it hadn't slid beneath my pillow, either. "Nate . . ."

The lightest touch grazed the curl of my ear. "Check your bag." The whisper slipped past my cheek, and faded.

Like he did come daybreak.

A ripple of sensation fizzed along my spine—along with a realization. "You used my phone?" I shot off the bed. "Sassy damn poet." I grabbed my bag, scrounging through yesterday's carnage for the device he coveted, and turned it over in my hand. Nothing seemed to have changed. Maybe he really did want a version of his own. "It's not happening, you know," I called out to the music of his soft laughter. "Asshat."

Nathaniel's chill touch brushed my ear as I glared at the air before me and grabbed my towel.

"No show for you." I headed for the communal bathroom on my corridor, swiping tights and a tee from my drawers, plus my vanity kit, as I pulled my door open, impressed with my ability to multitask, and nearly face-planted into a sweaty Kimberly.

She panted to the rhythm of her footfalls, not breaking her stride as I fell into step beside her.

"You're a runner?"

"You are a chatterer." She pulled an earbud free. "And you sleep in. How do you get anything done?" Her nose wrinkled, like the concept of sleeping offered her a direct insult.

"Night owl. I got my sonnet written," I lied, knowing I'd have to pull something out of my peach before class. "Isn't our draft due today?"

She nodded, slowing as we reached the bathroom door. "That came out fast."

"Inspired by the surroundings, I guess." I shrugged. "And I have the panda eyes to pay for it." I yawned into the back of my hand, waving my towel at her.

"See you in class." Her back already turned to me, I waved goodbye to her racerback.

One hot shower later and a deluge of frigid water right at the end as a secondary wake-up call, I was ready to face my ghost and the day all at once. A yawn hit me as I brushed my teeth, and I dribbled toothpaste bubbles down my chin. Okay, so maybe I was ready to face one of those, and after another coffee hit.

"Nate better be on a caffeine kick." Tea hour was over. It was time to coffee it up. I grabbed my things as the bathroom filled with chattering sisters. Ducking my way through a bunch of greetings I pretended to return, I headed back to my room.

No steaming mug, or any mugs, waited on my desk where I had left both this morning and last night's offerings.

"Nate?" I placed my things in a bundle on the floor, and walked straight to my laptop, tapping on the keyboard to wake it up. No, I hadn't shut it down. Shhh. And I paid for my lapse in judgement on more than one front.

Back soon.

Nate had added his own line beneath what looked like a complete sonnet in my folder.

"That's what you wanted my phone for, huh? You had to show off?" I waited for his snarky reply.

Silence filled my room.

I flicked water droplets from my hair, bundling it up into a messy bun on top of my head. "Poet boy, you had better be in here soon, or I'll . . ." I bit my lip.

147

Send you packing wasn't a threat I could lightly throw out there, regardless of whether he was present in the room or not.

"Dammit it, Nate. I have to go." I checked the time on my phone again as I stuffed my laptop into its case and shoved the strap over my shoulder. "I don't have time for this. Please be here," I begged.

The clock tower chimed its first of nine strikes.

"Oh fuck, fuckity fuck," I muttered, kicking on a pair of sandshoes, and grabbed the top notebook on the pile, along with the nearest pen, then a spare. There was nothing worse than running out of ink mid class, except maybe fretting about the ghost boy who didn't do as he was told in the meantime.

"Whatever happened to *don't leave the room and be a good ghost boy*?" I asked the room despairingly. "It would serve you right if I summoned myself another dead thing on Friday night, you know."

Nothing.

I bit back the scream that lodged in my throat and refused to leave as I shoved everything into my oversized tote and shoved the door open a second time, blessedly not hitting the Big Sister in the face for the second round that morning.

*

I couldn't focus on *anything* in class, and it wasn't only Kimberly who noticed.

"Miss Reeves. I trust you've completed your sonnet?" Prof. Topaz Corrisken asked, her voice a little louder than necessary at the end of our two-hour lecture while I tortured myself with a slow, inattentive death.

I jerked in my seat when Kimberly kicked my shin in a somewhat brutal maneuver. "That's the third time," she muttered, though I couldn't tell from her stoic facade if I embarrassed or amused her.

"Thanks. Uh, yes. It's uploaded to the drive." With little chance to do more than read Nathaniel's attempt and throw my own words down in place of what he had created—his were a beautiful world in words that questioned the existence of us all; mine were a pithy diatribe about the virtues of night-owl hours—I knew my work was below the standard expected. Still, I'd managed to upload them, and that was what mattered . . . right? "It's my first attempt, and the barest draft," I offered.

Her tight smile promised hell and damnation if my words failed to please as I expected. "I look forward to reading your endeavors."

"I doubt that in every form." I returned her smile and spoke through my teeth in a lost voice that Kimberly alone could hear.

She cast me a sympathetic glance. "Two days."

"To what? The end of my career when she reads the dirty draft I barely proofed, or until doomsday?" I quipped.

Kimberly tossed her head. "Two days until I can empower you with your own dead poet," she murmured, offering me a secret smile.

"Great." I forced my smile back, my thumbs already working across the screen of my phone as the article I was supposed to be working on became my new focus. To hell with the sonnet; I always sucked at poetry and wasn't art subjective anyway? As long as I got the cadence right, then Professor Corrisken had to give me at least a pass, surely.

This whole sleepless-with-my-ghost thing did not do wonders for my study habits.

"Your talent is there. We've been watching you. And you came highly . . . recommended." Kimberly's hard gaze reminded me of Erin, who dumped me in this mess in the first place.

Erin who bribed her. Or blackmailed, more likely. Their history had to be gooey, plus front-page newsworthy. A story I'd never be able to write, or if I did, it would never go to print. Not while Erin reigned as editor of the school paper.

"Good to know I have an aptitude in there, somewhere. Or that it comes naturally."

I threw that last barb out there, because the thought that we weren't able to write on our own bothered me on a deep level. More than piracy or plagiarism that usually ate at me. This was a study in stealing the *voices* of other poets. Mind, my own attempt was beyond creepy, and I'd be graded appropriately, regardless of my hopes to the counter.

"Perhaps." Kimberly's faint simple itched me in places that shouldn't have itched.

"I should get some sleep. Catch up. Prep for . . . whatever horrors you have planned for this weekend for us." I knew rush week was usually a week of um, festivities, but Kimberly seems to have a specific timetable in mind.

"It's one night," she murmured, running her nails across the back of my hand.

More itching.

Itchy, itchy, itchy.

"Emma!" Vivian called from the lecture hall doorway. "Coffee catch-up?"

"That's my cue!" I snatched my hand back from beneath Kimberly's coffin-filed talons and darted out of my seat, pleased when I didn't tumble my butt down the lecture hall steps. I grabbed Vivian's hand and pulled her away from the door.

"Whoa, since when did you move that fast?"

"I'm motivated." I made it around the outside of the

building and halted, glancing over my shoulder. Half of me expected Kimberly to be standing there, watching us, while the other half of my brain screamed *she's not omnipotent!*

"Since when? Is your deadline eating you? How's the article going?"

"Better than the sonnet." *Lie.*

"You're sonneteering?"

"Not really. Gotta go. Bye!" I took off across the commons.

"What about coffee?" Vivian yelled after me, loud enough to raise an army of dead poets.

I winced. "Raincheck!" I waved a hand over my head and dodged a raucous group of frat boys. My wince deepened when I spotted Thomas's plasticky-looking blond head amidst them, but the perfectly pastel twinset at his side bubbled laughter out of me.

She and Kimberly could be besties forever.

I covered my giggle and snorted instead. Ignoring the side looks that fantastical noise earned me, I scooted my butt back to the house, stopped to make a fresh hot chocolate, and headed upstairs.

"You drink a lot of that. It's not great for your . . . you know." Lacy wrinkled her nose and pointed first to her behind and then mine in an obvious judgy attitude on weight as she passed me on the stairs.

"I have a lot of . . . *you know*," I said absently, not really listening to the sister's snark.

Her overplayed gape, as I passed her clutching my prize, went unapplauded. I stepped into my room at the same time as Nate slipped through the wall in true ghost fashion, though I used the regular entrance.

He semi-solidified in time to make a lunge for my hot chocolate as my fingers let go of my peace offering.

My heart scampered in my chest like three squirrels

juggling acorns and coming up bare. "Day—you—see you—sunshine," I stammered, adding little finger flaps at the edges for emphasis. *I can see you.*

My skin prickled like I was falling. I reached out to grasp something—anything—but my feet were flat on the floor.

Nate offered me a wan smile and placed my hot chocolate that frosted over almost instantly on the desk. "Yes, I've been able to do that for a while now," he acknowledged.

I blinked at him, and his usual owl impression swapped teams. "You what? But I can see you," I blurted in a hush, then clapped my hands over my mouth. We stared at each other over my laced fingers for a breath as icy as his hot chocolate, me all wide-eyed and jittering on my toes; him nonchalant, leaning against my desk with a gaze that said *have you caught on yet?* "You little liar," I muttered as I lowered my hands. "How long, Nathaniel?"

I stalked forward until we stood nose to nose. Or at least nose to cravat, because up close and toe to toe he stood nearly a full foot taller than my regular five foot five inches.

Apparently two-hundred-year-old dead poets weren't all of the short variety.

"Didn't your feet hang off the end of your bed or something?"

I frowned up at Nate, pretending to measure him against any old historical picture I'd ever seen of bedrooms, but the only one I could manage was Louis XIV. His bed was *short*. And not half as sexy as looking at my dead poet. It took tilting my head right back to hold those mesmerizing violet-haloed eyes with their golden sparkle. Nathaniel Harker was just the right height to lean up onto my toes and—

We are not going there with the ghost boy.

"Sometimes. That depended upon whose bed I shared, I suppose." He shrugged like this pronouncement didn't offer a fresh face slap.

"Fine." I pointed a finger at his chest and actually poked him. "No. Phone. For. You. Dead. Poet. Boy." I poked again then pressed my hand flat. Hard muscle nearly bent my nails back. Not from gym build-up—the sort that Thomas bragged on about and taunted at every opportunity—but the natural, lean sort that was kind of a little bit . . . deadlier. "Christ, Nate. What else are you hiding in there?"

His hand closed over mine for the briefest second before I yanked mine away, panting. Nate's eyes darkened like midnight.

I held up my finger—an inoffensive one—proud of my control. "Don't answer that. I don't want to know." I did want to know, actually, but he didn't have to tell me right now.

Itch, itch.

"How long have you been leaving the room?" I demanded instead, continuing my one-way conversation.

He shrugged. "Every day. The house is interesting."

I bit back a groan. "Oh, fuckity. Nate. These girls will eat you, and not in the good way. You can't be seen, do you understand? They can't know you're here."

He nodded. "I understand, Miss Emma, so please, make me real."

"What?"

He nodded to my phone. "One of those."

"No." I shook my head, adamant as I slapped myself with wayward bangs. "We've been through this. You have to be a good ghost boy."

"Do I?" Mischief sparkled in his eyes. "How do you define 'good', Miss Emma?" He prowled toward me.

"Flirt," I muttered. "Pay attention, Nate. I need you to be serious for a moment. Please."

He stopped. "I was." A touch of pride glowed from his stunning cheekbones as he sparkled down at me, alight with his brand of mischief that never heralded good things. "I wrote your sonnet."

"I can't use that." I dropped my hand from gripping his chest and put it on my hip instead. "It's not fair. It's not my work." I shook my head in a pre-empt. "And I can't put your name on it either. Not for my assignment. Don't even ask. I'll find another way, I promise."

He appeared appeased. "Put me on your app. Neri. Make me a fake profile."

I stared. "How do you know about fake profiles? And that is a terrible idea."

"It is a brilliant idea. I read about them when I sto— When I borrowed your phone the other night. We make me a student from another time."

"Place."

"Whatever."

My mouth hung open. Apparently, Nathaniel's immersion into our culture was complete.

"Wait, what do you mean, from another place? You can't put on an accent." The corner of my mouth quirked and I fought it back. "Stop making me laugh."

"Stop pointing at me. That expression on your lips, Miss Emma, is a dangerous weapon." Nathaniel watched me with those hooded eyes and flipped my phone in his hand. "Come here."

"How—you pickpocket," I cried and clapped my hand back over my mouth in a personal volume reduction, checking my bag.

"Probably," he agreed, crooking his finger.

That shouldn't be as sexy as it is.

His come-hither factor didn't diminish as he eased across the room, looped an arm around my waist and drew me forward. Or maybe my own legs took me on that short journey back to him where he dangled my phone in front of my face.

"You aren't very good at this carrot thing, are you?" I asked when he handed me the phone straight back.

"Are carrots the new toy?"

"You have been binge-watching way too much." I tapped his stomach with my free hand. More musculature. More taps. *Stop tapping the ghost boy.* One more tap.

Don't caress the ghost boy, Emma.

"Are you done?"

"Maybe?" I looked up at him through my lashes.

"Only maybe?" His fingers turned small circles against my spine.

"Uh—" I could barely think when he did that. The contact sent ripples of sensation in every direction, spiraling outward.

"So it's settled, then." He looked inordinately pleased with himself.

My eyes narrowed. "Fine, a phone. One fake profile." Why was I agreeing to all this? We were back with the toddler and Candyland because I couldn't seem to keep my hands off him. Not that I wanted to. "Please stay in the room, Nathaniel. I'm . . . scared," I whispered.

Cool arms wrapped arounds my shoulders, pulling me in close. I experienced ghost-boy chest firsthand and it wasn't . . . cool. As in cool, the temperature. Not all over, anyway. And hard. But the longer I let Nathaniel press me to his chest where I fit kind of perfectly, his chin resting on the top of my head as he stroked light fingers along my spine and whispered lines of his poems in my ear, the less cool he became. In fact, he grew distinctly warm.

Like a not-dead, real poet.

"Nate," I whispered, pressing my hand to the place where my cheek rested a moment "You're hot."

"Why, thank you."

"Conceited ass."

"Better than asshat, spinster."

"If you say so. Seriously, that last isn't even an insult here."

"It should be."

"But it's not. Single life is . . . single life. We enjoy it. Revel in it. Okay. To the point I tried to make. You aren't as cold as you were before. Here, where I, um—" I made the mistake of looking up at him, and my half-assed explanation died on my lips.

"I know." Those eyes that started dark, lightened then hooded as he gazed down at me.

Breath stalled in my throat, or maybe he stole the last from my lips as I gave it freely. Warm hands flexed on my waist as his chin dropped and he lowered his mouth toward mine.

Too close.

"No." I shoved my hands at the hot spot on the washboard abs I loved to fondle and scrambled backwards. "No, no, nope. We are not doing this."

"Aren't we?" The hands at my waist flexed, but let me go, trailing across my belly button—blessedly coffee-free today—before they dropped, though his eyes never changed.

My lips tingled as he raised his fingers to my mouth and pressed gently. "Not yet."

Way too unintentionally sexy.

The smile from before resurrected. "Yet."

A growl left my lips. "Intolerable flirt."

His gaze dropped knowingly to track the path my hands had taken over his stomach and chest. "I'm not alone in that, little kitten."

"Kitten?" Any hackles I had raised, but he was right, I was ready to spit.

"You purred."

"That was a growl," I growled.

156

"Purr." The self-satisfied smile was back.

I bared my teeth, but that drew a deep laugh forward that rippled goose bumps along my arms. The shiver didn't eventuate, though I still wrapped my arms around myself in a single-person hug. I didn't understand why I avoided his kiss. If ever there was a time to let a poet of two hundred years ago take advantage, that was it.

But part of me wondered if *I* wasn't taking advantage of *him*. I hadn't lied; we weren't there yet, even if we were so close, metaphysically speaking. Or physically.

I wanted him closer. I wanted to trace my hands across his stomach and ghost-boy chest and . . . other things.

And I wanted to find out what his mouth felt like on mine.

But at the same time, I didn't. Because once we crossed that line, we couldn't go back. The fantasy bubble would pop and suddenly we'd be in a whole other world of hurt and . . . I liked where we were. Playing around the edges. The constant teasing. The flirting. The looks. Everything hidden even when it was right in the open.

Because this way, being apart but so close to Nathaniel Harker was safe.

The warmth of him still rippled across my flesh in the wake of his touch, the presence of him seeping deep into my bones as I pressed myself to the wall on the opposite side of the room. Nate watched me with careful eyes, as though measuring my response before he made another choice, or advance.

Did I want my dorm-room-bound poet to seduce me? It wasn't like he hadn't been trying, but I'd always pushed back on that front as though he was a genuine flirt. Maybe he was and this part of him came through that way, but still . . .

What does Nate's kiss feel like?

I'd never know. I couldn't know. Because I couldn't be attracted to the man who wasn't alive.

"I'll organize you a phone," I blurted, my mind jammed on a repeat moment of the argument from before. "Actually, I might even have one."

Surprise widened his features at this pronouncement. I darted across my room to the cupboard he often sulked in and hesitated at the door.

"Don't you dare lock me in."

"I would never." He had the grace to look appalled.

Brownie points for you, poet boy.

Waggling a finger in his direction, I dived into the bags that had been deposited by sorority sisters unknown and left packed. I hadn't bothered doing anything with them under the belief that I wouldn't need them either . . . and now I wondered how long I would be a resident at Phi Omega House.

Rule number one at The Actum: *the editor lies.*

Not only did Erin know everything that went on in her domain, but she also understood what motivated each staff member, even if that meant stretching the truth on occasion.

What truths had she stretched for me?

A rummage through my oldest suitcase the sisters must have *hated* lugging about the house yielded results. A brick of a phone—Nathaniel would be happy—with a slightly cracked screen that got tossed aside for the next best thing back in the ill-fated Thomas era sat in my hand. Even better, a charger that fit the slightly outdated device I thought hadn't died yet.

"Okay, this is not going to be a fast process." I backed out of the cupboard butt first, uncoiling the charger as I went. The thing seemed a miracle mile in length. "And it's far from the newest tech. But it should do—"

I turned around and my mouth hung agape.

Nathaniel lounged on my bed in his usual pose, though I was used to seeing him stretched out on my rug. I was also used to seeing him clothed. At least, with his shirt on.

Not with his cravat untied and draped loosely around either side of his neck. His shirt followed suit, displaying an expanse of chest and stomach that went on and on, with shadowed valleys that hinted at the planes of muscle I'd felt before. And the vee that slid either side of his hips and disappeared into his pants in lines my fingers itched to trace.

I pressed a hand over my eyes, trying to ignore the heat flushing from my belly that headed in both directions at once. "I can't unsee that."

"Do you want to?" His voice sounded closer.

Damn, ghost boy.

"You had better still be on the bed, poet boy. With the shirt done up. And the cravat," I added for good measure. Who knew what he'd do with that thing if I didn't specify. Mister Poet Harker was too creative for his own good.

Nathaniel said nothing for a while. I didn't hear anything, either. Just as I was about to open both eyes and mouth to—*rip him a new one, flirt right back*—he announced, "It's done."

"Done?" I dropped my hand and opened my eyes.

Nate still lay on my bed, his head propped up with one hand. An elbow sat beneath him in the perfect poet's reclining pose against my pillow. His shirt had been neatly buttoned up—each in their right hole, I checked—and his cravat was intricately knotted in a way I'd never seen before.

He smiled at me winningly. "Taa-daa."

"Smart-ass. How many knots do you know?" I stared at his cravat and tried not to recall the way he looked before. *Fail.* Nate frowned. "That shouldn't have been a hard question. Didn't you try to be a sailor?" I joked.

"Forty-three."

I blinked. "You know forty-three knots?"

He shook his head and curls bounded around his face. "I know forty-three ways to tie a cravat," he corrected me. "That was what you asked, did you not?"

My lips twitched. "Was that a knot joke?"

"Mmm. Come here. Tell me about who I am."

"Who you are." I stared at him as my lips spread in a wide smile. "Nathaniel Harker, I have been trying to work that out ever since you turned up in my bedroom."

He shook his head and crooked that same damn finger again until I edged nearer, still unsure why my stomach clenched down the closer I came to him. "I mean who I will be on your student app."

"The app." I stared at him, and then my mind clicked. "Neri?"

"The ones where you can tap on the person's head and talk."

"Chat."

"Yes. That." He grinned at me, and the pensive air in the room broke.

His legs tucked up beneath him as he made room for me on my bed. I cast him a quick look but scooted on to join him, until my back pressed to the wall. The oversized queen mattress was well and truly big enough for us both, but with him on it the space . . . shrank.

Nathaniel leaned into my side, and I let him scroll through my contacts. He seemed fascinated with Vivian, until I showed him the sorority's landing page, and how to cyber-stalk—nicely—the sisters he'd already seen on Ouija board day. He *oohed* and *ahhed* at the appropriate moments, made a few quiet comments in all the right places, and then we went further afield.

I held my breath when Thomas came up, of course—I could be "unseen" by him but not block him or any other student since we "shared a common ground" (campus) and "needed to co-exist in a harmonious space"—see Inerius's outdated ground rules run by the patriarchy. Honestly, if Kimberly needed a new obsession, I would happily point her at this one.

I figured the founders discovered the joys of weed or some other drug in the campus's poison garden at the back of the sorority the night they wrote that addendum for the app when it first came out. It made for a frustrating existence with my ex, but also curtailed any need to enter Inerius's dating scene after my chaotic, failed freshman attempt at romance.

Until now.

No. Ghost boy is off limits.

I cast a look askance at Nate as he scrolled through comments under posts and discovered the online creative community.

"You're going to fit right in," I murmured, my heart panging in my chest at the thought of him finding his people. "Though we might need to get you an updated look. And maybe a head shot."

He grasped his cravat like I'd suggested decapitation was on the menu. "I don't need an update. Why are you shooting me?"

I liberated my phone and snapped a shot of him. The pic worked better than I expected. No faded edges, glowyness or transparency was in sight. A good thing, as my Photoshop skills were basic at best. For all intents and purposes, Nate looked . . . real. Old-fashioned, out of this time or maybe dressed for a period play but . . . real.

"That's it." I grinned at the analogy that fit his fake-him story perfectly. "You're a theatre kid who's transferred for the season. Paperwork hasn't come through yet. We are waiting." I bit my lip.

While Nate mulled over that idea, I sent a covert message

161

to Griffin, who would be able to create Nate's profile in a more realistic way than I would be able to give him. Also, we avoided the necessary campus student screening questions, should I bribe him with the right about of information I scraped from my last interview in the dean's office. Griff was always poking around in there, looking for secure files and access to things he shouldn't have. It was one more person who knew Nate's secret, but if I threw up a fake profile without the correct tech support, Griff would likely come knocking and the process would repeat itself anyway. The bounce took less than a second and the response I anticipated arrived promptly.

I grinned and put my phone down. "Okay this is how we make this stick. You can keep some of the clothes. I'll find you others. Nothing too modern, I promise. What do you think?"

Nate looked at me and he *glowed*.

"I think I trust you, Miss Emma Reeves, more than I have trusted anyone in my life, and in death."

Now those were words worth dying for. Pity they sliced my soul full of guilt as I smiled back like every word he uttered wasn't a complete lie.

He'd find that out the day I broke his fragile trust, and sent him back. It was the only way I could keep my promise to make sure he stayed safe.

Live by Her Rules, Die by Her Rules?

My article died within its first paragraph rewrite on over a dozen occasions as I stared at my screen, my fingers lifeless as they hovered stiff and inactive over my keyboard. Kimberly's dire prediction seemed to have cost me my muse.

Keyboard, meet forehead.

I'd have the alphabet stamped across my face at this rate and my English lit class could compose sonnets directly from my visage.

Nate had started a new habit of breaking pencils on my behalf whenever he saw me struggling. Soon my desk was a veritable graveyard of graphite and painted wood shards. But while I suffered, he, on the other hand, was exuberant. Because for the first time in two hundred years, my dead poet existed.

And more than that, he was *seen* outside of my room. If only online, for now.

I couldn't work out if Neri was a blessing or a curse, but Nathaniel wielded that device—and the app—with a dab hand like he had been born in this century. Aided by *The Actum*'s tame geek department, my dead poet entered Inerius's creative community as Nathaniel J. Harker, complete with a cravatted profile pic and a small bio write-up he made himself and seemed to change—hourly—as often as the app allowed.

By the end of the first day, he knew half as many people on campus as I did—and after the number of interviews I'd hosted in my role as first a pleb at the campus paper and later as Erin's star reporter over my three years at Inerius, that was saying something.

Perhaps being locked away in a room for the past weeks hadn't been the healthiest choice for my dead poet, but when I considered Kimberly and her minion's ill intentions, what other choice did I have?

Nathaniel had no idea how vicious they could be, even if he did listen at the walls and witness the sorority's hazing tendencies, Ouija sessions aside. The pressures of sisterhood within Phi Omega House grew on a daily basis, though I ignored most, seconded away with Nate and living life vicariously through him in the strangest death imitating life socials of all time.

Plus, when it came to sorority life, I knew that that Kimberly could be as seductive as Nate. Her cultish-addictive personality type was a Jekyll and Hyde mirror that slapped the other cheek where his kind, poetic soul won through. Because under the guise of "a poet for all" lay an obsession that read in reverse "a poet's voice just for me".

I wondered that the others didn't realize that her grandstanding wasn't a necessary part of the ritual and what she would do when she understood that she didn't need us at all.

Any of us.

Before she stuffed her head full of other people's words and claimed them as her own.

As far as I could tell, that was her ultimate intent, regardless what frock coat and curly hair she prettied it up as or century she drew her inspiration from.

Not to use old, prepublished words but to take the inspiration from those poets who lingered in her mind somehow and use that knowledge, claiming them as her direct muse and then publish whatever spewed out later under her own name.

With the *Cult de Kimberly*—my bad, the Dead Poets Sorority fumbling along behind her.

And somewhere in all that, Nate was stuck in the middle with me, locked to the place where I summoned him. Neither were my own intentions as pure as he seemed to assume.

The thought of sending him back to the void he was lost in for two hundred years sickened me on more levels than I could name. But letting Nate wander all too innocently into Kimberly's hands, his gifts dispersed across the sorority's untalented cronies when they had never worked for their words in their life . . .

That would be a greater sin.

"Miss Emma. You are the most fascinating shade of green. May I?" Nathaniel held up my old phone and aimed the camera lens at my face, grinning, though his gold-flecked eyes cast his reflected worry back at me.

"No, you absolutely may not. Flirt," I grumbled, smiling as he no doubt intended to break my mood. His grin lifted me from my broodiness. I wanted to taco-slap him. Cutely. Kind of.

"Have you—"

My phone vibrated on my desk. "Hold that thought."

Erin: How's my star reporter surviving?

Erin: More importantly, how's my star's exposé going?

> **Vivian:** Wake up, pretty thing. It's time to fess up that you're ignoring the world.

> **Vivian:** It's not healthy to hide from everyone, cactus girl.

Vivian's messages came through on top of Erin's. I swallowed hard at the dual check-in that provided my personal renewed sense of reality far too early in the morning. Or was it evening? Nope, evening. Nate was real. Still real. My gauge of the world in my sleep-deprived state. Wait. Wake up? It was . . .

"Oh, fuckity."

After five a.m.

Also, my creeper of a best friend knew I liked my sleep even before Nate existed. I almost smiled, but then I realized this was Viv's way of nicely telling me to pull my head in, get my ass up and get my article handed in before Erin left me at Phi Omega House indefinitely.

Or put it back out into society and be normal.

"You do swear a lot."

I waved Nathaniel off as I hit reply.

> **Emma:** On its way. Be there soon. Initiation is this weekend. Should be a doozy to top it all off. Might have a secret admirer piece to add in. Poet theory.

> **Vivian:** I'll come finddd youuuu

> **Vivian:** No really, provide proof of life right now.

Emma: Too early. Dead poets ate Emma.

Erin: That sounds positive for the article . . . send me more.

I folded my phone in my hand when Nathaniel peered over the top of the screen. "Nuh-uh. You do not get to peer at people's mail."

"Mail." He contemplated that one before the pop culture reference dropped. "Oh—"

"Gotta dash. Be a good ghost boy, and—"

"Stay in the room," he finished for me with a small wave, though that didn't hide the pensive melancholy building behind those eyes. His all too pretty eyes.

I have got to get him out of this room.

I couldn't take any more of Nate's soul-filled eyes before I did something I'd regret, and that wasn't responsible of me when I had to look after my ghost boy. Something that both of us would regret at some future point.

Something I couldn't take back and that I'd remember for the rest of my life and that would be stuck with him before I inevitably sent him back to the place where he fell and never stopped.

For an eternity.

*

Nate's sonnet blared across the screen larger than life. Or rather, he was. Thank fuck that he hadn't put his name to the bottom of it or worse, watermarked the piece. I didn't put it past Griffin to show him how, now that he was on the college app as a real-fake person, though I was still the only person who knew he didn't actually exist. Griff just thought he was some random I needed to pull in from a different campus on the sly.

Neri's online student populace would be rabid to see their star reporter burn in a blaze of not-so-poetic glory for a faux pas this epic—if Griffin ever decided to let my secret slip.

The number of favors I owed towered above me, metaphorically speaking.

Oh Pulitzer, Pulitzer, how far thou art from my willing hands . . .

Nathaniel's language was contagious. I groaned at the sight of his words on the screen and slumped over my notepad . . . ostensibly filled with more of Nate's notes. At least I could hide them under my curly cut.

"Not bad," Kimberly muttered appreciatively by my side. "Maybe I should murder you and resurrect *your* voice."

I wasn't entirely sure she was kidding. A shiver rippled along my spine at the memory of Kimberly's soulless black eyes the night of the séance.

Hard pass.

"Might be faster," I muttered aloud. "At least I'd be a fresh one. If I screw up at initiation, you have my permission."

She cast a speculative look my way, and I shut my mouth.

"Good work, Miss Reeves. Very good, in comparison to your draft." Professor Corrisken waved her hand at the screen as she talked, the only one present, since her classes included notebooks for handwritten inspiration only. "This is an excellent example of a sonnet, if written out in a somewhat older style. There is inspiration clearly taken from Shelley—both of the Shelleys, and a little Byron mixed in."

I snorted into my notebook. *Byron? Nate would freaking hate that.*

Corrisken ignored my muttering to myself, thankfully.

"You see the structure? Ten precise syllables on each line that should appeal to some of your more . . . OCD natures."

I raised my head in time to see her look at Kimberly and wink.

Kimberly *tittered*.

What the . . . ? I started in my seat. No freaking way was there an affair happening under my nose and I'd missed it. Mind, I'd pulled a dead ghost boy out of obscurity and Kimberly didn't spot that so . . . anything was possible.

"Rein it in, you horny thing," I muttered.

"Stick to sonnets, pledge," Kimberly whispered breezily, through her talons jabbed my thigh in recompense.

I bit my lip through the sudden need to scream my scant evidence to the world, unsure if I wanted to rant to Erin or write it in my article. *I am not a career-ender.*

Even if Erin apparently was—Corrisken's in this case. I wondered how Kimberly would take that little slight if it happened, and how her vengeance would play out.

Not sanely.

Or perhaps I should run, with Nathaniel tightly in tow, as far as I possibly could from the madness of this place.

For the first time ever I contemplated actually leaving Inerius U for something else. For someone else. Because Nathaniel's safety had become that paramount.

Holy shit. I plagiarized my poet. Or had he plagiarized me? How the hell did one come to terms with another person claiming their work under your name?

I'm sorry, Miss. My dead poet wrote my sonnet for me.

Kimberly would be so proud.

I couldn't name him after all . . . ugh, this was such a mess. I longed for my keyboard to bang my forehead on, but neither item would take much more abuse without cracking. I had bets placed on which would go first. My phone buzzed in my bag as the class lumbered on. I reached for it regardless of the glare Kimberly sent me as her pseudo lover continued her lesson, and peeked at my phone. Surely today couldn't get any worse, right?

Wrong.

Nathaniel had found the relationship button. All of Neri had just been alerted to the fact he was dating . . .

Double ugh.

I closed my eyes as Kimberly peeked over my shoulder. She was as bad as him. Maybe they should get together. I let that thought fester for a full second before I took it back.

Nope. I would never give up my poet boy. He was mine to protect all over. Even if I had to protect him from himself.

Dangerous ground, Emma.

He'd done what I asked and stayed in the room, I thought, from the half selfie that showed one eye and part of my bedroom wall. Identifying enough for anyone—like my over-the-shoulder voyeur—who knew what the inside of Phi Omega House looked like, and the no internal photography caveat.

Kimberly, however, didn't make a single sound as Topaz Corrisken caught her attention with a little peachy butt wiggle while I sat numbly through the rest of the class, working on stipulations around how to corral my dead poet who was obviously busting to dive out of his—*my*—room.

Answer: let the ghost boy roam.

It was a terrible idea. A catastrophic thought. And yet . . . it kind of had legs. If he could prove I was able to trust him and change his damn relationship status away from *I'm in a relationship with my desk cacti,* then maybe we would be able to achieve something tangible.

Because my dead poet used the latinized plural form in a socials post. Besides, that was *my* desk cactus he photographed without either of our permission. I doubted he asked.

"Come on. You are in a daze. Being the teacher's pet today has gone to your head already, huh?" Thankfully, Kimberly didn't poke me this time.

"Pretty much." I packed up, and headed for the door.

Kimberly peeled away, a strange smile lighting her face. I took note as I pivoted around when a cup of bitter, warm ambrosia pressed into my back. A pair of dark eyes I knew well peered at me over it, concern similar to the look Nathaniel gave me before I abandoned him crinkled her face.

"Viv?"

"I'm force-feeding you too, in case he isn't." She pushed a toasted bagel in a paper bag into my hands and shook her head. Dark, straight hair highlighted with blue and purple strands she must have done herself recently—she hated hairdressers, always had—flicked around her face as she glared at me.

"Thank you. Wait. He, who?" I tried for nonchalant two sentences too late and came up with a shameface.

I'm shit at lying. Especially to my best friend.

"Don't even try it. I know there's a someone. A someone called Nate. Come on." Vivian pulled me away from the lecture hall where I plugged the doorway with my bag and bagel.

The stream of students who followed on when she freed me from my stasis chattered at my back.

"Try what?" I sipped my bagel and chewed on my coffee.

Viv gave me a *look*. "That. Girl, please. Tell me he's real."

I nodded as I backed into the crowd. "As real as the plastic cactus populating my desk that I'm apparently dating. Or, he is. Promise. Love you. Gotta go get initiated."

Vivian's gaze weighed on me as I scampered back to my self-captive hermit life in the sorority house full of dead

171

things, and wondered when Kimberly would make good on her promise to make me one of them.

Not *if*.

*

Wisps hung over the graveyard as though they waited for new victims to lead astray into the freshly dug abyss. Or—in the case of the sixteen Dead Poets Sorority pledges hopping from foot to foot in their thinnest nightdresses by design on an unseasonal summer's frigid eve, with all the soul sucked from the night—into Kimberly's waiting arms at the other end of the mini necropolis.

Before she departed, dressed in a long, black lace nightdress with a transparent gauze gown over the top, her alabaster skin and hair glowing beneath the high moon's cold light as though nothing touched her, she whispered fourteen fateful words:

"Find me after you've communed with your poet. Or don't find me at all."

Her eye caught mine and she offered a slow nod before she turned and waltzed through the crumbling gravestones set beyond Inerius's small ancient chapel and the poison garden behind Phi Omega House's daunting shadow that bordered on the edge of the grounds of Delta Chi Sigma, Inerius U's oldest frat.

Her ethereal form twisted and turned along the once marked paths now overgrown with an excess of weeds as she moved like a wraith who should never have been real. Then she, too, disappeared into the mists that wandered between the places where souls rested like she'd never been there at all.

Even knowing her bag of tricks and her intent, my skin still erupted in ghostflesh. I rubbed my icy arms.

One of Nathaniel's cold hugs would have been warmer than this.

"We're going to get frostbite." Rosa shivered beside me.

"Don't think it's the frost we have to worry about biting us." Hannah picked her feet up from the bare soil distastefully.

Bianca gave her a prod between her shoulder blades. "You heard Kimberly. Go find your poet."

The existing sisterhood were immune to tonight's initiation. As far as a hazing went and after Shyleigh's exodus, I had expected something far worse. *The night isn't over yet*. Still, the graveyard matched the ambience to Kimberly's poet cult-club, so there was something in that.

Rosa lifted her heels off the ground but didn't step forward. "What did you have to do for your initiation?"

I didn't wait for the inevitable answer I knew would involve a lewd sex-toy story, whether it was true or for shock factor. Maybe I could lend Bianca my desk cactus later if she enjoyed it that much. None of the pledges seemed to want to move, so I did, setting forward. Kimberly expected it, but nothing about this place scared me.

I'd always been a bit of a taphophile, though I had never had the time to discover the back row of Inerius U's graveyard since I arrived on campus. A personal deficit that I intended to rectify tonight.

My toes squelched in the mud beneath the dewy grass Rosa had complained about earlier. Time seemed skewed here, once I stepped into the mist's cool tendrils. I took smaller steps after my initial lunge off the mark to ensure I didn't end up peach down in the quagmire that surrounded the first, and most recent—if a century-old marker could be considered *recent*—graves.

Who knew if the sisters had watered the ground or if the campus graveyard behind the ancient chapel was always this boggy—I wouldn't put anything past Kimberly. I had no intention of ending up in an impromptu *Poltergeist* pool scene on my way to locating my dead poet's headstone when I already had a prime specimen waiting for me in my room.

"Head right." A ghostly voice I recognized all too well drifted to me out of the mist that wove its way between the headstones.

I nodded my acknowledgement as my path grew steadily more crooked, diverging from my intended goal as my feet headed me in the direction I wanted. Here, the names set in the stone deteriorated until I could barely read the inscriptions. Speaking aloud in this place seemed the grossest disrespect. I bent to peer closer at the headstones illuminated by the moonlight that the darting wisps reflected where the years began to read with dates set in the eighteen hundreds, counting backward.

Not the smoke machine the sorority employed back on my first night in Phi Omega House; this was the real stuff. Kimberly had lucked out with the perfect night for her initiation task. Somewhere behind me someone emitted a high-pitched scream that the mists quickly swallowed, followed by a resounding *splat.*

"First initiative fail." Lacy's gleeful voice reverberated across the graveyard.

"So much for respect."

"I'll have a word. Right, Emma. Turn *right*." Kimberly wafted between the headstones on my left, and vanished.

My heart pounded for the first time during the initiation event. If ever I had pissed her off, I would earn my comeuppance at some quiet hour of this night. I doubted it would be as loud and so publicly announced as the prior fail. Hair prickled along my arms and legs in a ripple of ghostflesh.

Against every instinct that told me to turn left, head

174

straight or run screaming back to Erin to tell her she could keep her recommendation and hide quivering beneath Nate cravat's, I sucked a deep breath of graveyard midnight air, and let it out inch by inch.

And turned right.

I'd entered my destination. The oldest part of the graveyard where I'd never ventured before. The taphophile in me cheered while my natural curiosity took center stage. Weeds grew thicker here. I tripped on something that grew across a path and kicked a toad. It warbled off to one side as I strode past, trying to pretend the sludgy goop on my toe was mud or ghost-boy goo, not toad slime.

A yawn slipped past my defenses despite the stunning, if misty, vista laid out before me. Dammit, I was trying to keep those at bay, but Nathaniel wanted to talk Neri, and all the friends he discovered while he perched on my bed last night. On my pillow, naturally. Which meant sleeping with my head on my knees while I mumbled "uh-huh" occasionally and he played with my hair.

His light, dual touches both warm and cool that flicked the strands around in a sweet massage left me leaning into his hand until I drifted in a not-quite slumber that left me both floating and exhausted. Bonus round: he quoted his newest sonnet to my sleepless brain. I couldn't remember a single word, but I knew I loved it at the time.

Nathaniel had a natural tactile empathy. A draw that flowed in both directions. When someone hurt, he opened his arms. When excitement hit him, he touched others. Or just me, because I was his literal sole point of contact. Not that I minded—and the more often he touched me, the warmer that touch became, like he was kind of . . .

Human.

Alive.

A morose thought to contemplate while I wandered

blindly about a graveyard kicking toads so I could commune with his kind and potentially resurrect a new poet bestie for him. The Kermit-colored beast residing in my chest hated the idea of sharing him with anyone, even one of his own kind. My ghost boy was *mine*, and mine alone. Damn Kimberly and her sisterhood. And my cactus. That could shrivel up and die, too.

Oops. That last probably wasn't PC in a graveyard.

I took a left along a wide lane between the newer graves, then a right. Slowly, the paths narrowed, the stones darkening with age. Two more lefts later I circled a headstone widdershins just to be contrary and to see if I could bring a faery into the mix as well before I planted my tush in front of my chosen headstone. I thought I had reached the farthest corner boundary from anywhere.

She said go right.

I might be over some of the founders' bodies. Ugh. I didn't want to commune with those. Blowing out a long sigh, I snagged a handful of vines and weeds, cleaning up the grave I sat on beneath the night's clear moon. My skin had long since lost all feeling, and the bugs and toads seemed not to cross the earth here, as though they considered it sacred ground.

Or haunted.

I huffed out a laugh and swatted away a wisp that decided to wander past. "Too late, little thing. I'm already lost."

So lost. I'd fallen so far down the Dead Poets Sorority rabbit hole that I didn't know which way was up, let alone could I find the entrance again. So far I'd been engaged by my editor to write an article—for which I had epic writer's block—on a secret sorority intent on raising Romantic era poets for the purpose of liberating their voices and capturing them as their own under the guise of inspiration. I had battled cake stands, sequined togas, potentially alienated my best friend, avoided my toxic ex on numerous occasions, moved houses and evicted a peer from Phi Omega House.

I'd broken into a locked library, stolen spell books, befriended a sorority head who I wasn't sure was as sane or as crazy as suspected, and I'd written a truly terrible sonnet.

Oh, and I'd raised a dead poet and kept him in my bedroom semi-successfully for the last few weeks.

No wonder I was exhausted.

Footsteps crunched across gravel—or old beer bottles, knowing the student body—somewhere a few rows behind me. My head snapped around and I started to talk randomly to my headstone. Just like the first night in the house, I had no freaking idea what I was doing, and so I chattered on in the hope that I passed.

Or that Erin's mystery bribe paid well enough. I'd sell a minor organ to know what she'd promised Kimberly to gain my entry into her sorority house.

"Uh, hi. I'm Emma," I addressed my anonymous, bramble-obscured headstone of choice for this evening's hazing event. Breaking my tenuous vow of silence, I pulled out some more weeds, winding the tougher strands around my fingers. Prickles bit into my skin, but I barely felt their bite. "It's been a while since I came out here, actually. I had a fascination with this place in my first year. Took some photos of the graves over there." I waved back toward the entrance where the fully dressed, pledged-in sisters waited for the failed pledges to return, sobbing. "I didn't come this far and I sort of ran out of time . . . I'm sorry to disturb you tonight," I informed my headstone. "It's not very nice of us to waltz around on your undisturbed earth. I did kick a toad off your burial site, though." Something cold brushed my cheek. I pushed my hair back and waved another wisp away. "Do these things annoy you? They are tenacious."

I was definitely picking up some of Nate's language. The man was contagious. My heart ached for him. So did my hands.

Itchy, itchy.

"No one has been around for a long time, have they? The campus should look after you better. I think I was researching a monk last time I visited. We used to have one here. A whole monastery. You probably knew them. They got up to the usual. You know, drinking sacramental wine, some campus shenanigans. The odd streaking dare through campus. I suppose they preceded some of the frat boys over there." I pointed in the direction of the original frat house on campus. "They had to have a benchmark somewhere. One monk was buried with one of his prized illuminated manuscripts. Took years, decades of work. Can you imagine the arthritis from that? The college found out. They wanted him exhumed. Others did not. Big hoo-ha from that. I'm sure you've seen enough in your time." I cleared off one corner of the gravestone. "Ah, there you are." Some of the stone crumbled away in my hand. "Oops."

Another scream—this one of frustration, not fear—ripped through the otherwise quiet night. I realized how little chatter I could hear. How far was I from the other girls? Had I been punked? I kept expecting the proverbial—or otherwise—blade between my ribs. But somehow, on this spot, I felt protected.

"Another one down." I tugged out a particularly tough weed that pulled sharply at my skin. "Ow. That stung." I wiped my hand on my pale nightdress, leaving a dark smear I didn't think was dirt. "Shit. Oops, sorry. You probably don't want a spinster swearing on your grave, right?" I smiled a little.

Somehow I didn't think this person would mind. The

grave had that kind of a vibe. Actually, it was probably some strict teacher who absolutely *would* mind, but I pushed that thought aside.

No zombie hand had reached out to grab an ankle yet and as I'd experienced a few years ago, this place had a sense of peace, though that had been during sunlight hours. Now, beneath the cold moonlight that I was acclimatizing to under Nate's tutelage, I still didn't get creeped out despite the perfect surroundings for exactly that.

"So . . . I guess I'm supposed to raise a poet or something. Or talk to you."

How Kimberly knew any of us would sit by a poet, I had no idea. The graves weren't marked, but I supposed that wasn't the point. She didn't intend for us to raise anyone tonight, surely, when she as our ethereal plotting leader hadn't managed that feat herself, at least to my knowledge. Just to see that we were committed to following directions and getting toady and dirt-ridden for the night. Maybe lose a toe or two to unseasonal summer frostbite.

My favorite oxymoron of the event to date.

No, seriously. I wasn't that cold. I touched the arm I could barely feel and the chill'd tendrils brushed my cheek again.

"Stop that," I murmured, smiling as I swatted the incessant wisp away, but when I looked up, there wasn't one nearby.

Frowning, I grabbed for the last of the weeds on the overgrown, now semi-cleared gravestone and gave a final almighty tug. The last stubborn one came out fine, and I was left staring at the script etched on the stone.

My heart froze in my chest, like the hot chocolates that habitually iced over in my dorm room in our personal dance as I stared at the name I shouldn't have been able to read. The faded letters were worn away as if time itself had erased

179

them, or perhaps had been rubbed over many times by those left behind.

But I didn't need to touch them, though I did, tracing each with my fingertip as my throat closed, and sorrow welled from somewhere deeper than I knew I possessed.

Lost but not forgotten

NATHANIEL HARKER

1804–1827

"Hello," I whispered.

*

I passed the sisters' test. Kimberly's test.

Most of us did. Two failed pledges stood outside the line of newly acclaimed sisters once we all trudged back to the house, through the poison garden in the world's biggest hint. Once we stood lined up like good girls—Nate would have laughed his perfectly knotted cravat off—the Big Sister in question placed a small, ancient book in my open palm.

Leather-bound and decorated with faded, tooled detail on both cover and spine, it was not unlike the spell books I'd played with in the locked library. When I flicked through the soft pages, however, I found every one of them empty.

"This is your Poetic Journal." Kimberly flashed too bleached teeth, her back turned to Hannah and Rosa where they stood off to one side, flanked by Lacy and Bianca while the rest of the sisters surrounded us in a giant circle of varying shades of nightdresses. It was cruel, making them stay, but I didn't have the heart, or the poetic balls right now to push her to make them leave. Not after my discovery. My emotional well ran dry. "Here is this week's homework: find your favorite inspiration. Take the poet you successfully communed with in the graveyard and call upon them each night. Next weekend, we will summon them together." She looked at each of us in turn, her sharp gaze lingering upon me. "And together, we will see who answers."

I swallowed bitter seeds that flooded my mouth. Not for the first time did that *turn right* comment sweep across my mind. She'd seen his name in my notebook back in class last week; there was no chance she didn't know about Nathaniel. Especially now that he was on socials. The question was . . . *what* did she know, and how much could I not reveal?

We'd already decided that Nate was part of an old bloodline and that his name came from a family heritage. Looking back now, maybe we should have changed it. But if he wanted to be known for his poetry, then we couldn't steal that from him too when he finally had a chance at life and the brand of recognition that he craved.

After his death. Because my dead poet wasn't alive.

I closed my eyes when Hannah let out an untimely sob. Untimely, because Kimberly's sharp smile pierced every heart waiting on that dire pronouncement. Breath whooshed from the girls placed on either side of me, their relief at their secure place in the sorority a palpable thing.

And objectionable.

"Ah yes," Kimberly murmured. "Our little friends who didn't make it." The sarcasm in her voice was neither sweet, nor subtle.

I opened my eyes to find Hannah in tears while Rosa, surprisingly, stared straight ahead.

"If she hurts my girl, I'll find out how ceremonial my blades are," Fae muttered darkly from down the line.

But like every other girl in her place, she didn't move. Including me.

"It's time. There is no shame," Kimberly said. Her voice dropped, quiet and low, and all the more terrible for it. "It's time you left the house. Don't walk back here again. Avoid the shadow, lest it remember you. I've heard these stones speak. Sometimes, they whisper." Her head tilted to one side. "Sometimes they scream. Off you go," she murmured.

I couldn't get a breath in. The air charged around us, still and frozen like Kimberly had cast a spell to eviscerate every speck of oxygen from the room. Neither could the failed pledges, from the looks of their pale, unmoving faces. They stared at Kimberly with their mouths open.

"You don't want us to strip?" Hannah blurted.

Kimberly's shoulders shook. The moment broke the ice as every girl in the line and the circle around me lost their poetic shit. Everyone except Fae, who glared at Kimberly's back.

"No, little lost girl," Kimberly whispered in the cracked silence that followed. "Walk home."

Hannah stared at Kimberly as though she had two heads, but Bianca and Lacy were on the ball. They turned the failed pledges about, walked them out the front door of Phi Omega House, and shut it behind them.

"That was nice," one of the girls whispered their awe.

Kimberly shrugged. "It's Friday frat night. The football team lost. And the polo team. Let's be honest. Varsity games aren't Inerius's strength. Both teams will be riotously drunk already. Isn't there a vendetta between them? Something about painting the campus in their team colors? I think they even have a points system for imagination." She flicked a hand behind herself, dismissing the failed pledges to their brightly colored fate. "Let's lock up for the night."

The sisters disappeared to the foyer. A heavy thunk as the

deadlock fell like a portcullis slammed into place left me in no doubt of Hannah and Rosa's potential fates.

Run run run—

Sometimes the stones scream.

It wasn't the first time I'd heard the sentiment about the sticky foundations of Phi Omega House that seemed to be its own living, breathing entity. Nathaniel mentioned it too. *Consider me a new convert.* The bitter seeds I choked on earlier broke across the back of my tongue. Kimberly ignored the hand that rose over my mouth. Even some of the older sisters appeared a little green.

"Now, I have a present for you all." Her smile softened as she proffered a sleight of hand, her preferred weapon of toddler distraction against her personal brand of bullying. "To our new sisters. You survived your night in the grave-yard. In a few hours it will be dawn. You've lost a night of sleep, and tomorrow there will be chores. I'm sure you can catch up with your rest later. Right now, I invite you to take one of these."

I blinked at yet another break in sorority tradition. But when she was attempting to raise dead poets, who cared about rules? At least, she didn't seem to care.

Each new sister was presented with a small, fragile bauble laid out on a matching ribbon. The hand-blown-looking glass was filled with something like smoke that swirled in eddies even as it frosted from the inside. My stomach cramped down on the need to run and run and run, but I had to stay and see this thing through.

The ribbon on my throat tightened as Kimberly's talons sliced across my pulse point. She made a bow at the back and snipped the ends of the choker with a tiny pair of scissors.

"Read. And next time, take the instruction more literally." Her nails dug into my skin over my pulse a moment longer before she released me and resumed her duties.

Air sank back into my lungs as I managed a full inhalation. The edge of the ribbon fluttered to land on my wrist. I picked at the scraps, prepared to flick them to the floor, but writing on the dull side caught my eyes.

with my dying breath.

Kimberly must have handwritten it over and over on every single piece. The sister tying each pendant to their pledge's neck whispered the words, and the pledge obediently repeated them. Even Fae, her eyes glazed as though she, too, craved the acceptance the sisterhood offered, murmured the chant, Rosa's departure already forgotten.

Erin, you owe me big time.

Nate, I will find a way.

I made my own pledge in my head so that when my turn came to utter the words, my veins lit with a heady obsession of their own. The ribbon flexed at my throat as though my oath held its own sort of magic.

And under Kimberly's eye, as she thought I accepted her the way she victoriously looked upon her new army of desperate literary wannabes, that same caress across my cheek, cool and welcoming left me smiling.

But not at her.

Where Would You Find Another Ghost Like Me?

Nate

Wanderer flees, alone he cannot see
An ancient wreck returned by wishes and hope.
Desperation calls, a ruined, violent birth
A creature of whispers, of stone and earth

Who calls upon whom in this endless dream
Of white noise that never stops when they scream
With voiceless sound. Clarity rent anew
When she who drew me forth joins those who would

Force savage words from what they do not own.
Lift up the lifeless rather than decay
In farce; their only wish to thief away
What they desire most but shall never have

Might, the voice to call their brethren to arms
And she a false prophet with wolfish charms.

The Poet's New Clothes

The Dead Poets Sorority sisters lack in a distinct area: an understanding that the dead are not as free as the living. What they hope to resurrect to complete their dreams will be filled instead with the belated, denied hopes of those who may or may not have achieved their own goals.

I couldn't print it, of course.

More lines were deleted.

Another blank page I stared at, wondering when I would give Erin what she requested. If I could, in fact, fulfil what I overpromised in the haste of my need to prove to myself that I *could*. But that tidbit of insider knowledge would earn me a walk of shame and Nate an eternity locked in Kimberly's boudoir . . . or worse. The pendant at my throat tightened every time I spoke to him, warming when I read his words aloud until I stopped reading him, at all.

Nate refused to give up on his tirade of flirtation. If I thought providing him with the phone he bartered in return for my sanity would provide me with both peace and an outlet for my ghost-sitting duties, all I found was a new rabbit hole to tumble down.

Two days after the graveyard incident, three paragraphs into a freshly deleted article that I hid from Nate's prying eyes and seventeen unanswered messages from Erin, I ached in places no sister should ever ache. The hurts were due to both sleepless nights and chores around the sorority house. Not that I'd put on my princess hat; Kimberly simply worked us.

Hard.

The problem with the dead is that they see the living as a conduit of hope for the years they have lost, and all the places they were terrorized in between.

Or not a all *that* terrorized. Not that I knew, as Nate remained tight-lipped and refused to speak on the subject. But when we lay face to face across my bed before the dawn and he faded, though I knew he remained where he lay, his cold touch upon the back of my hand, I recognized the haunted glitter in his eyes. The mark of who he was, who he had been.

Who he became after, before.

More insider knowledge that I could never share, not with anyone.

Delete.

"Have you found the boards yet? You can post some of your work there," I called over my shoulder as I straightened my hair and dabbed makeup beneath my eyes, though no amount of concealer could conceal the gray circles better suited to ghost life than reality. "Maybe we can swap places and you can go to class for me tomorrow," I yawned.

Nathaniel frowned. "Skip class," he murmured. "Sleep, Miss Emma. Now."

"It's Sunday. I don't have class until tomorrow." Or any more duties, thankfully. My knuckles were cracked from cleaning, like the rest of the pledges-turned-new-sisters, and my knees hurt for all the wrong reasons. If those ached, I wanted to earn it.

"So, sleep," he reminded me gently.

I poked him with an elbow that sped straight through him. "Nasty ghost. I don't sleep at night, remember? That's our time."

His face softened at the reminder. "But you need sleep." Petulant, stubborn Nate came out to play a second later.

"Sure I don't."

"I'll cuddle." He waggled his eyebrows at me.

"You're a flirt. A hopeless one," I informed him.

We hadn't spoken about the gravestone incident, even though I was convinced he'd defied my command and followed me. I didn't mind in part, because that meant he was there and I hadn't been alone after all. But a large part of me worried for his safety, over his abject, boundless curiosity, and what it meant if he left the house. If he could, in fact, leave the house, untethered.

The bane of the poet, I suppose. Or at least, the bane of *my* poet.

"Aren't you the spinster who refuses to yield to a lover?" Nate reclined on my rug in the middle of my room, his knees bent in a vee shape, cravat open, tossing his phone in the air.

If not for the still-stilted speech and his outdated dress, I'd assume he was any regular part of the student body, smuggled into my room under the *no boys allowed* rule that privilegeds like Thomas Carlisle ignored on the regular.

Social status, wealth and power came into play between the frat and sorority gig. Pity he didn't have the morals or the personality to complete the set.

Or the passion.

All the things the ghost boy in the middle of my room possessed in excess. I would never change anything about him, not even in my dream version, which matched kind of perfectly with the one on my rug.

A warmth spread through my chest at the realization, dashed a fraction of a second later by his words.

"Spinster? Are we back on that?" I scoffed, and pelted him with my squishy desk cactus.

Nate's hand shot out and caught the thing. Midair.

He turned his head at me and winked. "Dead poet reflexes," he said softly.

Color me cacti-impressed.

"Keep it up and I'm sure you'll score a date sometime," I bantered back, though the thought of him hanging out with some ghost girl on his arm from his own era left me rocking back on my metaphorical heels. I turned back to my article and hit delete on the blank page a few times for emphasis. It was definitely time to change projects.

"Why don't we go on a date?" Nathaniel shifted behind me, restless.

Or eager.

I froze in place. My hands locked at both knuckles over my tortured keyboard, my thumb stuck on the 'm' key that ran on for a line or two by itself. Finally, I noticed and pulled my hand back. "That's a terrible idea. You can't leave the building. Plus, you saw my last attempt at dating." I shrugged the cool spot away at my back.

"Come float away with me in the ethereal stream." His voice came from right behind me, a single cool touch on my nape where my hair was tucked up in a damp messy bun after the shower I took to wake myself up. "I am not Thomas Carlisle."

"I know that." Breath stuttered over my tongue at his seductive words, though I couldn't tell which part I liked more.

Damn dead flirt.

189

"Do you?" His deep murmur rippled over me. "I will not disrespect you, Miss Emma. Not your wishes nor your beliefs, not who you want to be. Bloom like the crocus beneath the winter sun. Be wonderful and surprising and everything this world doesn't expect of you." His voice threaded to a mere whisper while my heart thudded in my chest.

I don't want you to stop.

"It's easy to say that—" I started, turning, but his hands slid across the tops of my arms, skating over my skin until I shivered beneath his hold, and stilled. Every part of me tingled to the point where his fingertips rested over the backs of my knuckles.

"I will never tell you who you can or cannot see or befriend, or that what you think is strange." A smile lilted his tone. "But I would like to share more moments with you, discovering places and people and life and all the beautiful things . . . just with you. For you."

His touch disappeared, leaving me aching and bereft.

I closed my hands on nothingness and tried to make my Nathaniel-muddled brain activate.

"I know you're nothing like him. Not in the least. In all the best ways," I rambled as the omission stuck in my throat, or somewhere lower, like near my heart. *This is so dangerous.* "Nathaniel—" I swiveled on my desk chair, but when I made a half revolution, Nate reclined back on the shag-pile pink rug, his phone held over his face as he studied something on the screen.

The only change in this ghost-boy *spot the difference* picture was that his cravat was neatly tied in a simple but elegant knot that had not been there before.

"Thomas Carlisle would never have the brains for that maneuver," I muttered.

Nathaniel didn't look at me, but the corner of his mouth quirked.

*

"They kidnapped you and forced you to write bad poetry instead of revealing exposés." Vivian insisted on feeding me physically if she couldn't assist with my moral growth, though I suspected the scalpel and straitjacket—violet as requested, I would assume—probably weren't too far behind.

"Nope." I popped the corner of my soggy pastry into my mouth.

"They . . . made you wear pastels and twinsets and pledge your allegiance to literary conformation."

"What does that even mean?"

"She made you . . ."

"Since when did this become about a *she*?" I let out a brittle laugh that turned heads at the nearby tables of Proserpine's Venom like I'd snapped peanut brittle over my morning croissant.

Black and white poppies waved in a monochromatic field in the garden that never failed to flower outside the coffee shop. They blurred my vision and suited my mood. Or maybe Nate's, as I left him moping in my room. He hadn't been able to write, apparently beleaguered by too much chatter.

The phone hadn't done him any favors as he absorbed pop culture references en masse and binge-watched fairy-tale retellings on every streaming service on my laptop that the sorority could afford when I wasn't using it.

Which was all of them.

"It was always about *the* she. Big Sister she. Kimberly

Welles." Vivian pointed her floppy fry at me. It drooped in the middle, denying her point.

"Are you sure about that?" I asked, my mood sobering to a deeper level. "I know Kimberly is—" I hesitated.

"Cruel? Ducked? Evil?" Vivian suggested.

"Why is evil after—"

"Because she's all those things, and if you can't see that then you're so far up her peach-colored twinset that you'll finger-paint by pastel numbers the next time you try to write your article." Vivian raised both eyebrows in challenge and leaned back, chomping down half her soggy fry. "Now, eat. Crappy coffee doth not sustain you."

I didn't even flinch at the archaic reference, taking a bite out of my equally soggy jam-filled croissant to appease her. "Sure. Neither does two hours of sleep," I grumbled.

"Who are you shagging?" A fry waved in my field of vision.

"My desk cactus."

"Sounds fun. Is he?"

"Is he what?" I gathered my things. "I have to go."

I made it as far as pushing my chair back before Viv hooked her toe around my ankle in a not-so-sweet game of footsies. "Ow."

"Get used to it. Remember the cactus."

I blinked at her, Nate style. "The cactus?"

"How it arrived." Viv watched me expectantly.

I did, but I didn't want to go there. "Thomas was being himself."

"His self-righteous self, all show and pomp, and I knew it was going to happen, so I stuck . . ."

"Cacti on the door where he would ram his butt on it on the way out when I threw him out," I reminisced.

"Under supervision." Another fry poked in my direction. "Now, eat."

More croissant chomping ensued, though I did smile. "It was a glorious day for squishy cacti kind." If a somewhat heart-shattering moment for me. High school sucked for hearts. College, when I thought the boys would be . . . better, turned out to be twice as bad. "I should have just shagged."

"You would never have survived it. You're a romantic at heart, waiting for someone to blow your mind."

"Am I?" My croissant lowered. I stared across the small, plastic table as Vivian tugged me back into place.

"Yes. You are." She considered me as a smile spread across her face.

"What?" I frowned, brushing butter pastry crumbs off my front. "Are we done playing footsie now?"

"You're free to go frolic with your floozy." Viv nodded over my shoulder. I turned to follow her gaze and saw Kimberely heading toward us. Vivian returned to her fries, making a show of being unbothered and poking them into her mouth one at a time like a solo game of *fluffy bunnies*.

"That's so not a healthy habit."

She winked and stared pointedly over my shoulder. "*Ifow*," she muttered through a mouthful of soggy fries.

"Classy." Kimberly's talon pressed through my bra strap like a hypodermic syringe headed on a direct course for my veins. "Are you ready?"

"For?" I stared at my best friend who continued to fill her mouth with comfort food while answering the Big Sister I couldn't deny.

"Tonight." The poke became an insistent tap. "Sorority secrets." I could imagine Kimberly's saccharine smile as her sugary goodness dripped over me in a stain I doubted would wash off anytime soon.

Vivian gave a little finger wave, though her eyes communicated what she chose not to say. Her M.O. when the proverbial poet would spray the fan. I wondered when Kimberly would get her own cactus delivery stuck to her door.

Or mine.

"What's the rush?" I followed her out of Proserpine's and bent to pick a black swan poppy from the garden. Its frayed petals wavered as I took the taboo option despite campus superstition that held to the original Persephone ownership lore where picking a flower from Prosperine's garden risked the fate of an eternal waking sleep, trapping the traveler in the garden forever.

My future would not be defined by opiates and burnt coffee grounds, so I figured I was fairly safe.

Kimberly's sharply indrawn breath at my side revealed her superstitious nature. *Now that's something I can add to an article.* Something that wouldn't get the ghost boy in my room turned into a campus group-study project.

Did Inerius have a paranormals department? Kimberly should head it up, if that was the case.

I twirled the stolen flower between my fingers. On closer inspection, the black swan poppy's petals held a distinct burgundy berry hue. "Not the real thing after all," I muttered, rubbing the thin stem between my fingers as we walked.

Kimberly linked her arm through mine, dipping her head. "I want to run another séance tonight. Just a few select sisters."

I stared at the cracks in the path as we walked, counting the weeds that grew in the spaces between. "I thought the next was supposed to be on Friday." Maybe I heard wrong. I'd been up for twenty hours at that point, after all. "Wouldn't the ritual be more powerful with everyone involved?"

Kimberly hummed. "The intent is what's important, Emma. Not the voices behind the chant."

But isn't that what this is all about? The voices you want to steal away?

I cleared my throat and kept that thought locked firmly behind my teeth. Not all comments needed to be heard—at least, not in present company. Suddenly I missed Vivian's snarky outlook more than ever. A glance over my shoulder proved Prosperine's stood well beyond the reach of our long shadows behind us.

"I think I need sleep before we raise anything. Wait, who are we summoning? Or, what?" I tried to keep my voice light as my heart pounded traitorously in my chest.

"Who . . . I thought we might try some of the college's alumni from the graveyard."

"Really?" The smile that forced my cheeks wide must have looked psychotic, judging by the startled expressions on the students passing us who veered wide. I didn't know who turned out to be scarier: her or me.

"Yes. Someone from the long past. A relic of Inerius U. One of the founding families."

I held my breath.

"Benedict Mason." Kimberly sent me an amused glance, her eyes sparkling with that now familiar sense of obsession. "Rosa's chosen poet she left unattended the other night. I thought he might be useful."

*

The ghost of Benedict Mason whispered around the locked library. Or something did. At this point, I couldn't be certain the cold touches on my cheeks were Nate's familiar caress or something else, but the gathered sisters inhaled sharply and continued their chants in hushed voices long after the clock tower struck a single hour beneath a dark, moonless night.

Now that the pledges had been officially welcomed into the sorority, we had access to the full building, apart from the sisters' bedrooms, of course. No, this night with its cloud cover and unusual silence was perfect for raising a ghostie poet, should there be but one to raise.

Phi Omega House, I had learned, kept its secrets tucked in the tightest of crooks and crevices where only shadows dared tread. Or perhaps, the dead. And reporters desperate to complete their exposés.

Am I so desperate? My blank page tortured me. I made a silent pact to finish the article this week and send it off. Leave the sorority and . . .

Nate.

My reason for staying. My reason not to leave.

But if I didn't finish the article, then maybe I could delay having to send Nate back . . .

Ugh. I could send myself insane turning in circles like I had in the graveyard that night, looping about the headstones in a bid to locate the fae realm. Not that I needed to add any extra monstrous forms into the mix. My life was complicated enough right now.

Hell, I didn't even know where he disappeared to between daylight and sunset during the times he chose not to be in a corporeal form anymore. Nathaniel refused to come out to talk like he usually did, sending my low-level panic into serious overdrive. The concept that one day his time would run out and I'd never again see his curly head and flirtatious, soft smile gripped my heart with the sort of dread that made me want to vomit up the croissant remnants Vivian shoved into me earlier in the day.

And when I returned to my room, aching for Nate's comfort, he wasn't there. Or rather, I prayed to the muse that he was, and evaded me for his own reasons. Now . . .

If Nate wasn't present in this room, did he manage to

flit somewhere between the walls of this place? Some part of me knew he didn't stay locked away like I asked. Neither was it fair of me to deny him movement, even if his safety terrified me. Parent, I would never be. Not if this was the sort of daily panic that consumed one over their offspring in their absence. I swore he mentioned something about talking to the stones once, back when he first arrived.

The day I staked out the house, the stones felt . . . sticky. Cold, too. Not like someone peed on them, though I didn't doubt that happened, too. But, different. Like they housed something more. Did they talk back, as Kimberly claimed? Did they . . . scream? If he could commune with others like himself, trapped spirits, surely he'd tell them to stay put and never rise.

Which brought me back to our select circle gathered for the purpose of calling someone from their rest.

I hoped we failed.

"Benjamin Mason, join our voice. Be our strength. Lift us with your light," Kimberly whispered.

Or hissed. Her stage-show production of the first night took a back seat as even her ethereal energy seemed to waver tonight. Waning moon, perhaps? I'd forgotten to bring my star chart with me. Maybe the burnt coffee beans sucked the life from her as they did from us all in an epic case of one a.m.-itis.

"I did wonder if you marked the graves," I muttered out of the corner of my mouth without opening my eyes.

Cue talon poke.

"We are the voices of today. Lend us your words. Bring your voice to a place where transcendence is real."

The girls around me chanted, reading from the script Kimberly shoved between our hands in a pamphlet structure she must have pulled from some long-archived tome and printed out copies. I wouldn't put it past her to have changed the wording, but Nate had been unavailable on the topic when I poked the room for him, his phone long gone flat.

My mind kept drifting away from tonight's scheduled activity and back to the questions that had been bothering me since the graveyard. Those apparently required answers tonight, or so the reporter half of my brain seemed to think.

"What I can't work out is how you got me to mine. I mean, I wandered away, didn't I? I could have chosen any headstone to stop at. Any at all."

"Emma." The toe of Kimberly's heeled, pastel-pink fluffy slippers pressed over the arch of my foot.

I clamped my mouth shut, breathed through my nose, and resumed chanting with the rest of the sisters.

I'm not raising another dead poet. This won't work. It's not what I did for Nate.

Not that Kimberly would know, because she had never achieved what I had before.

Ugh, and I was back to turning circles. Seriously, her brand of insanity was contagious, I swore.

Intent matters. That's what Kimberly said earlier. Welp, I had exactly zero intent of raising any poet on this night, except managing the one who had better have his poet's behind lodged in my bedroom like a good ghost boy for freaking once.

I miss him I miss him I miss him—

Cold tendrils, so much icier than Nate's familiar touch stroked at my skin. The briefest caress from cheek to throat, and then the unusual caress dipped lower.

I did the only thing a girl could do when assaulted by an uninvited incubus in the making. The scream that ripped from me should have woken several centuries of the dead, poetic or otherwise.

"Nice." Kimberly snorted at my side. "Super classy, Emma."

"Sorry." I pried my eyes open to find every sister in the room staring at me, as well as some who hadn't been present when we started our secret séance. No one else seemed to have shared my otherworldly experience. "I— Something touched me." I stared at Kimberly, willing her to see the truth in my eyes, past all the stage production and bullshit. Zero response. *Okay.* I decided that to get a little truth, I had to give one. "That first night. I felt something. Not the rattling boards or the smoke ma— ah, the mist," I covered the slip as Kimberly's eyes narrowed. "Right at the end, something really cold touched me. Freaked me right out. I thought . . . I don't know. I thought maybe it was a draft. But it left me cold inside." I wrapped my arms around myself. "I thought it touched me again now. Maybe I'm freaking everyone out. Or just myself. Sorry."

Not all of that was a production to gain her trust. The cold thing *had* freaked me out, both times I encountered its strange presence.

Kimberly watched me, something dulling her obsessive spark. Maybe she never felt the house's strange touch or heard its talking stones.

Shit, shit, shit. Too much, too soon.

But dammit, this one was true. That she bought my bullshit more than she bought my honesty hurt. Weirdly.

"I felt it, too," Lacy piped up across the small circle.

I offered her a watery smile, unsure if her testimony— true or otherwise—would strengthen Kimberly's resolve. Especially with the way the blonde girl's gaze never broke away from me, even when I ignored her.

A rumble of agreement whispered around the circle. I fought an eye roll; Vivian would have a ball with collective-consciousness thinking on this one.

"Perhaps," Kimberly conceded. "We should let Benjamin rest."

A sigh left my chest and that earned me a sharp glance. "I'm glad we tried." I faked a huge smile. "Friday for the big one?" Hell, I sounded like an overused teleprompter for the next sales advert.

"We will see."

Yup, wore out my welcome right there.

I shuffled my bare feet—no heeled slippers on me—out of the library I'd been so desperate to get into, now keen to leave the premises altogether.

"Goodnight," Lacy whispered as she passed me, heading along the corridor to the stairs.

I stared after her retreating back. "Night," I muttered.

Apparently ghostly intentions drew sisters together. Mind, wasn't that the whole point of the sorority—a common ground, and growing together into better humans?

I shook my head as I padded back toward the kitchen, ready for a hot/cold chocolate top-up. If Nate didn't frost this one over, I'd know he was in a feral mood. Then it would be all about getting the truth out of him because that man could keep a secret better than anyone ali—

Well. Anyone I knew, anyway.

"I didn't mark your grave."

I ignored the voice behind me, not needing to check who it belonged to.

"That's not ominous at all." I poured hot water into the mug and topped it with crema. Someone had provided lavender syrup and I added a touch for the hell of it. It wasn't like he could drink it, so why not?

Kimberly laughed, the sound as cold as the touch in the library as I swiveled to face her. "I told the others where to go. Like I did with you. But theirs had luminous little handprints on them. Phosphorescence." She held up a glowy finger that shimmered even under the bright kitchen lights. "It's available to make kids' toys and some homemade makeup." Her nose wrinkled at the concept. "I didn't mark yours."

"Why not?"

"I wanted to see where you ended up."

"At a weedy grave where a toad tried to chew on my toes."

"At your boyfriend's ancestor," she corrected me when I gaped at her. "Am I wrong? You are 'the cactus', are you not?"

"Dammit, you did read my notebook," I muttered, letting my cheeks heat on demand as a cover for a much worse cold flush. *Fuck, fuck, fuckity.* "He's a transfer. Bit of a random, actually."

"How come he didn't start here? He'd be a legacy admission."

I shrugged. "Pressure. The creative in him fears imposter syndrome."

That explanation seemed to appease her, thankfully, because I was bang out of bullshit for two a.m.

"Understandable. Goodnight, Emma. Don't let the bedtime spirits bite."

"Ah, gross. I'll stick to my cactus, thanks."

But she was gone and I stood holding a lavender-scented hot chocolate I suddenly wanted to down alone, without the residual sisters loitering on the stairs in attendance. Preferably topped with a double shot of rum with a side of dead poet hugs in residence.

14

Darkest Night and Brighter Lights

The lavender chocolate steamed, but Nate did reappear. I'd already climbed into bed, my head on the pillow, when his cool touch brushed my ankles.

"It's not polite to be under someone's sheets when you haven't been invited," I murmured.

"Emma—" his voice strained.

I sat up too fast and the room blurred. "What is it? Did they summon someone else? Did you start to go?"

I reached for him when he shimmered, my heart dancing to an erratic beat in my chest. My breath couldn't keep up as I scrambled over the quilt I'd curved around me like a nest when he wasn't where he normally rested—slept was an oversimplification.

"No. No, that's not it." He shimmered in and out of existence right before my eyes.

"Bullshit. Look at you," I breathed, reaching for him again, but he darted away like one of those damned wisps in the graveyard that night.

"I can't look at me," he murmured. "Remember? I'm in me, not all-omnipotent."

"Now is not the time for philosophical semantics, Nate. It's three a.m."

"Closer to four. You napped," he whispered, hovering a few inches beyond my reach.

"For heaven's sake, tell me before I strangle you with your own ghost goop!" I hissed.

Surely my neighbors were asleep, but this wasn't like my normal nighttime conversations that Kimberly seemed to be all too aware of if I read between the lines correctly.

I had to be more careful. Her thinking Nate—the not-entirely-legacy admission—was my boyfriend, just became the least of my worries.

"Lavender."

That snapped me back.

"What?"

"You put it in the chocolate. Bitter, but sweet. I can—" His voice strained again, but not with pain. No, he was—

My ghost boy was close to tears. He drifted closer, his hands raised like mine were, framing my face without touching me.

"Emma. I can smell it."

"You can smell it."

"You're repeating me."

"I know, but I can't stop. You can—" I nibbled my bottom lip. "What's it smell like?" It felt like a test, but I had to know.

He closed his eyes and inhaled. Not here, but of a memory. "Sunshine. A path I walked along two hundred and three years ago. There were . . . butterflies. Black and white ones. I leaned down and picked a stem. The broken scent was sharp. This aroma is sweet, because it is mixed with—"

"Chocolate," I whispered. Of course nothing was straightforward with Nathaniel. How could I have expected it to be?

His eyes opened slowly. "The scent of you."

"Oh."

He watched me, all violet swirls and gold flecks, but tonight the swirls weren't dark at all, but a lighter shade.

Sunlight and lavender.

I shook my head of the fanciful notion. Nate's secret smile was back, as though he knew *exactly* what effect his words had on me. The magic he wound around us, like he could draw the memory out of the past and plop me right into it.

Maybe, for a moment there, he had.

"Scents are progress, right? This is good. Great! How does it work?" I searched his face that lost color and focus then slid back again. "Can you come back to me, please?" His anxiety slipped to me in the sort of panic transfer Vivian would love to study. "I can't— Were you present in the downstairs room tonight? Wait, did you watch me pour the chocolate? Is that what this is about—"

His finger pressed over my lips. "I wasn't here."

"You weren't—"

"I didn't stay in the room like you asked."

My own words echoed back at me as I stared at him and didn't try to talk around his finger this time. Well, for a full second.

"Where did you go?"

"Out."

"You went—"

"I wanted to see if I could leave the building."

A million and one jokes hit my tongue on that front. I said none of them, leaning around the finger that pressed to my bottom lips, and oh so slowly slid off.

Warmth.

I cleared my throat gently. "And . . . Can you?"

"Yes."

"Nathaniel," I breathed. "How does this—"

"I don't know." His eyes swirled, golden flecks of starlight studded on a midnight background beneath an indigo halo. "I did feel the need to return. Not strong, more like an ache that I could not deny. But there is something I want to do. Two things."

"What?"

"I want to see the library."

"All right."

He smiled at my immediate concession. "And I want to take you out."

"Out to . . ." I shook my head, waiting for the rest.

"Out." He frowned. "Did I say it wrong, Emma? I want to take you out," he enunciated clearly. "On a date. Like I asked you before."

"You're not joking."

"Not one bit."

I sucked in a breath. "All right. But only because I'm the one person you know."

"I know others." He tipped his head toward the dead phone he still hadn't charged. "They aren't as interesting as you. I Googled."

"Who?"

"Everyone. You. Other reporters. Students. Lois Lane."

"You little dead stalker." My lips twitched as I failed to suppress my smile.

"Perhaps." A shrug. "But Lois seemed interesting. I'm no Clark Kent, Miss Emma." He pushed his hair back from his face when his spiral curls flopped forward.

"Just Emma. Like you said before," I whispered, my chest tight at the confession. "I don't think I like being compared to . . . anyone."

"And yet it happens all the time. We compare ourselves constantly. In competition to those around us, who we strive to be. The unattainable." He took a step closer, his body less flickery, more solid now. "What we think we are supposed to be."

"I don't think I know who that is anymore."

The confession slipped from me, leaving me empty and bereft inside.

"Then we find out together." His fingers found mine, closed around my hand in a warm, firm grip. "Tomorrow."

I had a date with a dead man who I had to conceal in public. "At night. When you're . . . best at not fading. At least, not on purpose. And you need clothes. Different ones. The cravat stays home." I slipped into full planning mode.

He opened his mouth to object, seemed to think better of it, and nodded. "All right."

"Okay, next. Dinner. It's logical. I know you're not big on that. Hear me out. We could have a picnic. Moonlit, if that suits?" That he had started to experience scents opened a whole new door. My heart thumped again as I voiced the idea that flitted through my mind, and prayed he wouldn't knock me down. "We stay away from people. And maybe try the library on a different night."

"You'd let me out twice?" Nathaniel's surprise ate at me.

"I didn't mean to lock you away." I bit my lip, looking up at him as he solidified so close. Too close. "I— I wanted you to be safe. This is above my paygrade, ghost boy. I could kill a plastic cactus."

"You haven't yet." He leaned in, whispering, his lips across my cheek. A strange, cool warmth bloomed where he touched, then he eased back and I could breathe again.

"Give it time," I muttered ruefully.

"Sleep, Emma Reeves. I'll watch you."

That could be creepy, but it wasn't. Not from him.

"Dead stalker boy."

"Beautiful reporter girl."

I swore he smiled before he dissipated. When I pulled my quilt up and remembered the hot chocolate that caused the kerfuffle in the first place, the top hadn't iced over.

The mug I had left on the edge of my desk stood empty.

*

One pair of skinny black jeans, blue velvet lace-up boots I could not talk him out of, his white shirt that he arrived in and refused to give up, and a dragonfly-embroidered sports coat later, Nathaniel looked . . .

Real. Like a real, if geeky, albeit whimsigoth date.

Certainly not the sort anyone from the sorority had ever dated, but I didn't care a whit about that. He fit in with Inerius's creative community to perfection. We updated his profile pic—sans cravat for the first time—shortly before ten in the evening in the middle of the following week. Nate held out that long and not a moment later.

Because that's how long it took for my credit card to max out and his order of new clothes to arrive. I did the boots, then passed my phone to Nathaniel. It took him two nights to choose the rest, but we got there.

My ghost boy officially updated his first wardrobe in two centuries.

"You look amazing," I whispered as we slipped out the back of the sorority house, and walked through the poison garden. Being with real Nate seemed suddenly far less risky than ghost Nate in the eyes of the sisters, at least. "Remember not to fade and stay by me, okay? If anyone talks to you, try to either sound like you know what you're on about, or act drunk. I'll deal with anything else."

He beamed down at me. "Emma, you have given me more than I can ever repay."

"You're welcome." I clenched my teeth through my forced smile, feeling on the worse side of the *gift horse* idiom.

Nathaniel tucked our Inerius-branded red and white picnic rug under his arm and stretched out a hand. "I believe this is the current date etiquette . . . ?"

I stared down at his hand, my throat tight. "Ah, yes. Right." For all the times we had touched and that he lay in my bed while I slept, this simple, innocent gesture seemed more . . . intimate.

Deliberate.

"Is that okay?" I slipped my hand through his. The natural coolness of him gave way to the warmth I'd come to understand changed when we were closer. "Tell me if I do something—"

"You haven't done anything wrong, Emma," he reassured me. "I know he hurt you. I will not."

"Midnight hours and whispers in the dark . . ." Nathaniel's way of speaking was contagious, apparently, as well as the heartstrings that came along for the ride with his words. I stopped at the end of the poison garden and fixed my gaze forward, unable to take another step. "Maybe we should go back," I managed.

"No, we go forth."

"There's that language." A reluctant laugh broke free from me.

"Not what I've been berated for in a previous life," he muttered in a rueful tone. "Chastise me, o' spinster woman, whist thou spiteful tongue."

I snorted. "Baby, get ready. I'll blast you."

"I can take it." He puffed out his chest. Kinda.

"No, Jack Burton. You can't." He'd been on a sci-fi binge the last I checked, running through every Eighties film he could find, including developing a penchant for ancient Kurt Russell and Wes Craven films.

"Hmmm." His eyes sparkled as he looked down at me. "You are—"

"Stop it," I said firmly, though I returned his smile. "All right. I have the basket. And a hill picked out that's semi near people, but away. Are you ready, Mister Harker?"

"I've been waiting," he murmured huskily, his gaze darkening as he tucked me into his side. His hand unwound from mine.

I missed the contact almost immediately, though a breath tugged from my lips as he wrapped his arm around my waist to keep me in place against him. "Haven't you got the moves?"

"I made a list." He sounded inordinately proud of himself.

"You made a list. Miracles, I swear."

"You do a lot of that, Emma of the Interesting Insults." His light tone told me he didn't care, if he ever had.

Nathaniel Harker was an oddity, I suspected not only of his own time but of mine. That he'd been dead for two hundred years didn't faze him. That his works went unread—that was his Achilles heel. I understood, to a degree.

Of my own writing, I didn't expect anything to exceed my lifetime. Whatever I achieved in the years I had on this earth was what got me through. That was it. No long-term legacy plans, unlike his. But he died young, and I supposed those stolen years were what he wanted back. A life, or maybe something more. Fame that never faded with time's cruel grip. The immortality of published works.

"Your paper has an interesting structure," he murmured. "The people fight for their places daily, but their words are often flat, and not . . . art." His arm tightened around my waist as I guided him through a small valley of tiny man-made hillocks that separated the bar area on campus from

209

the frat and sorority houses. A small stand of trees and beehives for the science blocks sat beyond. "Do you enjoy working there?"

"I like to work. I like being busy. It prevents me from thinking about . . . the wrong things."

His brow dipped. "The wrong things like . . . talking to dead men in your bed instead of writing your words when they are due?"

I grimaced. That could refer to either my overdue assignments or my article. Either way he was right, but that wasn't what I'd meant.

"The wrong things like toxic exes."

"Ah. The Asshat Carlisle."

"You got it on the second round." I didn't wait for his answer, stopping on top of the tallest hill. Getting my bearings, I turned in a circle and located the student bar. "Right, that's what we want to avoid, at least for tonight. And that's the pizzeria. They have decent music." A solo artist on a Hawaiian lap guitar played an instrumental piece. The sound floated around us, over the soft conversation as I pointed to the quad that housed the major eateries. "And if we head over there we can bask in the literal glow of everything, hear a little of the chatter but not have anyone right on top of us." I pointed to a hill with a small garden bed nearby. It looked pretty and I hoped it gave off the right vibe Nathaniel sought.

But when we got there, he drew us back from the crest and down the side we'd just climbed up, standing above me.

"What are you doing?" I looked up at him.

His velvet boots had no heel, but in the skinny jeans and jacket, he seemed that much taller. "I want you to myself tonight," he murmured. "Is that wrong?"

You have me to yourself every night.

210

My heart danced in my chest again. "No, it's not wrong," I whispered as he laid out the rug and perched on one corner, letting him pull me down to ground level.

One hand automatically unpacked the small containers of food I kind of assumed he wouldn't want to sample anyway, but he'd said date so . . . I pulled out all the romantic stuff he would have seen in his pop culture immersive watch-through. Strawberries came out on top, along with a mini charcuterie platter, cinnamon popcorn and olives. The last item I extracted from the basket was a thermos.

"Chocolate?" he asked, making an approving sound when I nodded, not having let him have a say in this part. "Well chosen."

"Thanks. Uh, I wasn't sure if . . ."

"I'll give it a try. Or if I can't, you can." His fascination with watching me eat still freaked me out, which carried over to Vivian feeding me. Now I could add Nate to the *Feeding Emma* train.

He leaned across me for a strawberry and eyed it with a speculative glitter. "Tasteless or not?" His shrug was lighthearted, as though he'd accepted this sequence in his life—or death—and he took a bite. "Sweet," he murmured, still chewing, though his eyes locked on me as he offered me the rest of the treat.

"Uh, okay—" I nibbled one corner, giggling as juice ran away from me and I swiped at its trail before I wore the remnants. "You can taste it?"

"Every part." Stars reflected in his eyes as he leaned forward and flicked his thumb over the corner of my lips, then sucked on the pad of his thumb. "Waste not."

That's how tonight is going to go, is it?

I let out a shuddering breath. "I didn't think . . ."

Nate swiped something from the box behind me. "Catch."

I looked up in time to find a piece of cinnamon popcorn in dive-bomb mode. "What the—" It hit me on the nose and bounced off. "Ghost boy?"

"Do you actually have reflexes?" He grinned at me.

"Give me that." I grabbed for the box, but he was too fast.

I managed to secure a handful of the slightly greasy kernels, tossing them at him one at a time. He caught three in his mouth, but by the time the small box emptied, the blanket was littered with tiny puffed, fragrant corn kernels, and I was still scoring like the inside of a donut hole.

"Last chance," he teased, waving a cinnamon popcorn piece before me. "You've got this, Emma. Focus. Right here."

I stared at the transformation of a dead ghost boy of two hundred years ago to a young man who integrated fairly seamlessly—with some interpretive services—into daily student life. Providing he didn't phase in and out of sight.

Long enough that the popcorn bounced off my nose. Again.

"Boo." I rubbed the tip of my nose. "I feel you have an unfair advantage."

"What's that?"

"Tonight is not my night," I grumbled, picking up the crumpled popcorn kernels and placing them back in their snack box.

"Sure," he agreed amicably.

"What happened?" I glanced at him sideways. "You never simply agree with me, dead boy."

He raised an eyebrow, passing me a folded piece of paper towel to wipe my hands on once the cinnamon popcorn was cleaned up. "Are you supposed to call me that in public?"

"Are we in public? I thought you wanted privacy." I

tossed the cinna-bombed paper towelette at him, but he didn't so much as flinch.

So much for the perfect reflexes.

Nate's hand rose, his thumb stroking along my cheek. "I did."

What were we talking about?

A frisson of sensation rippled along my spine as he caught my hand and pulled me to my feet, his other hand still cradling my cheek. "Dance with me, Emma."

"Oh no," I protested. "I don't dance. Only when drunk, remember?" I was sure I'd told him. At least once.

"Show me." The command in his voice gave me pause.

"Did you—"

"Yes."

I gaped as his hands found my waist and he stepped in closer, already moving with the music that filtered between the tiny hills from the restaurants beyond our private space. "Nate, I really don't do this."

"Try, for me?" He drew us together, pressing our bodies flush, thigh to thigh.

"That got close fast," I mumbled, lost in him as I knotted my fingers in his shirt. "You might have noticed I suck at intimacy." One of my crutches was hanging on to things—and people—when I shouldn't. Thomas made that abundantly clear when we broke up. Before the cactus incident, not after.

"I hadn't, actually. We are intimate all the time, Miss Emma."

"Just Emma," I whispered.

Nate cocked his head to one side. Curls tumbled over his eyes and I swept them back when he made no move to do it for himself. The corners of his lips shifted, but he didn't smile. "Just Emma, then. For tonight. We are intimate all the time, and you don't shy away. We talk for hours. We fight and play and tease and mock each other. These are signs of trust." He leaned down and rested his forehead against mine.

My eyes drifted shut as we swayed in place. "I suppose so."

"Trust is earned, Emma. When you let me watch you sleep, it's because you feel safe. When you allow me in your room and don't cast me out, I am grateful because I trust you too." His hands flexed on my waist. "I cherish your esteem. Once that is earned, it is a priceless gift. Thank you." One hand drifted to my lower back, resting there lightly. "Let me show you how to dance."

He repositioned me gently, easing me into the hold with the same sort of grace he applied to his poetry. No rush changed our movements, as though he planned this all along. Maybe he had. For all I knew, Nathaniel Harker made a deal with the stars to sing for us tonight.

I leaned my cheek against his shoulder as he weaved us in a pattern I swore followed the path of the stars themselves. I kept my eyes closed, giving him my trust, and let him hold me in his embrace, my body soft against his.

Trust. Something I gave him freely, and offered too. We were thrown together by an accident of circumstance. That's all we were. Nothing more. Two people who should never have met, lives joined by a thread of time folded into a mismatch of errors. And yet here we were, swaying together beneath a moon that watched over us both.

And when Nathaniel stopped dancing, raised his hand from my waist to brush beneath my chin and tipped my head back, I let him. His breath brushed my skin and time just—

Stopped.

Everything stopped as his mouth connected gently with

214

mine. No more than a brush of lips on lips before he pulled back, my lips tingling with his coolness turned warm. Finally, I opened my eyes and fell into the stars in his.

"Tell me to leave," he murmured, brushing bangs back from my face with his thumbs. His gaze fixed on mine, dark and intense, flecked with gold and swirls of violet.

My breath shortened. "No," I whispered.

"Emma, tell me—"

I pushed up on my toes and kissed him.

Nathaniel froze. Then his mouth moved over mine, slow and seductive, all the things that defined him. Curious and sexy as hell, so damaged but also beautiful in those internal scars that made up all the parts of him. His fingers raked through my hair, tangled in the strands and pulled me impossibly closer.

A sigh drew from deep within me as his tongue traced a path across my bottom lip and slipped inside when I opened for him. A moan slipped from my mouth to his, and then I lost all sense of time and place and anything but him.

This was Nate. My ghost boy. I shouldn't be kissing him. I shouldn't be kissing anyone. But that's what tonight was—a prelude to this. All the teasing and testing and playing lcd to the ultimate trust fall.

And he caught me.

I tugged on his shirt, sliding my hands beneath his jacket. Heat pervaded my palms as I rediscovered what I knew about his hard body beneath. The strange warmth and coolness of him pooling as his touch spread over my skin. I'd never get used to that dual sensation, but I'd never not want it, either. Every inch of me craved him, ached to be bared, skin-to-skin with this man.

Need zinged through me as a soft sound lingered between us. His kisses grew deeper as he angled my head back, gliding his tongue sensually along mine. My throat ached, raw, and I realized the wanton moan came from me. His answer was an approving sound from deep within his chest that left me leaning into him.

My hand pushed to his chest as I pulled back, but he only let me steal a needy breath before his mouth was back on mine. I gave in to the all-consuming desire that heated me both inside and out while Nathaniel Harker kissed me beneath a midnight velvet sky, studded with perfect diamonds.

After a breath that lasted forever he drew back, one hand cupping my nape to hold me in place, his other tracing patterns along my spine. "I like this dress."

"And it's staying on." *For tonight.*

His wounded expression left me giggling. "First base, Nate Harker. It's enough for tonight."

"Is it?" He reached for me again, and my breath stalled. "You are the most intolerable flirt."

"Flirt? Oh, so much more than that, Emma." My name rolled sweetly off his seductive lips, darkened from our kisses.

"Oh." Words abandoned me.

His smile said everything I couldn't. "I'm not ready to go back yet, but I won't do more than kiss you, unless you ask it of me tonight. Is that fair?" He led me back to the blanket and kneeled in the center, drawing me down beside him.

My breath shortened the moment his hands tangled in my hair again, and I lost track of the stars, of time and the whole world.

I only cared about the parts that had Nathaniel in it.

His arms wrapped around me, the strange inner warmth of him growing as he slid his body alongside mine. The gentle pressure of his presence left me twice as breathless as I kissed him back. One knee pressed between my thighs, his hand gripping my dress at my hip.

"I like this dress," he murmured again. "Wear it again for

me?" The command vied with a request in his voice that hit the same heartstrings that always twanged when he asked me for anything.

I managed to nod before he found my mouth again, pushed his knee higher between my legs and rolled us. The stars disappeared as his weight pressed over me.

"Nate," I murmured, breathless.

"Let go, Emma," he whispered, fluttering kisses along my jawline as he pressed his knee between my thighs.

Sensation rushed through me, followed by a gush of heat. I gasped, winding his curls around my fingers. "We shouldn't—"

"We should." His gaze darkened as he lifted his head. "Do you want me to kiss you?"

His knee pressed again, then again. Pleasure rocketed through me in a steady pulse. I gasped at air that refused to fill my lungs, my hips already rising to meet the sweet pressure in exactly the right place.

"Please." I tipped my head back, parting my lips. "Nate—"

He didn't make me ask again, crushing our mouths together in a hard kiss that stole my breath along with my senses.

My orgasm rushed at me as he pressed his knee higher. I cried out into his mouth, though he swallowed the sound. Everything muted as I raised my hips off the ground, rubbing myself shamelessly against him. Bliss burst over me as I rode my pleasure out on him. Then I lay back panting as he watched me with fathomless eyes, a secret smile curving sinful lips.

"So beautiful, Emma." He kissed me slowly, sinking his weight against my body, grinding his hips against me until I gasped again, already oversensitized and breathless. "I want to kiss you until the sun rises."

217

He stole my next moan as I lost track of everything but him.

I'd finally found the man of my dreams, and he'd been dead for two hundred years. Not that my heart cared about that minor fact.

Consider me mind-blown.

A Toad for a Soul

The array of cold shivers that Phi Omega House held could be categorized under *deathly* to *empty soul*-based. Mostly they turned up on the nights that Kimberly hosted her séances, though they didn't seem to originate with the house's occupants—more the house itself. Sometimes, the light touches filled the coldest, darkest hours of the night when the halls were at their most quiet and the sisters slept safe in their beds.

I had learned which belonged to my dead poet and which didn't. Only his touches alone didn't scare me. That contact, I understood.

The others didn't have my permission, nor did I know where they came from, but the more séances Kimberly held, the more I experienced the cold wafts and tendrils that were most assuredly *not* from Nate.

And he still wouldn't talk about the places he experienced in between.

I ticked off my list of names, that I cross-checked with a nighttime wander through the graveyard—careful to avoid the southwest corner where Nathaniel's headstone was already overgrown with its contingent of weeds again, from the side glimpse I risked at it, as though Inerius's grounds were determined to obscure his presence from our reality, no matter how long he'd been dead. Knowing his habits of following me, I didn't want to challenge his perception of his new life by reminding him of what was lost, or draw Kimberly or the other sisters to his *"family"*.

The chance of one of them trying to resurrect him might be small, but it wasn't impossible. I didn't know what would happen if they decided to call his name at the next gathering and fluke-trapped him within the confines of their salted circle, nor did I want to find out.

Fortunately, Kimberly had moved on from her fascination with me and, along with our journalized sisterhood homework, she had added a task of designating each of us a poet as a *familiar*.

"Like the witch's sort?" Sarah Jane, a sister I didn't know well but who I remembered from the first night finding her door, piped up. She'd brought her cat with her to the séance, and refused to take it back upstairs when Kimberly glared in her direction. "Don't you think this would be better?"

Said feline was raised as an offering to the middle of our enlarged circle. Unlike last time the Big Sister hosted a dead poets gathering, the entire sorority was present for this meeting.

Kimberly's teeth pulled back in a silent snarl while several of the sisters tittered at the apparent absurdity of Sarah Jane's comment. "Do you truly believe *dead poets* require *cats* to speak for them in this instance?" she all but hissed in the poor girl's face.

"Uh—" The sister paled, but proffered the cat that took a swipe at Kimberly—all claws wisely retracted.

I doubted the thing would have fur come tomorrow if it managed to slice the Big Sister.

"The homework for this week is to bring your poet to life." Kimberly grabbed the poor creature's collar and twisted, lifting it out of Sarah Jane's hands. The cat mewled, scrabbling to get back to its owner as Kimberly towed it toward the front door.

I exchanged a wide-eyed glance with Bianca across the circle.

"Bye bye, kitty," she mouthed, though the snark that usually accompanied her comments was absent from her dulled eyes.

Kimberly's bullying had reached an all-time low.

Marlene, one of the successful pledges from my initiation batch, leaned forward before kitty could make his grand exodus to Sarah Jane's shocked soundtrack. "We haven't managed to raise a dead poet yet," she reminded Kimberly. "We were waiting for you to show us how."

Kimberly stopped. Anything I might have said in protest died in my throat as I snapped my mouth shut. Even I could have told the other sister that hadn't been the smartest move.

But when Kimberly turned back, she cradled kitty in her arms, scratching his chin, and smiled.

A hideous slash of lipstick and too whitened teeth flashed in a face born of unreleased frenzy.

"But one of us has raised a dead poet." Her smile grew wider as she started with Bianca, looking at every single sister in turn. "And she is an amazing liar."

Sisters froze in their places. My heart, so used to pounding in this house, stilled. Its regular thump absent, I tried to react, but failed. At least, not in the way I wanted to react. I'd always been the fighter not the flight risk, but all I wanted to do right then was run and run and run.

Right back to Nathaniel and get him out of this place I'd dragged him to that could be that much more dangerous than all the places he had been before, no matter what horrors they held. It had to be. Because Kimberly would entrap him and steal his voice.

My skin prickled like it might walk free of my bones as Kimberly turned to face me. Her demoness mouth opened wide and I half expected her to ooze slime like she did the first night she pretended to be possessed. And like that night, the coldest touch brushed the back of my arm, then my nape.

As if it noticed.

As if it warned me of the oncoming danger.

But I knew the dangers. We all did.

And yet we stayed for our own reasons, reasons that didn't really matter.

I have to get him out, now, now, now—

"Yes, she's right here." Kimberly stared directly at me as she spoke and I froze like the prey before the apex predator. Unable to hide, unable to run and protect the man I loved most. "She'll tell you everything you need to know about raising a dead man. Won't you . . . Lacy?"

"What?" I blurted into the strained silence that followed.

"Uh, sure," Lacy added a beat too late, and completely unconvincingly. "I'll talk about my um, dead poet."

The production was so poorly constructed, nowhere near Kimberly's usual standard, that the sisters chattered amongst themselves while Lacy tried to hold up her impromptu end of the bargain. Badly.

The sisters didn't seem to care after a while, gathering around Lacy and bombarding her with questions about her fake dead poet.

I slouched back in my chair, my arms crossed over my chest. "That's your worst piece of bullshit yet," I commented.

Kimberly laughed under her breath, still scratching kitty's chin. "Walk with me."

I had a good idea where this walk would lead, but I rose, anyway. My legs had gone to sleep after curling them under myself for the duration of the meeting that had been less séance-ish tonight and far more a rant for Kimberly.

"Why risk it all on a piss-poor production like that?" I stuffed my hands in my pockets as the coldness whispered around me. It was like we had brought the graveyard inside with us. "Why bother with the setup just to throw it away like that?"

"They don't care. Desperation breeds acceptance of the strangest things, don't you find, darling?"

I shrugged her pathetic endearment off. "That's fair." *Sort of.* I'd written some weird crap over the years. Inerius's students lapped it up in the name of gossip-mongering. "And when they discover how often you've lied to their faces?"

"Did I?" The corners of her mouth tilted in a derisive smile. "Lacy has worked hard to make a name for herself in the creative circles. Her poetry stands out—on rare occasions. Doesn't it make sense that she must have a patron muse to assist her?"

I blinked. "You're taking a woman's talents and saying they're the voice of a man dead a hundred years ago or more?" I asked slowly. "That seems . . ."

Bile rose to the back of my throat. Theft, in either direction, was still theft. Nathaniel's first question burned in the back of my throat, along with a diatribe about morality and plagiarism.

Run, little dead poet.

"Brilliant. I know." Kimberly clapped her hands near kitty and startled the cat that lodged its claws into her arm, though she didn't seem to notice the needle-sharp points in her skin.

"He doesn't like loud noises." I started guiltily, spinning on my heel to find Sarah Jane trailing us at a not that discreet distance. "And he doesn't like *you*." Her glare encompassed both of us.

I bit my lip, wanting to scream *I'm not a part of this*. But I'd been here long enough, attached to Kimberly at the hip, that I didn't doubt the sisters thought we were in bed together.

Possibly even in a literal capacity.

The thought that my morals were lumped with hers left me nauseated. *What the hell was Erin thinking when she sent me in here?* The answer hit me with a burst of clarity that I should have seen coming from the get-go: Kimberly wasn't the only rider with a first-class ticket on the vengeance train.

Just what kind of stakes did Erin have in this shit show?

That I'd bought into their vendetta, and hadn't listened to Vivian earlier, ate at me. Sure, I could still make a difference with my article, but *only* if I wrote it my way. *If* I did something useful with my words and used them to shed light on Kimberly's brand of crazy in a way that helped others not buy into that sort of toxic in a bid for perpetual popularity.

The way I'd bought into her cult-like persona, if only for a brief moment. How I'd participated.

Once.

The floor wavered beneath my feet. I grabbed for the nearest door frame, missing by the edge of my nails. One bent back in a shot of pain that thankfully woke me up. I took a large step back from Kimberly, a move that didn't go unnoticed.

I really didn't give a fuck. I was *done*, and I knew what she was about to do.

"Kitty doesn't have to stay." Kimberly reached the front door, but instead of using the main double wooden arched doors that we always used, she kicked open the cat flap set off to one side in the stone that barely allowed the overfed feline she shoved unceremoniously through to the other side. "If you want him, please, do follow. But that's your entrance from now on. Or don't come back in."

She leaned her back against the massive double wood doors, their arches reaching high above her head, and stared at Sarah Jane, unsmiling.

Unmoving.

I'd been wrong. Whatever I expected her to do, this would be so much worse.

Worse still, in that Sarah Jane didn't even question Kimberly's methods.

The crushed girl bent down onto her hands and knees and crawled through the cat flap, disappearing head and shoulders first. Which was where the entire, demoralizing exodus came undone. Sarah Jane stopped, and wiggled her hips.

"Help, please?" Her petition came out on the edge of a sob, like she held it back.

Kimberly watched the stuck girl, still unsmiling, and it hit me what was beyond wrong about this situation.

For the first time, she had no audience. Everyone else was back in the common room, attacking Lacy and vying for her attention about her not-resurrected poet.

The only other person here to witness Kimberly's bullying was—

Me.

I pressed my hand over my mouth as Kimberly strode forward, determination on her face as she stood behind Sarah Jane and lined up her booted foot.

Which was where I turned and fled. Cowardice hit me in the gut, and the cold touches were my constant companion all the way back to my room, where I slammed the door and locked myself in.

"Nate, we have to get out," I whispered.

To an empty room.

Nate had left the house. I was alone.

*

225

Two mugs of hot chocolate later, one semi-sulky returned dead poet and a droopy desk cactus on a rainy afternoon, we were back to square one where I bribed my dead poet into the dappled light and didn't sleep.

That was a lie. I hadn't slept in way too long, not in any real capacity. Already running on empty, my patience waned. My cactus bounced off the wall every time I found my cupboard empty.

The sisters no longer came for impromptu Ouija board sessions. I hardly left my room except for my classes, but only those when I had to go. Otherwise I used notes that Kimberly emailed me, and tried not to commune with her at all.

Or have any contact.

Not that I noticed that much, but somewhere in the back of my mind it registered that they would. Which was why, on the day I sent the draft of my article to Erin, I set a timer on my phone and sat back to wait.

Four minutes and twenty-two seconds later—the time I suspected it took her to skim the entire thing—she responded.

> **Erin:** The fuck is this POS? Have you been kidnapped by aliens? No one—especially not you—sends in a draft like this.

> **Emma:** I can't cover this. It's a heartbreaker. Deal breaker. Every breaker.

> **Erin:** That's what you do. Break all the hearts. Make them cry.

Emma: Is it? Because the only heart that's breaking right now is mine.

Emma: I can't do this, Erin.

I could almost hear her taking a deep breath across campus in her office, because like me, she didn't sleep so well.

Erin: I get it. But isn't the line: write what you know? So, write what you know. You're living it.

Emma: It's bullshit. And it's going to get someone expelled.

Erin: . . .

Emma: I'm not a bully, Erin. This isn't what I signed up for.

Erin: Why did you want to become a journalist?

Emma: To understand people. Their choices, their actions. Share discoveries of amazing things with the world.

Erin: And sometimes, tragedies. Even Lois Lane reported on the bad stuff, girlie.

Emma: That was never my goal. I wanted to write something mind-blowing. Career-making. Not whistleblowing.

Erin: So make it both. You have a brain. Use its full capacity. Be smart. It hurts? Make it freaking well hurt to write. Make it beautiful. Make it sting. But for fuck's sake don't send me shit or I really will sack you. Love, your editor and your friend (promise).

Emma: Thank you. Taco-slap me next time I screw up, okay?

Erin: Wish granted. 🌮

Emma: Also, I may have a new writer for you. I'll send you some pieces.

Erin: Is he engaged to a cactus?

Emma: Does everyone know?

Erin: I run a paper. If I don't know, I don't deserve my job.

Emma: Your new title is spymaster.

I laughed at the cringe of that last message, but she was right. I shouldn't have sent the article in the condition that I did.

"She hated it, didn't she?" Nate appeared—reappeared—behind me on the bed. His arms slipped comfortably around my waist as I squawked, and shoved my fist into my mouth. He laughed into my ear. "That little habit still fascinates me."

"I'm so glad it does," I hissed back, ready to dig my elbow into his ribs, but the moment I moved, he wasn't there anymore. "Wait, where—"

"Here."

I focused on the grinning, too-sexy-for-his-own-good ghost boy who'd returned to his cravat habit the moment he didn't have to worry about being seen in public again.

"That's cute. Said no one you scared, ever," I grumped. "The hell have you been, dead boy? I—" I closed my mouth, unwilling to complete the rest of that sentence.

Amusement lit his face afresh. "Me, too," he said simply.

I snorted. "For a dead man, you are way too empathetic."

"It comes with the occupation."

"Territory. The term is territory," I explained to his quizzical expression that only Nathaniel could pull off the way he did, eyebrows knitted, lips pursed, spiral curls tumbling forward.

I'd brushed some back from his forehead before I could stop myself. "I'm still mad at you."

"For running away?"

"For not coming back after," I whispered. "It's not the same thing."

"No. It's not." He watched me carefully. "You didn't take me with you."

"When?" I frowned. "I can't take you to classes, Nate. We've talked about this."

He laughed again, but there was no sexy humor in the sound this time. "As much as I would like that, no. To the graveyard. I would have liked to have . . . seen."

I stalled. Tried to breathe. "What, that you're dead? Do you need proof?" My voice rose because I *knew* I should have taken him with me. I knew that. But . . . I didn't. "I can't decide if that's the most morose, melancholy idea that I've ever heard, or the most narcissistic."

He shrugged. "All the same, I wanted to go. You didn't ask."

Oh, cacti. "Nate. I'm sorry." I reached for him, but he drifted out of my reach. Shit, this was really bad. "Uh, I can make it up to you? Take you if you want?"

"I went alone."

Double cacti.

"And how did that go?"

"You sound like my old lecturers. That's how they used to talk." His voice took on a distance I hadn't heard from him before even as he faded somewhere between my reality and wherever he went when he wasn't with me.

"What was it like, then? I mean, I know it was different, but the classes . . ." I hurried to cover my inadequacies, then drifted off, still far from adequate in my line of thought. "Wow, I don't think I should ever interview a subject ever again."

"Is that what I am to you? A subject?" We had barely talked since the night of the picnic, procrastination and apparently avoidance now being our combined thing. Nor had he kissed me since he left me at the door of the sorority at almost dawn after walking me back from the hidden place between the hills as the false dawn broke over the sky.

"Or my keeper."

That's not harsh at all. The title ran far too true the moment he voiced it. I hated the way it fit, how the double syllable rolled from his lips, the dull sheen coating his stardust gaze.

"Is that what you call me?" I let him tilt my head back, and lost myself in his eyes as soon as I found them again. "That makes me sound more like a prison warden than a . . . friend." I coughed that last out.

"A friend," Nate said slowly.

"Yep." I popped the "p" for emphasis.

"My friend, the keeper." His gaze lifted to pin me in place.

Everything in my mouth dried. My tongue clung to my gums. "Are we arguing the same point here?" I managed.

Somehow, I suspected we weren't.

"Are we?" Nate never struck me as a game player, yet here we were, dancing about semantics.

I liberated my lucky pen off my desk and toyed with it, though he never backed off and stood far too close, his fingers trailing along my jaw. "I don't want to leave you stuck behind walls of stone and wood," I said softly, clicking the top of the pen over and over. "I just want to keep you safe."

Keeper, keeper, keeper, whispered the stones.

"Lock me away in a jar of secrets. I only ask you to leave me but a breath of air." His words brushed my lips in an intimate caress.

Too intimate. Too much like a promise. Or a confession.

I pulled my jaw from his grasp. "I'm sorry," I whispered desperately. I'll— I don't know. We can find a way to make this work. *Please.*"

I looked up, but Nathaniel had already faded. My room was bereft of poets, ghostly or otherwise. I dropped the extra few inches to my mattress with a cry that I covered with two hands belatedly, my eyes darting about my darkened room.

"Nathaniel?" I whispered, pushing onto my elbows, then all the way up, my heart stalled against my ribs.

He's gone, gone, gone. The stones sang a different song.

"I— I'm sorry—"

"As am I." He materialized right in front of me, cupping my face in both cool hands that warmed the moment his skin contacted mine. "I'm sorry, beautiful Emma. I wanted you to understand the confinement I felt, being locked away alone. Not to distress you." His gaze roamed over my face, the edges of his stunning eyes crinkling.

I shook my head and didn't care that my voice matched my wobbling legs. "Don't do that again, please," I gasped, only a little desperate. "Don't go." I sounded like a child. I didn't care about how that came out, either.

Oh, God. I'd fallen completely for my ghost boy. I couldn't send him back. My heart would break, and I'd already gone through that once. Do it again, and there would be nothing left of me to shatter a third time.

Or anyone left to collect the fragments of me that the wind would scatter across campus like so many specks of ghost-boy dust.

But I might have to send him back.

There was no *might* about it. I couldn't keep him here. It wasn't safe, and it wasn't fair. We were on limited time. I launched myself at Nathaniel, almost breaking the moment with a hysterical laugh at the owl-eyed comical expression on his face a fraction of a second before he caught me. Lean, strong arms wound around my body as he cradled me to his chest and lowered us both to the bed.

"I won't leave you, and I won't let you go. Not even when the sun rises and you can't see me for a while," he promised in my ear when his mouth broke away from mine for a breath.

Mine, not his.

Then he stole my next breath, and I didn't mind at all.

Keeper, he called me. I wondered if that term made it into his poetry, too. Perhaps that page was a two-way door where we revolved around each other. I kept him in this world, *my* world with me, a place where we both needed him. And Nathaniel? He kept my heart across an impossible bridge, a divide spanning two hundred years and two people who should never have met but for a fluke of whimsy and curiosity.

I loved this impossible man curled around me, protecting me even from myself when I was supposed to be protecting him. My limbs shifted as the room lightened. Hours seemed to pass in seconds, though I was sure we lay together, entangled in each other for hours, whispering the secrets of life and death and the universe even though only one of us had knowledge of such things.

Secrets he trusted me with.

Keeper took on a new meaning.

The glass bauble on my sorority necklace heated against my skin as Nathaniel gathered me close with the apparent intent of actually sleeping with me—or resting—as he did. I closed my eyes to sink into his embrace; my mind stopped.

Blanked.

Enough to register the cold draft that brushed along my arm and might not have been a draft after all.

A reminder of the coldness this house held, and all its sticky stones.

That Nathaniel should not be here at all, no matter how much I denied the fact of the man I refused to let go.

I ignored all the nudges at the edges of my blank mind and pressed closer to him, ghost-sandbox style. I ignored the cold flicker along my arm that didn't belong to him.

And I ignored the feeling that, before I handed in the damn article that started all this, my heart would end up in more pieces than any dead poet could paste back together.

Huh. Nate's fanciful notions were rubbing off on me. All that could come later. What I ignored wouldn't hurt him—at least, not tonight.

I just wanted to steal another night of peace with him before I faced reality.

I closed my eyes and pretended to sleep until the sun rose, just like he did.

I stole the sorority shared key and took Nathaniel on a library date. I couldn't think of a better way to make it up to him after our fight, and he had asked to go. From the look in his eyes it wasn't *quite* what he had in mind but . . . keepers got to be choosers.

And I chose the locked library as our secret midnight date.

Mind, it was just me on my own who could have been caught, because while I crept through halls, Nathaniel walked through walls.

I met him at the door to the forbidden room, borrowed key in hand. The cool metal warmed as I twirled it between my fingers, then slipped it into the lock. Predictably, Nathaniel met me on the other side of the door, inside what had been a locked room.

"I could have let you in." He watched me pocket the key curiously.

"I'm surprised she didn't put wards on the room."

Actually, I was relieved. It made moving Nathaniel about that much easier, especially if we were to embark on more dates.

"Your arcane knowledge is growing." He flicked his fingers across the shelves and peered at the books in the glass cases. "This one is a fake."

I stared at him, then followed the crooked finger that beckoned me closer, taking his hand and letting him tangle our fingers together. "How on earth do you know that?"

He grinned at me, boyish and charming and mischievous all at once. "Because I recognize the penmanship. The monk who wrote this—you see this little squiggle, just here?" He pointed at a mark on the inside of the page, near the spine on the illuminated hand-inscribed manuscript. "This is the mark of one Alfonso Ignatius Lambusta. Wonderful name for a wonderful man. When he was sober. We had a lot of drunk monks then," he informed me. "He could replicate almost anything, at an incredible speed, or so it seemed. Come here. Look. See these pages? They're glued together. The book appears to be complete, you see? But it's really three or four pages you can flip to make it appear the manuscript is the right one, while in reality it took him maybe a few weeks to knock out the necessary work and that's all he ever did. He was paid his fee and moved on to the next ah . . . job."

I giggled. "You make it sound like the monks and the mafia had a lot in common."

"They possibly weren't that far apart in some ways." Nathaniel traced his fingers along the back of my wrist. "This room is . . . quiet."

I blinked at him, nonplussed. "Isn't a library meant to be quiet?"

"Yes, but . . ." He frowned, leaving the glass, case and trailed his fingers along the shelves again, then bent his head to listen. "I'll— Wait a moment." He disappeared between the books lining the wall.

The spaces between.

A shiver rolled over me. Wasn't that the epitome of the place he said he didn't want to return to? Not physically, I was sure his reality looked different but . . . gah. Ghost-boy realms would twist my mind into knots the moment I tried to understand them.

"Nathaniel!" I hissed. "Damn ghost boy. Nate?" I muttered when he didn't immediately reappear.

Then he did, bursting sideways out of the bookshelf, his ringlets bobbing about his face, eyes wide as he actually *panted*.

"What's wrong?" I patted at him, as much as one could pat at a ghost poet for comfort.

He kneeled to the floor, head ducked as he collected himself. When he rose, he seemed paler than ever. "The stones, Emma. The stones here. In this room, behind the shelves. They're silent."

I stared at him. "What?"

I'd become so used to the sticky, chattering stones that it didn't occur to me that there might be a place in the house where they *didn't* talk.

"Why would they be like that here?"

He shrugged, reaching out to tug on my hair lightly. "I don't know. Can we leave? I'd like to make tea."

"Tea. After silent stones and trauma." I shrugged. "Sure. I mean, that's not how I saw tonight going, but . . ."

Nate had already glided through the door.

I sighed. "Tea it is."

*

Before the college woke to the new day after our in-house library date, Nathaniel laced his fingers through my hair and kissed me until I couldn't remember the hour, what I needed to do, or my own name.

But I could recall his. Everything about him.

How he tasted, how warm he felt, his body pressed to mine, molded to me like that's how we were always supposed to be.

Nathaniel Harker had pre-dawn seduction down to an art. This world hadn't been ready for him back when he was alive, and Inerius U was *not* ready for him now.

And we still hadn't talked about how he danced with me for what felt like hours behind the hills when no one else watched. Then he kissed me until the sun almost broke the sky beyond the clock tower, walked me back to the sorority and kissed me some more.

Then, before anyone else could see, he walked away, his hands deep in his pockets, and faded as the sun rose.

The perfect date with a dead poet.

And then the silent stones in the forbidden library accosted him, and he made tea. Or I did, and we took it back upstairs and . . . here we were.

My life couldn't get more screwy at this point.

His kisses were addictive, but I couldn't let myself be more distracted by him, even when he reached for me.

"We have to stop."

"Do we?" His too-sexy smile said no.

The campus clock chiming five a.m. absolutely agreed.

I rolled on my side and picked up my desk cactus, already the worse for recent wear, and prepared to bounce it off his forehead. *Distraction required.* Or I'd never stop kissing him.

"That's not a bad thing, Miss Emma."

"Did I say that aloud?"

"Perhaps, Miss Emma." He wound his fingers through my hair and drew me closer.

"Just Emma," I said absently.

"Just Emma, then," he agreed. A secret smile lilted his voice.

237

I grinned into my hands, turning the squishy cactus over and over, letting him play with my hair. "I'm still not very good at this, am I?"

"You're very good at spinster-reporter life," he said solemnly.

"Asshat." I did bounce the cactus. "How do I make it up to you for being so boring?"

"Another date."

"Too fast, Nate. You're supposed to make me wait."

His sly grin rippled ghostflesh all over my skin. "Who said it was with you?"

"Oh, you—" I lunged forward and—

Slammed into the end of my bed where he wasn't, anymore. Warm arms wrapped around me from behind, tugging me back against his chest.

"You promised me time discovering the library."

"You are a geek." I wiggled in his arms, but he tightened his hold and there was no way I was getting free. "We did the library already."

"We did *your* library," he corrected me, affecting a shudder. "Now it is time for me to take you to *my* library."

I raised my eyebrows. "There's a difference?"

"Yes." More ghost-boy agreement.

Way too fast, Nate.

"Fine." I pursed my lips. "I want coffee first if we are librarying."

"You make that sound . . . naughty."

I rolled my eyes. "Only you would say it that way."

"Of course. That's the goal."

"What, to get into my pants?" I shoved half-heartedly at his arms, but sank back into the renewed warmth of his embrace as he cradled me into the pillows at the end of my bed and the nest I'd made there.

"How do we both fit into your pants together?"

I tipped my head back in time to discover abject confusion marring his beautiful face.

"Oh my fucking God. Priceless," I snorted, slapping his arm with my free hand. "No, it's another term, for . . . you know, wanting to sleep with someone. Me." Because I sure as hell didn't want my ghost boy sleeping around with anyone else—on top of the covers, or otherwise.

"We do sleep together," he reminded me, tucking my hair behind my ear. "The few hours you take I am always here, watching you."

"Creeper."

"Keeper."

"I wear it well." I offered him a salacious wink. His gaze coasted along my body in return, heating me inside and out.

"Pants," he reminded me.

"Oh. Um, sex. Getting into someone's pants means the same as wanting to, uh, you know—" I waved a vague hand.

"So, that's what you think I want with you, then?" He arched over me, dropping his mouth to mine in a searing kiss that left me breathless.

Heat flushed from my tingling breasts in a line straight between my legs as I let out a soft gasp.

"Yeah, that," I said faintly, losing myself in the ethereal sense of him that created a hard, strong frame behind me, but swirled around me all at once.

Nathaniel stretched me taut against his body, my back pressed to his chest. Our legs tangled together as he kissed me, so different from the teasing, light kisses in the dark on campus. This was a man in my bed with one intent . . .

And for the first time, he didn't need fancy words of seduction to make his point. His hands did that for him, skating from where he tilted my chin back, and drew my arms over his head. One thumb brushed the swell beneath my breast as I arched for him, needing *more*.

Light fingers traced circles around the places I ached for him to touch the most, but he didn't. At least, not quite yet. The muted sound that strained from my throat left him laughing softly into my mouth and I turned to jelly in his arms.

Those same fingers traced soft circles ever winding inward over my breast, through the thin material of my tee until my nipples made hard points. When his fingertips finally grazed them, I released a whimper against his mouth that he swallowed, his other hand arching my neck as he tipped my head right back to expose my body to his touch. His kisses remained slow while he explored.

His hand continued south, finding the hem of my Lois tee. Those long, artist's fingers, well warmed, teased the strip of exposed skin at my belly above my jeans as I wriggled in his embrace. The moan that tore from me was both wanton and slightly horrifying, more so when he pressed down with that same, teasing hand on my stomach, and stopped.

I mean, the kisses went on but everything else ground to a cunning and frustrating halt.

"Nathaniel Harker. You do not get to ghost-sleep in my bed if you stop right there," I muttered, wiggling my hips against the hardness of the very much *not* ghostly form of the man behind me.

His legs still tangled with mine, and his mouth touched the corners of my lips in the sort of intimate kisses that long-time lovers shared.

I swallowed a shattered breath and it exploded somewhere low in my chest instead.

"Don't I?" he murmured in my ear, playing with the top button of my jeans. "Would you miss this?" He kissed me again, still rubbing his thumb across the flesh below my belly button, and disappeared under my waistband.

My breaths stopped altogether as his fingers skated lower, dipping beneath my panties. Smooth fingers met tender skin. Without another word he slipped those same fingers between my legs and brushed them lightly over my clit.

"Nate," I gasped into his mouth, trying to press my thighs together—

But I couldn't.

He held my legs apart with his. While I thought we were tangled together, he'd been orchestrating something completely different. Nate's ankles hooked around mine, keeping my feet just far enough apart that I couldn't find the pressure I wanted.

"Let me touch you," Nathaniel murmured, stroking my aching flesh gently, and nowhere near as much as I needed. "Let me give you pleasure, Emma. I've wanted to touch you like this for so long."

I shuddered in his arms, mine wrapped around his neck, and nodded as his mouth grazed mine in the lightest kisses while his fingers toyed with my clit. The entire situation left me shivering in his hold. Though I strained to rub my legs together, turn around and press our bodies against one another, seeking more friction, the way he held me, exposed and at his mercy, turned me on more than anything else. It only took a few more strokes with his gentle fingers and I flooded my panties as I came for him. Heat suffused my cheeks as his name tore from my lips, but he swallowed that too.

Long, warm arms wrapped around me, crushing me against him as his kisses grew deeper. Nathaniel's hand slipped back to my stomach as he turned me around, cradling me to him.

"That is what I've wanted to do with you for so long, Miss Emma," he whispered, breaking his kiss to stare into my eyes as the sun crested the horizon, glazing my room in a rainbow of citrine and rose that I couldn't fully appreciate.

Instead I fell into a sunrise filled with violet spirals and golden flecks as the clock tower chimed the next hour and the one after that.

Not that I kept count.

My Fake Dead Poet Boyfriend

Nate sipped his coffee like a regular dead man and pretended to be a live one sitting in a plastic chair at Proserpine's Venom. Hell, he even waved at the odd student he recognized from the group chat he shared with a stack of other poet wannabes—who were blessedly Kimberly-free.

I'd checked in the name of ghostly safety.

I knew Nate wanted a little privacy, but he also needed to exist—in some form or other, freely—to be able to achieve that. With her . . .

He'd be no more than a bottle wisp in a mason jar trotted on out for special séances and when Kimberly wanted assistance with her homework.

Or more.

I suspected Kimberly's obsession wouldn't halt at a pithy thing like physical boundaries. She didn't cut the line at holding a dead man hostage, stealing his voice to replace hers or grandstanding with her rabid sisters. A little ghostly groping wasn't too far from the mark.

My cheeks heated as I recalled my own groping session from last night that ended with me snoring unsexily in Nathaniel's arms as exhaustion took over. Not just that; in his arms, I experienced that sort of safety net I craved with Thomas but never had.

Nate, on the other hand, brought with him a swath of mannerisms that died out years ago. Some might seem outdated, but his attentiveness warmed me. I only hoped I gave back to him as much as he provided for me.

Watching his face literally glow in the coffee shop at a quarter to ten in the evening, when I thought there would be fewer people—my decision-making skills on a Wednesday night sucked a sonnet's absent fifteenth line—made my literary week.

I stirred more sugar into my bitter, burnt beans than I needed, but hey, the coffee shop was called *Venom* for a reason.

"Enjoying yourself?" I murmured.

"You have no idea, Miss Emma." Nathaniel stared straight at me. His lopsided grin looked far less goofy and more in the realm of unintentional-sexy-geek, a spark of something undeniable flickering there. Awareness, intelligence, or a decent dollop of both. "Or perhaps you do?"

I shrugged, unable to contain the joy that reflected right back at him. "Perhaps. Have you given thought to the column concept yet?"

Erin said yes. Actually, she shouted it down the phone line on the provision that I never, *ever* send her a dirty draft like I had the previous week out of pure desperation. I agreed, she agreed, and now all I had to do was get the dead ghost boy across from me to agree and we were in business.

Nathaniel, however, hadn't agreed yet.

"The paper you write for is . . . campus wide."

"Yes." I nodded, trying to get bobble-head syndrome going for a party of one. "Which means that lots of people—read everyone—would at the very least glance at your work. If you write decently, which we both know you can, then nearly everyone will. That's how it works," I explained. "When I first started out, my first six months on staff, I was a nobody. Erin knew I could write, and she gave me some assignments. Nothing brilliant. What I didn't understand was that she was waiting for *me*. I had to step up, take one of those bland assignments that was batshit boring, and turn it into something amazing. Beautiful. It wasn't until I had a sports piece—and I freaking hate covering sports—that I got my literal break. Or my interview subject did. The assignment was to cover the stats of the current season via the number-two position player for the consistent wooden-spoon team of the league. What I got was an injured man who talked for hours about his passion for a sport I hated because I dated one of the more arrogant players who also sucked."

"Thomas." Nathaniel straightened in his seat, his expression wary.

"You got it. But Brandon didn't have any of the hang-ups his bestie did. The rest of the team absconded while he was cast and hospital-bound, and man, did that boy have some stories to tell. I couldn't print most of them but we talked for *hours*." I grinned. "But I got more information than I ever needed. What could have been a cut-and-dried piece of sports stats turned into a three-week series that made my freshman career and earned me a gold star."

"Fascinating." Nathaniel leaned forward. "You also have a glow when you talk about your passion."

I blushed, sipping the dregs of my burnt beans. "I think that's a good thing."

"It is," he reassured me. "Where do you keep it?"

"Keep what?"

"The gold star."

I spluttered coffee. "Dead poets unite, Nathaniel. You will be the death of me."

His smile faded. "I do hope not, my beautiful reporter." Cold/warm fingers laced through mine.

I clung to his hand, squeezing our knuckles together too tight. "All right. I think it's time for that tour of the library. What do you say?"

"I say that you are—"

"Stop it." I planted an elbow in his ribs. "No more flirting, Nate. Tonight was meant to be your night out."

"And I want to spend it with you."

"Can't account for taste." I shook my hair back, leading him along the coach-lantern-lit path toward the library. Midweek we had an hour or so before it closed, more than enough time for him to haunt the stacks. "What did you want to see?" He cast me an amused glance. "Oh, wait—everything."

Nate nodded, sliding an arm around my waist as I led him up the backstairs to avoid the front broad entrance to Inerius's oversized library where we could be too easily seen. I'd been ecstatic when I first saw the building in my freshman year, until I realized upon closer inspection that half the large rooms were empty, and the study spaces were just that . . . desks with empty bookshelves.

When I turned left on the small mezzanine area once we crept into the back entrance I often used, thanks to the library staff knowing my needy reporter habits—and that I didn't have a printer of my own—I tripped over my own feet. Nathaniel turned right instead and nearly walked me through a wall.

Because he *had* walked through the wall.

"You know, you can do that, but I can't," I said crossly, staring at the white slab of painted brickwork, waiting for him to reappear. "Do these ones talk?" I rapped my knuckles against the stonework.

"No. Did I mention that?" He affected the same vague outlook he usually pasted across his pretty-boy dead face whenever he wanted to avoid my questioning. A habit that truly shit me up the proverbial wall, even if it wasn't the one right in front of me. "Why don't you use the door?"

"What door?" I folded my arms. "I go this way, ghost boy," I reminded him, keeping my voice low.

"This door."

He rapped on the wall in a hollow place near the top corner of a join slightly above my head. The wall creaked, and swiveled—the slightest amount—in place.

My mouth fell open. "How did you—"

Nathaniel watched me with a mixture of impatience and bemusement. "I used to live here a long, long time ago, Miss Emma. Not all things have changed."

"Apparently not." Mimicking his owl eyes, I followed him through the wall and let it close behind us.

Beyond the wall—I swore that needed to be on a shirt— the bricks weren't the painted, modern facade that covered the rest of the empty, overpopulated Inerius U library space. The faintest flicker of blue preceded us. I frowned, wondering if this place was haunted with wisps, like the graveyard, but I didn't see the light again as I followed my ghost boy. No, this hallway came from something that time forgot about. Something like . . . Nathaniel.

He hummed a tune I didn't know, the notes lilting softly back at me as he trailed his fingers along the darkened brick. No lichen or moss—the horrors—grew on the wall like I kinda expected. There was nothing dank or musty about the hallway that looked like it hadn't been used since the last time Nathaniel walked these halls, but the dim lighting suggested that they did get used on some very rare occasion, if not much.

If ever.

Forgotten, like so many other parts of Inerius U's history.

He followed the bricked corridor's soft glow as it led us downward a few steps at a time, plateauing through shadowed sections, and then turned a corner that opened into a—

"It's a book nook." Nathaniel turned on his heel. A proud-as-freaking-punch smile graced his face as he fluffed out his dragonfly-embroidered jacket.

I stopped and would have caught one of the insects, had it lifted off the garment and swanned about the room to land on my tongue.

The room wasn't tall, exactly, or huge. Only big enough for maybe thirty people if they stood clustered together within its cramped walls. But the books—those were stacked tight along the walls on dark, glazed shelves that reached to the short ceiling.

"It's like an underlibrary," I whispered.

Nathaniel scooped an arm around my waist. "It gets better." His lips brushed my ear for a moment, then he released me, leaving me standing alone in the entrance to the strange room.

His hand caught mine, laced our fingers together and towed me toward the far corner in a diagonal line from where we entered. The heel of his hand thumped on a book-shelf at the same height that he hit the painted wall, and the shelf moved.

He towed me through that shelf into a short passage that had a star network running off it, each dimly lit. I strained my eyes, and started wandering, my mind running with article options.

Nathaniel's grip tightened. "Not tonight, Lois Lane." His eyes laughed at me when I tugged futilely at his hand. "Tonight is a library date. Come back and explore another time."

There will be another time?

"That's so mean." I wiggled my nose.

"Later," he sing-songed in my ear, and pressed a kiss

to my lips. I leaned into him but he was gone in another instant.

I tripped after him, a giggle tearing from my lips. "I really wanna be mad at you."

"Definitely later for that." Another room, almost identical to the first book nook followed on, but this one had a layer of dust on a giant table that clearly hadn't seen use in some time.

But this one, unlike the last, was occupied.

The same pale glow the shade of neon lapis lazuli drifted around the shelves. No—not around, *between* the shelves. Which shouldn't be possible. I leaned deeper into the room, peered at the glow that shifted just like the wisps, but didn't have quite the same movement.

Where they bobbed, this shadow slinked—I was well past the realm of skeptical with my ghost boy in a forgotten underlibrary at this point. My hand brushed the warm air an inch from the shelves that hadn't been disturbed in who knew how long in this space as the glow grew brighter and brighter.

A ripple, like water, only it didn't lengthen the shadow's form—and it gave a little wiggle, like a lure.

Or a tail.

Then it hit me—I was looking at the wrong end.

A smile crooked my lips as I reversed my path and headed for the shadow's head, or where I thought it would be, moving across the row of shelves with it, tracking its strange path as it leaped and flowed, bobbing along. My hands patted the air, trying to make sense. One paw came into view, then another. An eye, then an ear, and finally, whiskers—

"Minnie!" Nathaniel cried over my shoulder, scooping the ghost cat into his arms and cuddling the glowing beastie like it was his favorite thing in all the world. "Oh, Minnie. I have missed you, you wee little—" He kissed and snuggled at the phantom cat while I coughed my heart back into my chest.

"Holy hairballs, poet boy," I managed when my heart slowed enough to allow me to breathe. "Give a girl some warning before you burst right through her like that."

"Did I slime you?" He glanced over his shoulder, still petting Minnie.

I shook my head. "No, but it was a close thing." I hadn't been but I resented having the cat hair scared out of me while I was doing some ghostly perving. "Was she around when you were, uh—" I still wasn't clear on conversational etiquette, so I shut my mouth.

"When we were alive?" Nathaniel filled the gaps for me. "Yes. She was the library cat. We spent many hours together. She liked to be fed by hand and was a very fat kitty, weren't you. *Pss pss pss*," He made kitty noises at her.

I snorted. "Sickly sweet."

"She is beautiful. Aren't you, Minnie? Come visit me in my room sometime, pussy."

I bit back a comment about cats in the sorority house. "That would be my room," I said, as he placed the ghost cat on the ground.

She sashayed between his legs in a neon figure eight and disappeared right through the shelves without sliming them.

I pointed at him. "Minnie needs to teach you how to do that."

"Mmm." Nathaniel hummed thoughtfully as he circum-navigated the table that stood in the middle of the room with a degree of reverence, ready to resume his interrupted underlibrary tour now that Minnie had disappeared. "Critical thinking." He shot me a sideways glance. "That's what we studied in this room. What we were meant to study. I usually slept through this class and a friend of mine took notes that I copied out later."

"Were you such a party animal?" I reached out to swipe my hand through the thick layer of dust, but Nathaniel caught my wrist in a firm grip that drew a different sort of gasp from my lips.

"Leave it."

The command in his voice was undeniable. I nodded and he released me, gesturing to the next corner of the room. "Three more to go."

I followed him through the network of strange, hidden rooms, each a place where he had classes, got drunk with friends or wrote poetry in books and hid them amongst the shelves in the hope that one day, someone would discover him even years after his death. His friends, too.

I stared at the old volume he tugged free, its leather-bound edition faded but soft, pages slightly crackled. The words had faded too, but I still knew his hand as I read each line he had added in along with his friends.

"Your penmanship is beautiful," I murmured, tracing the backs of his fingers as he quoted the words, unwilling to touch the page lest I disturb the fragile words, and they frittered away, never to be seen again.

See? Fanciful. Like him.

Nathaniel sighed, closed the book with care and tucked it back into its hiding space. "Maybe one day, when these words are gone, someone will come down here and curate these works. It's like the place has been forgotten."

I reached across to flick a light switch and hoped that I didn't turn the lights off upstairs as well. The plastic knob nearly broke in my hand as I worked it. "At least, someone in the last century knew. Very early in. I don't know how long back, though." It had definitely been a while, looking at the fixtures.

The place was probably high on the fire-hazard list, filled with dusty carpets, old books and wiring the local contingent of rats likely chewed on. I shivered at the thought.

"Turn off the lights." The command was back in Nathaniel's voice.

"Hell, no. It was pitch in here a second ago." Even the residual glow from my phone seemed to do nothing for this forgotten space.

"Please, Emma," his voice softened.

I gave in. "Don't you leave me alone," I cautioned. "I'll never find my way out."

"Keep turning left. That's how you get out. It's one big circle beneath the top level. Then the hallway will take you back to the stairs where we entered."

"Oh—oh." The lights died and I stood alone in the darkness. "Uh, Nathaniel?"

A warm touch coasted across the back of my neck. "I'm here."

"Thanks." I started, staring into the darkness that revealed nothing at all. Not even the tiniest pinprick of light. The void I stood in was all-encompassing. I struggled to breathe. For the first time I wondered that I wasn't claustrophobic. "I— I might need those back on," I tried.

Then I stopped talking as his hand cupped my jaw from behind, tilting my head back. He kissed me the same way he had that left me so breathless in my room the night before. Only here, I couldn't do anything but feel him pressed against me, and then—

Nathaniel was gone.

I let out a cry that soft, cool tendrils muted. His phantom touch that I couldn't see, only experience, even when he wasn't really *there* left me shivering in a different way from before. I backed into the dusty table in the room, turned around and found myself face to face with him. His cool lips touched my cheeks a second before his hands tangled in my hair and his mouth crushed mine in the sort of connection I'd always craved.

The sort that drew a moan from my throat that I tried to snuff out, and failed.

That was okay. He swallowed it anyway.

I didn't realize he moved us until my back butted against the bookshelf where I had entered this room, I thought. In the fathomless darkness, it was all too easy to get turned around. His hands pressed to my hips as he broke the kiss.

"Stay here, Emma. Don't move for me. Will you do that?"

I reached for him, but he'd already disappeared. "All right," I promised the air, knowing he could hear me.

Light fingers—warm, not cold—grazed the tops of my thighs at the hem of my short denim skirt. I clapped my hand over my mouth even though there wasn't anyone around to hear me as Nate's hands snaked upward beneath the worn, soft denim. His thumbs traced patterns on my inner thighs, coaxing my legs apart.

I did as he commanded in silence, balancing on the toes of my cowgirl boots, letting the shelves behind me take my weight, and prayed I wouldn't end up with a hundred old volumes toppling down on both of us.

Nathaniel might have the knack of dissolving into ghost nothingness, but I hadn't mastered his trick yet. Nor did I want to, and find that I was front-page worthy, dead in a secret library cache beneath a pile of ancient tomes.

Not how I wanted to go out, with my skirt up around my waist and my panties—

"Oh," I managed, around the hands pressed over my mouth.

Nathaniel's fingers weren't just clever with a quill, and his mouth didn't just quote pretty words.

Nate's hot mouth found my wet flesh, his lips and tongue exploring my slick, needy pussy as I tried not to scream prematurely into my hands cupped over my mouth. A finger traced circles around my entrance, teasing my hole, then pushed inward. My knees buckled, but Nate's other hand pressed to my stomach, holding me up.

Broad shoulders supported my thighs, spreading me open as his mouth never stopped teasing and tasting me, drinking me in. My entire body clenched as I came for him seconds after he started.

"You are easy to pleasure, Emma," he murmured, lapping at the mess I made for him. "Come for me again?"

I moaned, scraping my nails along the bookshelves. "Please," I whispered, my mind stretching for anything else, but that's all I had to say. To beg him.

"Mmm." Nathaniel bent to his task, teasing my slit with his tongue. His lips wrapped around my clit as he sucked and teased the tiny nub until I whimpered, then he pushed two fingers inside me.

My legs trembled as I leaned back, closing my eyes in the darkness, and let him play and explore. He held me gently in place as I writhed between the shelves and his clever fingers until I squeezed my thighs tight at his shoulders. That tongue of his made its own patterns on my swollen flesh until I cried out, not even sure if I made real sounds or uttered meaningless words.

Everything built and built as he played my body with the same ease with which he filled parchment with his own brand of poetry, until I bent in half over him, my fingers tangled in his hair. His fingers slammed into me, over and over until I clenched down hard, milking his hand as I came a second time. His name dripped off my lips like a heartbeat I couldn't do without. A promise.

"Nathaniel."

I shuddered as he slid up my body, gathered me against him, and kissed me hard.

I tasted myself on his lips as he offered the sweetest kisses that soothed me through the aftershocks still fluttering through my body. The dichotomy pinned me against him, a frozen butterfly in its death throes. Then we were falling, and I clung to him in the darkness, him my only anchor to anything until we collapsed on the floor in a tangle of limbs, lips and tongues still entwined.

And in the darkness, he whispered a promise that no one else could ever break, no matter what evil came for him or stole him away.

"I love you, Emma Reeves. In this lifetime and the next, or the one beyond, nothing can take that away from me. Here, right now, I have you."

I opened my mouth to say the same words back, my truncated, unromantic version, but his mouth covered mine in a slow, deep kiss, and I knew he didn't need to hear me say anything at all.

Then he held me in the darkness until my breathing slowed, and I could feel the soft smile in the way he touched my face, memorizing the lines he traced.

*

We had a dawn habit to break.

My metaphors were worse than ever after hours of lack of sleep, snuggled in our new hideaway beneath the library. Somehow that space seemed more liberating and safer than anywhere else on campus. So much more *Nathaniel-coded*.

What was not safe, however, was the walk back to the sorority house when the early morning sparrow-fart joggers were already out on their first lap of the morning.

Unlike the night when Nathaniel and I shared our moonlit

picnic, this morning meant we were seen. And greeted. And stopped to talk.

Which was fine when they were his friends. Not as good when they were mine.

Or sisters.

"I didn't know you had a boyfriend," Lacy cooed as she pranced closer to us in colors a unicorn might have vomited up after an excess of cocktails the night before. For a before-sunrise event, she wore neon everything, complete with a lurid green G-string that disappeared between her butt cheeks over the top of her tights in a fashion choice that even the Eighties promised to forget.

I swore poor Nate's eyeballs may have bugged out of his head. We'd have a discussion about butt floss later. Right now, I had to save this fiasco.

"Yes, I do—Kimberly already knows," I started, trying to get off on the right foot and using the wrong one.

"She does?" Lacy's eyes rounded like dual cue balls on the wrong side of her face. If she and Nate stood side by side, they could have a matching set. "Bitch never shared. I'm Lacy."

Nate watched her extended hand and squeezed the tip of one finger after a moment's hesitation. "Very pretty," he said politely. His hands quickly returned to my waist, squeezing gently.

I pressed my lips into a firm line. "Okay, we're shattered. Going to head back up."

Dammit. That came out wrong.

Lacy's mouth made an "o". "You know the rules—"

"—No boys in the dorm," I finished the chorus with her.

She grinned and waved, her phone already in her hand.

I dropped my head into mine. "We are screwed," I muttered, my tired voice muffled.

"No, Emma." Nathaniel turned me around in his arms.

256

"But sometime, when you do let me into those pants, you will be."

I groaned. "Oh, my God. That was terrible. Stick to poetry, okay? It's much prettier. Speaking of—don't flirt with my sisters."

He smiled and dropped a kiss at the corner of my mouth. "I promise not to flirt with anyone but you."

"Better not, ghost boy." But I smiled as we checked around and crept inside the back of Phi Omega House through the poison garden entrance, managing to avoid everyone else. I closed the door behind us. "Okay, I didn't lie. The nights are starting to hurt me. I'm exhausted. But I didn't want to give up time with you."

"Nor I with you."

"Mmm." I snuggled into his chest. "Keep talking like that and I'll stay up forever."

"I wish that you could."

My heart panged, and I cleared my throat. "Want coffee? I'll go make a double batch. Or chocolate. I could do with the sugar hit."

"Perhaps feed yourself at some point, too. Don't forget to live, Emma," he warned me gently. A frown crossed his face as I disentangled myself and he pulled me back. "Wait."

"Do you want lavender? Mint?" I guessed. "Or are you on a new flavor kick?"

"No, something more important than that." Again with the hesitation. Nathaniel reached into the pocket of his jeans that he rarely swapped out now, and pulled out something small, placing the warmed metal piece into my hand. "I want you to have this," he said quietly.

I turned the tiny pin over in my palm. Three letters linked together in white and green enamel.

"What's DCS?" I asked, rubbing the pad of my thumb over the cutouts in the metal.

"Delta Chi Sigma. My old fraternity." Nate closed my fingers around the pin and pressed my hand to my chest. "It's yours."

More than my hand over my heart, where he held it, it hit me what he'd done. The back of my heel scraped against the necklace Thomas had given me that I'd kicked under my bed weeks ago when he tried to invade my room, never wanting to see it again.

My mind screamed *no* but . . . something in Nathaniel's eyes quietened me. "Now, Nathaniel? This isn't something you should give to me. This is something you'd . . ."

"Give to the girl I love. Who, in my time, I intended to marry."

Oh. My. Poetic. God.

No little "g" about it. I literally swooned, and the dead boy of my dreams caught me.

"I won't ask, because I can't in your world. I know that much about what we are." Nathaniel's eyes radiated with their strange gold and violet intensity. Not full of sadness, like I might have expected, but desire—to make every minute we shared count, perhaps. "I need you to know how I feel. What you mean to me, Miss Emma."

I swallowed hard, unable to form words for once, and let him kiss me without fighting him on it or snarking back. The gift he'd presented me with was clutched in my hand as another secret held tight between us.

Can We Ever End up Together?

Thomas: You need a better boyfriend than that weirdo.

Emma: Are you drunk? Why are you date-stalking me?

Thomas: Everyone knows who you're dating. It's embarrassing to me.

Emma: I haven't been your problem for a long time, Thomas. Go to sleep.

Thomas: I only slept well when you were here.

Emma: That was two years ago. Get laid with someone else.

Thomas: I only want you. Can we please try again?

Emma: Go to sleep, Thomas. You won't remember this in the morning.

Emma: Don't die or anything stupid.

Emma: Thomas?

My chest ached on nothingness as I stared down at my phone and waited, but Thomas seemed to have taken that second-to-last instruction to heart. Some long-archived part of me wanted to rush across campus to his frat and check that he hadn't passed out in a pool of his own vomit after yet another failed polo game.

After all, he was still human, even if it earned him the Asshat Ex of the Year award with the highest honors. Still . . . maybe I should check on him. My hand hovered over my phone. I squished my eyes shut. *No.* I knew better. *Toxic, toxic.* He might be drunk, my ex, but I left him for a reason. Reasons that Nate outlined for me on many occasions. At the end of the night I was human, he was my ex, and I cared, dammit.

Once.

My room remained conspicuously empty of any dead poet, the one I craved for my own strangely adjusted sleeping habits. Nathaniel had taken to wandering the campus in his less noticeable form, but I still freaked out at the thought of anyone seeing him.

My keeper.

The title still rankled. It had a Kimberly-esque tinge to it that I hated, even if he said it in a different way. I took the opportunity of an empty dorm room—ha, I didn't even remember what one felt like—to sit in front of my blank screen after sunset. When the glariness got to me, I pulled up the original draft I'd made that night.

The night when I accidentally summoned Nathaniel Harker from the depths of obscurity. Even now that seemed an age ago. Half a page of writing decorated the screen. It was the only version I had saved rather than deleting everything in sight the moment I word-vomited onto the page. Surprisingly, I didn't hate it.

Two read-throughs later, and I was in the zone. My fingers worked quickly without Nate's regular distractions and lines of excess poetry flung at me from random corners of the room.

And for once, the article flowed.

My eyes ached by the time I pressed save—a bad, old habit born of using cloud-based programs all the way through high school that saved live versions for me—and closed my laptop. I could proof it in the morning. Right now, if I wanted to wait until Nate returned sometime this evening, I needed fuel. Not the pod sort the sorority kitchen provided, either. I checked my phone.

If I hightailed it across campus now, I could make it to Proserpine's. My mind made up, I grabbed my trainers, threw on a hoodie and left a hastily scribbled note for Nate on my desk.

> Gone for coffee. Wait for me here? I'll be back soon.

After sitting for so long on a fast-numbing butt—both cheeks—getting up and walking through campus at what had to be close to a run felt good. Students still milled around after their last class of the day, and the bar on the other side of the hillocks where Nate and I had our picnic date was pumping. I shied away from that side of campus, taking the less brightly lit path toward the coffee shop. This side of the college was far more populated during the day.

At night, it still had some die-hard caffeine addicts needing fuel for pulling prospective all-nighters, especially with assignments due and exams encroaching for the end of semester. Maybe I should be joining them on more than one occasion to meet my own extended deadlines. Plus, there were long-term connotations to consider with my current dead poet situation . . . but deadlines were easier to deal with. Pun. *Ha*.

Studying the haggard faces surrounding me, I knew I had enough of my own to worry about, but Nate and I had hit that happy honeymoon period where nothing seemed to make a dent in the metaphysical armor that surrounded us.

That our peace offered a tentative version of happiness should have bothered me, but didn't. I ordered my coffee and stood at the side of the empty shop alone, turning my phone over in my hand. It buzzed twice, and I flipped it back.

Nathaniel: Hast thou rejected me, fair maiden?

Emma: *snort* I went to get coffee. Left you a note. Lovelorn?

Nathaniel: Probably. Are you coming back soon?

Emma: Feeling needy? I'll get you a cookie.

But even as I teased him, I grinned, knowing that he hated me being away as much as I had earlier when I found him absent. Though I'd thrown myself into my work as a distraction and gotten words, good words at that, down, I had actually missed Nate's constant quotes, his creative campus discoveries of the day, and attempts at seducing me.

A warmth that had nothing to do with the heating in the underpopulated campus café at this hour started low in my belly. I grinned down at my phone as my name was called too loud for the unoccupied space. I pocketed my phone, grabbed our coffees, and headed back toward the long walk through the poison garden.

I'd taken all of two steps when my name echoed along the path at me. Wincing, I turned on my heel and managed not to wear my coffees.

Vivian stood a few paces away, staring at me, no smile in sight. "When do I get to meet him?" She didn't come any closer. "Or have the sorority claimed dibs on that, too?"

My internal wince became a true outer one. "No one has dibs on anything. Well. Except maybe me on him." That sounded terrible. "Sorry, I've been writing. Words flow from fingers, not the mouth tonight."

Her lips finally twitched. "Riiight. Tell your editor that when she sends you copious notes and you ask her why."

Cue deeper wince. "This would be the second attempt."

Viv paused in her berating of me that nearly overrode my half of the weird conversation. "Did you just tell me she rejected something you sent her? Has that actually ever happened before?"

"No?" I grimaced this time. *Gotta vary the expressions up.* "These are gonna get cold. I should . . ."

"Go. Yeah, I know." Vivian's voice ran as flat as before.

I thought I would have preferred if she grumbled or bitched or was even resigned to the situation. But her no response/no comment attitude? This sucked worse than anything else.

"Sorry. I sneaked him into my room. He's plenty patient but he's a bit needy and, you know, he can—"

Walk through walls. Write poetry that went out of style two hundred years ago like it's his birthright. Kiss like a god, and has the tongue of one.

And of course, the coup de grace: *Oh, I forgot to tell you. He's dead.*

I studied the plastic tops of my takeaway coffees for too long a moment in the hopes I'd get away with this.

Viv fake-coughed into her hand. "Are you okay?"

This was my chance. I could fess up everything on this deserted stretch of campus ground, away from Nate, from Kimberly and the sorority, the house with its strange, sticky stones that probably listened as well as they chattered, and tell my best friend everything.

I held my breath and for a moment, I thought she did too. Then I forced a smile.

"Yeah, 'course. I'll see you after class tomorrow sometime, okay?" I turned away, heading for the sorority house's back entrance.

"Tomorrow. On the weekend." Viv's blunt tone stopped me mid retreat.

"Oh. Yeah." I grinned guiltily over my shoulder. "After that, then."

She said nothing else as I walked into the garden, and that hurt more than anything. On my side as well as hers. I hated the lies, and I hated the omissions. But telling anyone about Nate's true nature—apart from the necessary—would hurt him more, and that's what mattered most.

I could lie to myself all day. The last few weeks had become a study in perfecting that.

An overgrown rhododendron brushed the backs of my

knuckles as the back door to the house came into sight. I sighed my relief. The fast walk across campus grew long in the last minutes as I quickened my pace and wished I'd double-stacked the takeout cups so my fingertips didn't burn quite so much. I almost made it past the aggressive plant when a shadow stepped across my path.

"Na—Fuck!" I yelped, and bit my lip hard enough to taste the tang of body fluids that were supposed to stay on the inside. I stared at the too-tall shadow as I danced backward and managed not to sprawl on my ass at close to midnight. *Winning.* "Wait. Thomas?"

"I told you I wanted you back." He lumbered forward, one arm stretched out, zombie style.

Why am I suddenly attracting dead-like men?

Not that I wanted more dead men. Just one.

I didn't know what hit me first—his slurred words or the ninety-percent proof breath. If I had a lighter, the poison garden would be ash after he breathed all over it.

"I thought you passed out," I said as my heart slowed. "Kinda hoped you slept okay."

My mistake, offering sympathy to a narcissist.

"I'd sleep better with you in my bed. I miss you, Em," he murmured, reaching for me.

I danced around him, prepared to sacrifice the stupid coffees that had been the bane of my existence tonight. Why did I even leave my room? If I had stayed, I could have been cuddling with Nate by now, and teaching him about something else. I looked longingly at the door, and attempted to step around Thomas.

He sidestepped right into my path.

I sighed. "Thomas, this is silly. We're years along the breakup path. I don't think of you, and you don't think of me. Remember?"

He shook his head. "I think of you a lot."

"Well, that makes you a solid creeper. Move, please," I added sharply.

His eyes sharpened, and I held my breath, lest his wash over me again. I didn't need a whiskey-breath bath, and even though I didn't think Nate could scent much, I didn't want to have to shower, although at this rate I might anyway.

Thomas leaned forward and brushed his fingers inside my hoodie, pushing the unzipped material aside. "Who gave you this?' he said sharply, sounding sober and more like himself.

I raised my hand to cover the frat pin Nate gave me. I'd put it on my shirt every day since, knowing what it meant to him while trying to deny what it meant to me.

In my time, I'd give it to the girl I intended to marry.

So I rearranged some of his words, but that had been the gist of our conversation. I knew women didn't attend universities back when he was alive, and I wasn't sure on their customs, but regardless of whether or not Nathaniel Harker held to convention, his words held true. And with no one around to tell him otherwise, he could do as he damn well pleased.

Rather like Thomas, who turned a variety of emerald to lime shades as I watched.

"The belladonna is over there. It could do with some fertilizing," I added helpfully as he clapped a hand over his mouth.

The moment he turned away, I ran for it. My feet hit the black slate steps to the sorority house and I slipped between the heavy doors at the back, pressing my back to them, and managed to lock them before the sound of him retching on the botanicals reached me.

I hoped he wouldn't pass out in the garden or eat anything that would seriously hurt him but right now I was glad to get my behind away from him.

For the first time in what felt like an hour, no one challenged me as I climbed the stairs to my bedroom, kicked open the door and collapsed on my bed, pushing my coffees into Nathaniel's waiting hands.

I shed my hoodie and my trainers, and curled into an Emma-shaped ball in the middle of the bed, my arms wrapped around my knees. "I'm never leaving the room ever again," I rasped as the shakes set in. All I could inhale was Thomas's fetid breath and taste the obsessive wrongness of him.

Nate took less than a heartbeat to respond, placing the coffee cups onto the floor for the pink bear rug to mind. He slid onto the bed beside me. A heartbeat later his arms wrapped about me too, engulfing me in the dusty scent of leather-bound books and midnight secret rendezvous.

"My favorite thing," I murmured.

He laughed softly. "I'll take that as a compliment. Who scared you?" It came out so casually that I almost—almost—told him.

Instead, I shook my head and burrowed deeper. "No one important. Can we watch something, please? I need to get out of my head."

His hands glided over my body. "I can provide you with a distraction."

My elbow jabbed his ribs in a gentle effort of its own. "A different sort of distraction. Please? You pick."

Nathaniel huffed in my ear. "Later?" He leaned in and inhaled me, then pulled away. "Why don't you shower," he muttered, his voice tight. "Then we can watch something."

I bit my lip. The stench of Thomas's whiskey-soaked breath stuck to me as much as I feared, apparently. "I can do that," I conceded, grabbing my vanity kit and towel. "Please don't go anywhere. I really—" I bit my lip, a breath shy of doing some serious begging.

I don't want to be alone tonight.

Nate brushed hair back from my face. "I'll be here when you get back, my Emma."

My breath caught in my throat at the tenderness reflected in his eyes. *Emma.* His Emma. Somehow, all his flirtations set aside, the simpleness of that statement hit me right at heart level.

"Thank you," I murmured, horrified when my voice cracked. Gripping my kit, I scampered out the door and along the hall to the communal bathroom, which was—thankfully—empty at this time of night.

The house held a sort of hum, like a livewire, as I turned the shower on as close to scalding hot as my skin would allow and stood under it for a few minutes, drowning myself in steam and heat. A shuddering breath tore from my lips as the tears started, racking from me in great shudders.

I thought I did enough to push Thomas away.

I thought I could leave my ruined heart at his feet years ago.

And now he was back, seemingly intent on filling whatever hole currently occupied his drunken attention. My hand wavered on the glass door to the shower. I'd left him in the garden. What if he actually chewed on something poisonous? The flower beds were rife with inedibles. It would be such a Thomas thing to do. Then, intentional or not, I'd be guilty by association, even if it was in my head, if he was hurt.

I closed my eyes as the tears streamed faster than the water that cascaded over my cheeks.

He's not my problem. He's not my problem.

The mantra gained strength with each iteration.

"He's not my problem," I whispered to the ether, praying Thomas—someone—heard me.

Steam swirled around the bathroom in chaotic eddies as I washed my hair and scrubbed my skin until all I could smell was soap on soap on soap. My skin burned under the heat, but I couldn't stop. The pain reminded me of what it felt like when Thomas broke my heart in the first place.

In an effort to maintain my torturous mindset, I finished up my bathing routine with a run of frigid water set on pure icy cold and doused myself until the shivers set in and the steam dissipated. Then I left the shower, patted my hair to some semblance of dryness, and wrapped the towel around myself, having forgotten a change of clothes.

"Nate will have to learn to turn around and not peek," I muttered as I poked my head out of the door and checked for a clear coast.

Not that it should have mattered, but I didn't want to run into Kimberly tonight. The floor itself seemed to ripple beneath my feet and the house's strange energy left it more alive than ever.

"Eyes away, Mister Poet, please?" I slipped back into my room to find Nate perched on the edge of my bed, tossing his phone in the air, and I put on an act, tugging at the edge of my towel and playing with it. Nathaniel's gaze followed my movements, but he didn't play along as usual. The butterflies that already rioted in my stomach stopped. I gripped the edges of my towel tight, trying not to drip all over my shag-pile rug, and make my bear wet, and stopped. "Are you okay?"

His gaze coasted up my bare, rivulet-running legs until it landed on my face, but man, did he take his time getting there. "I'm fine."

I blinked. "Don't you use the F-word with me, mister."

He laughed, and put the phone on my pillow, pushing himself up from the mattress. "I was worried about you. He upset you, didn't he."

That wasn't a question, and I didn't need to ask which *he* we were talking about.

"Yeah, he upset me." I managed a lopsided grin. "But I'm here with you and that makes it . . . all right." Not that I ever got to my coffee that was probably lukewarm at best by now. Maybe I could ask Nathaniel to ice it.

"He is worthy of the asshat title." Nate glided closer, and upon inspection, I discovered his feet weren't contacting the floor. Maybe half an inch off, but it made all the difference in his grace.

"You'd better not do that when we leave the room," I muttered. "Someone's going to twig."

"They can take a whole branch if that's what they need." He landed—literally—in front of me, long-fingered hands brushing my waist.

It took me a second to interpret that not only had he understood the colloquial expression, but twisted the thieves' slang to fit his own meaning.

"Look at you, all grown-up and being the modern poet."

"If you like." He reached out and trailed his fingers along the front of my towel until he reached my midsection. "Turn around."

Ghost bumps erupted over every exposed part of me— and there was a lot of that on display. "What?"

"Face the mirror, Emma." Nate's voice dipped low.

A frisson ran along my spine as I twisted on the spot to face the oval mirror that sat above my set of drawers opposite my desk. Nathaniel's hands reached around me to catch my wrists in a gentle hold. He lifted them to place on the top of the drawers.

"What are we doing?"

"Distracting you. And me."

"You're . . . angry?"

"Perhaps. I don't like that another man upset you."

Not angry. He's jealous.

Or protective.

A shudder similar to the one I experienced in the shower rippled over me, this time for a very different reason.

Nathaniel's hands glided along my arms in reverse, starting at the backs of my hands and trailing upward until he reached my shoulders. "Stay there," he murmured.

"Where are you going?" I asked our reflections.

Violet and gold eyes met mine over my shoulder. A hint of a smile that disappeared as fast as it came on left me gripping the wooden drawer top until I was certain my nails would embed little half-moons all over its surface.

Nate shucked his jacket onto the bed and flicked the buttons of his shirt open one at a time, never breaking eye contact. My mouth dried watching his progress, or lack thereof, as his knuckles brushed my towel-covered spine, then his shirt followed the jacket's trajectory.

I traced the shape of his shoulders with my eyes, the tight planes of muscle there that seemed to come naturally to his body. The carved, heroin-chic quality to him that left his body ripped and lean and angular, yet a work of pure art at the same time.

Next to him, I wanted to curl in on myself. My hands left the drawer top, and gripped at my towel. "Nate, maybe this isn't a good idea," I hushed—

To nothing at all. The air behind me stood empty.

"Dammit, I wish you wouldn't do that," I hissed as his fingers, that warm/cold dual touch, brushed my cheek.

"I'm right here, my Emma."

"Then show me," I whispered, my eyes stinging again, but I had nothing left to cry. Raw and unnerved, I closed my eyes when his unseen touch ghosted across my collarbone, then pushed at the top of the towel.

"Hands on top," he murmured in my ear.

My heart thumped a traitorous rhythm as the warmth of him framed my back. To know he was there but not see him if I opened my eyes broke me. "I don't know if I can do this," I said, uncaring of the desperation that entered my voice.

"Let me soothe you, curious girl. Don't you want to know what it's like just to feel? Open your eyes. Watch." His disembodied voice shattered something within me. Maybe it was the request in there, not the demand, but I did as he said and watched.

Nothing.

My own reflection stared back at me as I tried not to hyperventilate while his hands took an invisible tour over my body. Over the towel at first as I gripped the wooden furniture top with my palms, flat, then with my nails digging in when the tie between my breasts untucked and unfolded. The damp cloth dropped away from my body to leave me bare.

Fingertips traced across the swells of my flesh, tracing a path across my breasts, then my nipples, tweaking the sensitive nubs to hard peaks as I watched. I moaned softly, shifting my feet apart when his denim-covered knee pressed between my legs. It didn't escape me that even though Nate wasn't visible, I could feel every inch of fabric between his flesh and mine. Heat rushed between my thighs. Which meant that he still wore clothes while I . . .

Did not.

He nudged my thighs apart and I let him, leaning back into his embrace. I didn't know if he floated or if we did, but I let him take my weight, giving over all my control in what might have been the craziest decision of my life. The lightest touch of his thumbs brushed beneath my breasts. My nipples pebbled to harder peaks, begging for attention, but he avoided the dusky flesh that ached when he ignored them and coasted one hand lower, over my stomach.

The other, he lifted to my chin, holding me carefully in place, like I was some fine porcelain doll he feared to break.

No one's ever handled me like I was important before.

A whimper tore from my throat as he traced the soft flesh between my thighs. I tried to clamp my legs together, but he pushed his knee forward, holding me open.

"Nate," I gasped, writhing a little. "Either touch me, or don't. This . . . I want you so much it almost hurts."

The confession tripped from my lips at the same time as he rubbed his fingers lower, like he knew exactly what he was doing. His lightest touch stroked the tops of my thighs, collected some of my messy slick there that left my cheeks flaming to spread over my pussy. I closed my eyes at the ease with which my body let him toy with me, the dampness on my inner thighs adding to the raw discomfort of being touched, even though I knew it was okay to let go and enjoy this part. I still struggled with it.

Nate circled my clit with his fingertips until I gasped, digging my nails into the top of the dresser.

"He never seduced you properly, did he?" Nathaniel's voice held a degree of dark humor that lasted a full second, before he sank two fingers deep inside me.

I arched, biting back a cry he muffled beneath his hand that clamped over my mouth, just in time to avoid the entire sorority hearing our midnight playtime endeavor. My thighs trembled as he worked me hard and rough. I panted behind the hand that cupped my chin, tilting my head up so I had to watch myself in the mirror.

Eyes bright, but dozy, breath coming fast, I stared at the disheveled image before me. All damp hair that clung to the woman with stained cheeks, her tongue flicking out to lick fingers she couldn't see.

This can't be me. I can't be her. She's too—

My body clamped down on his intruding fingers, hips rolling with the motion at the onset of my orgasm. But I couldn't look away, locked into the space where he could see everything, but I couldn't see him. My pleasure dripped down my thighs as I cried out into his hand that covered my mouth and sucked on the fingers he offered.

"Beautiful," Nathaniel murmured in that same soft voice, his lips brushing against my ear. "I knew you would be, watching yourself like this."

I cried out again, my body trembling as I fell forward. He caught me with one arm wrapped firm around my chest, though the other hand never stopped playing the way he wanted, pumping in and out of me fast enough that I could hear the gushing, wet sound. I found his shoulder, broke all his rules and dug my nails in, clinging to him as I screamed my release against his skin.

The leather-and-books taste of him filled my senses. I sank back, letting him hold me as he slipped both arms around me and carried me back to my bed, where I trembled while he wrapped both of us in the blankets.

The next time I opened my eyes and twisted to look at him over my shoulder where he was tucked in, spooning beside me, and still half dressed, his eyes were visible again. But now they held a darker shade of violet than ever before.

Like a dark-moon sky full of secrets and promises that only he knew, and would never tell.

"Distracted?" He leaned in and kissed the corner of my mouth.

I turned around for a full kiss, needing his reassurance, as a breath unsexily hiccupped from me. He didn't seem to mind, cupping the back of my head to hold me in place while he deepened the kiss.

"Absolutely distracted. Thank you," I managed. "I think I owe you."

"You never owe me anything. That's not how it works, Emma."

"I think it does." I wound one finger through a corkscrew curl then back out again. His hair bobbed about with a mind of its own, I swore. "You're all settled in, huh?"

His eyebrows rose. "Were you up to dancing or a walking date, or did I not do it right?"

I snuffed out a laugh behind my hand. "You did it all right," I reassured him, running my fingers over his shoulder, exploring. "I can't walk anywhere."

"Good." He nudged my cheek forward with his chin, the light prickle of a five o'clock shadow I hadn't noticed before grazing my skin as my heartbeat ramped up again. "I picked something."

He understood both the initial assignment and the unspoken one. *Gold star to my ghost boy.* But that still left me needing to do more for him. I wanted to make him feel as legless and as jelly-like—in all the good ways—all over as I did right now.

But also, I didn't have the energy to fight him on it. It turned out he had selected a rom-com that neither of us really watched, more distracted with each other instead. In the end, I rolled over, facing away from the TV, and studied his face instead.

The night filled with small, innocent above-the-covers touches and light kisses. Nothing serious or the sort of flirtatious seduction that he insisted on at a daily level, but it was enough, like him.

He was always enough.

Always.

Occasionally, he cringed at the odd quote that filtered

through to us. I laughed, tapping my empty coffee cup against his shoulder. "You could write it better."

"I would be too flowery for your time. Your audience." The term sat oddly on his tongue, it seemed, but he appeared pleased with it.

He'd enrolled himself—to my greatest horror—in a media class as a late semester starter. I couldn't attend with him, but Griffin could, the only other person on campus—in the world—who knew that Nathaniel Harker shouldn't be at Inerius U at all.

"Maybe. Or you could lend authenticity to period pieces. Write and costume things set in your own era."

Nathaniel's nose wrinkled as we ignored the couple fighting on screen in their breakup period before they got back together and fell in love all over again. Or maybe they never fell out of love in the first place. I hated the miscommunication trope with a passion.

"I already lived that life, Miss Emma. It's not one I'd return to."

"Not all it's cracked up to be, huh?"

He tugged me in closer. "I like the freedoms afforded to lovers in this life."

His mouth descended over mine in a gentle kiss that fast devolved into something deeper, reminiscent of our playtime in front of the mirror earlier.

"Oh," I managed.

And then he made sure that I didn't speak for a long time at all.

Where Art Thou, O Dead Poet?

Our date of the week involved walking through the grave-yard at midnight. I'd thought the place cold and lifeless when the sisters invaded the hallowed grounds for their own twisted bout of fun, but the gray granite populace seemed even more so with one of its own kind walking through its plots at my side.

Thankfully, the cold touches stayed away. Those seemed not to like Nathaniel's company out here.

"Here." Nathaniel crouched to tug away a net of matted weeds from an ancient-looking gravestone. "This was one of my professors. Lovely man, brilliant mind. Could quote every Roman philosopher verbatim and sing in Sanskrit. Used to do naked runs—" he checked sideways at the term for an approving nod before he continued his story "—when he got drunk. Helped with *hazing the freshmen* back then, too. Once, the frat brothers tossed one boy's clothing into the tree near the house after he had to do a full lap of campus. When he came back, Gregory was underneath, also naked, with his hands laced, and called out, 'Would you like a leg up, my boy?'" Nathaniel laughed softly. "His bread always was buttered on the other side. Such a card."

"He sounds amazing," I murmured when Nathaniel

straightened and wrapped his arm around my shoulders, tugging me inward to him. "Rules and regulations prevent that sort of relationship today."

He shrugged. "I don't think it was ever meant to be that way. We just were."

I rested against his side, and slid my hands inside his dragonfly jacket. "Do you miss them?" I gestured to the graveyard full of the friends and professors he had pointed out for the last hour, regaling me with anecdotes.

He shook his head, curls bouncing around his face as I watched, still fascinated by their determination to exist. "No. They are a memory. You are now," he said simply.

"Suck-up," I muttered, pressing up on my toes to kiss his cheek.

He turned into the kiss, cupping my nape and holding me close. "Better?" he asked, as though knowing how much I didn't want to be here tonight, but walked with him because I knew he did.

I nodded, safe in the circle of his velvet-dragonfly-embroidered arms. "Much."

"Come on. There's more." He led me to the right-hand corner as if drawn there by a golden thread.

I held back for a moment then gave up. He'd come here for a purpose, and I knew we would get to that same spot I'd sat and talked to a stone bearing his name eventually, no matter how long I resisted.

"Are you sure?" I called when he stood a few feet away, stock-still.

"I'm sure."

He drew me into him and wrapped his arms around my waist, drawing me to his chest as he stared at his name and death date etched in the stone where I had cleaned the mess away. The weeds had grown back, resisting my efforts of that night that had drawn their own speck of blood

278

beneath the cold moonlight, as though I never changed anything at all.

As though he never changed anything, and yet, here he stood, his chest pressed to my back, chin resting on the top of my head as he hummed softly.

> *"For thine flowers will wilt, thy bones shift to dust,*
> *The world will turn on. Every day that*
> *passes the sun rises anew*
> *And you are lost but never forgotten,"*

he whispered.

I shivered and gripped his arms tight. "One of yours?"

He nodded, and squeezed me closer. "One I wrote for a close friend I lost months before my own existence ended. I . . . dropped deep into melancholy myself then. Many of us did. He was a bright light in the darkness, one I thought may have changed the world. But he . . ." Nathaniel swallowed. "He is not buried here."

He took his own life.

"Oh, Nate." I closed my mouth on my too-brief assessment of his loved one. "I'm sorry. But also, you're wrong."

"On what?"

"Your existence didn't end. You're here," I whispered.

He kissed my temple. "I think I'm ready to go back now."

"G-go back—" I started, my heart stalling in my chest cavity long enough for his eyes to meet mine, and hold. "Oh," I whispered, relief swamping me at the truth I saw there.

He's not leaving me. It's okay.
I don't want him to leave.
Don't leave me.
Please.
Not ever.

I found his cold hand and warmed it with mine as we walked back through the graveyard in silence, leaving the ghosts of his past buried beneath old, unturned earth and the weeds that obscured their names.

And his.

*

My sleepless umbra of the last month finally caught up with me. I mixed up my classes, poured tea into the coffee machine, much to the sisters' conglomerate abject horror, and ended up with Nate's phone instead of mine.

Which I discovered when I tried to text Kimberly to tell her I wouldn't make English lit because I was halfway across campus where I thought I had a third-year editing class for a group project that needed to be finalized the following month.

I knew I was doomed when I was the only one who turned up for a meeting that had been held the previous week . . . and no one let me know because I'd missed so many, canoodled up with Nathaniel. It did appear that Thomas had managed to leave the poison garden under his own steam—or was otherwise locked in the sorority basement, but I didn't think so. He held no intrinsic worth to Kimberly, so I was off the hook with him at least, for now.

All to say that left me stranded across campus, and miles from where I needed to be. I flipped Nate's phone over in my hand and wondered which would sustain more damage if I banged my head on it. Not that it would help my fatigue—I bumped into the nearest wall and leaned my back to the structure, letting my eyes drift shut as it held me up. If I slid down said wall and sat in the sun for a minute, maybe two . . .

I'd be asleep.

I dragged my eyes open with a monumental amount of effort, and pushed off the wall as the phone vibrated in my hand. Seeing my own name on my screen in reverse left me giggling at least.

Emma: Miss Emma. It appears we have swapped phones for the day.

Nate: Oops?

Emma: Are you coming back soon?

Nate: Are you always this needy? Wait, how did you unlock my phone?

Emma: Griffin gave me a few tips.

Nate: On hacking? That's cocky.

Emma: Perhaps. I'll see you after class.

Nate: xxx

I shook my head at the strange conversation, amusing myself with seeing our names and messages in reverse for a few minutes while he replied. Letting out a long sigh, I extracted my tattered, printed-out schedule for emergencies—like today—and checked my next class. I might miss the one with Kimberly, but I'd make media ethics afterward. A lecture I could snooze through and still pass, thankfully, as I might need it. Today was one of the few evening classes I couldn't skip.

That meant more time away from Nathaniel, but he'd have to wait. One night wouldn't kill what we had. I yawned my way across campus and stopped for my coffee top-up after the fiasco in the kitchen this morning. The scent of Earl Grey and espresso burning together would forever haunt me. That scent made even Proserpine's smell good.

"Emma?" A soft voice stopped me mid unsexy caffeine guzzle.

I turned, the cup still to my lips. Still guzzling, and attempted a smile. Rivulets of coffee trickled from the corners of my mouth and created a mosaic across my chest.

Of course, today I chose to wear my Lois tee, my *white* Lois tee, and she now wore coffee stains from one end of her little chibi facade to the other.

Maybe I could make it a campus fashion statement, though I doubted it.

"Rosa, hi." I patted at myself in an attempt to appear civilized.

She held out a handful of napkins and said nothing. Vivian had passed me a toasted bagel earlier in the week in a similar vein. With her, I got it. There would be retribution later. Plus, she understood my reasoning for being locked away behind the sorority's heavy doors. Rosa, however . . .

Her silence unnerved me.

"Thank you." I crumpled the stained coffee cup and napkins in one hand and binned them as soon as I found a trash receptacle. "How have you been?" I asked more quietly as I started to walk. Rosa fell into step at my side after a moment's intense stare-off.

She didn't answer.

"Were you safe getting home that night?" Her exodus had been on my mind when I wasn't getting *distracted* by my captive ghost boy. "I worried about you."

"You should leave that place. It's evil." She turned to face me full on and for the first time I noted the tears glazing her eyes.

"Rosa?" I stared right at her, a lump in my throat. "Please tell me you were safe that night." My heart thumped heavy and slow in my chest. Too slow.

"It's not safe there. Why don't you come with me?" She grabbed my arm in a hard grip and pulled me sideways into the long afternoon shadows that had grown while I crossed campus to the coffee shop, desperate for my caffeine hit.

"No. I can't." I pulled back, frowning at her. "There's something I have to do."

"There's nothing you need to do. Be free. Live your life like you should. Not under her influence," Rosa insisted, her tears breaking their banks as they cascaded over her cheeks. "Please, Emma. Come with me." Her nails dug into my arm, biting into my flesh.

"Let go." I tugged backward, hard enough to free myself.

Hard enough to send Rosa reeling until she crashed into another girl who caught her and made soothing noises.

"I told you she wouldn't leave." Hannah's baleful eyes rose to meet mine. "Selfish, spoilt bi—"

"I think you've made enough of a scene, don't you?" Kimberly spoke from behind me, hovering right over my shoulder like a twisted angel of death, but somehow worse.

Both girls' eyes widened.

I gritted my teeth and forced the smile and the words they needed to hear to back off before she hurt them more than she already had.

"I'm fine." *A partial truth*. "I need to stay in the sorority."

For Nate. Or maybe I'm just full of poet-poop. "Thank you for your concern." *I sound like Kimber-bot 2.0.*

Pass me my twinset now please, in a shade of watermelon.

Kimberly's talons tapped my shoulder as Rosa and Hannah walked away, talking quickly to each other. I squeezed my eyes shut.

This is hell. This is true hell. I've stepped out of life and entered Kimberly's dystopian future where she—

"Have you seen Nathaniel today? He wasn't in your room when I came by."

I turned and blinked at her. "You . . . checked my room. For my f— boyfriend." I fake-sneezed. Convincingly. I prayed, because hope did *not* cut it with this woman.

"Of course. You have homework due." Her smile could have cut certified safety glass.

"I do?" My mind raced to find the necessary cause, but I came up blank. "Any chance you covered for me, or do I still have time to hand it in? I've got no idea what I've missed—"

She laughed, and the tinkling sound that came out could have shredded a sorority outcast. "Oh, nothing so important. Just the homework I set you. Remember?"

I didn't, but that was kind of her point. "I'm sorry. I've been—"

"All loved up. Yes. We figured that out."

"We?" I swallowed. "I'm sorry. House rules and all."

She shrugged. "We all break them, Emma. Now, your ex-boyfriend who defaced the poison garden the other night, however . . ."

I winced. "Please say he's not my responsibility," I begged. "I've been trying to get rid of Thomas for two years. There's a . . . nasty history there."

"He won't be returning," she assured me. "I had words with the dean. Action has been taken."

I blinked at her. "Wait. Do you mean—"

"Thomas is leaving Inerius U under his own steam. I'm not that powerful." She waved a dismissive hand in my direction. "He's free to transfer wherever he wishes with the dean's approval. He even gets a letter of recommendation. But he cannot terrorize my sorority. We protect our own, Emma. Is that understood?"

I could have earned myself a decent strip of gravel rash for the descent of my open jaw that aimed at paver level. "Yes, ma'am," I said smartly.

"Good." Kimberly patted me, looking at my ruined shirt. "You've had a day." She put me out of my misery. "We have another séance, a full summoning very soon. I need your best notes, Emma. In your journal. Will you do that for me?" The frenzied, obsessive glint returned to her eye.

Hidden and shadowed, but I'd seen it before. The same dulled spark lingered behind her eyes, never quite absent.

Maybe I should have run and taken the out Rosa had offered, and made Hannah's day in letting them "rescue" me. But I couldn't leave Nathaniel alone. I'd never forgotten the first time he left Phi Omega House and how he said it called him back to it. Something told me that Kimberly wouldn't give up her prize so easily.

"Yeah, sure. That sounds good," I lied, backing up. "I've got ethics. Catch you after?" I had no such intentions, but hopefully it would deter her from following me.

A *just in case* sorority clause.

Kimberly perked up like she hadn't saved me from two of her failed pledges minutes before. "See you later," she called, waving one hand a little too fast.

I nodded, my fake smile aching as it started to slip from my face. I turned in the direction of my afternoon ethics class and dragged my feet despite the caffeine I'd injected earlier, wishing I could run the substance intravenously.

Half a dozen hours later, I dragged myself back past the same spot, though moon shadows, not the long afternoon sun, covered the locked-up café and the poison garden once the campus clock tolled the hour a happy ten times. Late summer storm clouds coalesced overhead, their soft growl the most recent threat to my sanity.

My cruddy, never-ending day continued in the form of a forgotten tutorial and a late-night catch-up group meeting for the one I had abandoned—their words, not mine—weeks before. As a result, my head roiled with more information than it could reasonably hold tonight, but I had my second wind and trotted through the garden, banishing Thomas's shade and refused to consider his fate.

We protect each other.

Her trust in me was misplaced. I swallowed the remaining cache of lies that webbed around me like some twisted horror story. My ethics course had been all about clarity in media. Huh. A laughable statement. I hadn't been able to snooze through the class at all, and I missed batting about the virtue of a strong code with Vivian, who devoured moral philosophy as a bedtime snack.

I missed Vivian all over, actually.

But right now, the person I needed most was Nathaniel.

I crept up the stairs, ignored the strange smell emanating from the kitchen and hoped I hadn't bunged the coffee machine up so badly that I'd be inhaling the burnt Earl Gray and espresso mix as a penance for the rest of my days, and pushed my door open.

"Nate? I have phones to swap," I called to my ghost boy.

My absent ghost boy, as I stood alone in my cold, empty room except for one blue glowing Minnie who sat face to face with my faux bear like it was the strangest thing she had ever seen.

It was pink, had fake teeth and was semi-cross-eyed so I'd give her that.

"Hey, Minnie." I waved absently at the ghost cat. "Good to see you out of the library."

Funny, how a dead man could fill a dorm room with presence enough that I missed him physically when he wasn't there, but a phantom cat and a fake bear rug did the job just fine in a pinch.

"Dammit, Nate. I asked you not to leave. Asshat," I added for good measure, grabbing the hem of my coffee-sticky Lois tee and yanking it over my head. It wasn't like he hadn't seen it all before. And . . . other things.

I stripped when he didn't appear, hiding my frown beneath my hair.

Nate: It's me. I'm back in my room. Where are you?

I started when my phone—my actual phone—buzzed on my desk. On charge, where he had thoughtfully left it.

"Okay," I groused, grabbing a towel and wrapping that around me. "I'm going for a shower. Back in five," I called to the glowy ghost cat in case I read the room wrong and he was present after all.

But somehow I knew he wasn't.

The lump in my throat grew as I showered fast, didn't bother with makeup and changed in a still-Nate-free room. Even Minnie had vacated. The building storm outside left me on edge as I tossed on a cream peasant dress that stopped halfway along my arms in puffy, soft cotton sleeves with a peek-a-boo neckline tied with a beaded feather string. The skirt consisted of crocheted lace in layers that hung above my knees.

I padded through the sleeping house barefoot, checking

287

first the library, then the kitchen—which still smelled odd. My fingers brushed the stonework as I passed, clinging to the sticky surface that never seemed to stay clean, either inside or out of the old sorority house.

Outside, outside, outside . . .

I blinked once and chose to listen to the talking stones. I mean, they might be telling the truth.

A Soul Lost on a Stormy Night

I found the staircase to the rooftop, my fingers trailing the chattering stones, but their whispered message never wavered.

Up up up—

Or perhaps it did, and I interpreted their words differently.

Or maybe Vivian really would get to order me that custom pink straitjacket after all.

Or—

I pulled the door open, stepping out onto the windblown rooftop of Phi Omega House situated between the twin belfries that overlooked all of Inerius U, lined up with the clock tower like someone had marked out ley lines on a map.

Hell, for the Gothic look of the building and the fact the stones *talked* to me like they did to a dead man who shouldn't be alive in the first place, maybe it was well marked on the grounds.

Below, in the opposite direction, the poison garden spread out like a living organism stealing back an inch of ground at a time. Beyond that mess lay Proserpine's Venom, plus the rest of the campus buildings. The graveyard, with its unmarked walks and names I didn't know before, etched its mark into the furthest point along the boundary line near the old chapel.

And above us, the sky rattled and moaned like someone had dared to wake a slumbering god in the midst of summer heat. Unspent electricity prickled my arms, raising hairs that stood on end in a silent salute to the oncoming storm.

But none of that held my attention.

I stared at the back of the man who stood at the far end of the rooftop, his silhouette outlined by the sheet lightning that illuminated the darkening sky, where he balanced on the building's very end. Curls whipped around him, untamed, his white shirt loose and as wild as the storm that tried to throw him from the precipice.

He'd dressed in some of his old clothes, the ones I first met him in, sans the jacket, though he'd kept the black jeans. Even with his lean build, he made a formidable silhouette, standing at the storm's threshold, leaning into the wind.

A scream stuck in my throat as I watched him sway at the edge of nothingness at all, flanked by two stone gargoyles that remained sentinel above any passerby too stupid to be out in this monstrosity of a roiling mess.

Like us.

"Nathaniel—" His name caught in my throat even as my logical brain told me that a dead man couldn't die a second time.

My heart couldn't risk losing him like this.

Not here, not today.

I lunged forward but a huge gust chose that exact moment to beat me back. A cry ripped from me as I stumbled backward into the door, still fighting my way forward.

"Nate—"

He turned, and my despair went on hold.

Indefinitely.

The man I knew transformed into something so much more than the whimsical poet who had lain on my rug quoting throwaway, flirtatious lines at me. The man who strode toward me now, heedless of the storm's whim as though he commanded it, stared at me with a piercing intensity built of midnight-dark eyes flecked with pure lightning. His shirt hung undone to the waist, his cravat absent. Nothing about him looked like the neat and immaculate Nathaniel Harker I thought I understood.

The version of him that I loved.

"I was looking for you—" My words died on my lips as he stepped into my space and speared his hands through my hair, though his longer limbs held me at arm's length. "Nate, I couldn't find you. The stones, do they speak to you?"

Why that seemed important to know in this moment, when the wind that sliced at us threatened to throw us off the rooftop together and ripped at our clothes, I had no idea.

"Who is he to you, your Thomas?" Nate demanded, his voice low and rough.

I stared back at him, my mouth hanging open. "That's what this is? Jealousy?"

"Who is he?" Smooth fingers massaged my nape in sensual circles, so different in their pattern to the tempest building behind his eyes. "I need to know."

"Nobody." I choked out the single word, shouting over the wind. "He's no one to me. I— He accosted me on the way into the house. He was drunk, sick with . . . I don't know. Like an obsession. I hated it. The feel of him near me, touching me. Breathing on me," I confessed, fearing my voice was too low to be heard.

It didn't seem to matter.

Nathaniel tugged on the roots of my hair. "No one?" he repeated, pulling my head back gently, a controlled gesture as he dipped his head close enough that he shared my breath. Close enough to brush our lips together the faintest amount with every word he spoke. "Tell me you're not still in love with him."

"I'm not. I promise," I whispered, praying he heard me.

A single breath that belonged to only one of us shattered between us before his mouth claimed mine in a frenzied kiss of lips and tongues and desperation that spoke of all the heartache and shattered innocence coursing through him. His hand on my nape pulled me closer until I arched in his arms.

His tongue sought entry, pushing past my boundaries without requesting permission. Tonight was different for us both. A gasp left me as my hands knotted in the soft folds of his cotton shirt, and then I pulled him down to me, as needy as him to be closer than our clothing allowed. He met me head on, thrusting his tongue roughly between my lips, forcing my mouth wider. This kiss wasn't gentle, and it wasn't sweet, or seductive. Tonight Nate was demanding, controlling his desire tightly.

I wanted him to unleash it.

A deep sound reverberated through Nate's chest. He broke the kiss, pulling back to tear his shirt off over his head one-handed. Then his mouth was back on mine as he folded me against him, edging the waist of my dress up. One hand closed around my breast, his thumb pinching the sensitive peak through the thin fabric until I moaned.

The ground disappeared as I fell in his arms. The world spun on its axis as though the wind caught us and tossed us off the edge in freefall. For a moment, that's what I thought had happened until my butt hit the cement beneath my feet.

I scrabbled upright. "No." I shoved at his chest even as his hands skimmed up my thighs, pushing my dress up and easing my legs apart. I made no resistance to that effort, but I shook my head all the same.

"No?" he repeated, stilling as he arched over me even as

my hands trailed up along his stomach, tracing the places of hard, defined muscle there, the fine edges of ink that wound around his ribs.

"You gave me so much before." I licked his bottom lip, keeping my eyes locked on his intense gaze before I lost my nerve. "Before the mirror."

When you held me after and I didn't want to move from the safety of your arms.

I'd never experienced so much love or arousal in my life. Nathaniel gave me everything he had to offer. If tonight was going to go like I expected he planned, or maybe he had no plan and was running on adrenaline alone, then I wanted to make sure I gave that same sense back to him.

He watched me, his entire body still and taut. I squeezed his arms in a silent plea. He jerked his head once, dipping his chin to crush our mouths together, then drew back, letting me touch him.

I pushed at his shoulders until he eased onto his heels, running my hands along his chest, and lower as I crawled to my knees. Nate's mouth opened as though he might object to my kneeling on the cement rooftop beneath the stormy sky at midnight, but I couldn't think of a more apt place for us.

Making sure his eyes were locked on mine as he stood tall above me, I reached up to toy with the tie that held the front of my dress together. One tug on the long string and the front panels parted, exposing my bare flesh to the night air.

I shivered, though not from the cold as he looked at me. The darkness in his eyes deepened, and I arched my shoulders to improve the view. The sound that rumbled from his chest I took as a male noise of arousal when his fingers dropped to trace lightly over my décolletage, lacing through my hair as I leaned forward to undo his jeans. His hands cupped my bare breasts, toying with my nipples as I mewled, pausing to try to concentrate on my task through my pleasure.

"You don't have to do this," he murmured.

I smiled and placed a kiss on his abdomen. "I want to."

He didn't stop me after that, his hands tangling in my hair as I freed his thick cock from the tight confines of his pants. A hiss escaped him that I heard above the storm's roar. My hand closed around his velvet length, gliding along the hardness I ached to swallow.

The hand on my head pressed forward in a gentle pressure, and I leaned in to lick the tip of him, keeping my eyes locked to his. The strained shudder that I earned from him as I learned the shape of him in my mouth at first and then deeper, was worth the discomfort shooting through my knees.

Nathaniel tugged on my hair, shifting his hips with a soft groan that helped me find the rhythm he liked, teaching me what I needed to know as my hands went on a little tour of their own. I pushed his pants away while I learned how to use my tongue to please him. His moans melded with the storm's unreleased fury, fingers digging into my scalp when I hollowed my cheeks and sucked harder. I swallowed around the length of him that pulsed in my mouth, wiggling closer to take him deeper.

Nathaniel growled above me, and tugged me backward.

I threw out a hand to catch myself but he kneeled and caught me before I had to, flicking my dress up to skate his hands beneath, finding my bare thighs and—

"Naughty, my Emma. What if you hadn't been able to find me tonight?' he murmured against my ear. Nathaniel pushed his jeans further down and settled me over his hips, kneeling on the cement, and shifted me to straddle him.

"I knew I would. I'll always find you," I said against his

mouth. My mind flitted back to where he stood at the edge of the storm, like he might throw himself into its center and never emerge. "I thought you would—"

"I won't leave you."

His straining cock probed my entrance. I whined into his mouth when he kissed me again, no longer holding back in his desire, only in how fast I could sink along his length. Long-fingered hands clamped on my hips, until I rocked over the very tip of him. My whimpers increased when he slid a hand across my stomach then lower to play in the silky wetness between us. His thumb rubbed my clit until I pulsed around the tip of him. Violent stormy eyes met mine as I rocked on him.

"Nate, please, I need—"

I pressed our mouths together to contain my scream, rocking against his fingers where they stroked my sensitive nub. His other hand gripped my ass, squeezing hard as he pulled me forward and rocked me back, but he wouldn't allow me closer than that.

"Please, Nate. I need more," I begged, rolling my hips in time with the way his fingers played me.

"Come first," he growled. "Then I'll let you have what you want."

A shudder worked its way from my tailbone to my lips. Heat slipped through me, my hands slapping his shoulders with the force of my first orgasm. I dug my nails into him for purchase, clinging to him as he kissed me hard and deep. The intense sound that rumbled through his chest in victory brought me out of my orgasmic haze as he gripped both of my hips and pushed me down.

I saw white.

My head tipped back in a wordless scream, the overwhelm too much to handle. I clamped down, my walls leaving butterfly kisses along his length as I rocked to the rhythm he set. Breath evaded me as he left me in a constant state of freefall, yet never let me go to tumble on alone.

I clung tight to his shoulders, his name on my lips though I could never form a full word as lightning rippled in white sheets across the sky above us, and the first heavy drops of rain splattered over our skin.

The scent of petrichor surrounded us as Nate filled me again and again, his own roar building as he gripped me close, strong hands careful on my body, though he never refrained from his powerful rhythm. Then he drove into me faster, harder from below, pounding deep. I lost all sense of everything other than the rain pouring down my face, welling in heated pools between our bodies everywhere we joined. Thunder imbued the air around us with a cacophony of sound that blared out everything else and yet left us in a sphere of silence at the same time.

I shuddered over him as my next climax swept through me, his mouth on mine as I tried to say the words I wanted to tell him, but he stole my breath a second time. My thighs tightened around his hips as I pushed down, taking his cock as deep as I could, needing him that close. *Closer.*

His thumb strummed my clit again. The overworked nub pulsed too much. I whined into his mouth, but he refused to let up. My pussy clamped down on his cock within seconds, but he never broke his rhythm. This time, I knew, he would take himself with me.

"Nothing more than this. Who we are," he rasped in my ear as he dug his hands into my hips and pinned me in place. Water streamed down his face, plastering his curls to the sides of his skull before he crushed our mouths together in a last, desperate kiss.

I shivered over him. "Nate, I love you," I whimpered into his mouth.

Strong hands crushed me to him as I rolled my hips,

riding out my strongest orgasm that refused to end. Our bodies crashed together beneath the storm's vengeance.

His roar filled my mind as he arched over me, and the world whitened out again.

Mine. Forever.

"I love you," I screamed into the maelstrom, daring its violence to contradict me and steal him away for daring to voice the words.

His hands cradled me as he held me through the worst of the storm, of who we were together.

What we could survive.

And when I opened my eyes and kissed him softly, he held me fiercely and began to move within me again.

Sleep Is for the ~~Wicked~~ Dead

Nate lay on his back on my bed, writing frantically, while I tweaked the article I wasn't sure I could hand in, tapping at the keys of my laptop in a listless fashion. The stones in the walls stopped talking once the storm passed, as though its violence offered some sort of conduit to whatever lay within the house's foundations.

Or perhaps who resided inside it.

The scribbles at my side—along with the odd modern curse word interspersed with some archaic, flowery language—hit all the right and wrong buttons at once.

"How come you get to make words while I sit here, tap tap tappitying?" Nate's language had integrated into mine seamlessly.

"Because I have no deadline. You worry about the things that matter little and panic over those you cannot control, Emma." He placed his pen and paper on the edge of my desk, pushing up onto one elbow to brush my hair back from my face where I slumped over my keyboard.

I bared freshly whitened teeth at him. There was nothing like procrastination to make sure I was bleached, plucked and primed within an inch of sorority regulation. "You even manage to look romantic, all stretched out. My posture sucks."

He patted the bed. "Then come here."

"Did you just *come-hither* me?"

"Perhaps." The glitter in his midnight gaze never quite returned to his usual violet swirls and gold flecks after our rooftop rendezvous. Nate crooked a finger in my direction.

I bit my lip, glancing at my screen. "I have to have this in by tomorrow . . ."

"You know you're not sending it in, not even if you deem it perfect."

My brow dipped. "How do you know that?"

"Because it would mean the end of this." He caught my hand and flicked his wrist, pulling me off my chair and into his arms.

I crashed into his chest in a tangle of arms and legs as he trapped me against him. Long, ink-stained fingers soothed my hair, and traveled in swirls across my semi-bare shoulders where the spaghetti straps held my gingham cornflower dress up in a crisscross pattern.

"You're still a distraction." I shoved half-heartedly at his chest.

A laugh rumbled at the point of origin there. "A pretty one, I hope."

"Far too pretty." I toyed with one of his curls that bounced back more corkscrewy than ever after our sojourn in the rain. "You're right. I don't want this to end."

"Does it have to?" I swore he made puppy-dog eyes at me.

I tugged one curl too hard, and he winced. "This is impossible. I can't keep you, Nate. You're not a pet, you're a person."

"I'm glad you noticed." His impish grin did nothing for the anxiety bubble growing in my gut.

Minnie wandered across my desk, knocking my desk

cactus off, and broke a mug. She pivoted to return the way she had come, and disappeared.

"Ghost cats," I muttered.

"Cute, though." Nate ignored the extra degrees of chaos in my room.

I sighed, returning to the problem at hand. "You have no social security number. No birth certificate . . ." I trailed off.

Well, he might, just not one from this century, or even the last.

"Your friend did an excellent job of creating me on paper before," Nate said. His quiet interruption to my tirade halted me midstream.

"You want a hacked life forever? I mean, you can't die, right? Won't people notice when you look like this in forty years? A hundred? When does it become test-tube land in a science building, Nate?"

"Vampires get away with it." He beamed at his apparent logic.

"Vampires are not real." The Netflix account had been a huge mistake.

"As far as you know." He booped my nose.

I stared. "Don't do that. It's demoralizing."

"You, Emma Reeves, are cute."

"I thought I was beautiful, according to you."

"My quote. I'm allowed to alter it." His grin never faded as he rolled us on my bed so that he caged me in with both arms.

"I'm not getting any writing done tonight, am I?" I sighed as my procrastination attempt blew right out of my control and into his.

"You weren't writing anyway." Light kisses feathered over the bridge of my nose.

"You were," I pointed out.

"I can write anytime. Besides." He leaned down to

whisper in my ear, his lips traveling lower to tickle the slope of my throat. "You are beautiful, Emma Reeves."

I waited for the rest of his line, but it didn't come. When he pulled back, his eyes were pensive. "Are you okay?"

Nathaniel watched me like he tried to absorb every part of what he saw before him. "The storm called to me," he murmured. "The stones, too. They . . ."

"Talked," I croaked, finishing his thought. My mouth dried.

Upstairs upstairs upstairs.

Their echo twisted through my mind until a scream blocked my throat with the intrusion. "What did they say to you?"

His fingers traced the edge of my jawline. "Up, up, up," he whispered.

I heard the same words.

My hand trembled on his arm. "What did those words mean to you?" I dug my nails in when he didn't answer straight away. "Nathaniel?"

"When I was alive, we believed in beauty wherever it was found." He stroked my cheek with the pad of his thumb, then rested it on my lips. A gentle gesture at silence, perhaps, or reassurance? With Nate, I couldn't always tell. His frame of reference outweighed mine by two hundred years and the distance had never seemed so far as it did right now. "In the human form." His thumb pressed down on my bottom lip until my mouth opened on a slight gasp. "In words of endearment. In nature's brutal power. The storm knew me, Emma. It asked me . . ." He swallowed and closed his mouth.

"What?" I spoke around his thumb, my tongue flicking against the tip.

His unformed words hissed between his teeth, but he didn't pull away. "The rooftop seemed the place to be closest to its heart. I wanted to be there, amidst the violence of it. Because in that same savagery, I found a reflection of myself. Of what I feel for you."

"Nate." I reached for him. "I'm sorry."

"Don't be." He rested his forehead to mine. "Love can be beautiful, and sweet and serene. It can also be brutal and potent and furious. That does not mean it lacks beauty." His eyes searched mine, a silent entreaty that I understood what he said.

"Love aches," I whispered back. "It stings and clenches and half the time I want to puke out of fear of loss and repeating old mistakes or making new ones to the same end. But also there's . . . this. Where we are here, and quiet and everything is still."

"Perfect." His cheek rubbed against mine, his skin soft, bristles rough.

"Beautiful," I agreed to the matching rumble of approval in his chest, and I knew I'd understood him.

But all that didn't explain the anguish coursing through his eyes when he stood at the edge of the building like a malevolent spirit about to take flight and soar away from me forever.

Love can also lead to fear and loss.

I'd experienced it before and that heartbreak coated my rose-colored glasses in a spiderweb of fine cracks that I could barely see beyond.

"Nathaniel, what did the stones say to you?" I repeated, my voice low, the barest whisper. I already knew what he was going to say.

He stilled, warm hands turned cool. "I waited for you, Emma. I read the messages from Thomas. The ones you sent back like you still cared for him. It . . . burned. Here." He pressed my hand to his chest where his heart didn't thump reassuringly beneath my fist. He banged our hands together

302

there in a parody of the missing beat. "Like I could still feel. And then, I didn't want to feel anymore. Nothing at all. The stones helped. They called out to me in whispers I thought that only I could hear."

I shook my head frantically. "It's not only you. I hear them too. They've been . . ." I searched for the right word but of course that evaded me so I stuck with the one that I'd used the entire time I'd been around the house. "Sticky. They've felt sticky to me ever since I arrived. Right before I found you."

"You called to me too." The hand cradling my cheek slid back to cup my nape. He pulled me in, closer. "You drew me out of the darkness, Emma. Don't send me away. Don't send me back." His eyes searched mine and for the first time in over a day the flecks of violet I knew so well flickered with their usual brightness against the gold in his eyes.

"I—" The lie stuck in my throat. "You know I—"

"Promise me," he whispered, *begged*. "I want to stay with you."

"I'll find a way," I blurted, sliding my hands up his arms to knot in the cravat he'd taken to wearing again like a fragile sort of armor against reality. "I'll find a way to help you, Nathaniel. I promise."

He kissed me, sweet yet hard, soft yet deep. I fell into him and swore my own heart stopped, if for a moment's grace for him. When he let me go, the anxiety bomb that had been all too ready to burst in my stomach was absent. His arms curled around me as he propped himself up against my headboard, reclaimed his pen and paper, and swung my laptop to face me.

"Write, Emma Reeves. Revel in beauty wherever you find it. Rebel against limits and enforced order. Divulge your secrets. Don't tell mine." He kissed the tip of my ear and went back to his poetry, one arm looped around my waist, his paper balanced on his knee as he scrawled in a fine hand.

And I returned to staring at my screen.

One tap at a time, I began to add notes to the deadline I promised my editor and made my work worthy.

*

My article still sucked and I refused to acknowledge that Nate might be right about my refusal to complete it. Instead, I made notes in my Dead Poets Sorority journal about Nate's concepts of romanticism, figuring that covered what Kimberly needed anyway.

Not that Erin would be particularly interested in our love story; tactile love and her didn't get along well at the best of times. I had everything she needed to put a pin in the side of the Kimberly-shaped shadow that hung over Phi Omega House. I just . . . couldn't hand it in. Because then I'd have to fess up to both myself and Nate that I had lied to him and there was no happy ending for either of us.

There couldn't be.

Hi, Erin. I'd like you to meet the ghost boyfriend I accidentally dredged out from the depths of the nineteenth century. Would you mind drawing up a chair for him?

Knowing Erin, she'd see headlines and dollar signs and put him on staff under strict contract. But Nate's freedom would never be his own, and regardless of whether or not he acknowledged that, one of us knew and that was enough.

Tomorrow's impending Monday morning meeting itched at me. Due to my sorority incarceration assignment, I had managed to avoid going into the actual office, but that also isolated me more than my hermit tendencies had done on my behalf in hiding from the sisterhood and my best friend.

And the failed pledges. The list grew.

"You think loudly," Nate informed me, breaking through his tirade against Byron, whom he was hating on this week worse than ever. Seriously. If a poet could have PMS, this was it. BMS, maybe. *Bad Meter Syndrome.*

"And you don't?" I retorted, tossing a gummy bear at him. He caught it deftly, left-handed—damn those ghost-boy reflexes—and popped the candy into his mouth. "What was so wrong with Byron, anyway?"

Nate sighed. *Loudly.* "Unremarkable. Unexceptional. Everything is dark, dark, death, death-dark." He drummed his heel on the baseboard of my bed in emphasis. "Where is the beauty in such things?" he cried. "Poetry is supposed to be about the flow and allure of the world around us, not break it down into the shadows of the realms no one is supposed to see."

I bit my lip. *But you saw them.*

Those words stayed trapped firmly behind my clenched teeth.

Nathaniel waved his hand in my direction. "Come here."

A sigh of my own left me. I knew better than to interrupt his Byron-esque tirade. "All right," I said, cautious of his mood as I settled in the vee of his open knees.

One arm slid loose around my waist. His other trailed along my spine to my hairline then traveled in reverse. Gold and violet eyes met mine, glittering in a sea of midnight shadows.

"Do you want to hear about the realm I should not speak of, where there is nothingness forever? Where time ceases to fade and all falls and falls and falls, Miss Emma? Should I tell you how cold it is there, where the souls have departed and what is left, the remains of some cognitive form are threads of consciousness? That terrifying cold is what awaits beyond," he whispered, leaning into me.

The hand on my spine flattened, not allowing me to

draw back from the horrifying imagery that spilled from him, locked away for far too long. A shadow passed over us and I *felt it*—the cold touch that whispered from that first night in the house, something brought across from the place he spoke of where souls frittered apart and stones screamed into the void where only those beyond could hear their cries.

A shuddering breath escaped him, and cool hands gripped me tight.

"Or should I speak of the girl and the light, the one who brought me forth from a place of no end to a place I knew not but know now? These are the words I wish you to hear, where time flows as it should and my soul is once again whole. Because of you, Miss Emma." Warmth flowed into his hands, chasing the shadow away that claimed him so fiercely in its darkness.

I sucked in a harsh breath and let it out on a choking sob.

"I'm sorry. I scared you." He held me against his chest, but I pushed free.

"I wish you had told me sooner." I glared up at him. "Secrets aren't healthy, Nathaniel. Perhaps in your time you needed them, but here—"

"You lie to your friend, you do not speak to her and you cast out the man who came back to you, who hurt you," he said softly.

I recoiled in his arms. "Is that how you see me?"

"No. But your world still has secrets even if you don't always see them for what they are. You simply call them something else." He stroked my cheeks. "Are you all right?"

I nodded, the lie weighing heavy and cold in my chest.

I wish you'd told me sooner.

But he hadn't, keeping that secret tucked away within him, like the talking stones.

"I don't think I can keep up with a dead man," I murmured, sinking into the refuge of his soft cotton shirt so I didn't have to look at him, and played with the ends of his cravat.

It was funny in a *not* funny way—what Kimberly sought with her sorority, I'd found in Nate. Not in the stolen words of a resurrected poet but in talking to a man who understood what true Romanticism was, and lived its truth.

His truth that then flowed through me as he taught me to believe in the beauty of the things I glossed over in our busy lives. In this world of white noise and complicated relationships that he broke down so succinctly. Because in the end we were still human and still the same peoples who he knew and understood when he lived and walked and loved and breathed.

Like he did now.

Only, we were noisier.

He let me hide until after the sun set and we didn't have to anymore. Even then he still held me until my eyelids drooped. "Sleep, Emma." He kissed the top of my head. "I won't be long."

Covers I didn't need were drawn over me, but fatigue left me achy and limbless. Maybe the conversation from before had been too heavy, but I didn't think it was the subject matter that wore me out.

"Where are you going?"

"To the graveyard."

"Let me come with you." I tried to sit up but his hand on my shoulder pushed me back.

"No, my Emma." His quiet voice returned and I knew I had to listen to him even if I hated it. "I would like to walk alone tonight."

I opened my mouth to object, then shut it again and nodded. He faded from sight and I knew he would be safe without me. The room cooled before my brain caught up with the program. "Nate!"

"Emma?" He reappeared, frowning. "I promise I will return soon."

"Just— Don't go near any rooftop ledges. Please?" I clutched my sheets like a child and begged for the meaningless promise I needed to let him go.

The corners of his mouth twitched. "Of course. Whatever you want."

Meaningless promise thus bestowed, Nate dropped a sweet kiss on my lips and disappeared.

I waited until the room grew cold before I pulled out my journal and wrote out everything he'd said.

Word for word.

The Inside of a Snow Globe

The Actum's Monday morning pre-meeting post-breakfast circle chattered with the energy of several over-caffeinated hyenas. Griffin winked at me and doodled cacti on his page around my name and Nate's, laid out in a heart shape. I wanted to claw his drawing apart but violence before the meeting was generally a prohibited activity.

Janie and Rhapsody compared stats on last week's winning polo game—no Thomas in sight on their fact sheets. A well of endless guilt yawned in the pit of my stomach that no amount of sorority coffee could fill. I hadn't had time to duck through Proserpine's on my way to the office this morning.

Erin spared me part of a glance as she strode through *The Actum*'s doors, her laptop strung over one shoulder, and an oversized thermos in her other hand bearing fluffy-looking anime characters clutching knives.

It suited her personality to perfection.

"All right. Let's get started. I have a hole in my feature for this week." She didn't look at me, and I held my head forward when Janie and Rhapsody glanced my way. "What have we got?"

"I heard Thomas Carlisle got kicked off college grounds," Janie piped up. "That's why the polo team did so well."

I shook my head, hating the omission that led to the lie that were my first words to the team I hadn't seen in weeks. "With his wealth? Even if he lost every game, his family would never allow that."

Erin nodded at me. "Didn't you used to date him?"

"Enough to want to take out a restraining order. I'll pass."

I doubted he'd talk about the circumstances he left under. Maybe I should have put my hand up for that one to check the submission before it went to print. Before I could say anything else, Rhapsody stuck her hand in the air.

"I'll take it."

"Got you." Erin flipped her laptop open and made a note. "Sports. So, we won something. What was the party like afterward?"

Janie and Rhapsody exchanged glances. "I want to say epic, but they were kind of . . . stunned. The whole thing was done and dusted before midnight. They trained the next morning, squelching about after that epic storm."

I started in my seat. Every eye drew to me.

"Good night not to wander about campus," I blurted.

The eyes traveled back to Janie and Rhapsody.

"Write it up," Erin said. "I don't care how small it is. But we need something bigger. If no one broke anything, pissed on a statue or defaced the dean's office, that makes it a fairly tame week. We need something more. Who won an award?" Headshakes circulated the small group. "Got fired? Ousted from a frat? Hooked up?" Desperation entered her voice. The paper taco on her lap twitched.

"There's been a spate of random attacks on campus's security," Griffin offered, covering his mouth with one inked hand.

Erin sent him a withering glance. "Was it you?"

He patted his mouth and doodled more unsuspecting cacti on his notes.

She shook her head. "Has anyone got anything actually newsworthy for this week's edition? Because this rag is going to earn me a meeting with someone I'd prefer not to screw with and that means you're all on coffee rations for the rest of the month."

Janie and Rhapsody gasped in unison. "You wouldn't," they said together.

Erin's teeth ground. I heard every single one grate from across the circle. "I will," she promised. "Get me what I need. You have . . ." she checked her watch ". . . four hours. Make it count. Emma, stay."

And now I am also jobless.

I squeezed the flash drive in my pocket and made a decision, sliding my hand free. "I'm all yours."

"Thanks. That's . . . cute. Where's my article."

"On its way. Nearly done."

"It was due yesterday."

"Sororities and séances don't really play by deadline rules."

"And yet offers for references do." She folded her arms over her chest and stared at me across a half-moon circle of empty plastic chairs. "You never don't deliver, Emma. Not in all the years I've known you, and not for all the shithouse assignments I've thrown your way. What gives?"

"A dead man?" I mused, and the corners of my mouth turned up. "I think that's our problem. We keep chasing the big one, right?"

"Yes, that's what journalism is. Current events, what's happening now."

"Is it, though? What if what we need is a series that

311

runs through on a weekly basis. One that readers can get addicted to."

Erin's arms loosened. "I'm listening."

"Remember the polo-boy series I did?"

"That was an unintentional boon."

"Right, *but*—" I let my idea build steam. "One interview, and I had enough material for three weeks' worth of print."

Erin sighed. "Emma, you can't even give me one article after what, four, five weeks of research?"

"It's been hell on earth but sure. However, I wasn't thinking of me."

Erin sat up a little straighter. "Your ghost writer."

I smirked. "My ghost writer. I think we have something special. Can I share this with you? But promise me you *won't* show it to anyone else. At all. Got it? We need their okay first."

Erin's eyes glittered with the refracted light of a thousand sapphires as she scooped Nathaniel's diatribe on Byron out of my hands. "Personal, a little on the nose but . . . oh, my God."

"Right?"

"*Who.*" She looked up at me. "And how soon can I get more?"

"Uh-uh." I shook my head. "Hand it back. Contract, an offer, and I'll take it to him."

"Mm-hm. I'll email you the terms. Can this person work to a deadline?" The barb lay heavy between us.

I knew she was pissy at me, but right now my focus was on getting Nathaniel his first paid deal. I'd worry about parts like a bank account later. If she bought into him.

"I'll make it happen." I grinned Cheshire style, clutching the prize that Erin's eyes coveted as I pulled the pages to my chest.

Nathaniel might be mad at me for showing off his work but wasn't that where we started in the first place? He wanted not to fade into obscurity. I could make that happen while he still existed in my time and fulfill at least one item on his wish list.

"Make sure that you do. I'd hate to not offer that reference when it's time." Erin's face stayed completely blank as she threw those Pulitzer puke-worthy words at me.

"I will." I filled the air with my promise, and gathered my things. "Also, it's not just you I'm late for with things. It's kind of . . . everything," I apologized, glancing at the clock.

"Emma," she called as I darted toward the doorway, already guzzling a cooled coffee that Griffin passed to me on my way out that, though impossible, I swore held a tang of Earl Grey.

I'll never escape it.

"Yeah?" I glanced over my shoulder to find her staring at me.

"I heard about him. The odd bot. He's not— There's nothing wrong, is there?"

I could have laughed at her. Howled the entire office down at that sentiment. Whatever she could have asked, that was the least of all the worries on my overburdened platter that started with her assignment and would end when I handed in the completed article currently stuffed in my jean pocket.

"It's fine," I assured her. "He's fine. All is fine, fine, fine." I hadn't used the F-word that much in months. "I'll drop that article in later, okay?"

"When?"

But I'd already hit the stairwell, taking the steps two at a time. I blasted out of the office doors, straight past Vivian who held out a bagel that I didn't pause to grab, waving my coffee.

"We need to talk, Emma! Stop, for heaven's sake, you crazy woman!" she shouted to my back.

Good to know we've broken through the silence stage.

"Next time," I yelled back without slowing, and powered on to my next class.

*

Green goop poured from Kimberly's sleeves while smoke wound its way around my ankles. I tried not to inhale the crap that would end up asphyxiating us all if she didn't manage to summon her new dead poet boyfriend sometime soon.

The other sisters watched on, eyes wide with a mixture of horror and awe that reflected in the girl next to them as Kimberly moaned and professed love to the next dead spirit supposedly in attendance.

"We should have kept the Ouija board thing going. That was so much better than this." Fae yawned in my ear.

I nodded, zoning out as I scribbled notes in my journal. Talking to Erin this morning had sparked something and I hadn't had the chance to get back to the idea of approaching Nate with more than the series concept. We had talked about an initial column sure, but what if we created him—actual Nate Harker, the character—and wrote the column from his point of view?

Dead Poet's Corner, perhaps, or something along those lines.

I kept scribbling notes until my chair jumped forward. I frowned. That wasn't part of Kimberly's regular bag of tricks. The chair jumped again, then the toe of a steel-capped boot hit the back of my heel.

"Owww," I muttered, blinking back the insta tears that blurred my vision. "That freaking hurt."

314

"So will she if you don't pretend to suck up her ghost goop," Fae muttered. "Look *up* if you value your mortal existence."

"We have one of those?" I glanced up and found Kimberly's face an inch from mine. "Holy ghost balls, poethood. That's a weapon." I shuffled my chair back to its original position from where Fae had jaunted me forward.

"What words do you have for me tonight?" Kimberly whispered in her dramatic voice as the temperature plummeted in the room.

Hairs rose on my arms, not in the least from the heat in her narrowed eyes that were far from vague or possessed. She'd set her makeup thick for the stage production, but it more heavily reminded me of a cheap fortune teller.

Not that telling her so would win me any dead poet points.

"Uh, sure." I offered her the book, thinking through what I'd put in there to date. My conversation with Nate about death, and what came after. Subjective nonsense without a starting point of reference and a handheld guide. The Romantic movement conversation.

Now, that could actually be interesting. I'd laid it out as a narrative, no speakers in play, so if she read that aloud there would be no incrimination and it might be what she searched for. Plus my ideas on the column, which she'd know for exactly what it was.

Other than that, I barely used the journal, half as much as I saw the other girls scribble in theirs.

My fingers curled around the glass ball at my throat that went with my journal. It hadn't heated up since Nate and I were together last, and he had been absent more nights than not when I crept back into my room in the last week. I thought of stalking him in the graveyard, but also, boundaries. If he wanted space, then I should, reasonably, give that to him.

That didn't mean I didn't ache when I dealt with his absence.

Christ, I sound like a lovelorn poet.

Maybe someone should tank me up with whiskey and turf me into the poison garden to see how I fared in the morning.

"Before the sun sets I am little but death," Kimberly read aloud.

What in the sticky stones is that—

Oh shit. *Stop.* My brain screamed profanity that never made it to my lips as I sat stock-still in my seat.

"Those are my scribbles." I waved a careless hand even as my heart thundered in my chest.

"After shadow falls from your bequeathing breath, I am held in place by beauty and grace." She didn't pause where he did when he read those lines to me as he lay in my bed while I tried to sleep, but spent my hours watching him, face to face.

Gods, it felt like an age ago that Nathaniel and I were simply a reporter on assignment and a ghost boy sharing a bed together on top of the covers and fully clothed.

Now . . .

"This is excellent inspiration, Emma. You must become our next guest to summon her poet. Like Lacy." Kimberly's voice slid into my subconscious.

I nodded, not really listening, lost in the memory of who we were weeks ago and who we'd become now. Nate was currently locked away in the relative safety of my room.

"Sure. I mean, wait, no—" I panicked as Kimberly's smile grew wider, and her green goop dripped to the floor, tonight's show over.

Not that it mattered. They had a new centerpiece to stare at.

"Of course, you have your own pet dead poet, don't you?" she whispered.

She knows, she knows, she knows—

My brain fought its confines, an ache spreading from the top of my head in a blinding slice. I winced, pressing my fingers to the arch of my eyebrow. *Not now.* I hadn't had a migraine in months and this was not the time. Not at all. I had to concentrate.

"What was his name? Nathan. Harper?"

"Nathaniel Harker."

The correction of his name tumbled forth before I could rein the urge in, and I knew my error the moment I spoke.

Or misspoke.

Because she hadn't. Not at all.

She knew his name all along, as she always had since that day in the English lit lecture hall when I doodled his name across my page. The day Viv asked me about him, and I couldn't answer either one of them.

"Yes, the dead man and the living one. Why don't you resurrect his namesake for us, Emma? I think you should lead the next séance for us . . . tomorrow night."

"Tomorrow?" I whispered faintly.

"Tomorrow." Kimberly's fangs were on show as the sisters edged forward, their desperation reflected in the glitter in their eyes that matched hers. Even Fae shifted somewhat apologetically at my side. "Why wait? It's not like you have a captive ghost around here, right?" Her fake laugh bounced off the walls and shattered. "I might even have a few chants we can all use together. To help capture him for you, of course. Like a tiny glow bug in a jar."

The shard of her humor fell over us all as the remaining girls tittered, not hearing the crackle and crunch of her ruined humor that died a short, brittle death.

I nodded and threw on a smile deserving of Erin's pride in her star reporter.

Pulitzer, I am coming for you.

A fake séance I could pull off, if she could.

"Tomorrow it is."

*

"Don't go."

Nate cuddled my desk cactus, petting its spikes that looked somewhat the worse for wear for his additional attention.

"I can't not go. It's the job."

"The job is done."

But I can't leave you.

We stared at each other, at an impasse. I didn't know what would happen if I made Nathaniel leave the house but I had the impression that the stones needed him to stay. That somehow he was locked to this place, like Kimberly in her twisted way.

Maybe Shyleigh, Hannah and Rosa got the easier end of this—being cast out as a failed pledge could be the better route, but I was committed and I had to see this thing through. Besides, if Kimberly did something atrocious tonight, then I could add her behavior into my exposé.

The lies I told myself. I swore the walls listened and absorbed every one. The moment I left this place I'd be happier than an editor swanning about on a cutting-room floor.

"I'll be fine," I muttered. "You work on your piece, okay?"

The contract had come through from Erin. We both screamed. Nathaniel's voice made an excellent and clear soprano, actually. His hands shook as he read through the terms and with a bit of an interpretation service, we got there. Okay, a lot of one.

"Is this what you want me to do?" he'd said, skimming his gaze over the clause that defined the work.

"Isn't it what you want to do? Talk about who you are, what you wrote?"

"Or what I write," he whispered, his fingers linked in mine.

"You still shouldn't go tonight." His expression turned mulish as he changed the subject back from my *not so* sleight of hand.

If I repeated *I'll be fine* one more time, he'd find something *fine* stuck so far up his poet hole that the only words he'd be quoting for the rest of his immortal existence would all start with the letter F.

"It's a fake séance where I pretend to bring back a dead man who is already alive." I leaned over and pecked his cheek. "What's the worst that can happen?"

*

"Was that it?" Kimberly crossed her arms as my Byronesque chant that I didn't remember using to hail Nate from the poetic underworld trailed from my lips.

"Uh-huh." I toyed with the pendant at my neck that sat cold in my hand. "And I did some Brontë. I think."

Kimberly's lips actually pulled back from her teeth. "We are invoking *male* poets, Emma. Not female ones."

"Shouldn't female voices be stronger than male?" Not that I gave a shit or believed any of it at all. Hell, I could almost feel Nate's virtual eye roll from across the building even with a floor in the road. I knew he'd be seconded away within the walls, eavesdropping like a bad little ghost boy.

The corners of my mouth twitched at the thought, and Kimberly zeroed in on the movement. *Mistake.*

"The male voice has overrun us for so long," she hissed in my face, a wild-run danger noodle at the end of its too-short nope rope. "Females need to stand tall and be inspired by those who came before us!"

"You mean you want to take the voices of the past and recycle their words to fix your own ineptitude." Bitterness broke across the back of my tongue as I longed for the safety of Nate's arms and the sweetness of his gentle words. He was right; I shouldn't have come.

Some part of me who still believed in fairy tales wanted to take him and run as far as we could from this place of twisted rituals. But fairy tales never ended so well. There was always heartache, a moral at the end that ruined everything, and someone always died.

I slid my hand in my pocket, angling my phone toward her, and prayed the recording was still active. If her little temper tantrum kept going, I wouldn't have to do a thing. She'd hang herself and I'd be able to quote her verbatim.

Her sharp smile grew. "Finally, some bite." She patted my head like I was a puppy and she the proud mother. "I knew you fitted in here better than you thought."

My heart slammed into my chest. "What?"

"Didn't Erin tell you?" Kimberly walked around me in a circle, her finger on the top of my head as the other girls stared. I didn't dare move, let alone shake her off, in case I attacked her. "She was my first failed pledge. My very first walk of shame. I have a picture of her in my bedroom. It's framed. I even made her sign it."

Fuckity. No wonder she hates you.

I kept my opinions on the inside and carefully donned

my reporter hat. This was the interview of the century. But I was doing it for me, for my piece, not something someone else set me up for. "And knowing that, you let me in?"

"I wanted you here." Kimberly completed her revolution of me and tapped my nose with her pointer finger, her psychotic smile proud as poetic punch. "I knew how valuable you'd be to the sorority from your work at the paper. All those articles delving deep into the minds of others, and all while working with such a mediocre woman as Erin? And yet you still managed to stand out. Now here you are, about to hand over to me the poet of my literary dreams."

I am not your minion. But I kept that little comment locked away behind tight lips.

"With the descendant of one of our own poets you're going to raise," Lacy piped up from the staircase.

I noted she hadn't joined the circle, sitting off to one side. Kimberly hadn't mentioned banishment, exactly, but I wouldn't put that past her.

"Is that what Erin promised? That I would raise a dead man?"

"Poet," Kimberly corrected me. "No, of course not. I'm not stupid enough to believe a lie that obvious. She offered me something I couldn't possibly refuse."

I kept my snarl off my face. Just. "What's that?"

"A repeat of her first walk of shame. Before the entire campus." Kimberly paused for effect. "In daylight."

Holy shit. Erin. What did you do?

I cast about desperately for a topic of distraction and came up with ghost goop. *That'll do.*

"Nate isn't, you know, connected to the spirit realm or anything," I murmured, tugging at the pendant on my Dead Poets Sorority necklace that seemed determined to strangle me with every lie I uttered.

"But he is creative. He's on Neri with his writing." Lacy

smiled shyly, fangirling over her crush like half the campus. Apparently.

I winced internally while my heart pitter-pattered. Nate having a fan hit his personal goals. While that would please him, the attention and who it might bring to his door terrified me.

"Séance, ladies," Kimberly muttered, but Lacy wasn't done.

"Maybe he could read and summon for us."

"Well, he's his own man . . ." I deferred the line of questioning. "Maybe Kimberly can have a go at raising the ancestor?" I held out the book to her and crossed my toes in my shoes. The pages at the back that Nate had written in were blank now. I made sure of that.

"That man could rock one of those skinny leather ties, like an Eighties rock star," Lacy gabbed on.

"He's more of a cravat man." I shook my head, desperate to stop her line of thought before she went too far. "Besides, I don't think they had those in his time."

The room stopped.

Lacy slunk into the stairs as Kimberly gained at least a foot in height. I swore. Or maybe I drooped as weeks of sleep deprivation finally took their toll in magnificent fashion.

Fuckity fuck.

Kimberly had set a trap, with Lacy holding the lure, and I walked right into it.

"In his time," Kimberly repeated. "I did wonder why you were so absent when you first arrived. That night. You managed to summon him then, didn't you?"

A gasp rippled around the room. Cold tendrils brushed my arms in warning a mite too late. All this time, and the house chills hadn't been malevolent at all, like the screaming stones. The whispering, sticky stones. The warding stones.

They'd been trying to tell me something.

I hadn't listened.

Now, here we were, facing off like two opposing players over a pucking poet. Only, I didn't know where my goal posts sat, while Kimberly had hers square in her sights, with Nate positioned right between them.

"I didn't mean—" I started, my belated recovery far too late to save Nate's metaphysical ass.

"Of course you did." Kimberly returned to petting me with her talons.

I wanted to pull each of them off every time she touched me, and stick them in places that poets should never know about.

"It was a one-off event."

"Liar." She smiled, and I returned it by rote. "We've all seen him around. You even made up a nice little social profile for him. How *fake* a dead poet can he be?" Her coffee syrup tone left the house's stones screaming their latent warning and me on edge.

Someone coughed. I looked over my shoulder to find even Lacy seemingly a little green. My glance became a glare and she sank lower on her step. *Yeah, I know what you did.* She'd set a trap with Kimberly and I walked my reporter ass right into it, too desperate to get what I wanted to see the dangers that were right in front of me the whole time.

So convinced that the dangers couldn't be as bad as I thought they were.

Nate tried to warn me. The house screamed at me.

And now, too late, I listened. Now, when they all fell silent.

"What do you want?" I whispered, stretching my fingers around my pendant in a grip so tight that I expected the glass to shatter into a thousand shards that would pierce my skin at any second.

"I want him," Kimberly said simply. "I want your poet here, in this room. I want him to be mine."

I stared. Someone shifted.

"Ours," she corrected, though not a single feature on her face moved. A shiver unrelated to the house passed over me. She could have been the one without a soul for all the emotion that didn't pass through her. "We want him as our muse. Our inspiration into a new era of enlightenment. Of romanticism. A transcendence will take place."

Theft. She's talking about stealing Nathaniel's voice. Caging him and never letting him be free.

All the things he wanted, he would never be able to have now that they knew he existed.

"No." I backed up a step. "*No*," I said, louder this time. "I don't have that sort of control over him." Not an untruth, and the best I could do on the spot.

"Then you'd better figure it out. Here." Kimberly placed a stack of small, leather-bound books almost identical to our journals into my arms. Books I recognized from her personal stash at the sorority library. "You'll need these for tomorrow night. Or I'll find a way to raise your soul from the underworld. By then, it's the only way you'll see this place again."

The room hung on her every word while I gaped. Did no one else hear her threat to end my existence? Did I over-reach with that one? My hands shook on the stack of spell books I didn't need as I took the stairs past Lacy, two at a time, to reach the poet I wanted to protect above all.

He has to leave.

I have to send him back.

The heartbreak I thought we had mended together frac-tured on the spot. The pain hit me so hard that I was shocked my legs kept moving, surprised the entire room didn't hear the roar that filled my ears.

A cold touch gripped my ankle. I stared down at the small form huddled by the side of the stairs. No one else watched us. All of the sisters were too busy congratulating Kimberly on her magnificent coup de grâce in the room below.

"I'm sorry," Lacy whispered. "I didn't know."

I shook my head. "You knew."

Her hand dropped away, and I walked on alone, prepared to lose everything I thought I had gained in the world.

Sending Nate back broke every promise I'd made to him, but he had to understand. He *had to,* otherwise his existence would likely be as a pet locked away in a display case in Kimberly's bedroom, with his name on a plaque on her wall.

While I traded places with him, and played the dead part.

22

Sharing Is Caring

Bile filled my mouth as I crept into my room, and warm arms enveloped me.

"I told you not to go," he berated me desperately, pushing hair back from my face as I dropped the spell books I didn't need. *"I told you."*

"Now is when you say that you told me so?" I coughed a laugh into his shirt that might have been a sob. "Nate, you have to leave."

"No."

"She knows." I looked up at him through a sheen of salt that blurred his beautiful features. "You aren't safe. I'm sorry. I couldn't keep you safe like I promised."

He stroked my cheek. "I should have protected you from the world, not the other way around."

"I always fought against a patriarchal system." I hiccupped into his hand. *Super unsexy.*

"You run your own system, Emma. You are its queen. Don't let anyone else tell you otherwise."

"See, this is why I love you," I whispered back, my breath hitching.

His eyes darkened as he reached for me. "Fuck her."

I laughed, a hollow sound that reverberated so deep

inside me that I lost a part of myself. "Now you conquer the vernacular. Perfect."

"As are you." His tender kiss started gentle and grew deeper, fingers lacing in my hair.

The knock rattled my door in its frame.

"It's got to be her." I yanked back from him, my lips tingling. "Bed. Get under something. *Now*."

"I will not hide from her." He drew himself up.

"This is not the time to act on your ego, poet boy. I will not lose you like this," I hissed.

"Emma?" Vivian's voice echoed through the thick sorority door. "I know you're in there. Let me in. This has gone on long enough."

"Different threat. Fade," I ordered. We looked at each other, my panic reflected on his face. I flapped my hands. "Hide. Do something."

"She can't be that bad, can she?" He wrapped an arm tight around me and glanced over his shoulder at the door. "I mean . . ."

"Yes. She really can. Go. Now," I said firmly, grabbing the cupboard door and pointing.

His face fell. "The cupboard? Again?"

"Yes. Love you. Bye."

I shoved the door shut and turned my back to it, leaning on its extra-cold surface that Nate iced, because he could, as Viv barged her way in.

*

"You, stay where you are." I pointed to Vivian, who sat obediently on one side of the bear rug, then turned my attention to my poet peeking his head through the cupboard door, literally. "You, come out and wait there. No, don't even try it. You wanted to stay, so you can stay," I warned Nate when he attempted to fade into his eternal nothingness after a single look at Vivian's set jaw and flashing eyes. "If I have to face her, so do you."

The pair of them looked across the hideous shag-pile rug like the other might pluck their eyebrows or set them alight for fun. I wouldn't put anything past Vivian, who had sneaked into the sorority house after bribing the sister who nearly caught her. Working in a reverse timeline, she'd also dumped her cold coffee in the garden after finding out from Griffin at the paper that Nate wasn't really a student at Inerius, when Erin wasn't available to pester, once she hadn't been able to locate Nate in class. Any class. Because she also couldn't find me, which was when she got the coffee in the first place.

Hence the glaring across the pink faux bear, and the threat to eyebrow mortality.

To be fair, in Vivian's case the former might be true just to see what sort of reaction she would earn from him. But I liked Nathaniel's eyebrows where they were, and so I sat between them.

I'd also locked the bedroom door, and placed Vivian under a permanent vow of silence. For her part, she was still drinking in the dead man on the other side of the rug.

I considered her control admirable.

"What if—" she started, leaning forward enough to flick a finger past me to wiggle the air beyond his cravat.

Said cravat crumpled. Nate skittered backward, horror etching his face.

"No contact," I warned her. "Back to your space. I said it was an accident."

"Keeping him here wasn't."

I pursed my lips. "Given. But also, dead poet. Wouldn't you?"

Nate posed to look pretty.

"That's fair," Viv acknowledged. "And Kimberly? Is she your fault?" She peered past me, her eyes narrowed. "My girl isn't to be screwed with."

"I'm not responsible for anything." Nate held his hands up in surrender. "Also, you're scary."

"Thank you." Viv sat back, her mission accomplished.

I sighed and looked across at Nate. "Do you need to go back in the cupboard?"

His hands fell.

"I didn't think so."

Vivian smirked. "This is the cacti replacement, huh? All the things that Thomas Carlisle is not."

I winced. "We don't use those words in this room," I cautioned her. "There are . . . repercussions."

"What, like fabulous, frenzied sex after you've made up from your lovelorn tiff?" She looked between our matching, heated faces and snorted. "So freaking predictable."

"All right," I said hastily. "We are sitting in the antiverse's nest, and we need to understand what we are going to do."

"What *you* are going to do—" Vivian began to correct me, while Nate braided tiny plaits into my rug.

"Yes. That." I smiled brightly.

"—is fix this." She waved at Nathaniel, who watched her out of the corner of his eye. His mouth set in a hard line, but he didn't say anything.

Not what I wanted to hear. "I get that, but—"

"Send him back where he came from, Emma. Do the right thing." She slapped her hand on her knee.

Nate and I both jumped.

"I don't think—"

"You didn't think, and that was the problem. Don't tell me you don't know that. He shouldn't have stayed *in the first place* and now look at the mess." She stared at me in exasperation. "I freaking *knew* this had happened."

"You predicted I had drawn a dead man out of the void of eternal death?" I pursed my lips and looked at her. "I call bullshit."

"I knew you did something stupid. Falling in love with someone you can't stay with qualifies as stupid. Worse than cactus boy."

"The cactus resents that remark."

"He can't stay."

"I *know*, Viv," I snapped. "I know, all right? I don't know how to—"

"He wants to stay."

Nathaniel's quiet voice filled the room.

Viv and I blinked at him. *Owl time.*

"Or doesn't *he* get a say in his own future?"

I bit my lip and reached for Nate's hand without looking as my eyes prickled.

Itchy hands, itchy hands—

Vivian made a goose-hissing sound. "*He* can have a say in his future when it doesn't put the life of the woman he loves in mortal danger. Or hasn't she told you about that part yet?"

I studied the filth between the shag pile. "You sneaked in."

"I snuck in."

"That's not grammatically correct," I started.

"I don't care," Vivian snapped. "It's been weeks! Weeks of feeding you bagels because the boy you fell for doesn't eat! He doesn't sleep. You're exhausted. He. Is. Dead. You can't be together! Be reasonable. Please. One of you?" She stopped talking to me and beseeched the only other person in the room.

"All right."

My head snapped up so fast that the room swam. I rubbed the back of my neck, willing back the wave of nausea that would have flattened me if I hadn't already been sitting. "You don't mean that."

Nathaniel stared at me through steady gold and violet-flecked eyes. "I will do whatever it takes to keep you safe, Miss Emma."

"Swoon," Vivian muttered from across the rug.

I shushed her with a hand. "It was meant to be the other way around," I murmured, willing the tears not to come, but they did anyway. "I was supposed to look after *you*."

"And you did." He gathered me into his arms.

I settled against his chest, automatically searching for that place where his heart should beat, but didn't. "Tin man," I murmured.

"If you say so." He held me tight, then looked across at Vivian. "What do we need to do?"

She cracked her knuckles to my wince. "Project management is my skill set." Her gaze dropped to meet mine. "If you'd told me earlier, this mess would have exit strategy written all over it. But it doesn't, so we had better make one." That was as close as she would come to saying *I told you so*. I nodded my apology, knowing she wouldn't take that, either. Vivian held my gaze for a moment before her mouth softened. "Kimberly wouldn't set you up to fail. Not when she wants what you want. Show me everything."

*

Four hours later we had tried a variety of binding spells that neither worked nor incited the stones to speak to us. I figured that when we got close to something important, the little chatterboxes would do their thing. Until then, it seemed we were on our own.

Nate entertained Vivian, fading in and out of reality while she gasped and cheered quietly. The household got up around us, but no one bothered us. I figured Kimberly had given me a twenty-four-hour grace period to do what I needed, and then I was screwed.

Our ghost poet in residence offered to make me tea, but that involved him leaving the room and I refused point-blank.

He did it anyway.

Which was how we found the spell that did work—the moment he came back.

"Miss Emma, your coffee."

Vivian took it from him and maneuvered him into the little salt circle where I had removed the rug, just like the first night, as I looked straight at him from my place on the bed.

"With all that I am and all that we be, I take thy lover's power from thee. I bind you from movement, I bind you from harm. I bind you to this place, I bind you with this charm." My throat clogged. I was supposed to say the chant six more times over, but there was no way I'd get them out. Plus, I'd patchworked the whole thing together from some of my words, his and what came from Kimberly's books.

Nathaniel stared at me for a moment. He half faded, frowned, and leaned forward. One step out of the circle that strained every muscle, and his gaze drew back to mine, oh so slow.

"Emma. What did you do?"

I closed my eyes as tears slid down my cheeks. "I locked you to the house in full. I think. So you ca-can't leave." A hiccup of monumental proportions choked me as he sank to the floor and landed on it. He didn't disappear through the boards. He didn't fade or run or sink or any of the things independent Nate might do.

I'd made him my dead boy poet pet.

It wasn't even funny or cute.

"I'm sorry," I rasped, sliding from the bed. The spell book dropped onto the floor. I ignored it and crawled to him.

"Stay away," he muttered, forcing his body to turn from mine.

"I'm sorry—"

"Stay away from me," he growled.

I cast a desperate look at Vivian, whose face reflected the pain he experienced, though her expression was laced with determination.

"Take it off," she whispered. "Let him be free."

I wanted to keep apologizing, but I picked up the next spell book and trawled through it instead. "I don't know how."

Nate's drawn, panicked face would haunt me forever. No matter what the end result of this revolting, ridiculous day was, how he looked at me now *hurt*.

"I'll find it," I whispered, flicking frantically through the pages until I came to what I thought was the opposite spell and added my own words.

"Emma, it's not working," Nate said tightly. "This hurts." He pressed a hand to his chest as though he couldn't breathe.

Not that he didn't need to, but couldn't—something.

"This one requires candles." Vivian yanked open my desk drawers and rummaged through their contents. Failing to find any, she grabbed my cactus, sat it in the middle and wrote his initials on it. "I'm sorry," she apologized, and lit the tip. "Chant, bish," she muttered.

I chanted, fast and frantic, reaching for him. Our

fingertips touched and he tumbled forward, right over the puddle of fast-melting cactus.

"Fuckity!" I yanked him sideways and we sprawled together in a pile of soggy, sweaty poet and limbs that seemed to connect to more than two people at once. "I never want to do that again. It was so wrong."

"Wrong, absolutely. Don't do it again." Nate cupped my face and kissed me hard.

The room disappeared. Everything disappeared. I could have been in the void with him and I wouldn't have had a clue, all because this impossible man didn't want to leave me.

His heart might not beat, but mine cantered on at double time, racing enough for both of us.

"When you're ready," Vivian muttered as we broke apart.

I panted softly, unable to look her way. Actually, I didn't want to. All my remaining minutes needed to be spent on Nate. Viv could wait.

"I'm not," I breathed.

"Me neither." Nate squeezed my hands. "But for you, we do this."

"That's a terrible reason."

He kissed me again. "Better?"

"Uh, sure?" I blinked up at him.

Vivian snorted. "Wake up, Emma. We don't have a lot of time."

Damn my ex-roomie for a reality check we both definitely needed way too much.

Nate touched his forehead to mine. "I'll be back soon."

"What? No, don't you *dare*—"

Viv and I were alone in the room.

"Damn dead ghost boy."

"Who you'll join if you don't figure out a way to fix this," Vivian rolled on with her commentary. "Binding spell."

"Got that."

"The original summoning."

"That too." I hefted the notebook—my notebook, not the one that Kimberly gave me.

"And a banishing spell." Vivian passed over an extra spell book, open to a middle-ish page, without looking at me.

"Where did you get that?" I gaped at the spell I'd seen in the sorority library weeks before, and my stomach plummeted.

A ritual to cast out unwanted spirits from a dwelling.

"It was in the pile. Start doctoring that baby up and hide it."

"What? Why?"

"Because." She tsked at me. "Your ghost boy might change his mind. Kimberly might storm the room. The sisters might steal you away a few hours early."

"Might, might, might," I muttered, affecting one of Nate's sulks.

"Oh, you do love him, don't you? No, no waterworks. Be strong. Fall apart after he's gone. Expose the sorority. Goals, girl."

I stared at her, right through her determination and saw—

Nothing but more determination.

"How do you do that?"

"I am a cyber machine from the future." She winked. "No, really, I'm looking forward to the drama. I've ticked my ghost poet box for the day, I might get to see a banishing in process, and I'll have my first therapy client for the next decade or more after this. What more could a girl need?"

I sniffled. "How about a best friend who's about to crack and crumble because she can't do this?"

Vivian squeezed my arm. "We can do this. Promise."

"You need to leave." Nate squeezed through the stones and stood behind Vivian, his brow dipped, every curl wild.

Her eyes bugged for a second before she reclaimed her calm at the surprise ghost-boy attack. "Why?" She turned sedately on her heel, and I knew she was an inch from slapping him with the melted cactus. "We need to have a talk about your ghost etiquette."

"The sisters are barricading the house. Did you come in through the front door?" He waved a hand behind him in a vague fashion that I'd become used to, though his tone drove a sense of urgency through us all.

"I didn't crawl through the cat flap," Vivian replied tartly.

"Go, now." I squeezed her tight.

"Remember the list," she whispered and slipped out the door, checking in both directions before she crept away down the hall.

"Should you follow her?" I locked it behind her, resting my head against Nate's chest. His hands sank over my waist and I knew every moment I didn't send him back was utter folly, as well as selfish as hell. *Definitely picking up all the ghost poet lingo.* But I also couldn't bring myself to send him back yet.

"Wait for me," he murmured, and slipped back into the small spaces where the sisters couldn't find him.

Moments later he returned and laced his fingers through mine, towing me toward the window. "Count for me."

I gave him a glance that said he was out of his dead poet mind, but he wasn't looking.

Campus appeared the same to me—students wandering about the grounds, milling like so many ants with their important purposes, while we were locked away in our tower room. An attempt to leave at this point would hurt only one of us, and I could survive Kimberly's wrath. Maybe.

Nate, on the other hand . . .

I squeezed my eyes shut just as he nudged me. "See?"

Vivian waved her phone at me, pointing at the device she held above her head from where she popped out from behind a giant blackberry shrub.

"Oh, crap. Where is my—"

Nate passed me my phone as it vibrated.

Vivian: Do it. Now, Emma. This is one you'll regret forever.

I stared at the screen, the device creaking in my hand, and I wanted to dash it into the wall just to see how many pieces it made when it shattered, all because I knew she was right.

But which path leads to regret the most?

Sending him back and losing him, or keeping him and wondering forever if I did it wrong?

Miserable, heartbroken and grieving in advance, I tossed my phone onto my desk and let Nate lift me off my feet. He curled with me on my bed. "We can't stow you away in the graveyard? You should go." I wrapped my arms around him. "Hide somewhere they can't find you. Be you. Be beautiful. Amazing."

"No." He kissed my temple. "I will not leave you."

I nodded. "I won't leave you, either." *Not until we have to.*

The borrowed minutes stretched out. His kisses grew more urgent, the edge of desperation tanged to his sweet, leather and soap taste. I let him lie me back, let him steal more minutes as his body glided over mine. The distraction was perfect.

What could have been tears and heartache transformed into an hour or more of the sort of slow lovemaking that left my body zinging with need and tender from his moments of roughness.

I devoured every touch, memorized him as much as he did me. Every soft sound he made, the light kisses that caressed my bare skin. How his strange eyes darkened like midnight before the storm.

"I want to go with you," I tried, arching up into him.

Hands fisted my hair as he drove his hips deep, his mouth muffling my cry, and stilled. "No, Emma. Not to that place. Not for someone like you."

"What's wrong with me?" I begged, digging my nails into his shoulders, then letting go when I realized I'd marked him.

"You are so alive," he rasped, and his mouth crashed over mine until the midnight star-fall in his eyes consumed me.

He held me afterward, too, his touch tender. The perfect, attentive lover. I shivered, pressing myself closer as I rested my head on his bare shoulder. "I'm glad your friend left."

"She'll shred me after this. Or send me off with a section 12 order. To a psychiatric ward. An asylum," I clarified when he watched me, still bemused.

"You would make sources of all the inmates, learn every one of their stories," he murmured, tracing my lips with the pad of his thumb.

"Story . . ." I closed my eyes and flapped a palm at my desk. "Oh, hell. Vivian may have to take a number. Erin will— I haven't sent in . . ."

"I'm sure she'll understand." Something in his voice turned me from my frantic search for my phone.

"You were listening," I accused him.

"From within the walls. A . . . safe space." He enunciated the words carefully as he traced a hand through my bangs and tucked a wayward one behind my ear. "Show me what you wrote. Let's fix this part."

"You want to help me write the article?" I stared at him.

"Now?" The sun had almost set. Another night's sleep lost, but I didn't care. Nothing unimportant mattered right now. "It's so close . . ." A lump built in my throat. "Nate, I'm not ready to say goodbye."

"Then don't, not yet." He held me gently and placed my phone in my hands. "Call your friend. Be beautiful for me. In every way. Not how you look." He soothed the inevitable argument that sprang to my lips, impending doom or not. "But in all things, you are so very beautiful. I have no more words." He kissed me again and my body, still tangled with his, jellified.

"All right, you win." I laced our hands together and squeezed his fingers then sent a message off to Erin.

Emma: I'm going to be late sending my submission. Something catastrophic came up.

Erin: Like your fake boyfriend's pending exile to her cave of horrors?

Emma: Does everyone know?

Erin: Vivian came by. You have two days. Make it spectacular.

Emma: I know what she did to you. She'll do the same thing to Nate.

Erin: . . .

Erin: Then make it count.

She didn't reply straight away. I sighed while Nate scrolled through my article over my shoulder. Just as I had given up on Erin as a done deal, my phone vibrated again.

That was it. All I got back from my badass editor who took Kimberly on and survived. I'd have to wrangle that story out of her another time. Right now, I had a ghost boy to banish. I really couldn't put it off any longer.

"You put everything we are into this."

I twisted on one elbow to look back at him. "Huh? Oh, article. For context. I was painting Kimberly as the bad guy. That was the original brief. But also, for heart . . ." I trailed off at the heat emanating off Nathaniel. The necklace at my throat tightened and I tugged at the ribbon. "Is it that bad?"

"You've put us into this story without my permission, Emma."

No Miss Emma. For all the times I requested he use plain old *Emma*, suddenly, now, I missed the minor honorific.

"It's an introduction," I reassured him quickly.

"Do you always display your love life so overtly?" he growled, one hand gripping my bare hip.

It didn't escape me that we were having this fight while naked, if under a light bedsheet.

"No, this would be the first time." I frowned. "I can take it out."

"But you were going to submit it as is. What will you do with my words once I am gone? Will they also go under your name, as Kimberly would have you do?"

340

I gaped at him, my blood running as icy as the hot chocolates he used to freeze when he sulked. "No. *No.* I would never do that to you, or to anyone else. Mind, I also wouldn't put my own work up under someone else's name and blindside them in class so they ended up having their work thrown up on the screen when I had *no choice* that day. I had no idea how to react to that!" I ranted, weeks of exhaustion and pent-up emotion boiling over.

Nathaniel made an all-male noise in the back of his throat as he gathered me close. "Did they like it?" he murmured, watching me carefully.

"Loved it," I admitted, grudgingly. My rage cooled somewhat. "But you shouldn't have done it without asking me."

"Kind of my point."

Too late the penny dropped on an inept poet wannabe. Me, not him. Because he outclassed us all, by far.

"Oh," I said in a small voice. "I'm sorry."

"Good girl." He tapped my nose with the tip of his finger and followed that confusing move up with a kiss that left me boneless beneath him.

"Those two words should be illegal," I muttered. "I'll change the article. I promise. And your words will remain yours forever. I'll—" I didn't want to go into the legal ramifications of copyright when I had a different ritual to perform. "I'll make sure you're protected. Please, Nate." Suddenly, it was so critical he heard me that my chest cramped. "Do you trust me with this?"

He cupped my cheeks in those long-fingered hands I loved and rested his forehead against mine.

"There is no one I would trust more than I do you."

Messages of Breath and Light

We dressed each other slowly. Nathaniel went first, picking out the sweater dress I wore on the night I met him, tugging the stretchy material over my head. He fluffed my hair around my shoulders, pressing kisses to my bare skin until every part of me was covered and then he found my mouth again. Finally, I pushed him away with reluctant hands, and worked on his shirt and pants.

Whoever said undressing their partner was the most intimate of moments never tried the action in reverse.

He stood still while I drew the front panels of soft cotton together, then worked on his pants. Finally, I looped his cravat around his neck, and tied it neatly as he'd shown me on many occasions.

"I don't think I've ever seen anything sexier than a woman who knows how to handle my cravat," he murmured, a smile in his voice as he watched me with the sort of longing I knew was reflected in my own eyes.

"I promise that's going on a shirt."

"You can't replace Lois."

"She's well and truly coffee-stained at this point." I patted his cravat. "You're all done."

He held out the small book with my adjusted banishment spell bookmarked in its pages. "I trust you."

I stared down at the tiny square of tooled leather, and shook my head. "I can't do this, Nate. I can't send you back to that— to that—" *Literal hell.* A place he had said pulled his soul away and left what remained of him falling. *Forever.* "No." I backed away.

He strode forward. "And I won't let them take your light from this world, Emma. You are the most wonderful creature I've ever beheld. Stay, and live," he whispered. "Write all the things I cannot. Amaze and bemuse. Shock, and ruin their expectations. Win your Pulitzer Prize."

"You are too much, Nathaniel Harker."

The corner of his lips quirked. "Wait until you find the stack of sonnets under your mattress." His arm looped around my waist as he drew me into him, his hold unbreakable. "Near your pillow. I added one for every day I was here, waiting for you."

"So many hours wasted." My stomach fell into freefall at the horror of it. "Nate—"

"Shhh, Miss Emma. Make this a beautiful choice."

"Why must you be so damn grown-up?" I whimpered into his shirt.

"I am two hundred years older than you."

"If we're counting."

"There's that spinster I fell for. The woman everyone wants to be, but who holds herself untouchable." He rocked me gently side to side as I hiccupped into his shirt. Minnie curled around his ankles and rubbed her head against his shins. I didn't begrudge her interruption.

"Not a spinster."

"You'd better not stay one." He looked at me seriously. "Emma. Listen to me. I need you to love. Be loved. Offer your love. Fall in love. Many times. Leave your heart open. Let it be broken, because without that risk how will you know if there is true love around you?"

His fingers massaged the back of my neck. I made a strange, strangled sound at the back of my throat. "You make saying goodbye impossible."

"Then don't say goodbye," he whispered. "Tell me that you love me. Read the words. Keep my poems. One is for you, and you alone."

I glanced back at the bed. "Will I find it in the pile?"

He smiled, tracing the line of my jaw with his thumb. "I hid it on your phone. You'll find it, don't worry. I'm not that talented a hacker."

"Smart-ass."

"Probably."

He stepped back into the circle of salt. "Read, Emma. Before they come for you."

I nodded at the sense in his words, knowing that Vivian would approve. "Are you sure?" I stalled, still seeking a fresh option. Any option, other than this. Starting the incantation seemed so . . . permanent.

He nodded his silent brand of encouragement as I let out a last, restricted breath, then started.

And stopped.

Instead, Nathaniel's voice filled the room, smooth and sweet and heady.

> *"A month's moon I waited and she*
> *came to me each night,*
> *Serenaded by whispered words hidden in the stones,*
> *Her mind ablaze with wondrous light*
> *And I made of naught but borrowed flesh*
> *and bone—"*

"Do you really think now is the best time?" I gasped, letting my inappropriate giggles crash into the sobs that broke free.

Golden flecks spun in a violet galaxy. "Time means little if there is naught but love to wield it."

"Stop," I grumbled half-heartedly. "Or I'll quote you in the article."

He grinned; both of us knew this part would remain forever omitted, and never make it to Erin's desk, or any other.

"I love you, Emma Reeves. Please, serenade me into the darkness." His smile remained, though the shadows behind his eyes beckoned, inviting.

My voice stuck in my throat as I began the chant. Seven times I was supposed to read the incantation through. I wondered if, like with the binding spell, it would only require a single pass to take effect.

"Goodbye, thy fiend, I tell you to go,

When you will not listen when I say to you no,

No longer welcome, I bid you decay,

Never again to see the light of this day,

I send you away, unwelcome spirit.

Turn from me and enter the darkness.

Turn away, be forever set free

To roam in the realm so far away from me."

My voice cracked on the last cruel word. Nathaniel didn't waver but offered me an encouraging nod. I swallowed hard and started again.

"Goodbye, thy fiend . . ."

I hated that the words didn't match who he was at all,

but misrepresentation was the least of my worries tonight. Nathaniel twitched within the salt confines as I spoke, his teeth clenched.

I'm doing this to him. Causing him pain.

My words faltered, died.

"Be strong, my spinster," he whispered. Even now, his strange sense of humor glimmered through the darkness where I'd send him with no chance of bringing him back. "Serenade me with your curse, dear maiden I love," he murmured. Glittering eyes met mine, and he stole my breath for another reason entirely.

Somewhere in the house's lower levels, a different chant rose, shimmering along the foundations until the entire building trembled.

"The sisters have started." My mouth hung open as I crumpled the spell book in my hands. *I waited too long.*

"Then hurry, my Lois," he whispered. "Send me away and dream unholy thoughts."

Any other time, I would have giggled and started a ghost boy tickle fight at the risk of sliming my mortal soul. Right now, I wanted to crash-tackle him out of the circle and rub salt in a thousand cuts on Kimberly's skin.

"I send you away, unwelcome spirit—" My words clashed with whatever ritual Kimberly invoked downstairs.

The house shook with the dichotomy of my banishment spell and her summoning that clashed on the same plane all at once over the same soul. Nathaniel dropped to one knee, fading from sight as my heart leaped into my throat, only to snap back into existence at a level of clarity that seemed less real than anything I'd seen from him before.

But all the more solid and real for its unreality.

"Keep going," he rasped, forcing himself to stand. One hand reached for me, or perhaps to push me away.

Every movement strained, as though he walked under water.

"It's working," I gasped.

He nodded, pushing against an invisible barrier. "Don't stop, Miss Emma." His voice was barely audible above the shaking building. A paw slipped out from inside the cupboard. Even with her ethereal powers, it seemed that Minnie wanted little to do with this next part. I didn't blame her.

Stay safe, phantom feline. The thought of losing them both at once shattered my freshly cracking heart.

My hair lifted away from my face in a static effect, and his curls wafted about of their own volition. The turmoil started slow, but as I chanted through my rounds of the banishment spell, the internal storm roiled until I screamed the words, my voice long turned hoarse.

"Don't stop," he spoke as the room stilled.

Quietened.

He flickered again.

Gone, then not.

My heart shattered.

"Nathaniel," I begged, my cheeks damp as he smiled.

The smile of a dead man who knew he could not live.

"No—"

A roar filled the house as every girl below our floor chanted louder. Cold tendrils worked their way along my ankles, up my knees and along my wrists, their devastating ache luring me forward. I broke from my stasis, and stumbled into Nate's circle.

"Don't go," I sobbed. "I need you."

"This is who we are." He kissed the tip of my nose, the barest contact that left me with a fresh ache I knew would never heal.

"Who we should be together," I begged, gripping his hands tight as he faded before me, wavering in and out of this existence.

One breath I held, then another. A child's wish that all would be well.

"Say the words, my Emma," he murmured, stroking my hair back from my face.

I whispered words I'd already said six times through numbed lips, no longer hearing them, though he seemed to understand my meaning, regardless of what I said. How I said it, how many times.

"You might free my soul, but I bind my heart to yours, always," he whispered in my ear. Cool lips brushed the corner of mine and then—

Below us, the girls' chants grew to a crescendo. The entire house rattled, but theirs were not the only voices that made up the white noise I shouted above. The stones had woken, adding their own chatter to the cacophony.

It comes, it comes, it comes—

Away, away, away.

He was gone. Then not. Back again.

My heart strained in my chest.

I shook my head to free myself of the overwhelm but it refused to dissipate.

"Keep reading," Nathaniel called, his voice rising above the chaos as the whirlwind buffeted us both. His arms banded about me tight. *So real.* "Don't stop!"

"Goodbye, thy fiend, I tell you to go—"

Was this the seventh, or the eighth? Which iteration was I on? Did it matter? I'd keep reading until the spell worked. That was the plan, right? I started my chant again as the voices from downstairs ramped it up another notch. Minnie darted around the outside of the circle in a lapis neon blur and disappeared beneath my bed. The house rocked, as though it had grown legs and lifted from the very foundations to walk away across campus and settle beside the gravestone bearing his name.

It comes, it comes, it comes—
The darkness, it comes—
"No longer welcome, I bid you decay," I gasped.

Nathaniel's smile strained for the first time, his form wavering as the stones screamed together. And yet, when I stopped chanting and he spoke, I heard him as though the storm slid us into its eye. We stood in the center of calm, granted a moment's pure reprieve amidst the chaos.

"Turn away, be forever set free, to roam in the realm so far away from me—"

He gazed at me, his eyes full of pure yearning, for all he could have had, all the should-have-beens. It wasn't fair that this was what was taken from him now, when he could have been so much *more*—

"I love you," I whispered, my words run dry as he formed solid, as real and human and *alive* as any man.

Soft lips brushed mine, his eyes a swirl of golden stardust on a bed of moonlight.

"I am dead, and you are—"

His form flickered. Darkness filled the salt circle I had broken.

With nothingness.

"Nathaniel!" I screamed.

That strange, quiet moment resumed, and he was gone.

My final chant collided with Kimberly's, and the house could take no more. Its foundations groaned, the stones screamed, and everything around me turned to nothing but a cacophony of screams before the entire building rocked like it would never be still again.

I clung to the floor, my throat raw with Nathaniel's name on my lips, but I knew he wouldn't—or couldn't—return that the space in the circle would remain empty. The air within shimmered as I strained toward it while the house gave one final, almighty shiver, lurching to its deepest original foundations.

And then fell still.

Even the stones stopped screaming. Not a single whisper left them, like they, too, were muted, their voices torn away by our clashing spells.

Silence filled the air around me, and it was worse than anything else. Because Nathaniel Harker was gone. It was as though when the magic was stripped from the walls of the house, all his presence left too.

And though my body shook and trembled in the aftermath, knowing that Nathaniel would never come back was worse.

So, so much worse.

I clung to the floor and wished the stones would talk to me once more.

But they didn't.

All the Promises I'll Never Break

I choked on the silence of sticky stones in a void of magic that pummeled my eardrums well after the event ended. Every part of me ached but seemed numb at the same time. A gray haze covered the upper floor, so thick that for a moment I thought I was back in the graveyard, about to be accosted by wisps.

I reached out in front of me and grasped nothingness.

But the air wasn't cool enough for that. My hands slapped downward, and hit the tattered bear rug. My vision cleared a touch as I blinked exhausted eyes. Somewhere beyond the house, the campus tower clock struck an early hour of the morning. Not dawn, not yet, but not far off, either.

The false dawn. That's why I couldn't see. Everything looked the same. But without Nathaniel here, what did any of it matter? My butt hit the floor next to the bear's head that looked distinctly out of sorts. Its eyes didn't sit straight anymore, and some of its teeth were missing.

"Hard night," I muttered.

It didn't reply.

Probably a good thing. I didn't have the heart to destroy any more possessed creatures.

My heart compressed on that thought. I leaned over, one

hand clutched to my stomach, though I didn't retch or puke like I thought I might. The floor lurched, or maybe it was me. Footsteps pounded the hall outside my room, rushing up or down—I didn't care.

No one screamed; no one raised an alarm of any sort. Somewhere downstairs, something cracked. I remembered the way the building creaked and rocked at its foundations. *I'm probably not safe here.* But I couldn't bring myself to care. At least Vivian had gotten herself out earlier. I could call that one a win. Someone I cared about.

The house dropped away, leaving me lost inside my head. For a solid minute, my only companions were my chaotic, jumbled thoughts. I wondered if I had been the one who fell into the void, rather than Nathaniel.

Nathaniel.

The slicing loss of him hit home in full. I slapped the salt-singed bear too hard. It flattened out. More collateral damage. Everything I touched died. Like my poet boy. "No—" I choked on a tang of metal and salt.

I loved him.

And it hurt. So damn much to know he was gone. Hell, was he any safer there than here? I'd never know.

Tears stung my eyes. Every part of me itched, a thousand cuts like the ones I had wished on my enemy biting at my arms. The air was loaded with the death of magic where Kimberly's spell collided with mine. Instead of charging the house with extra juice, it was like the cataclysm stripped everything away, leaving everything in it—including people—bereft of life. I'd been standing right in the middle of the stone and salt circle when the spells collided.

Or exploded.

Whatever the hell we did. We broke something.

Hearts. Minds. Morals.

The world.

I didn't give a shit. I'd lost him. Everything.

My palms hit something sharp. Some of the stone wall along the edge of my room had crumbled. I slapped my palm on the pile of rubble a second time, then a third, taking the pain in and storing it. That would bruise tomorrow.

An obscured figure wandered out of the haze in the hall, beyond my door that hung crooked on its hinges, toward me.

"Fuck off, Kimberly. You've done what you set out to do." I ran my fingers through the fine, dry strands of my hair as I sat on my pathetic shag-pile rug. *Nathaniel used to flirt with me here, all stretched out, and smile that secret smile of his.*

I bit back a laugh at the memory. *Inappropriate, Emma.* Maybe I could add a paragraph or two to the article. Good thing I emailed that off as a backup before we cast the salt circle. Who knew how that would have corrupted the file.

I couldn't think of the B word. It hurt too much.

Voices called out, permeated the haze surrounding me. Maybe if I strained hard enough and blocked out the world, I could hear him, too, like I had the stones. Once. Then I remembered that they had stopped talking to me, at least for now. Maybe they were in shock at what I'd done. Just like he had been. The betrayal on his face tore at me, though I didn't want to let the memory of him go.

Thinking of him hurt, too.

The footsteps neared. I found a rock with a sharp edge, ready to hurl it, but my hand lay limp on a pile of stone dust as though it didn't belong to me. My fingers opened and the stone tumbled out.

"Go away," I managed. "You've done enough."

Voices called out from below, torch lights searching

through the haze. I ignored them all. I shook my head, but the words someone said over my head didn't make it to me.

After a few breaths, that faded a little, I coughed up a few spots of blood that seemed to originate from where I'd bitten my tongue at some point. I swirled the bright red about in my palm and it stained the skin, melding with the gray stone matter.

"Out, out, damn spot." I tried to mangle the quote, and didn't do half as bad a job as I hoped.

Nothing worked the way it should. I didn't care.

"Hell is murky. But I don't think that's the way to scrub your sins away, dear spinster."

The words sank into my overcooked brain as I processed the voice. Dusty bare feet appeared in my field of vision before my head jerked up—and up.

To the tan breeches beneath the filthy frock coat so much worse for wear, though not more than its owner. His shirt hung in tatters, displaying a whole lot more chest than I was used to seeing. The new dawn light wavered through the haze filtering into my room, past the shattered stones, the ruined circle where I had banished him.

Through the cries and sobs and conversation from the floor below that I ignored, I stared into a face I barely recognized yet knew all the same. His corkscrew hair hung in every direction, and a smear of dark fluid crossed one cheek. But his eyes—

Those were the darkest brown, filled with sorrow and understanding and love. Eyes I could fall into and never emerge from again.

"Nathaniel?" I craned back as he scooped two strong, long-fingered hands beneath my arms and lifted me to my shaky feet.

His hands never left me as I cataloged every inch of

him, noting the pale skin, the warmth of him, the way he smiled—sweet and all him, yet wary.

As though he didn't know me, and was scared of my reaction to him.

Conversation went on vaguely around us, as though a great crowd gathered, although I neither saw nor really heard them. Those people stood at a distance to us. We remained in the center of our own void, a place of swirling peace, a pace apart.

I raised trembling hands to graze over his cheeks. "How are you here?" I whispered. The muted crash and thud of ambulances and paramedics hit me hard, or at least, the absence of their noise did. "Wait, are you here?" I had to say goodbye? *Again?* "Don't be cruel."

"I'm here, Miss Emma," he murmured, resting his forehead against mine as he held me close, tucked into his body.

"Just Emma." My hands slid up the tattered remains of, his ruined shirt, inside his frock coat. "You can't be. I sent you back."

"And yet here I am." His crooked smile did strange things to my heart. *Hope.* That indelible emotion that I wished I'd banished along with him. Only, I hadn't banished him. Not properly.

"I think we broke the world, or a small part of it."

"Probably." He tilted his head so that when he spoke, his breath brushed my lips, so close he almost kissed me, but not quite. "I was here, then gone. I was . . . elsewhere. Nowhere. Falling for so long. And then I was back."

"I'm sorry," I whispered. "I sent you away."

"You did as you needed to do, Emma. Now I am with you," he said, drawing me closer.

My impossible dead poet.

"You're not supposed to be here," I muttered, my headspace still messed up. "I screwed up."

"Are you upset because you failed to send me back?" He stroked my cheek, his newly deep brown eyes drinking me in.

"Is this the color they always were? Back then, before you—" My words stalled in my chest. In all the weeks we'd been together, I never asked what color his eyes were when he was alive.

"Before? They were dark." He brushed warm lips against my cheek, pressed his first kiss to the corner of my mouth. "Believe, Emma. It is okay to believe."

"Hope hurts," I said flatly. "I know I hit my head. I know I want you back so much I'm hallucinating. Or dreaming. Vivian will have a field day with this." I groaned, pressing my hand to his bare chest beneath his singed shirt even as I pushed up onto my toes and let my breath mingle with his to the measure of his slow, steady heartbeat.

Breath.

Heartbeat.

I yanked my hand back as a yelp ripped from my lips. His hands, locked around me, didn't let me get far.

"You— You're—?"

"I'm here." He held me tight, and crushed me to his chest. I closed my eyes, memorizing the sound of his heart reverberating inside his chest. "I don't understand, Nate. Are you still—"

"I'm me, Emma. You sent me away. They brought me back."

"But you were gone." I frowned. "It can't have been that easy."

His smile slipped. "Not quite so easy. They gave me a choice." His eyes turned pensive and I *knew* it was him.

Then his words hit home. "They?" He had never mentioned anyone else in the spaces between before.

Nathaniel watched me with those brown eyes I both knew and didn't.

"The stones," he said simply.

My mouth opened. I started to say something, then remembered the absence of the stones' voices, and shut my mouth again, nodding instead. "Okay."

His lips turned up at the edges. Not a lot, but his secret smile returned. "I must remember to be banished more often if it makes you this amicable," he murmured.

"Don't you dare."

"Cross my heart," he said seriously. "The stones . . . They offered me two paths. One, to remain here, but not. Or to come back."

I blinked at him. "I don't understand." Maybe the magic ate my brain cells too or made my synapses die out. "Please be obvious."

"I didn't understand either. We . . . talked . . . for some time," he said in a stilled voice that I knew meant he didn't have the words to describe what he had seen. And if Nathaniel Harker had run out of words, then we were in trouble. "They told me I could stay as part of this place, drift between the spaces in the cracks, the walls. Be here, but not. It's . . . difficult." He sighed. "I wouldn't always be here, more a voice in the walls." He leaned in to touch the walls and I let out a cry.

"Don't! They're silent," I warned him, but his hand was already pressed to the broken stone.

Nathaniel's head bowed. A moment later, he looked up at me. "They're talking now." He held out his hand. Reluctant to feel the sticky stones silent and dry as they had been before, I let him capture my palm and place it to the stones.

Back back back

Home stay stay stay

I breathed out. "They're talking."

He nodded.

I managed to inhale properly as my room began to

brighten. "And the second choice they offered you?" I scooted closer to him.

"The second." He stared down at me, his dark eyes fathomless, unreadable. "They offered to allow me to remain as I was. As I am. The cost is my immortality. I return as you see me now."

I raised a shaking hand. "You get to live the life you wanted to have that was taken from you?"

"Yes." He nodded.

"But you gave up the chance to see life forever. To see everything, always from inside here. But you chose . . . mortality. Again?" I stroked the stones like an old friend and they whispered to me.

He nodded again. "Yes."

No limits. Eternity over a short life, even entrapped. It was a choice few could make.

"Why would you do that?"

He reached out to cup my cheek. "Because of you."

My first tear fell, unbidden. "Nathaniel," I whispered.

And then he held me as the world returned, busy and chaotic, running feet and rushing sisters. We left the house that crumbled and creaked and chattered around us, even if no one else seemed to hear it except for Nathaniel and myself. Then we stood outside, his arms wrapped around me as students gathered.

Photos were taken. More people on campus than I'd seen at any point asked questions and poked at us and shouted but I didn't answer any of them. My reporter hat had nothing to do with today. I didn't care. Neither did he, warding them away as he held me tight to his chest while we stood below a house of cracked stone, and let everyone else be frantic around us for once.

Without us.

And not once did he let me go.

Not even when Erin and Vivian launched themselves at me in a dual full-body attack. Nathaniel gently pried them off me as Vivian whispered, *"I told you so,"* and I returned, *"Bullshit."*

Erin burst our safety bubble first. "Where's the batshit-crazy bitch?"

I didn't want to think about Kimberly, or her contingent of dead-poet-thieving sisters. "I don't want to see her ever again." Apparently, I was still in the dead poets denial crew. "Please fetch me a sandbox so I can bury my head for the next decade. I don't want to face the world."

"That won't be very productive." Nate tsked me. "You won't be very nice if you're not writing."

"Truth." Erin pointed a finger at him. "That needs to go on a shirt. Or a mug."

"Agreed." Vivian pecked my cheek and patted Nate's frock coat. A plume of stone dust decorated the air between us. "I'm going to sort Kimberly out. She won't be bothering anyone for a long time. I got you, boo. And you. Be good to our girl." She fixed Nate with a hard stare that had ashed mere mortals.

He winked.

I coughed to hide my giggle while her eyes narrowed. "Play nice," I reproved him. "She's saving our asses."

"No hat?" Nate patted my head.

Erin looked confused. "I received your article. You'd better give me full exclusives. And you," she added to Nate as Griffin appeared at her side. "I expect to see you at the next Monday morning meeting. Your voice is . . ." She made a chef's kiss gesture and wiggled her assets.

Nate watched with interest until I poked him. "That sounds . . . interesting?" He looked down at me.

"You don't need my permission. You're your own man," I said softly, then frowned. "Oh, hell. Questions. We need a write-up on the sorority. Something appropriately vague but satisfying by tonight." Erin gave me an approving nod. Panic built in my chest on a different front. "I have no idea how to make you real, Nate."

"You did." He kissed the tip of my nose.

"No, you don't understand," I hissed. "You don't exist—"

"Sure he does." Griffin held out his phone. "See? He's got an employment contract with *The Actum*. Erin has co-signed. I can alter other things, too. We can arrange something?" He looked at me shiftily, then away. "Ah, student number, transferred in from across the coast last week. I backdated it. Say, you want a roommate? I sleep weird hours and I can teach you programming languages."

"I don't think I remember what sleep is." Nate tipped his head on one side. "Would you like to know how to write a sonnet?"

"I'll try anything, bro." Griffin held out his hand and they bro-bumped.

"What just happened?" I asked Erin.

"Your boy exists." She looked on in awe. "He's kind of addictive."

"And he's mine."

"Share," she reproved me. "On Mondays, he's ours."

"For an hour." I squeezed Nate's waist. "Otherwise, this *not so* dead poet is all mine. The sorority can go to hell."

"I don't think they'll be much of a problem." She nodded over my shoulder.

I peered through the clearing haze to where Vivian talked quickly to a single waiting paramedic she seemed to know, whose hand was resting on Kimberly's head where the latter was strapped to a stretcher. Apparently, the downstairs group took a much worse hit than I had, with their ceremony.

The failed pledges who had been walked out of Phi Omega House surrounded both Vivian and the paramedic, chattering away faster than the poor woman could take notes.

On the stretcher, Kimberly stirred. Vivian patted her head. I started to ask if she was okay, then changed my mind. *Not today Emma's problem.*

Plus, Viv promised she'd take care of that threat. I trusted her to take one for the team.

Phi Omega House would take on a change of leadership after this. The whole of Kimberly's cadre would take a clean sweep, most likely, if I got the page time and headlines I'd be begging Erin for, not to mention the thank-yous that were due in her corner after what she offered in order to gain me time in the Dead Poets Sorority.

Nathaniel broke me out of my reverie, his arms wrapped around my waist as he chatted with Griffin about weird, normal boy stuff, interspersed with the odd, archaic reference. His chin rested on the top of my head while Erin mumbled notes at me about the next run of articles and how we could cover everything in a major bumper edition.

I was good with everything but for right now, the white noise swept around me, warded away by the very alive poet who stroked his fingers through my hair and tucked me against his warm chest that housed his beating heart for the first time in two centuries.

Eventually, while they all chattered between themselves, he leaned down, brushing his lips across the shell of my ear.

"You are beautiful, and I'm not dead. I know what we should do this late summer eve," he whispered.

I tipped my head back and met his mouth with mine.

"You never did make good on that promise, poet boy," I murmured.

"A new promise now, my Emma." His eyes glowed dark, and for the briefest second they reflected gold and purple in the strange light before he kissed me.

Perhaps there was a little bit of the ghost boy left in my poet after all.

EPILOGUE

Vivian

When Wishes Granted Equal the

Destruction of Dreams

My patient murmured insensible things as I checked over her vitals. Too thin wrists twitched in her sleep, rattling the belts attached to her bed. I could pull up the zipped sides of her enclosure, but I didn't think we would need them this evening. IV lines ran from the catheter secured to the back of her hand. Machines that lined the back of the room bleeped in their steady, soothing heartbeat rhythm to match hers.

Nothing else made a sound in room three of Inerius's Manicomium House.

Blonde curls turned dull already after her weeks of incarceration in the building's lowest levels. Cheeks once rosy lost their high gloss without any sort of sunlight to lift her. From soft, plump lips, now turned cracked and dry, tumbled the mangled words of long-dead poets that merged with their live thoughts as though all of them existed inside her head at once.

Kimberly Welles was my first patient, and Inerius U's best-kept secret.

Nathaniel Harker barely made a dent compared to the enigmas housed within these limewashed walls.

Hardly anyone knew this little level existed. I'd been introduced during my first week at the college when I stumbled upon the five locked rooms by complete accident. I'd been seeking the mortuary—read the hidden bodies donor program for student accessibility and study—on a coffee run delivering lunches like a good little freshman trying to earn extra credit and suck up somebody's cactus.

All the things I was *supposed* to do back then. Instead, I nearly became a personal study session of my own. The only thing that saved my first-year peach was my ardent curiosity of the processes I discovered behind locked doors.

When I promised Emma a straitjacket to examine her crazy but brilliant mind in a joking voice, I wasn't really joking.

Not even a little bit.

But now I had a new patient to study. One who belonged here long before her magical mishap at Phi Omega House.

My hands drifted over Kimberly's skin that I personally kept clean and sanitized. Her arms emerged like two thin sticks from beneath her paper thin medical gown. Seeing as Kimberly was such a special girl, she had earned herself a dose of special attention.

And her parents, understanding the cultish lifestyle their offspring ran on with and the odd aftereffects of the Dead Poets Sorority's outcome, had happily donated a new wing to Manicomium House, along with a wad of cash large enough to cover my residency for the next few years.

A nursemaid's allowance intended to ensure their daughter's care while they swanned away and left her in the bowels of what was essentially a glistening oubliette, and my honors study thesis.

After the Dead Poets Sorority's and Emma's spells collided to crack the literal fabric of the dead in sending Nate back and resurrecting him all at once, Kimberly seemed to be the sole—ha, soul—collateral, apart from the now slightly crooked building and its strange, cold stones. Emma called them sticky, and Nate promised me they screamed into the silent void after asking him questions.

A tidbit he kept from Emma.

The things we do for our tender loved ones. And the secrets he shared with me on our weekly sessions that I hoarded away for myself.

I swore I could hear the stones' whispers emanating from the building, as though the new cracks within cornerstones' foundations allowed a select few to hear their strange soft voices, collecting the memories of those who passed within their walls, secreting wisps of each personality like their personal Hotel Inerius.

Maybe I owed one of those straitjackets to myself for even thinking such things. But more interesting to me was the girl on the bed, who rarely woke, and when she did, the most fascinating things tumbled forth from her lips.

Kimberly Welles's case was beyond special. The invoking conjuration that she chanted mashed into the banishment incantation that Emma created out of her patchwork knowledge of how she attained Nate in the first place. And what brought Nathaniel back to our plane seemed to shatter the presence of every poet that Kimberly had ever tried to resurrect—it appeared her personal séances numbered in the dozens. Their fragments lodged deep into the depths of her own psyche.

Or maybe they were figments of her frazzled imagination,

and she quoted verbatim that which she had already memorized.

A stroke of genius, or the ultimate line into creativity? That's what I wanted to unravel inside her mind.

My little pet project.

I stroked back the lank curls from her face, noting they needed a brush. Another item for my list as part of tomorrow's job. I'd become Kimberly's sole carer in this room. Just the two of us. I smiled down at her as I stroked her hair. Here, I fed her, bathed and washed her, and made her pretty again. Sometimes, her eyes opened, and she stared into the mirror opposite with the same vacancy as the dolls my mother forced me to play with as a child.

I wondered which face she saw when she did—the one she wore, or the one that matched the voice that she spoke with at the time.

Sometimes she cried; others she sang with the sort of joy I drank in, eager for more of her insanity. Words tumbled freely from her lips. I recorded every one to study each night, comparing my notes against old articles and Nathaniel's draft of the compendium he would publish as a new book soon to be released. The dead poet collection, brought to life. His fame from another era. Immortality, a world in words.

Just like him.

A sort of parody of all the things Kimberly intended to capture.

I patted her forehead once more and checked the room temperature. "You're fine, pet. Sleep tight." I flicked the leather belts buckled around her wrists. "I'll see you in the morning."

I leaned over to press a button above her head on the machine that still bleeped softly. Her only other company once I left for the night, and those were late enough. Even Emma had noted my absence, but I wrote it off as part of my thesis for this year.

Not that I lied, exactly. I had notes galore on Kimberly, and my study of her new . . . abilities would be my access pass into the academic world.

Kimberly's head turned toward me, her eyes opening with the sort of lucidity that was rare in her.

"The moon shines upon those who strive for greatness but fail most often in the light." Knowing blue eyes fixed on me, bright and open.

I started, my heart pounding, and stared back at her.

But after a moment her eyes resumed their dull color and the light left her.

A breath of genius or not? That was always the question. I scribbled her quote hastily in my notebook, pondering the words. Were they meaningful, or not? I couldn't guess at which poet she drew inspiration from tonight, but the line would make a decent tattoo. I had to laugh. Maybe we could become besties, and get matching ones.

I left her room without another word and swiped my card to lock her door, sealing her inside as I did every night. Three more swipe doors and I locked the ward down completely, ignoring the sounds the other patients made behind in their rooms.

Kimberly was our only really silent one. But the others weren't mine to worry about. I left my white jacket and yesterday's recordings at the unmanned desk with a smile and a promise. *I'll be back tomorrow.* A promise I made to myself and the cameras that watched, with their little red light. The only thing I was allowed to take outside of Manicomium's lower levels were my notebook and that day's notes. Even those had to be written in my own personal shorthand, indecipherable by anyone else.

I waved goodbye to the cameras that watched everything—even the Dead Poets Sorority when it was active—and headed back to my dorm. Emma was on a date with Nathaniel, celebrating the prelaunch of his book, which meant I had time to do a little research into Kimberly's quote of the day.

Emma Reeves wasn't the only one obsessed with her own dead poet. I had a collection of them stuffed into one living girl.

I trod campus's paths with a slow gait, turning Kimberly's words over in my head as I passed Phi Omega House. Or what would become 2.0. Plenty of the students fought against the policy to resurrect—ha—the crooked house on its crooked mile to recreate what once was; many of the original sisters cadre amongst their number. I kind of liked the way the Gothic house leaned now, though the internals had already been fixed so the place was structurally livable again. Emma's room was not the only part of the building that had taken damage, though that and the living space where Kimberly hosted her final attempt at a séance had been a dual ground zero.

She and Nathaniel had become official in relationship status on campus—no cacti in sight. Nathaniel had taken up residence at *The Actum* as one of Erin's newest recruits, finally giving life to the paper's internal pages with his insight on social structure, though he often hosted a Sunday reading of his poetry and had created a viral following for himself. He and Griffin had settled in too, by all reports. I didn't pretend to understand that strange relationship by any means but I added it to my list for my next session with the not-quite-dead campus poet in residence.

Someone had righted the gargoyles that crouched over the entrance, judging each soul that set foot beneath the building's long shadow. As always, I felt their presence keenly as I walked under where their claws reached over the Gothic building's facade, reclaiming their grumpy placement.

From the corner of my eye, even though it wasn't close to dawn yet, I swore I saw one of their stone wings move. The softest sound, less a crack than a leathery creak. Other times when I walked beneath the stone struts they sat on at night, where they should have been, the platforms stood empty.

When I returned shortly after dawn broke, their pedestals were always filled. My strange companions in a world where a dead man walked and poets spoke through a bland girl's mouth.

Nathaniel Harker wasn't the only thing that Emma's spell brought to life.

ACKNOWLEDGEMENTS

Dead Poets Sorority has been the most incredible whirlwind, Gothic ride. From the moment Nathaniel dropped into my world, it hasn't been the same—in all the best ghost-boy ways. I've always loved graveyards, but now I can't go past one without looking for a headstone like his and wondering what stories lie beneath the earth.

The people who share my love of serenity amongst head-stones the most are my husband and kids, who are so used to my dire need to stop on the side of the road the moment one comes up that we haven't stopped at before (the older and more obscure, the better). Our favorite so far has been the Necropolis at Glasgow where we spent hours beneath gray skies amongst ancient crypts. Tony, and offspring x three, thank you for every word you hear me type at all hours, when I get up early or wander about the house at random times and for the need to pull over because I spotted a graveyard at four hundred meters even though I regularly turn us up dead-end streets by accident. Thank you always for enduring and for all the stories and trips to come together.

One person set me on this spectral path. My best friend who I published with so many years ago—Faedra. Thank you for sharing random daily thoughts, vibing the vibe—IYKYK—talking books and romance and authors and all the random things. You are my daily sanity check and I love you to pieces.

Steph Campisi—thank you for your words of wisdom and treading the path before me. I appreciate all the chats, especially with another Aussie! It's meant the world having someone share the corner and to listen to who understands every step. Massive appreciation.

My lovely lady from the Love on the Beach Christmas book signing who shared pictures with me of her coffin-shaped stunning manicure. The moment I saw those I knew exactly where I was putting that inspiration to work. Loved seeing you again.

The taco slapping. This caused contention across servers and edits. It's a thing. I promise. Please look up Dwayne Johnson and Kevin Hart battling it off. Tag me. It's hilarious. I can procrasti-watch all day. It's therapeutic. Maybe.

Andie and Jenny. You are my sanity check every day. I'm not half as organized as you, Jenny, and I want to grow up to be you, Andie. In the meantime, I'm collecting capybara stickers until we can open a bookshop café together.

Rachel Hart. You gave me the chance to write this story. Nathaniel and Emma changed over time, and they grew a lot in the process, but they wouldn't be who they are without you or your guidance. I am beyond grateful for everything. Nathaniel's dragonfly jacket is for you. Maybe the boots.

Maddie Wilson, thank you for the hours you put in reading my words and bringing Minnie to life, plus being my gothicana/romantasy hero in so many ways. Also for fangirling over the Easter eggs. I'll never give up hiding Nineties references in my books.

Speerzie, you're the best signing neighbor a girl can have.

My Discord networks. I live there, as well as my reader group. Thank you for providing a place where I don't have to think before I type. Truly a relief to have that space that's open and honest.

Readers, thank you for making it this far. For having a TBR pile and for the hours you spent reading this book over another. Nathaniel and Emma's world: Phi Omega House, the gargoyles, the storm scene, the underlibrary, the graveyard and the wisps, *that* epilogue . . . those are written for you. Thank you for reading. I fangirl over you, too.

See you next round.

Sofia xx